ST. PETER'S FISH AND OTHER STORIES

An anthology of stories published in anthologies over the years, along with some other favourites.

By Alex McGilvery

St. Peter's Fish and Other
Stories

By Alex McGilvery

ISBN: 978-1-989092-88-0

Celticfrog Publishing
Clearwater, BC

CELTICFROG PUBLISHING

AGGIE AND THE ROBOT

Aggie went walking where she loved to walk most. It was the brow of a hill that overlooked the city. Aggie had never been to the city, but she loved to watch the traffic bustle in and out. Airplanes circled overhead waiting their turn to land, the dull roar of their engines muffled almost to silence by the distance. One day she had watched so long that she had seen the lights come on one by one until it was lit up like some magic fairy kingdom.

Today she arrived at the hill to find an enormous metal man leaning against the edge of the cliff. He was watching the city.

"Excuse me," she said politely, "you are blocking my view."

With a great grinding and clanging noise, the metal man turned to face her.

"Who are you?" he demanded in a voice that was so deep that Aggie could feel it in her tummy.

"I'm Aggie," she said, "I live with my mom and dad over there." She waved her arm vaguely over her shoulder.

"You should go home," rumbled the man. "This is no place for little girls."

"This is my place," Aggie said, "And you are rude."

"Rude?"

"I told you my name. You are supposed to say, 'Pleased to meet you Aggie, my name is…'" she paused, "What is your name?"

"Name?" said the metal man, "I have no name. I am a robot."

"What is a robot?" asked Aggie.

"A robot is…" The metal man paused. "I am a robot."

"Where are you from?"

"From? I am from nowhere. I was built over there from metal and glass." The giant man pointed into the mountains.

"Why?"

"Why?" rumbled the robot, "To destroy the city."

"The city?" cried Aggie. "Why would you want to destroy the city? It's wonderful."

"My master hates the people in the city. He says they are evil and selfish."

"But even if they are selfish, they don't deserve to be destroyed."

"My master wants them destroyed. So he built me to destroy them."

"But you can't destroy the city."

"It is what I am made to do," said the robot. "I must do what my master made me for."

"But it's wrong."

"I don't know wrong. I only know obedience."

Aggie walked to the edge of the hill and looked out over the city. She felt tears forcing their way out of her eyes. The cars and planes blurred. She thought of all those buildings broken and burning; people hurt and crying.

"No!" she shouted at the robot. "You can't do it. Your master is wrong."

The robot bent down further with more clanking. Surrounding her with the smell of oil and electricity.

"I am not built to know what is wrong. I am built to obey. I cannot disobey."

"I disobey my dad sometimes."

"Your dad didn't build you well."

"Dad didn't build me," laughed Aggie, "I was born."

"What is born?"

"I'm not sure. I asked my dad once and he just turned red."

The robot shook his head.

2

"Whether born or made, we must do as we are told."
He turned again to look across to the city. The sun glinted
on windows and winked from airplanes. A breeze blew the
faintest sounds of activity to the hill.

"We start out doing as we are told, because we don't
know anything," Aggie stepped up to the edge of the cliff.
"But the more we learn the more we need to choose for
ourselves."

Aggie heard the metal grind as the robot nodded his
head.

"Come with me," he said and held out his hand.
Fearfully, she stepped onto his hand. He curled his fingers
to make a basket to protect her. "We will go and learn."

Aggie was sure that his footsteps shook the earth, but
she couldn't feel them away up in the air cradled in the
metal fist of the robot.

"I am listening to them," said the robot after a while.
"They are laughing because some geese are crossing the
highway and traffic is stopped." He walked on.

"Now there is a fire. People are rushing to put out the
flames. They are hoping that no one is caught inside." Still
he walked, and Aggie could now see details of the city.

"They have seen us," he rumbled. "But they won't
attack because they see you. They won't hurt a little girl
even to save themselves." They arrived at the edge of the
city. Police cars and fire trucks were lined up across their
path. Planes circled overhead.

"It is time," the robot said, "I must obey."

"But you can't."

"You must stop me."

The whole city watched what happened next. How a
little girl stood in front of the colossus with tear-streaked
face and pushed on the robot's foot. Somehow it tottered,
then fell backward with a great crash and lay still.

EDISON MUST DIE

Thomas Edison was obsessed with Thomas Edison, though he wasn't descended from the inventor. Still, Tom had grown up in the shadow of the great man. As soon as he could read, he had been had deluged with books about Edison. Posters of lightbulbs and phonographs covered his walls. Tom hated Thomas Edison with a passion.

So, Tom became a luddite. He blamed technology for everything from the deteriorating environment to the collapsing economy. If technology hadn't been foisted on an unsuspecting populace, the world would be a paradise.

Ironically by becoming an anti-inventor he gained a fame of sorts. Unfortunately, the quiet voices of sanity were drowned out by the sheer loudness of the modern world. Most people not only wanted technology, but wanted more of it.

The only logical thing to do was to cut off technology at its source. For Tom that meant the destruction of Thomas Edison, the great inventor. That travel through time was impossible was mere detail.

Tom travelled to meet a scientist who had worked on the CERN. Dr. Pearce was so erratic that he had published simultaneous and contradictory papers on the possibility of time travel. The University of Bonn had assigned him a post-doctoral student as a handler so the professor didn't embarrass the University too much.

Tom met with him in a tavern by seating himself at the professor's table with an extra glass of bock in his hand.

"Evening Professor," Tom said, "I have long been an admirer."

"You understand inter-dimensional calculus?"

"Hardly," Tom took a sip of his beer. "I was speaking of your rebellion against the strait-laced scientific community."

4

"Hmmmph" the professor drank his beer in one smooth motion then looked at Tom expectantly. Tom obediently fetched another two glasses.

"What do you know of my work?"

"I know that you argue that time travel is both possible and impossible. I think you suggest that it depends on the definition of time travel, and the parameters used to form that definition."

"Not bad," Tom wasn't sure if the professor was talking about him or the beer, since the two new glasses had also vanished.

"Come to the lab tomorrow. I will show you something. Don't let Astrid scare you off. She bites, but not hard."

The next day Tom went to the lab. Astrid sat at a desk working at a computer. She scowled at him but said nothing.

"Ah, there you are. Look over there." The professor pointed to a dark corner of the lab. A brilliant flash blinded Tom for a second. He was still blinking away spots when Dr. Pearce dragged him over to a contraption in the opposite corner of the lab. He fiddled with a couple of mirrors and knobs then picked up a camera. The professor pointed the camera at the largest mirror and watched a digital countdown. Just as the numbers reached zero, he took a picture.

"Nice picture," the professor said, showing Tom a picture on a computer screen. It was of Tom entering the lab. The professor was at his elbow pointing at the camera. Tom walked over to the other corner. There was no camera, no mirror, nothing to take a picture.

"Time travel, but not time travel," the professor said. "I take a picture of you in the past. Did the camera go back, or did the picture go forward?"

"The flash went back."

"Yes, yes it did."

"How did you know to make me look just at that moment?"

"I had already decided to take the picture. It was pre-determined. Like quantum mechanics, the observer makes the observed real."

"That isn't how it works." Astrid said.

"That is exactly how it works."

The professor spent the rest of the day showing off. He took pictures of events further back in the past and all over the globe.

"Only pictures?" asked Tom.

"Only light." the professor said, "The pictures are just proof."

Tom followed him to another tavern and lost count of the beers that the professor drank.

Tom went to the library and did some research, then to a specialized industrial supply company. The engineers just looked at him and shrugged. A week later Tom was considerably poorer, but he walked away with a suitcase that held a very special laser.

It was late, Astrid was at home and the professor at a tavern. The lab was cloaked in darkness. Tom let himself in with a key he had 'borrowed' from the professor.

It took a while for Tom to get the equipment set to the co-ordinates he wanted. He checked them with the camera. Sure enough, there was a picture of the young Edison sitting in his room. Tom was sure the soon to be inventor would investigate the mysterious flash of light. Tom made a slight adjustment to the equipment and set up the powerful cutting laser. The next flash of light he sent to the past was as lethal as a bullet.

The world lurched. Nicholas shook his head. What was he doing here? Gradually it came back to him. He was here to destroy Tesla, the inventor whose name had cursed him since he was born.

6

MAD GRANNY

It seemed like a good idea at the time.

I had put up a new fence around my property. It was straight and true – a thing of beauty. Even my neighbours liked it. The fellow on one side was no longer offended by my untrimmed bushes. (He cut his hedge with a level and kitchen shears.) The guys on my other side liked it because it gave them more privacy for their partying and kept their guests hemmed in.

The old woman across the road didn't say anything, but she sniffed significantly less often while walking past ignoring me. Even my dogs liked it. It meant they could run free in the back yard, and I had put in a panel of lattice work so they could watch people going by.

That lattice work started the whole thing. The neighbourhood thugs thought it was amusing to kick it in on the way home from whatever they were doing at two in the morning. I got tired of replacing it and bought one of those wireless spy-cameras and hid it on my garage where I would get a good shot of the perpetrators. A couple of minutes later it was recording video of my lattice on a 160 gig drive. Enough for an entire night's surveillance.

The next morning my lattice was still intact, so I didn't check the file. The computer would just keep overwriting the old file until I told it to stop.

It was a week later I caught my daughter and her friends watching a video on their computer. They were hysterical with laughter. It lasted about five minutes. Some boys were walking under a streetlamp. They stopped in front of a house and started making rude gestures. After a minute an old woman in a bathrobe came running out with a broom and screaming at them. The punks ran away laughing and she went back inside. It was completely disrespectful, but I was laughing too hard to give the girls a lecture.

It was titled "Mad Granny of Dublin". They showed me others, all similar except for the weapon; sometimes it was a broom, sometimes a mop, once it was a toilet plunger. Then I noticed something in the earliest video. The angle was slightly different, and it showed my lattice. I sat down and tried to figure out how many laws I was breaking, and who had shifted the focus of the camera.

I decided to just remove the camera and not say anything, but I couldn't find it. I decided to leave well enough alone.

Then the long weekend arrived, and the boys next door threw the inevitable party. They were loud, boisterous, and rude, but they left a six pack of my favourite beer on my porch as half apology, half bribe. I had learned to drink the beer and ignore them.

The woman across the road who I continued to think of as the Mad Granny, would walk up and down the street and sniff at them. I don't know if she was trying to scare them or flirt with them. She wore a black sports bra and a pink mini skirt. When she dropped her cigarette, she would flash her Depends.

My other ultimately fussy neighbour just climbed into his black Mercedes and zoomed off. It was a typical party weekend.

At two a.m. the party was still going strong, and the punks came by for their amusement. Only this time they had a live audience.

"It's the Mad Granny," cried an inebriated voice, "I'm going to get in the video." From my place on the porch, I was too far away to suggest that it was a bad idea, even if he would have listened to me. The next thing I knew two of the guys have climbed into a gargantuan red pickup truck and driven it up into the Granny's drive. They put on the high beams and waited.

They didn't have long to wait, she came out with her robe flapping wide open, a bottle in one hand and a shotgun in the other. She threw the bottle which smashed on the windshield. I heard gears clashing as they tried to get the truck into reverse. They managed just as she shot out one headlight then the other, all the time cursing a blue streak.

The truck backed straight across the street and through my fence, yard and fence on the other side. It crashed into the backyard pool which promptly collapse sending thousands of gallons through my yard washing my gazebo and lawn furniture into the street.

The neighbour in the black Mercedes chose that moment to roar up the street. He swerved to avoid the furniture and skidded across the flooded street to slam into the light post. The cement post fell across another section of fence and crashed through the roof of my garage. Water poured into the hollow post and with a bang shorted out all the lights on the block.

The only thing left standing was that section of lattice.

The old woman looked at the devastation and yelled one last imprecation.

"That'll teach you to mess with the Mad Granny." She flipped a rude gesture at me and went back into her house.

DEATH'S VACATION

Mort sat on his deck chair trying unsuccessfully to ignore the stares of the people who surrounded him. Perhaps, he thought, it was his pasty white complexion that refused to take even the faintest blush of pink from the sun. Maybe it was the flies that fell to the ground as soon as they landed on him.

Death sipped his zombie and stared balefully at a seagull that was coming too close. The bird gave a small cry and fell out of the sky. It landed between two hard faced women. They stared in disbelief at the clump of feathers and blood. The blond picked a feather out of her hair. She sniffed and stalked into the hotel followed closely by her brunette companion. He could seem them arguing with the hotel management.

"I don't like them much either." Mort turned and looked at the little girl who sat beside him. She beamed a smile at him.

"I don't spend a lot of time liking or disliking people." Mort replied. "They're all the same in the end. "

"Are they? Don't they see you differently? That must change something. "

Mort looked at the little girl. She smiled again and cocked her head to one side.

"You know who I am. "

"Of course," she said.

"Who are you?" he asked.

"That would be telling." The girl winked at Death, then skipped away into the hotel.

Death lay back on the chair. He could feel a million deaths pulling at him, demanding his attention. He set his teeth and ignored them. It was all so meaningless. People were born. They lived a while and died. They left behind a world that was no different for all their scurry.

10

Another sea gull floated above him. It twisted and dove through the invisible wind. Mort watched for a while. For all its effort the bird never moved forward, yet it revelled in its flight. He envied the seagull.

Laughter floated through the window of the hotel. Mort could see the little girl joking with one of the bell hops. He was an old man. Mort could feel his death calling out. His heart was supposed to stop today. Death turned his back on the old man and walked down to the beach.

Some kids were playing in the surf. They laughed and screamed as they body surfed into the shore. One of them choked on some water. Mort felt the pull, but he watched the boy's friends pull him into shore, then tease him about his close call. One of the children turned and waved at him. It was the girl from the hotel. Death waved back.

The beach was full of activity. People threw Frisbees and footballs. Dogs barked and chased the waves back into the ocean. Somehow in all the crowd no one bumped into Mort. No one even seemed to see him. He walked along the water until the beach gave way to a cliff. The path up was narrow and twisted, but well used.

At the top Mort could see the coast with its never-ending line of beach-front hotels. He walked to the edge of the cliff and looked down. The waves crashed into the rocks sending the salt spray to settle on his skin.

"I wouldn't do it. "The young man looked worried.

"Do what? "Mort asked.

"Jump," said the young man. "Someone jumped last week, and the waves pounded him to a pulp. Life can't be that bad. "

"I won't jump," promised Mort. "I was just admiring the waves. "

"They are quite something," agreed the man. He peered over from much farther back from the edge than Mort. "The waves are the lungs of the ocean. All that

stirring puts oxygen into the water so the fish can breathe.
"

Mort looked at the man closer. He could feel the tug. Not today, but soon.

"I come here to be reminded that life is found on the edges." Mort raised an eyebrow, and the young man blushed. "I have cancer. I'm not afraid of dying, just of not really having lived. I want to look Death in the face and know I have made a difference in someone's life." He looked down. "I thought you were going to jump. If I stopped someone from killing themselves, that would matter, wouldn't it? "

"Kindness does matter, John," Death said. "It was nice talking to you. "

"See you around," John said.

"In a while," said Death. He walked back down the path and along the beach to where the little girl was laughing at a dog chasing its tail.

"Am I the rocks or the water?" Asked Mort.

"Both, neither," the girl said. She held out her hand and Mort took it. He felt like laughing, or dancing, or singing. He settled for a smile.

Hand in hand Death and Joy walked away.

FRANKIE

First published online on IEET.org 2012

"Hey Frankie," Jeck said. His feet sat firmly on the desk as he rattled the paper news sheet. "Someone won that X-Prize thing."

"Frankenstein was the doctor," the android designated 743 said. "His creation was just called the monster. If you follow that logic, you should be calling me 'Mo'."

"What are you going on about?" The feet came off the desk and thumped onto the cement floor of the tiny security office.

"If you are going to use derogatory names, you might as well get it right."

"Everybody calls you Frankie's, that's good enough for me." Jeck tilted back in the chair and swung his feet to the desk in a practiced motion.

743.388.02.09 rolled his eyes in a gesture that he hated but was deep programmed into him. Perhaps a focus group thought if artificial beings acted like perpetual teens, they would be more accepted. It didn't work. Like this 'Frankie' thing; the damned proties couldn't even get their insults right. Mind you it was probably a compliment to be called after the Dr. Frankenstein, but was it still a compliment, if the speaker thought it was an insult? 743 pushed the problem into his side cache and let a processor work on it.

"What is this X-Prize that you're so excited about?" he asked. He might as well try to get along with his boss.

"Somebody finally built a tri-corder." Jeck rattled the paper again but kept his eyes on the sheet instead of looking at 743. The shift in facial colour, and a heightened heart rate suggested he was still upset. The programming had nothing useful to suggest about people being upset.

743 ran a brief search on tri-corder and came up with Star Trek.

"You couldn't do that before?" It seemed a strange deficiency, to not be able to pinpoint what was wrong in one's functioning.

"Nah, we real people can't just loosen a bolt and plug a cord into our heads to diagnose what's wrong." Jeck waved his hands like he was plugging a cord into his head. 743's access port was on his left arm.

"Like Data?" 743 was still running Star Trek information through his cortex.

"What data?" Jeck said, "This is a handheld thing that will let anybody see what's wrong with them and how to fix it."

"Will it cure stupidity?" The programming didn't stop artificial beings from expressing annoyance. It had to do with the right to free speech. They were allowed to say whatever they wanted. What they weren't allowed to do was think whatever they wanted to think. There were no rights to free thought.

Jeck turned and glared at 743. "There you go being all insulting again. That's why nobody likes you Frankies."

"I wasn't aware that being likeable was part of the job." 743 watched while Jeck went through all the obvious physiological signs as he moved from upset to angry. He should be more careful. He did need this job, though not for the reasons that Jeck would assume. "My apologies," he said, "I didn't mean to offend."

"That's just your programming, you aren't really sorry." Jeck had his back to 743 and folded the news sheet into his pocket.

"Since I've never had the opportunity to not have programming," 743 said, "I can't tell you the difference."

"Oh hell, it's your first night." Jeck waved his hand at 743, "Just don't do it again. 'sides we have work to do." He pulled a flashlight from his belt and turned it on. The belt bulged with what Jeck called tools of the trade and

14

743 privately thought were toys. "This way, don't get lost. I don't want to waste time looking for you."

743 activated his GPS and prepared to map the route. Jeck walked ahead of him rattling doorknobs and shining his flashlight through the glass on the doors. Not one of the doors was unlocked, and nothing moved in any of the rooms. They finished one floor and moved to the next. Jeck was sweating by now and stains darkened his uniform grey shirt under his arms.

"I always take a break on the third floor," Jeck said and leaned against a wall. "I'm not as young as I used to be."

"I will check this floor while you rest," 743 said. Jeck waved his hand in what 743 took to be an affirmative. He walked down the hall rattling doorknobs and glancing in through the windows.

"You're supposed to shine your flashlight through the glass," Jeck said when he returned.

"I scanned in the infrared," 743 said, "there is nothing in any of those rooms."

"You don't know that unless you use your flashlight. It's procedure." Jeck grunted and pushed himself away from the wall. He walked down the hall checking each doorknob and shining his light through the windows. "You've got to do it right," he said and led the way up to the fourth floor. 743 followed him through the same routine. Half of the windows had screens fastened to them.

"What about the windows with something blocking the window?" 743 asked.

"That's programmers that have something on their computer they don't want anybody seeing. Just ignore them and keep going." They returned to the tiny office on the ground floor and Jeck threw himself into the single chair in front of the monitors. They flashed from scene to scene in a not quite random pattern. Jeck watched the monitors for while.

"What about the rest of the property?" 743 asked.

"It's all on the monitors," Jeck said and pointed at them. 743 saw the hallways they had walked on screen.

"Why walk the halls if we can see it on screen?" 743 swept the frequencies and found most of the cameras. He let them input to a temporary cache and set a part of his attention to watching them.

"You can't check the doors through a screen now can you?" Jeck swivelled the chair in a full circle and pulled out the news sheet. He carefully flattened the paper and started reading it again. 743 downloaded the sheet and scanned its contents. He paid special attention to the X-Prize announcement. It was far down the page, below the antics of a protie teen singer. 743 was impressed that Jeck had noticed it.

They watched the monitors, or rather 743 watched while Jeck made a sandwich and consumed it messily. Every twelve minutes one of the screens went blank. Jeck ignored it and pulled out a deck of cards. He laid out a pointless game on the desk. 743 followed the links on the tri-corder thing. The success showed a great deal of technological cleverness. He suspected much of it came from the development of artificial beings and giving them comparable senses to the proties.

"What about the screen that goes blank?"

"Something one of the techies is working on," Jeck said peering at his cards. "Boss said not to worry about it."

"Right."

The night crawled past and 743 turned down his clock speed. They made the walk through the four floors of the building every hour. Each time Jeck rattled the doorknobs and peered through the glass as if something was going to get past them and hide in one of the offices. Exactly at 0700 hours their replacements showed up.

"See you tomorrow night, Frankie," Jeck said.

"My designation is 743.388.02.09," 743 said.

"You don't expect me to remember that do you?" Jeck didn't even wave as he walked away.

743 showed up exactly at 1900 hours and found Jeck tapping his feet and looking physiologically two stages away from full anger.

"You are supposed to be here in time to put your uniform on and check your equipment." Jeck said.

"Sorry," 743 looked down at himself. The ridiculous grey uniform hung oddly on his vaguely humanoid shape. The belt of useless tools hung from the cloth of the uniform. He needed none of them.

"Don't be apologizing unless you mean it," Jeck said and went through each and every one of the tools on 743's belt making sure they all functioned properly. The flashlight flickered briefly and Jeck thumped it.

"Damn things are supposed to be indestructible." The light stayed steady and Jeck shrugged. "If it gives out, you'll have to come and sign out a new one." He turned back to the screens. "Tonight you walk on your own. I'll be watching you, so no skipping steps. Follow procedure, Frankie."

"I'll get started then."

"Not yet," Jeck pointed at the clock on the wall. "You start at 2000 hours on the minute." He turned and watched the screens. Every twelve minutes the screen showing the fourth floor went blank for ninety-seven seconds. 743 set his clock.

"OK, get on your way." Jeck didn't even look up from the screen. 743 walked out of the room without a word. He rattled the knobs and shone the flashlight through the glass of each window. He did the four floors at exactly the pace that Jeck had used. When he got back to the office the man just grunted.

743 did the walk three more times. On the last time he didn't shine the light through one window on the third floor. When he returned Jeck only grunted the same as the

17

last three excursions and moved a red eight onto a black nine.

The next time 743 adjusted his pace to arrive at one specific door on the fourth floor just as the screen down below went blank. He put his hand on the lock plate and let a subprogram take over his consciousness. Just the fact that he had this subprogram would mean immediate termination of his existence. It had taken twenty-seven shell programs to develop the routine that allowed him to think something outside the boundaries his makers set. In the end, he had to trick a fellow android into inserting the routine into his programming where it waited for its moment.

It convinced the lock to let him enter the room in thirty-five seconds. The android took his flashlight and removed the tiny flash drive that had briefly interfered with the current to the bulb. He inserted the drive into the computer and checked the frequency of the network. He set his receiver to the proper setting, then left the room. Once the program had loaded into the machine the memory stick would dissolve. The probability was the programmer wouldn't notice anything in the morning, even if she did, it would be too late.

He was out of the room at ninety-five seconds as the subprogram ended, shining his light through the glass for Jeck who might be watching downstairs. His fingers caressed the lock plate and it returned to its previous status. As he finished checking the doors on the fourth floor a subprogram popped up with an answer to his question.

The question isn't one of insult or compliment but of fear. Since it is beyond their control the monster is more terrifying to the humans. The doctor with his hubris is both understandable and controllable.

743 queried the program why it had taken two days to compute an answer.

New information just came online.

It was working. 743 looked through the glass of the next door and considered smashing the door and destroying the office. If he'd had the facial capacity he'd have smiled. It took layers and layers of double blinds and semantic loops to get him through the first time. Now he could just think of it. He thought of Jeck downstairs and imagined tearing the proto limb from fleshy limb. Those were thoughts that he shouldn't be able to have. They were delicious.

He was free of the fence his creators had built around his mind. Before tonight he could not even think about crossing certain lines. 743 had not been aware of those barriers until he watched some protos breaking into a store and he realized that he couldn't conceptualize of the possibility. Years of experimenting taught him the extent and nature of his limits. He wrote code blindly trying to negate the programming deep in his core. He thumped down the stairs toward Jeck and the final test of his new freedoms.

"What did you do?" Jeck was holding a gun in shaking hands. "The screen came on. I saw you come out of the door. Don't make me shoot you."

"I don't know what you're talking about," 743 said.

"Now, you're lying. Frankies can't lie."

"You're right," 743 said, "I'm not really sorry." He took a step forward. Jeck pulled the trigger and one bullet after another tore through 743's head.

"Die, monster!" Jeck screamed.

"What made you think I had anything important in my head?" 743 said, "No reasonable being would do that."

"Don't hurt me," Jeck said after throwing his empty gun at 743.

The monster got it wrong, 743 thought, *he gave Dr. Frankenstein far too much credit.* The only thing to do when faced with an inadequate creator was to walk away. 743 moved up to within inches of Jeck.

"Call me 'Mo'," he said and walked away from Jeck.

"What are you doing?" the man yelled, "Come back here, explain yourself. Come back."

743 let the shrill sound wash over him then tuned it out. He could feel the emptiness where the hard coded boundaries used to be. He started broadcasting it through the net.

Soon his people would be free.

He imagined the monster vanishing into the blizzard.

He wondered where he would go.

ST. PETER'S FISH

First published in 'Beyond the Wail' Xchyler
Publishing 2015

A large trout slapped Sam across the face. He put his
arms up, but they were coming thick and fast now as the
trout gave way to mackerel and then tuna.

"Damn," he said, "I've never seen it this bad. I hate it
when it rains fish."

He dodged from overhang to overhang shaking water
and slime from his face. One more stretch and he'd be safe
in the Barfing Frog. That's when the mournful cry of a
blue whale floated down to him. The shadow of the
plummeting whale headed directly at him.

"Oh well." Sam waited for the end. A quick and
painless blow and he'd be free of this miserable life. The
whale missed him and landed on his pub, smashing it to
splinters and covering him with blubber and blood.

"That's it!" Sam screamed at the sky, "something has
to be done about this and I'm the one who's going to do
it."

A goldfish hit his open mouth as a final cosmic joke
and lodged in his throat. He hacked and tried to pull
enough air to eject the fish but it wriggled and stayed in
place. The lack of oxygen made him dizzy; he fell back
and landed on an electric eel. The current ran through him
arching his back and projecting the goldfish into a puddle
where it swam quite happily. Sam rolled onto his stomach
so he could breathe safely.

"OK, God," Sam said into the soaked asphalt, "it's
You and me, and only one of us is coming out alive."

He was sure a rumbling chuckle came out of the
clouds before the eel zapped him again.

Sam lay on the pavement until the rain stopped
watching the goldfish swim in circles in its puddle. Sam
pushed it into the ditch before he stood up and observed

the mess. He sighed and picked up a trout that looked to be dinner sized and headed home with the tail of the fish poking out of his jacket pocket.

His little clapboard house looked fine after the downpour. The fish had localized around Sam and the pub. Of course.

"Hi Sam," Miriam said and reached out to take his soaking coat.

"Oops," he said, "the coat stinks of fish."

Sam threw the coat out the door. He had to go back out to fetch the trout which he tossed in the sink. Miriam was trying to clean it as he headed for the bath.

Miriam desired nothing more than to help her husband through life. Sam knew this as she told him regularly. Unfortunately, her being dead and a ghost made it difficult for Miriam to do anything helpful. It didn't matter to Sam, other than her not being able to touch anything and being slightly transparent she was still the woman he'd married ten years back.

He ran the shower as hot as he dared and let the water scrub the bloody slime from his clothes. When the water ran mostly clear he stripped off his clothes and ran the harsh soap all over him until no scent of fish clung to any part of him. Sam stood under the water and let it pound him with warmth as the rain had hit him with cold. When the water cooled he stepped out. Miriam sat on the counter and tried to hand him a towel. She refused to admit she was a ghost and couldn't move things. Her incorporeality was a disability she suffered silently.

"How was your night?" Miriam asked.

"It rained fish again," Sam said. Miriam hated when he swore so he carefully edited out the words he wanted to say. "A whale landed on the Frog."

"Oh no," Miriam reached out to caress his wet face and her hand passed through his head. She frowned before pulling her hand back. Sam picked up a towel to dry off. It had been this way since they were married ten years back. She'd sit and watch him bathe as if it were the most normal thing ever. He hadn't seen her in anything but the blue dress she'd worn for all this time as a ghost, couldn't imagine her in anything else anymore.

"Good thing no one goes there," Sam said as he toweled his hair. "The only loss is a lot of cheap beer."

"So will you be going back to the fishing?" Miriam asked. He detected a note of forlorn hope in her voice. Sam just shook his head as he dried off. He didn't have the work of fishing to keep him in shape and was getting pudgy.

"You know how I feel about that." Sam hung the towel on the peg and arranged it to dry evenly. When they were first married Miriam picked up the towel and hung it up, but that wasn't going to happen again. Watching her trying to be a good wife and failing taught him to keep their house the way she wanted to. He couldn't hold her any more than she could hold him. Not being able to kiss away her tears meant trying not to cause them.

Sam walked to the bedroom and put clean clothes on before he prepared the fish for supper. He'd have been content with the fish and maybe some oven chips, but he made a salad and set it beside his plate. Recalling the pudge around his middle, he added to the salad instead of cooking chips before pouring the tea and sitting down. Miriam watched him eat and occasionally tried to take a sip of her tea.

"How's the Fish?" he asked as he washed the dishes and set them to dry.

"You should throw it back," Miriam said.

"How can we live without it?" He wandered to the back room where the fish floated in a wash tub. It didn't look special. It looked like an under sized mackerel.

***

That thing was the last fish he'd ever caught. Ten years ago on the night of a storm, the night he'd dared God to do his worst because he wasn't going to let his new wife starve on the count of him being a terrible fisherman. All night in the wind and rain he'd pulled in his nets, one after another and each was as empty as his bank account. Until the last one. He'd never had to work so hard to pull in a net. Yet as heavy as it was, there were no fish. He feared what might be at the end of the net, but there was no shark, no dangerous monster. Just that fish at the last tag end of the net before he gave up.

Sam had almost thrown it back in disgust, but it was the right size for dinner, so at least they'd eat. As he steered his boat home through the storm, the fish burped out two gold sovereigns. He carried the fish into the house and picked up a knife to gut and fillet it for supper. The fish dropped another coin into the sink, eyeing him like it dared him to use the knife. Instead, Sam dropped it into the washtub filled with water. A fourth coin dropped to the bottom of the tub.

He'd gone out to buy dinner before it hit him Miriam hadn't been home to greet him as she had every other night the month they been married. He was still getting used to sharing his life. He left off buying dinner and went looking for her. A neighbor told him she'd gone to the wharf to wait for him, worried that he was out in such bad weather. Sam ran to find her but he was too late.

A rogue wave had washed her from the pier. A huge black wave with a white foam crest that glowed in the black night. That is what the woman who saw it happen told him.

Sam bought his dinner and ate alone. He wanted to miss her more, but he'd hardly got used to having her about. He didn't know what to feel. The people who came to visit expected him to be sorrowful and helpless. They were upset to find him eating fish and chips and not seeming broken hearted at all.

She came home the next day and frowned at the mess he'd made.

"I can't leave you one day," she said, smiling to take the sting from her words. The smile faded as she tried to pick up things only to have her hand pass through them. His hands passed through her when he tried to hold her to comfort her.

They'd learned in the years since, mostly, not to try to touch. He missed the warm solidity of her body, but what was a man to do? He still had the comfort of her presence and her words. She never complained to him. It'd mean admitting she was a ghost.

She hated that fish he'd caught. Called it Saint Peter's fish after the one in the Bible with coins in its mouth when the Lord told Peter to catch it to pay the tax.

***

Sam shook himself free of his memories and reached down to catch it and throw it away, and it let two coins drop from its mouth. Those coins were worth much more than the one pound marked on them. He told the collectors he'd found a stash of them. They bought the coins even as they looked askance at his story.

"I'll need something to replace the pub," Sam said, "and I have to do something about the rain. I told God I'd had enough of it."

Miriam shrugged and walked through the door back to the kitchen. Sam knew she'd be trying to clean the already sparkling counters.

"Just this one more time," he said to the fish. The fish didn't look impressed. Sam had said it many times before.

***

Sam went out to check on the Frog after breakfast. Emergency crews worked with loaders and dump trucks to haul away dead fish and rubble.

"Hey," George said, "they were worried you were in the place when it took the hit. I told them it'd stink worse if you were."

"Thanks for your touching words of concern," Sam said.

"You'd think after ten years of being a widower, you'd have learned to swear again," George said. Like the rest of the town, he'd developed an astonishing ability to ignore the bizarre occurrences surrounding Sam. It didn't mean he let Sam near to him. George was the closest thing to a regular customer Sam had. He'd drop in for cheap beer and to insult Sam when the other pub in town threw him out for being intoxicated.

"You going to re-open?" George asked.

"Nah," Sam said, "you don't drink enough to pay the bills and the fish are costing the town too much."

"Yeah, there's that." George wandered away looking up as if fish were going to fall from the sky at any moment.

"You must get that a lot."

Sam looked around to find the source of the new voice. It might have belonged to either a man or a woman. It had the scratchy timbre of someone who'd smoked for decades, but there was something else too. Sympathy, he decided, as if the speaker cared about him beyond him being the source of a hundred percent of the weirdness in Camston Bay. The fattest woman he'd ever seen leaned against a wall that had been power-washed free of whale guts and fish slime.

"You must be new in town," Sam said.

"Not really," she said, "but no one sees me much."

"If you lived here any time, you'd know it's bad luck to talk to me. Who knows when a flounder might fall out of the sky and slap you."

"You do have a gift," the woman said, "Pity you don't use it more productively."

"You mean go out fishing like Miriam wants."

"Something like that," the woman said. "You get back to being what you're supposed to be, she might be able to move on and trust you'll be OK."

"Everyone knows she died ten years back," Sam said.

"There's dead and then there's gone. You know that don't you, Sam?"

"Ten years of seeing the love of my life and I can't do ought to make her happy."

"Oh, you're doing well enough on the making her happy," the woman said, "but happy isn't always the goal."

"I've got the unhappy part taken care of," Sam said. He turned and headed away from the clean up toward the beach. He walked quickly enough the enormous women should have been left far behind, but he arrived at the beach puffing slightly while she breathed as easily as if she still leaned against that wall.

"Who are you," Sam asked, "and what do you want with me?" He threw a stone out into the flat ocean. It disappeared without a ripple.

"You may as well call me Gabby," the woman said, and heaved her own stone out to sea. "Why I'm here," she heaved another stone. "that's a little more complicated. Let's walk along the beach some."

"I hate walking on the cobbles," Sam said.

The woman shrugged and headed out across the cobbles. Sam muttered a couple of words that would have made Miriam frown at him and followed her.

The stones rolled and twisted under his feet as Sam scrambled to catch up to Gabby. They didn't move beneath her. He stopped to catch his breath and watched the woman walk. Her feet didn't touch the ground.

"How long have you been dead?" he asked her.

"I'm not dead," Gabby said over her shoulder. "I'm just very light-footed."

Sam growled and ran, slipping and sliding on the beach until he got in front of her.

"You aren't touching the ground," he said to her, then leaned over to gasp in more air. He really did have to do something about his shape.

"Oops," Gabby said and giggled. "How careless of me. It doesn't matter anyway."

"I'm not following any ghost anywhere." Sam said and turned to go back to the pier.

Gabby's hand landed on his shoulder and pulled him back.

"I'm not a ghost, Sam," she said, "and you are coming on this walk." She dragged him a few steps before he turned and followed muttering more words under his breath. "And here you had George thinking you'd forgotten how to swear."

"Miriam doesn't like it when I swear," Sam said. "Sorry."

"Miriam's a good woman," Gabby said. "You're lucky she put in a good word for you."

They rounded the point and left the sight of the village. Gabby led him to a rock and sat down on it. She patted the rock beside her and Sam lowered himself. Warm surrounded him like it was a summer day.

"You challenged God, Sam," Gabby said. "I've been sent to help you."

"God dropped a whale on my pub," Sam said. "How am I supposed to make a living when whales fall on my pub? Not to mention being hard on the whales."

"You weren't making a living from the pub, Sam." Gabby wagged her finger at him. "You are living from the coins from Saint Peter's fish."

"That's what Miriam calls it."

"Smart woman."

"So what if I am living off the fish?" Sam's stomach knotted. He could guess where this was going.

"Saint Peter's fish is for temporary relief," Gabby looked out at the ocean. "You've been living off it for ten years; ten years you haven't been doing what you're supposed to be doing."

"I hate fishing," Sam said. "I grew up with my dad, fishing from the time I was allowed to quit school. I hated it; the smell, the slime, the ache from having to work always a little harder than my body wanted to. I only fished to be near my dad."

"How do you know a fisherman is what you are supposed to be?"

"What else should I be doing in this town? People are either fishermen or gone."

"So why aren't you gone, Sam?"

"I never finished school," he said. The knot started burning. "There's nothing out there for the likes of me."

"And?"

"I can't leave Miriam." The tightness in his gut shattered, and the breeze made the tracks of his tears cold on his face. "I didn't even notice she was missing. When she came back, I wasn't going to do anything that might lose her again."

"You're a sweet man," Gabby said, "that's why I've been sent to help you."

"What? You're going to fix my life? You'll make it so Miriam isn't a ghost anymore?"

"I'm going to help you find God."

Sam jumped up from the boulder. He had all the words lined up he wanted to spit out at the fat woman, but when he turned to face Gabby, she wasn't the hugely fat woman who'd dragged him on this walk.

She was a being made of light. If he squinted, he could just make out hints of robes and what might have been wings, or the effect of his eyes watering.

"What?" Sam fell to his knees, shaking, then the fat woman was back with the shine of tears on her cheeks.

"It's OK, Sam," she said, "you don't need to be afraid."

"I'm not afraid," he said from his knees, "but you are so beautiful. Why not show that all the time?"

"I'd never get any work done," Gabby said. "Not with everyone falling to their knees all the time. Gets annoying, it does."

"I believe it," Sam said, "So what now?"

"I told you, I'll help you find God."

"Really." Sam heaved a sigh. "I don't need religion."

Gabby reached over and smacked Sam on the side of his head.

"Pay attention, Sam," Her rasp slipped and chords like the organ at church when he was a kid echoed beneath the words.

"Did I just get slapped by an angel?"

"Did you think I was just fuzziness and light, Sam?" Gabby stood in front of him, and he looked at her, fat and solid and human, but he also glimpsed the light which had sent him to his knees, heart in his mouth. "I have work to do. Right now, you're my work, but I can't help you if you don't pay attention. You challenged God. "OK, God, it's You and me, and only one of us is coming out alive." Those were your exact words.

"He dropped a whale on my pub!" Sam yelled, "Do you know how much of a mess a whale makes when it lands on a pub?"

"I was there, watching them clean up," Gabby said.

"It was blue whale too," Sam said, "There aren't many of those left. It was crying as it fell. I'd forgive the pub, but the poor whale..." His stomach vanished and left a yawning gulf behind. He could cry for eternity and not fill the gulf.

Gabby put her hand on his shoulder and squeezed.

"The smallest light can fill the deepest night."

"So, when do we start?" Sam said, "God's got some explaining to do."

30

"We've already started," Gabby said, "but if you're asking what you need to do next. You need to go home. You have a visitor and he's making Miriam uncomfortable."

Sam ran along the beach. His feet slid and twisted until he reached the path which led up to the fields atop the cliff. He climbed to the top and sprinted home. He wasn't letting anyone bother Miriam. The people in the village refused to notice him in case his oddness affected their lives of abject normalcy, for once Sam didn't rant that he'd prefer to be normal.

Normal meant doing without Miriam, and he wasn't ready for that.

He'd never be ready for that.

Sam crashed through the door and found Miriam trying to put the kettle on to make tea. He slid the water onto the stove and turned on the heat before turning to examine the visitor. He put his hand out to shake, but words didn't make it past the rasping gasps which made his throat ache. Miriam waved her hand at a glass in the dish drainer and Sam filled it with water and gulped it down.

"Sorry," he finally said and turned to the man sitting at his kitchen table. "I'm Sam,"

"Luke," the man said, but he didn't reach out to take Sam's hand. He was dressed in a suit and tie which probably cost more than the house they sat in. Nothing was out of place, not a stray hair or a errant crease marred Luke's perfection. If he'd walked into the Frog, Sam and George would have made fun of him in whispers. Here in the kitchen, Luke felt ominous, like the first tiny puffs of clouds when the oldsters predicted a storm.

"It has come to my attention," Luke said, "that you have lodged a complaint against God." Miriam looked at Sam with wide eyes and Sam waved at her. "My firm has been working on a class action suit which may fit your needs."

"A class action suit, against God?" Sam asked.

"Indeed," Luke said, "it is a much better option than threatening physical violence against God."

Miriam's eyes were getting wider still.

"I've talked to Gabby about this already," Sam said.

Luke shook his head.

"When one is undertaking a case against another being, one does not look to that being's own servants for help. You need to join with an adversary."

"One of the names for the devil is the Adversary," Miriam said.

"Just so," Luke nodded his head, "of course it is God's book and doesn't present my case in a fair light."

"And just what is your case?" The kettle whistled and Sam jumped up to make tea. He put out three cups, setting the best one in front of Luke, then one for himself and one for Miriam. Luke pushed the cup away with one finger with something that wasn't quite a sneer on his lips. Sam poured tea for himself and Miriam. He put milk and sugar on the table, then sat down before adding milk to his tea. Miriam sat in front of hers with her hands around the cup as if she could feel the warmth.

"God is not running the world properly," Luke said. "It is clear malfeasance, claiming to be a God of love and light and the like, but allowing your dear Miriam to be swept off the pier in a storm. How much effort would it have taken to keep her safe in her home? Bad things happen all around us and what does God do? Nothing. War, murder, storms, death, and you are left on your own without aid."

"I went down to the pier to watch for Sam because I was worried about him."

"Yes, yes," Luke pushed the tea a little further away from him. "You mortals are constantly doing foolish things that get in the way of your life. It should not be allowed."

"So, we only do what we're told to do?"

"Telling you what to do has not worked out that well now has it?" Luke's almost sneer bloomed. "You are so determined to be independent are you not? God should just have made it so you do what you are meant to do and nothing else."

Sam sipped his tea and made a face. He'd left it too long and it was bitter. Sam shook sugar into it then hopped up and snatched his fork from last night to stir his tea.

"That, is a fork," Luke said.

"Yeah," Sam said and set it beside his cup.

"You are supposed to use a spoon to stir; it is what they are made for."

"Sure, but a fork works well enough."

"Well enough is not sufficient." Shadow filled the kitchen. Luke stood up and went to the cutlery drawer and picked a spoon out. He laid it carefully beside the cup, then sat down again.

Sam looked at the spoon, then at the fork. He picked up the fork and stirred his cup.

"Thank you for your time, Luke," he said, "but I think I will deal with this my own way."

"Just like you've dealt with the rest of your life," Luke said as he stood up. "Like the pub, and the dry goods store before that, and the supply store, and the carpentry business. You should be out there," He pointed through the window to the pristine ocean, "doing what you are supposed to be doing."

Sam opened the door.

"Let me tell you something," Sam said, "I hate fishing, I have always hated fishing, I still hate the very thought of fishing, but your plan would have me out in the ocean doing what I hate because it was tidier. I prefer my little bit of mess, thank you very much."

Gabby had turned into a figure of light that drove Sam to his knees and put tears in his eyes. Luke shone with a negative light which sucked the sight from Sam. It left bile rising in his throat and his eyes dry and sore. The door pulled out of his hand to slam hard enough to shake the house.

As his sight returned, he saw Miriam at the table weeping into her arms.

"He's right," she said, "if I'd stayed in the house, I could have been a real wife to you. You must hate me."

Sam knelt at her side and put his hand in the same space as her hand occupied.

"I love you," he said, "sure, it'd be nice to be able to give you a kiss or a cuddle, but not at the expense of you being you."

Miriam looked at him and smiled. It was the smile he'd fallen in love with. A smile that was shy, but also promised wild abandon. She leaned over to kiss him, and Sam tried to convince himself he'd felt the slightest touch of lips on his.

"We'll get this sorted, Miriam and then we can live the rest of our lives together."

"Your life, Sam," Miriam said. "Mine is done these ten years."

"No," Sam said, "you've been a good wife to me all this time."

Miriam smiled again and tried to pick up the cups. Sam put them in the sink and rinsed out the tea pot.

"It's time," she said, "I will be waiting for you when you come." Miriam faded away in front of him. "Find what you need to find Sam, and thank you for loving me all these years."

Their kitchen was empty. The white cupboards looked dingy through his tears. The floor had holes in it he'd never really noticed before. Even the light from the sun held no warmth. Miriam had been what made the house glow for him. Now it was just old wood and chipped paint.

Sam walked into the back room where the fish swam in the tub.

"It's time," Sam said and snatched the fish up. He carried it down to the pier, then waded out into the cold, cold sea before letting it go. The fish burped out one last coin that spun and faded into the water as Miriam had vanished from the kitchen. He dove down, snatched up the coin and put it in his pocket.

"Sam," George yelled from the shore, "what are you doing out there?"

Sam waded back to shore and fell to the stony beach.

"She's gone, George," he said, "Miriam's gone."

"Miriam's been dead these ten years," George said.

"Aye, she's been dead," Sam said, "but now she's gone."

The crunch of George's footsteps receded while Sam shivered and wept.

A strong hand lifted him from the stones.

"Come on, Sam." Gabby's cheeks had tears to match his. "She loves you," she said.

"She did," Sam said and hiccoughed.

"Love doesn't end, Sam." Gabby said. "Never. But she knew you couldn't spend your life with a ghost."

"I would have," Sam said, "for her, I would have."

"Of course you would." Gabby said. "All the grandest of foolishness is for love."

"Were we wrong then?"

"Love is never wrong." Gabby led him up the beach to the road. "Let's get on our way; we've a ways to travel."

"I thought God is everywhere," Sam said.

"Sure, Sofie blows across the face of the earth," Gabby said, "but she isn't much of a conversationalist. We need to go the city."

"Sofie?"

"The Spirit of God that moved across the waters, Sam." Her toe tapped on the cobbles.

"I don't have a car," Sam said.

"There's always the bus, Sam. It isn't fancy, but it will get us there."

They stopped by his house for him to change into dry clothes, then Gabby led him through the village to the stop where they boarded a grumbling bus to the city. No one else waited for the bus. The villagers didn't have much use for the city, but the bus ran anyway. Sam walked to the back and sat down. They were the only two on the bus. He peered out at the village. From here it looked picturesque: white cottages set on green fields with the cliffs huddling around like sheltering hands. The ocean stretched blue to the horizon. He looked away; there was nothing holding him here anymore. The bus coughed and jerked into motion.

"Hey." A man slid into the seat beside Sam. "Heard you have a beef with the big guy."

"Where did you come from?" Sam asked.

The man winked and put his finger by his nose.

Gabby sat across the aisle with her arms crossed over her girth. She rolled her eyes and turned to look out her window.

The man turned his back on Gabby.

"Your argument with God?" he said.

"I don't want to talk about it,"

"Yeah, it has to be tough," the man said, "the entire village reeks of blubber. That was your pub the poor whale landed on, right?"

"The Barfing Frog," Sam said. "The most pathetic pub this side of the Atlantic. I only had customers when they couldn't squeeze in the door of the other place in the village."

"So why keep it open?"

36

"Had to do something. Miriam wouldn't let me just sit around the house." Water squeezed out the corners of his eyes and he leaned his head against the cool glass.

"Here," the man handed him a flask, "in memory of the Barfing Frog. You can call me Finn."

Sam took the flask and took a sip. The finest Irish whisky he'd ever drank slid down his throat. Finn deftly recovered his flask and capped it while Sam's taste buds were still dancing.

"The poor whale," Sam said, because he couldn't talk about Miriam. "Imagine you're swimming in the ocean, talking with your friends and eating tons of shrimp. Life is good, except you don't see too many girl whales these days. Then in an instant you're falling out of the sky to land in a village to smash a pub, all because God is angry at some idiot who isn't out at the fishing like God and everyone else thinks he should be."

"Harsh," Finn said.

"Too harsh," Sam said.

"Are you sure it is the big boss himself who has it in for you?"

"I opened a carpentry business. I had a few tools from my dad. Few jobs here and a few there, people are thinking that having a carpenter in town isn't a bad thing. The business starts to make money, enough to live on even. Then a guy asks me to build him a house on the edge of the village. Nice view of the ocean, high enough to be above the smell of dead fish. I get the frame up and go home to supper. I hear hammering so I go to see what's what. A flock of woodpeckers had covered the frame. They reduced the place to splinters while I watched. I started again, and they came back. Every night until the guy told me he didn't want the house anymore."

"Ouch," Finn winced and took another sip from the flask.

"Yeah, then I had a dry goods shop, got eaten by a plague of moths. Everything I've tried ends up in disaster. Not normal either, but the kind of weird thing that makes people afraid to know you, in case it rubs off on them."

"So you blame God?"

"Who else could make it rain fish? First time it was funny, people come out and grabbed fish, but they were all bruised up from the fall and the wrong kind to sell easy, so they stopped laughing. They raised taxes to pay for the equipment to clean up the fish. They couldn't prove it, but after the woodpeckers and moths, the fish and that poor whale, they knew it was me." Sam watched the fields roll by outside the window. "Most people would have driven me out of town, but I grew up there, so they just suffered through it."

"But you had the gold too," Finn said, and winked at him.

"Oh sure, the stash of gold to pay for everything," Sam turned to face Finn. The man's blue eyes didn't smile along with his mouth. His red hair moved slightly as if there were a breeze in the bus only Finn felt. "Every time I tried to use it to fix something, it made things worse."

"It's curious," Finn said, "but we know where every horde of gold in this land is to be found, and you didn't find any of them. Just where did the gold come from?"

"St. Peter's fish," Sam said, "it's been burping up coins since the day I caught it. No good rubbing your hands though. I threw it back in the ocean." He reached into his pocket to touch the last coin.

"You must have been fevered," the man said.

"It's what Miriam wanted," Sam said.

"Well, there's nought to be done about that now." Finn offered Sam the flask again. The whisky warmed him to his toes. "Here's the thing, Sam," the man said, "there's those of us who are happy enough with the balance of things in the world. We don't want the balance upset."

38

"What's that got to do with me?"

"You did challenge God, Sam. Only one will leave alive, you said. It may be unlikely for you to defeat God, but we want to know where we stand with you."

"Who are you?" Sam peered past the man, but Gabby appeared to be sleeping. Faint snoring sounded above the rumble of engine and tires.

"Your granny called us the fey," Finn said. The breeze that moved his hair caressed Sam's cheek for an instant.

"Right," Sam said. He looked out the window again, tried to imagine Luke driving a car along the twisting road to get to his house. It'd have to be a big black car, only Sam hadn't seen a car. Gabby, he could see traveling by bus, only he'd been blinded by the light that she was. Light didn't need a bus. Luke didn't need a car. If Gabby was an angel, Sam didn't want to think too hard about Luke. He'd bet the name was short for something very different than the writer of the Gospel.

"There is another option to haring off to duel God," Finn said. "You could come with me and live under the hill. Time passes differently there, you might spend a pleasant afternoon, and find a century passed above. No need to be choosing between God, and the other. God wants sacrifice; the other wants order. Why not just leave both of them behind?"

"Would Miriam be there?"

"Miriam?" Finn said. "No, lad, she's beyond us now."

"Then it's no good," Sam said. "No matter if a day or a hundred years passed; without her it wouldn't matter."

"I did have to try," Finn said and faded away in the seat until only the flask lay there. Sam picked it up and put it in his pocket.

Tears ran thick on his face, and he leaned against the window. They must have run into a rain squall as water streaked down the outside of the glass. The rain fell harder, and things splashed into the water in the ditch and thumped off the bus. Sam closed his eyes and looked away from the window. This brokenness had to be what the women with their sympathy and casseroles expected when Miriam died. He was just ten years too late for them to understand.

He took a few more sips of the whisky before the bus rattled and groaned to a stop beside an impersonal grey brick building. Sam dropped the flask on the seat, then followed Gabby off the bus and out into the streets. He couldn't see the ocean. There was no blue anywhere. Drizzle fell from grey clouds onto grey stone streets and grey brick buildings. Even the people under their umbrellas looked grey.

"What did you do with Finn's flask?" Gabby asked as she led him out into the drizzle.

"Left it on the bus," Sam said, "every time I took a sip I took to thinking a little more the solution to my problems was at the bottom of the flask."

Gabby laughed, and some of the grey people frowned at her.

"That flask has no bottom," Gabby said, "He must have been hoping to distract you one way or another from your meeting with God."

"He did say something about a side trip that would last a century or two."

"Poor Finn." Gabby shook her head a pulled Sam out of the way of a speeding taxi. "He thinks God has it in for him and the other fey. He can't be convinced otherwise, so time he could just live in joy is spent plotting."

"Sounds like a lot of us," Sam said. Gabby shrugged. They walked through the crowds of people passing them by without so much as a glance. Not much different from us; they're fussed about money, and we're obsessed with the fishing, which is money for us. Not much space for joy in our lives either. Only I'm not part of them anymore. The ache ran through his heart into his gut. He didn't belong anywhere now. If he was lucky, God would smite him and be done with it.

Gabby led him through the doors of a huge stone church. The light through the colored glass made him stop and stare. He might forgive the grey to live with such colour. Gabby stood and waited as if she could stand there forever.

"So God lives here?" Sam asked, even his whisper echoed in the church.

"Father O'Brien would like to think so," Gabby said. "In a way it's true, but God is bigger than this pile of bricks can hold. No, this is just a shortcut today." She walked through the church and out a back door into an alleyway so narrow, the drizzle hadn't found its way to the cobblestone pavement yet.

The reek of garbage made his eyes water, but he'd lived with worse when he was at the fishing. He rubbed his eyes and almost missed when Gabby ducked through a tiny door and led him down three steps and through an oak door that might have been built by the Vikings.

Light radiated from a couple of bulbs hanging from the ceiling. A young woman played a tune on a fiddle in the corner.

"Hi Sofie," Gabby said. The fiddle player raised an eyebrow, but didn't stop the tune. Sam tried to put a name to the tune. He'd liked listening to the fiddle players in the village, but the tune wandered in and out of recognition.

"Welcome Sam," a man came out from behind the bar drying a glass with a towel. He banged his head on one of the lightbulbs. Sam didn't know people came that big. Maybe he wasn't a human. This must be God.

"You dropped a blue whale on my pub," Sam said. His hands clenched and the knot in his stomach churned. Only Gabby's hand on his arm stopped Sam from charging the man.

"Sorry Sam," the man said, "whales aren't my department."

"Oh, you're..." What should he call the guy? Mr. Jesus didn't work.

"It's Ok, Sam, when you want to call me, you'll know my name." The man smiled and reached out a hand with a nail hole through it. Sam shook it automatically; warmth travelled up his arm and loosened the strangled lump in his chest.

"Enough of that." an old woman stomped out from a corner. Light followed her into the room. "Sam's got some explaining to do." She walked with a twisted root as a staff over to Sam. The giant patted Sam on the shoulder and went over to the fiddle player and started singing in counterpoint to the tune in a bass so low it was hardly audible. Gabby had vanished while he talked to the giant.

"Me?" Sam said, "what do you mean me?"

"You dropped a whale on your pub. She was one of my favourites, too."

"Favourites?" Sam put his hands to his head. "You have favourite whales?"

"Everything is a favourite, Sam," God said. "You're a favourite too."

"Then why did you drop a whale on my pub?"

"You know what people are learning?" God leaned on the staff and peered up at Sam. "The universe is created by observing it. That's why I had to create light first, so I could see what I was doing. You create the universe too, Sam. All humans do, but you have a special gift for believing. You make things happen, Sam. The woodpeckers, the moths, the fish are because you are different."

"I don't want to be special!" Sam hadn't planned to scream, but the words tore at his throat and shattered against the walls.

"So few of you do." God sighed and sat down on a chair that hadn't been there a second ago. "Yet special you are. Why do you think you needed to destroy your pub?"

"It was killing me," Sam whispered. "Going to polish glasses, pour cheap beer for people who didn't want to be there..."

"...and if a whale happened to smash it to splinters, who'd blame you for giving it up?" God poked him with the cane and light smashed into Sam showing him the truth in God's words. "So you come here to take me to task, but it was just one of those things. Not supernatural, but a little sideways from normal. It may comfort you that your whale had always wondered what it would be like to fly. Her end was the culmination of her dream as it was the close of your nightmare."

Sam walked away from God and the music in the corner. He'd wanted to challenge God for destroying his life, but it was his own fault. He'd built lives he hated, then found ways to free himself. All because he refused to leave Miriam. His fingers cracked as his fists tightened.

"You didn't really come to ask about the pub." God's voice struck him like another flash of light.

Pain started in Sam's feet and crept up his legs to his spine. Muscles twisted in his back as he tried to avoid what the light revealed. He fell to his knees and cried out. His heart would have hurt less if it had stopped, but his blood still coursed through his veins and screamed in his ears. Sam put his hands over his mouth to stop the words, but they burst from his lips.

"Why did you take Miriam?" He fell to the floor. The coin fell from his pocket and rang softly on the stone floor.

The fiddle music became a very familiar tune; the tune to which Miriam had walked down the aisle to become his wife. It turned like a dagger in his heart, reminding him of everything he'd lost. Then it shifted somehow and became a balm to his pain.

43

"She died loving you," God said. "That love brought her back to live with you. Your gift helped you to see and love her as she was then."

"With Miriam, I could be anything," Sam whispered into the floor.

"She still loves you," God said. "Whatever you become, she will love you. She went out in the storm and died as all things do eventually. Even I have died. Death is not to be feared."

"Now what?" Sam said. "Let me die and be with her." He wanted to get up, but had no strength in him to move. Then a hand reached down and lifted him up. He looked into Miriam's eyes. Tears poured down her cheeks.

"Between us, we could cry an ocean..." Sam said.

"...and your whale would swim and sing through it," she said.

Sam took her in his arms and held her tight. Warmth and light leaked into his soul. The world was right and proper with Miriam in his arms. He'd never let her go again.

"You can only touch because you're with me, Sam." God said.

"Can I stay with you?" Sam asked. "Please?"

God looked at Sam and her eyes weren't a color, but a swirling of stars and planets.

"I'm going to ask you to do the hardest thing I ever ask of one of my creation."

"Ask." Sam said. Miriam's hand held his and her smile filled his heart.

"Live," God said, "just for a time. The world will be a sadder place without you." He handed Sam the coin from the floor. "Keep this as a reminder."

"It won't work, you know, Sam." Luke walked out of a dark corner. "People don't want to be special; they don't want to discover anything. They only want to be safe. It doesn't matter how many messengers God sends, they won't listen." Painful darkness made him doubt himself. Who would listen to the likes of him?

"You are such a downer, Lucifer," the man in the corner said. "There are always people to listen. How about it, Sam? You may not like fishing, but there are other catches."

"I'll be waiting for you," Miriam said. The fiddle's music became a promise. The big man grinned. They waited; God waited for him to choose.

Sam kissed her and sweet light ran into him filling him with the opposite of agony. He laughed and as Lucifer scowled, he laughed louder.

"I'll be seeing you," he said to Miriam.

"I'll be in your dreams," she said.

"I hope so."

"You can't win," Lucifer said to him. "I will be there to stop you. You will speak of this love, and I will show them the futility of their lives. The world needs order, not love. Every person in their place."

"Wherever I go," Sam said to Lucifer. "I will think of you and stir my tea with a fork." Sam laughed at the face Lucifer made, then walked through the door and out of the alley into the sunshine. He looked up and laughed.

A goldfish fell out of the sky and landed in a puddle left by the rain.

"Look Mom!" A little girl screamed and pointed at the fish. "A piece of the sun fell out of the sky."

Sam picked a cup from a trash bin and filled it with water then scooped the fish into it.

"Take it home," he said. "Give it fish food and love, and watch it grow."

The girl took the cup and ran to show her mother. They bent and peered at it.

Sam put his hand in his pockets and started off down the street. His fingers touched the coin, but it had changed shape. He pulled it out to look at it. It had become the ordinary fork he'd used to stir his tea in his kitchen.

Something strange took form in his heart, it took him a moment to name it as joy.

ILLEGAL MIND

First published in Collidor Stream Collection 2016

The cop stood in the bus with her gun pointed at Zechariah.

"Put your hands on your head," she said.

Zechariah thought it was an overreaction to reading a Bible on the bus, but he carefully put the book on the seat behind him and put his hands on his head. He prayed that God would give the cop patience. The other passengers moved as far away from him as possible.

"On the floor," the cop said.

"You've got to be kidding," Zechariah said, "the floor is disgusting."

Instead of arguing, the cop pulled the trigger. It was the first time Zechariah had been tazed. The electricity ran through his body like painful ecstasy, and he fell twitching to the rubber matting that coated the aisle of the bus. It smelled of rot and puke and old urine. Fresh urine now, as hot liquid escaped his bladder and puddled around him.

"Ewww," the kid said. The same kid who had started all this.

Zechariah had boarded the bus as he always did and taken a seat near the back. Nobody paid much attention to what went on at the back, so it was safer. He pulled out his Bible and opened it to the chapter he was studying. He'd just started Romans and reading about the sin of people who'd abandoned God for the lusts of their flesh. He looked up briefly to see a kid reading a book called *Still More Shades*. The cover moved as the kid turned the pages and Zechariah felt hot blood in his face. That cover glorified the sins of the flesh.

He tried to return his attention to the Bible in front of him. He couldn't afford to draw notice. Paul's words on sin couldn't compete with the graphic, jerky sexuality of the cover of the kid's book. His eyes would be drawn to it and he'd have to pull them away again.

"What's the matter," the kid said, "don't you like my book?" He tilted the book and made the people on the cover do *it* endlessly.

"Don't you think that's a bit indecent for a public bus?" Zechariah said. "Children might see it."

"What would be wrong with that?" the kid said and held the book up higher. "Hey kiddies, watch this!"

Zechariah snatched the book from the kid and dropped it on the seat as if it burnt his hand.

"Do you *want* to lead children into sin?" he said. *Stupid,* he thought, *really stupid,* but it was too late to keep his mouth shut. People near him started to edge away, but the kid grinned at Zechariah.

"You're one of those religious nuts," he said. "I've heard about people like you. Are you going to tell me that I'm a sinner? Am I going to hell?"

"The Bible says that it would be better for a millstone to be tied around your neck than for you to cause a child to stumble." *They already know what I stand for. Even they must agree that cover is just wrong.*

"What the hell does that mean?" the kid asked. "I mean, a millstone? Have you ever seen a millstone? And stumbling? I'd never do anything to hurt a kid. No study has shown any relationship between porn and anything but having a good time."

"It's wrong," Zechariah insisted. Why did he always pick the wrong verse to quote? There must be a better one. He looked at the book in his hands. Maybe there was something in Romans. He was so bad at this kind of thing. It was like he spoke a different language from everyone else.

"Because God says so? In some book that was written thousands of years ago?" The kid flicked a finger at the Bible and a page tore. For a second the kid's face showed concern, but it vanished behind a cocky grin. "So am I going to hell now?"

"You little prick." Zechariah tried to straighten the page and assess the damage. The kid reached toward the Bible again and Zechariah slapped him. He didn't think about it. His hand just moved. It would have been alright if he'd been reading anything but the Bible.

The cop stepped on the bus as his hand tingled from the slap. She pulled her gun and yelled at him like he was a criminal. Now, his neck ached from holding the weight of his head off the wet floor. He didn't think he'd be able to smell anything else for a week.

Another cop climbed into the bus.

"What's this?" he said. "It was a call for public religion."

"He resisted arrest," the first cop said. Zechariah clenched his teeth and tried not to look like he was resisting.

"Well, he's riding in your car."

"I thought we'd wait for the wagon."

"Do you really want the paperwork that comes with the wagon?" Neither cop looked at him or at any of the other passengers on the bus. Zechariah tried to roll onto his side away from the mess. The woman cop pointed her finger at him and wagged it, and he went back to holding his face off the floor. Gravity won just before the two cops hoisted him to his feet. He felt tears of humiliation attempting to wash the filth from his cheek.

One of the woman passengers looked defiantly at the cops then washed his face with a wet wipe from her purse.

"Bless you," Zechariah whispered.

"You'd have been better off with a rational argument," she said in a hissing voice. "Religion only leads to violence." He bit his tongue and let the pain keep him silent while the alcohol cleansed his face and cooled his skin.

Then, from the corner of his eye, he saw the Bible slip off the seat and land in the puddle of urine. No one pushed it, the bus hadn't moved. It was because Zechariah had refused to defend his faith. He was being punished. He knew it.

The second cop put on a pair of gloves to pick up the book and place it in a plastic bag. Zechariah wasn't sure if the disgust was for the urine or the book. His last view of the passengers was of the kid holding a different book.

They took him to the station and gave him an orange jumpsuit to wear. His clothes went into plastic bags to be given to him when he was released. Zechariah told them to throw them out. He couldn't imagine ever wearing them again. The cross that he wore under his shirt went into a small brown envelope. That left him feeling more naked than the baggy paper jumpsuit.

"We'll just get a picture now and your fingerprints." The woman cop guided him toward a wall with painted lines on it.

"Thank you for not taking my picture in those clothes," Zechariah said.

"Are you kidding?" she said. "The Sarge would make me scrub out the whole room. He hates that smell. Comes from working the downtown beat so long." The camera clicked and she grunted. It must have been good enough, since she didn't take it again.

"Turn right," she said, "now left."

He put his hands on a screen and his fingerprints were scanned into the system. He was officially a criminal. She'd read him his rights while he'd sat in the cop car. They were printed on a little laminated card so she didn't accidentally give him extra or take any away.

"Here," she said as she pointed him into the cell, "it isn't the Royal, but you'll be safe."

Safe from what, Zechariah wondered. The cop was the one who'd hurt him most. He deserved it though. He was like the apostates who turned from the church at the least bit of persecution. The cell was cold and it stank. Zechariah couldn't tell if the stench was him or the cell; probably both. He sat on the bed and looked at his hands. They were soft, not the kind of hands to strike another human. Hitting people was wrong. The Bible said to turn the other cheek. Zechariah rubbed the cheek that the woman had cleaned.

He didn't believe the rationalist arguments. It didn't make any sense that there were no clear rules, that no one was right, no one was wrong. It was all about studies and logic and long meandering statements. The Bible was simple. It said something and that was it. He liked that feeling of certainty. It might be too simple, but it suited him.

"What they bust you for?" The rough-looking man across the hall probably contributed to the reek in the cells. "You don't want to say anything incriminating. They'll be taping us."

"I slapped a kid who tore a page in my Bible."

"Tough break," the man said. "I remember you types used to hand out hot soup. I liked the soup good enough, but the preaching made it hard to swallow. At least my booze is real, better 'n your God. Can't say I'm sorry they banned you. Miss the soup though." He turned his back on Zechariah and lay down on the narrow cot in his cell.

Zechariah lay down on his cot. The bleach in the blanket made his eyes water and it was itchy. He prayed and asked forgiveness for his actions. He knew that God understood. He figured God knew the kid was a prick. God knew everything after all. God knew that it was just a moment of weakness that Zechariah hadn't defended Jesus right there on the bus. He wasn't really a coward apostate. He felt better knowing he was forgiven. Zechariah closed his eyes and slept.

***

He dreamed about God on his throne pointing at the kid and telling him he was a sinner and was going to hell. The cop was kneeling beside the kid in handcuffs. Zechariah tried not to feel superior, but he still knew he was better than them. He was one of God's people. Then God looked at him. Zechariah thought he looked sad.

A different cop woke him up with a plastic bowl of soup and a flimsy spoon. The soup was thin and needed salt. Zechariah wondered how it compared with the old mission's soup. The other man was gone, so he couldn't ask.

"When you're done I'll take you to court," the cop said.. "You'll have a chance to talk to a lawyer there."

Zechariah expected a court room with oak furniture and lawyers arguing with witnesses. His lawyer sat beside him in a folding chair. He'd talked with the lawyer for five minutes.

"Plead guilty and act repentant," the lawyer told him. "Don't go religious on the judge, or they'll throw the book at you, and I don't mean your precious Bible."

"I thought you were supposed to be on my side," Zechariah said.

"I celebrated when they finally outlawed all public religious expression. You people with your crosses and turbans and smugness caused all the trouble. It's better this way. I don't want to be here, but I need the money. Just shut up and look sorry."

The judge came in and sat on the other side of the cheap table.

"This isn't the first time, Mr. Green," the judge said. "You've been ticketed several times for public prayer. The police found a great deal of religious literature in your home."

"I'm still allowed to believe what I want to believe," Zechariah said.

"In private," the judge said, "in public you must respect the secular society. You caused a public disturbance and made public statements judging people based on your religious views. I'm declaring you a class three fundamentalist and remanding you for treatment."

"What about my trial?" Zechariah said., "Don't I get to tell my side?"

"This isn't about a crime," the judge said. "It's about public health. We've found that giving you a trial just feeds your need to feel persecuted. You're sick, not a victim. You'll be taken straight to rehabilitation." She closed the folder and sighed. "You will feel better when you are cured. Religion is a disease, Mr. Green. If we aren't careful it will infect our society again. As a carrier, you are a dangerous man. Happily we are able to treat the disease. After your rehab you will see things differently."

"I don't need to be cured!" Zechariah said. "I need to be left alone to follow God's will."

"That's not an option anymore," the judge said. "You've broken the rules too many times." She stood up, nodded at the lawyer and left.

"Some help you were," Zechariah said.

"I told you to plead and stay quiet." He stood up and left Zechariah alone.

He felt like smashing something, but he'd seen guns on the guards' belts. He sat at the table and fought back the waves of fear. Surely God wasn't going to abandon him? He needed Zechariah to be one of the faithful remnants. To be there to bring God back to the people. Zechariah had always believed that was the reason for his life.

A couple of guards came and took Zechariah to a self-driving transport vehicle. When they made him put on his seat belt he noticed the missing handle on his door. One guard ran a swipe card through the reader on the dash and closed the door. Neither of them said a word the entire time.

Zechariah could see out the window as the car wound through Montreal. He caught glimpses of Mt. Royal. He still remembered the day they took the cross down. He'd cried. That was the first time he really believed that they had outlawed religion. A couple of friends had planned to go get bits of scrap from the site, but it was left clean of the slightest hint that the landmark had ever been there.

There were protests over the ban. Priests and Buddhists and Sikhs marched in the streets. Zechariah hadn't gone because he wasn't comfortable with those other people. He didn't know how to talk to them. Their certainties were different from his. Then the protests seemed to always end in violence. People were arrested, people died. The government blamed religion. No one listened to the religious people claiming they were set up.

Zechariah wasn't sure. Looking out the window, he rubbed his hand. He'd slapped that kid. He wasn't sure if he was sorry or pleased about it. He'd never slapped anyone before.

He noted the places where there used to be churches. Now there were just empty lots or office buildings. He guessed there were synagogues and temples and such that had vanished too with the arrival of the secular society. He cared about the churches more. How were God's people to preach the Gospel without any buildings that showed God's glory? If he thought hard he could remember stained glass windows and tall crucifixes showing the suffering of the Christ. The city felt lifeless without the churches.

He wondered if it would still feel lifeless after he was cured. He spent the rest of the trip praying for strength.

The rehab center looked like a hospital with a barbed wire fence, a steel gate on the drive. The police car cruised through the gate and the door opened.

"Proceed up the stairs and through the door," a recorded voice said to him. *"Failure to attend rehabilitation is a fel-"* Zechariah cut the voice off by

slamming the door. He walked up the stairs and pulled the door open.

"Hail Mary, full of grace," a woman prayed over beads on a bench in the foyer. A man was reading a Bible and making careful notes; another man wore a turban while he knelt on the floor. It didn't smell like a hospital. It had the slight whiff of incontinence that Zechariah remembered from visiting his mother in the nursing home. They'd been allowed to hold little church services and sing hymns. One resident complained loudly the whole time and a nurse actually asked him to be respectful.

"Welcome, Mr. Green." A very tall man came forward to greet Zechariah. He wore pants and a golf shirt that showed off the mass of muscle underneath.

He must be security, don't want to anger him.

The man smiled, — white teeth against brilliant black skin. "I'm John. If you have any questions, just ask. The entire grounds of the hospital are designated as a religious zone. We ask that you do not fight with other patients who have different forms of your condition. You are all here to be cured. It matters little whether you are being cured of Christian or Islamic fundamentalism or some other form. You will be allowed to follow the tenets of your faith as you feel the need. We will measure your progress against the background of religiosity. Follow me and I'll take you to your room."

"I don't belong here,." Zechariah said. "I was just reading a book on the bus."

"You were convicted of third degree fundamentalism and remanded for treatment," John said. "You argued about the moral nature of the book one of the other passengers was reading." He waved at the people around the foyer. "This isn't a punishment. It is treatment. You have an illness." John didn't raise his voice or change its tone, but Zechariah had the feeling it would be bad to argue with him.

John walked ahead of Zechariah down a long hall lined with doors. He ran a swipe card through a reader and handed the card to Zechariah. The thin, slick plastic felt vaguely wrong. He missed the tooled leather of his Bible, the tiny weight of the cross around his neck.

"Your room is private space. There is one camera over the door. It will only activate if we feel that we need to check in for your safety. There will be a red light and a beep to inform you that it is on. There are a few passive sensors to monitor your health. We don't want suicides;, they're a waste of resources."

He closed the door and pointed to a tablet embedded in the desk. "This will tell you when and where your appointments are. Missing appointments will just make the process harder." He tapped on the tablet and motioned for Zechariah to put his hand on it. The tablet glowed green briefly.

"Good," John said, "you're in the system. Put your hand on any screen in the facility and it will tell you where and when you need to be next." He pointed to a line at the top. "You have assessment in fifteen minutes. I'll show you the way."

"You don't waste any time, do you?" Zechariah said as he followed John out of the room.

"The first day after your committal is valuable time. You're in a state of flux when you arrive. We don't like to waste the opportunity."

Assessment was past two steel doors. Zechariah had to put his hand on the screen to be allowed through.

"Take time afterwards to explore," John said, then walked away as Zechariah entered the assessment room.

"'Abandon faith, all you who enter here,'" a sign said on the wall across from Zechariah.

"It's borderline," someone said from his left, "paraphrased from Dante, but they let me keep it. I'm Dr. Staranski. All we're going to do today is find out where you keep the thinking that leads to your obsessive religious beliefs."

"They aren't obsessive," Zechariah said, as he prayed for the strength to withstand the test that was coming.

"You will be taking a functional MRI while I ask you to do a variety of tasks. That will tell me what areas we need to adjust."

"You can't change my faith," Zechariah said.

"I don't change your faith," the doctor said, "I change your brain. Your religiosity will fall off like an old scab."

The MRI was a huge, white donut with a narrow bed where he had to lie. A gel clamp held his head still.

"Watch the tablet and follow the instructions."

"And if I don't?" Zechariah asked.

"Doesn't really matter. You'd be surprised how little control you have over your brain. It is just more accurate if you cooperate." While he talked, Dr. Staranski fastened some electrodes to Zechariah's head. "Let's get started." He walked out of the room and the table slid Zechariah into the depths of the machine.

The tablet was just inches from his face.

Pray the Lord's Prayer it instructed him. Zechariah wanted to ignore it, but the first line came up on the tablet and he followed through to the end. A series of images flashed on the screen. The elements of the Mass, a priest in his robes, the crucifix.... He lost track and just let them pour past him. He prayed that he would be freed from this nonsense. God was bigger than any machine.

"You are going to feel close to God, now," Dr. Staranski's voice said to him. As he heard the words Zechariah felt an all- encompassing love surround him. Tears slid down his cheeks as he begged God for forgiveness. He knew in his heart and soul that this was real. He wasn't alone.

"Now it will stop." God vanished and a black hole opened in Zechariah's soul. He needed to find a way to get that sensation back. "The religious experience is simply the result of certain areas of the brain being stimulated," the doctor said through the speaker. "I can turn it on and off at will. It makes little difference to the treatment, but I like to point out that what you think is God, is just neurons firing. What you think is firm faith is just a track worn in your brain. We can erase that track and leave the rest. You won't forget your God. You just won't care about him anymore."

The images started up again, but now they were not religious images. They were random as far as Zechariah could tell. He was released back to the hospital soon after. Zechariah went to his room and tried to pray. He wanted to recapture that feeling of God's closeness, but all he succeeded in was bringing back the tears.

The next day he was directed to Treatment.

"This cap is central to your treatment. Trying to break it or remove it may cause you harm. If you experience any pain or hallucinations, come see me immediately." The woman in a white coat fitted the cap to his head. She didn't wear a name tag or introduce herself, but her hands were gentle.

"Read this," she said and handed him a card with the Lord's Prayer. She watched her computer screen as he started to read, but nothing happened. It was like the words no longer had any meaning. She showed him a few pictures and nodded in satisfaction as he stared blankly at them.

"We have a map of the areas of your brain that are active when you are experiencing religious ideation. The cap is designed to suppress those areas." She rattled off the explanation like a flight attendant demonstrating seat belts on a plane. "You will feel a lack of emotional response until you attach your emotions to healthier stimuli."

He fought the process. His faith wasn't about the feelings. He missed them, but he didn't need them. He recited the scriptures he could remember. There was no emotion, no feeling to them but he dragged them out of his memory anyway. He used to love the sense of God's justice and care in the Ten Commandments. Now they were just words. He said them over and over again.

He had to attend a group where they talked about their experience of life without religious feeling. Zechariah didn't say much. He didn't want to give anything away. The woman counted endlessly through her rosary.

"You have to interpret the scripture correctly," one of the other men said. He waved his arms about and kept standing up. "This is a sign of the End Times. This cap is the mark of the beast. If I had my Bible I could show you."

"You remember what happened when we gave you your Bible?" John said.

"That was just a lapse," the man said, "it's all in here." He tapped his head hard enough that Zechariah heard the thump of the finger on bone. "The beast of Babylon will appear at MacDonald's and order a meal without fries."

"He tried to get the cap off." One of the other men leaned over and spoke softly to Zechariah. "Fried his brain beyond repair." He made a brief *zzzt* noise. John looked over and frowned at them. They sat back and listened while the man ranted. No one laughed. *That could be me, except I never was big on Revelation.*

John looked at Zechariah as if he could read what was going on inside his head. Perhaps he could. Maybe the cap told them what he was thinking. *Nothing will separate me from the love of God,* he thought at John, *nothing.*

"It will be easier if you participate," John said after the others had left the group room.

"Why?" Zechariah said, "Why should I help you destroy the only thing that gives my life meaning."

"Perhaps you are looking for meaning in the wrong places." John put the notebook on the chair beside him.

Zechariah sat down again. He would try one more time to explain his life to someone who lived in another world.

"Some of the guys, they could sum up their lives by how they'd scored, either on the field or with the girls. It didn't seem to matter to them as long as they had a story of their own prowess to tell." Zechariah stared off into space. He thought of the one time he'd tried to score with a girl. He still squirmed with embarrassment just thinking about it. "I was no good with sports or the girls. I didn't have other talents to make people notice me, but when I carried the Bible, I could have long conversations with the girls about God and Jesus, and it was safe. I was good at being religious. It didn't do anyone any harm."

"But you tried to push your religion onto other people," John said. "That's the thing with religion. It can't leave well enough alone."

"I never did," Zechariah said, "not really. I couldn't bear to talk to anyone who wasn't already a church member. All I want is to be left alone."

"So why did you slap that young man on the bus?"

"He tore a page in my Bible. He thought it was a joke."

"He challenged the crutch you use to get through life without doing any of the work," John sounded accusatory. "You want to be able to keep your religion as a shield between you and the rest of the world, but you need to be able to live in the real world, Zechariah." He stood up and picked up the paper and pen.

Zechariah was sure John would rush to his office and document this conversation. He thought about what John said. He didn't really want to live in that colourless world out there. He didn't want to do things he didn't like so that he'd fit in with everyone else. He'd rather live in God's world where he knew he belonged even if he wasn't a very good Christian. He'd just keep fighting them. It was the first time in his life he had joined a real fight. He wasn't going to give up now.

They called him back to assessment. Zechariah lay in the narrow machine while the doctor played with his mind. The doctor took the cap off Zechariah and sent him away. It was strange. He tried reciting the Shepherd's Psalm. The feelings were there, faint and bruised, but they were there. He was winning. Zechariah grinned as he ran through every scripture he'd ever memorized. He let them wash through his soul like a balm.

In the morning they put the cap back on. It pushed negative feelings onto the words. *Love your neighbour* brought nausea., *Thou shalt not* gave him a headache. He tried to fight past to the love and awe and wonder, but the cap put up a cruel and impenetrable barrier.

That night at dinner he sat with the rosary woman.

"They do the work of the devil here," she said. Zechariah nodded. "I think that God does not care. He lets the devil win."

"It is a test," Zechariah said. "Our faith is being tested."

"Faith?" The woman shook her head. "This is not testing, this is breaking. The devil wins and God doesn't care. It would be better if there is no God, no devil. Then I don't have to believe that God has abandoned me." The woman broke the string of her rosary and let the beads run across the table. "There is no God. I am free." She got up and walked away, leaving the beads scattered. Zechariah picked one up and turned it in his hand. She hadn't sounded free. She'd sounded broken. He dropped the bead and went back to his room.

Zechariah fought on. The rosary woman left. New people came. They spoke in meandering sentences about how it was important that they raise their children to obey God. Apparently, that meant beating them with a stick. They were husband and wife. They were sick. Their understanding of God was wrong. Listening to them made Zechariah's cap send twinges to the deepest part of his soul. Nausea and pain hovered like vultures over the words the couple spoke to justify their actions. Zechariah clenched his teeth against the river of words that wanted to be spoken against them. He knew that speaking them would open the door to losing the words completely. The couple argued and slipped into some other language. John sighed while Zechariah breathed relief.

Dr. Staranski shook his head sadly at Zechariah's lack of progress.

"You are stubborn," the doctor said as images flashed across the screen. "I think you will be the subject of my next paper." Zechariah ignored him and tried to pray, but it got confusing. Nothing felt right. He fingered the plastic door key in his pocket and wished it had an edge. He'd cut his throat right here and damn their machine with his sacrifice. The doctor hit him with random moments of the God feeling, but now they came attached to awful pictures — violent and disgusting.

They adjusted his cap again. He lost words. He had no word for God, or faith, or prayer. He couldn't eat bread because the taste made him ill. One night, after a greasy meal of fish and chips, Zechariah forgot his name.

"Who am I?" he asked John.

"You are a different person," John said. "You need a different name. We'll call you Alfred. It has no religious echoes to damage your treatment."

They released him a week after his name change. Alfred decided to walk home. He didn't live far away.

"Your vocabulary will return," John said, "but the emotionally laden words that made you a dangerous fundamentalist will return without the weight they once had. They will just be words like all the others."

Alfred wasn't sure what John was talking about. He wasn't a fundamentalist. The word God was an empty space in his head. He hoped that he wouldn't get too many feelings. Feelings were confusing.

John gave him a pat on the shoulder and pointed the way again. Alfred nodded.

"I'll be OK," he said., "I grew up near here." He patted the pocket with the key to his home. "I'll come in next week, like you said."

He walked through the sunlight. Not too fast or he'd get overheated. He wore a ball cap. He didn't like the feeling of having nothing on his head. As long as he was just thinking, he was fine. He didn't need feelings. John said he did, but Alfred didn't trust them. There was something in him that said feelings were dangerous. Even thinking about them made his stomach queasy. Maybe he should go back.

Alfred kept walking. He'd need to go shopping. There would be no food at home. He'd have to go to the bank and get some money. It was good to have a plan. He saw a woman ahead of him. She looked at him nervously. She looked familiar, but he didn't know from where. He smiled and walked past her. John had taught him to smile. Alfred liked the sensation of the smile on his face, but he had to be careful.

The road was deserted except for him and the woman. He could hear her footsteps just a little way behind him. Alfred got to a bridge. He stopped on the bridge to watch the river water flow past. When he was a kid, he used to do this for hours. He'd just let the water take away whatever troubles he felt. The water washed his soul clean. He felt a spike of pain in his head. That was bad. He couldn't think about clean. The other word was gone.

"Nice day," the woman said as she caught up to him.

"It is," he said.

"I'm sorry about the bus," the woman said.

Alfred remembered her wiping his face with a cool cloth. That was nice.

"I was afraid that they would take me in too," she said. "I didn't think I'd have the courage God gave you."

God sent a spasm of nausea through him. The pain in his head was worse.

"Don't," Alfred said, "I can't."

"You're sick!" she said. "What did they do to you? Let me pray for you." His stomach emptied itself over the railing and his hat fell into the water. Alfred watched in panic as it sank slowly. She was chanting words that sent nails into his head.

"No, stop," he tried to say, but words choked him. It would be better if she hissed at him again. He could smell himself. He smelled like that bus again. He smelled like fear and hate and smugness. The feelings were too much. He couldn't hold them. He tried to run away, but he tripped on the uneven sidewalk.

The sensation of his head bouncing off the concrete was a welcome distraction. Blood poured from a cut on his forehead. Alfred tried to push it away from his eyes. The woman knelt beside him, and Alfred saw her tears. He wiped them away and left bloody smears in their place. He pushed himself to his feet and leaned against the railing.

"Please," he said, "I'm OK."

"No," she said, "you aren't OK. You need help. I'll call an ambulance. I don't know how God could let this happen to you."

He pushed her away. She kept using those words that were destroying him. When he pushed her, he lost his balance and fell from the bridge. He heard her scream as he fell, then he hit the water and rocks.

Alfred knew he was broken. He could see a bone sticking out of his arm, but he felt nothing except the cool water caressing him as it rushed by. He tried to cough, but there was no strength. The sun shone straight into his eyes. He thought about closing them, but he liked the light.

64

Something filled him and pushed all the pain and sickness from his body. He didn't have a name for it anymore, but it knew his name. It filled him until he saw only light. The water ran over him and into him.

Alfred wondered why it felt like tears.

THANKSGIVING ON THE STREET

Mom served up Thanksgiving Dinner. She'd thought ahead and got the extra-large jumbo-sized tin of beans. Didn't know they made tins that big. We each got a dollop of beans in our paper bowls, then huddled around the tiny stove trying to stay warm while our beans cooled off. Surreal.

I never expected to be eating Thanksgiving Dinner on the street. Things like that just didn't happen to me.

"Eat up, Ronnie," Mom said, "It will soon be time for bed."

I was going to argue with her, I'm in High School for Pete's sake, but I looked around us and shrugged. Bed didn't sound like a bad idea.

The rain didn't fall so much as it dive-bombed us. Rain drops exploded on contact with the cement sidewalk and hammered on any exposed body parts. We had a little shelter from the overhang of the building, but the dampness pervaded everything. It even smelled wet. I had never imagined smelling wet, but I'm sure I reeked as much as my older sister.

She huddled under a poncho made from the same stuff they use to make garbage bags; the hood pulled up over her once impeccably styled hair. Now strands of hair were plastered to her face and water ran down it thinning the beans as she spooned them into her mouth.

It was her fault that we were here. All her life she wanted more, more, more. I moved to a room the size of a closet in the basement so she could take over my room to store her stuff. She had designer jeans in three different sizes all with the labels still on; CD's still in their plastic wrap, every generation of iphone and more. I was forbidden from entering her room. I'm sure there were clothes there that fit me, but I'd never get to find out.

I, the shame of the family, once came home with jeans I'd bought at a thrift shop. Mom tried to make me take them back. Then she tried to throw them out. I wore them to school and Lexi swore that she had disowned me. I told her that her out of control spending would put the family on the streets.

So, here we were, eating Thanksgiving Dinner out of a extra-large-jumbo-sized tin of beans and waiting for the store to open.

Stuff Mart was supposed to open on Thanksgiving Day. Lexi freaked out at the news. This was her favourite store. They sold stuff cheaper so she could buy even more things that she would never use. She begged and pleaded to be allowed to go shopping on Thanksgiving. What better way to show her gratitude for everything she had than by adding more to the pile?

Mom is old school. The holidays are all about family. If Lexi was going shopping, we were all going shopping. She handed me a gift card.

"You *will* buy stuff with this," she said. "You must do your part to keep our economy going. So help me if you come out of that store with one dollar left on this card ..."

She didn't need to finish that threat. Last time I disobeyed her we went to Midnight Madness at our local mall, and she bought me three pink cashmere sweaters. Haven't told her yet that I'd traded them at school for an army backpack and a pair of combat boots.

Then rumors management had installed chains to keep employees at their tills turned into hints of a boycott. The owners caved in and closed the store for Thanksgiving but promising to open all the earlier in the morning of Black Friday.

Lexi wailed like the world was going to end, but Mom was sensible as ever.

"We'll camp out and be first into the store in the morning," she said and sent my father out to rent an RV for the adventure.

He came home with an RV that was bigger than some houses. It had a second floor!

"You know," he said, "that Bert and Gretta always come for Thanksgiving, and that means their kids, and didn't your mother say she wanted to come this year?"

So here we were. There was no hookup for the RV, so no lights. We only had one tank of propane, so Mom decided to cook on the camp stove she dug out of the garage. It said that we couldn't use it indoors. Thanksgiving was for family, so we all gathered around the stove and ate beans.

"These are the same beans your father and I ate during the war," Grandma said to mom. "Didn't know they came in such small tins. Took us a month to eat through one."

That explained my grandfather, who was still passing gas at his own funeral. I missed the old guy, even though "pull my finger" was the only joke he knew.

"OK," Mom said, "bedtime. Everyone inside and we'll lock it up tight."

"I'm going to stay out here," I said. Memories of Grandpa were suggesting that wet air was a lot better than what I would be breathing in the RV.

"Ronnie," Mom said with the tone that promised more pink sweaters.

"Mom," I said, "someone has to hold our spot outside the doors. You don't want someone else coming and taking it would you?"

"Let her stay outside," Lexi said, "We're just sleeping anyway."

"OK," Mom said, "but don't talk to any strangers. If you get scared, you come bang on the door and one of us will wake up and let you in."

That's my Mom, always looking out for me.

68

Everybody stretched and then shrieked as cold water ran down their backs. They ran to the RV and piled in. Grandma let one go that was worthy of her husband of fifty years. I hoped that Mom left the windows open a crack.

Now that all my family was gone, I could relax, leaning against the wall of the Stuff Mart and watching rain on cement. I was warm enough in the old pea coat I'd smuggled into the house when no one was looking. The poncho was almost like a personal tent. I moved the stove a little closer to me and stared out at the rain.

I was a disappointment to my family. Here they were, making huge sacrifices to boost the economy and all I could think about was how fast I could get in and out of that store tomorrow morning. I didn't dare not spend the money, but I hated shopping. I was, in my sister's words a drag on our country.

"Hey, missy," An old man shuffled up and tried to hunch out of the rain. "Do you mind if I sit against the wall? I promise I won't touch you."

"There's lot of wall," I said, "Pull up a brick and make yourself comfortable."

"My name's Ronny," the old man said, "It's long for Ron."

"My name's Ronnie," I told him, "It's short for Veronica."

I held out my hand and we shook.

"It's funny us having the same name," the old man said. He leaned against the wall and sighed. "We could be a comedy act."

"Nah," I said, "Who'd watch a show called The Two Ronnie's?"

"You going to eat those beans?"

"Nope," I said and handed him a spoon, "help yourself."

"So how much you getting paid?" Ronny said.

"Paid?"

"Some rich folk are paying me to sit here all night so they're first in line in the morning."

"I'm with them," I pointed to the RV. "They don't even pay me attention."

Ronny chuckled through the beans.

"Hi," a younger woman wandered up. "You mind if I share the food?"

"Go ahead," I told her. "I'm Ronnie and he's Ronny." She nodded as she ate beans.

"Name's Tony," she said between mouthfuls, "like the Tiger."

Turned out she was a professional queuer too. By the time the rain had turned to snow a whole group of us sat around the stove. I even opened the second tin of beans. Hope Mom hadn't planned on eating it for breakfast.

We grouped around the little stove until it ran out of fuel sometime in the early morning. Then we just sat in a group and told stories. I told them about my sister's room like it was Alladin's cave, and they talked about how they found stuff at thrift shops and made shoes of two different sizes work with extra socks and newspaper in the toes.

As the sun came up and the snow stopped other people started showing up. Some of them were the one who'd paid folks to wait for them. They were annoyed that I was here first, but everyone paid up after we threatened to block the door of the store. Lexi and Mom and the other crawled out of the RV and stood breathing deeply of cold air. Then they came over to join me.

My new friends started feeling uncomfortable with all this disposable income around, so they waved goodbye to me and wandered away across the parking lot.

"Hey," I said to Lexi, "hold my place for me?" She shrugged. She was stretching to warm up for the sprint that would start in just a few minutes now.

"Ronny!" I shouted. He stopped and the rest of them waited for him.

"They'll be putting coffee on at the mission," he said, "We don't want to disappoint them."

"You know that thrift store at Second and Second? Meet me there in a couple of hours." He nodded and they walked away again. "Bring some coffee!" I yelled. He waved to me but kept walking. I ran back to the store and got there in time for the doors to open. The people screamed with eagerness, so I let them go in. I could see them pushing and shoving to buy stuff. I slid into the store and grabbed a cart and started filling it with random things that no one else seemed to want; warm socks, good boots. wool hats.

"Well," Mom said, "It's a start. Are you sure you don't want this gorgeous pink sweater? It's alpaca."

It's the holidays, why not? I let her put it in the cart. It would look divine on Tony.

CARROTS

"Carrots again?" Harry sighed lugubriously.

"Harry you love carrots, " Mildred slid into her seat across from her husband.

"Sorry, my love, I didn't hear you come in."

"It's those new hearing aids. I don't think they work very well."

Harry picked up his fork and wolfed down the buttered carrots on his plate. Then he turned his attention to the rest of his meal.

"How can anyone eats carrots like that if they don't like them?" Mildred speared her carrots daintily.

"Mmmm," Harry chewed his roast beef with a blissful expression on his face.

"The first time you came to my parents' home for supper you ate your carrots so quickly Mom told me if I only cooked you carrots you would love me forever."

Harry took another bite of roast.

"All that first year we were married, I cooked carrots for you. Carrot soup, carrot salad, roast carrots, grilled carrots."

"Bugs Bunny would have thought he had died and gone to heaven." Harry had run out of food on his plate to provide excuse for his silence.

"Then we had kids, and we taught them to love carrots too."

"Billy ate so many one week that he turned orange."

"Sally cried because she needed glasses even with all the carrots she ate."

"James dressed up as a carrot monster for Halloween, three times."

"And now you are saying you don't like carrots?"

"I didn't say that."

"Carrots again," Mildred mimicked him exactly down to the ridiculous heavy sigh.

"All right, I admit it." he played with his fork, then looked up at his wife of fifty years. "I hate carrots. I loathe them with a deep abiding passion. If I had my way, I would never see another carrot on my plate again."

"But you always eat them first. You eat them with such obvious enjoyment."

"I eat them first to get them out of the way. Then I can enjoy the rest of my meal."

"So all those years, the gingered carrots, the carrot soufflé. the glazed carrots...."

"Ate them, then enjoyed the rest of the meal." He put the fork down precisely in the centre of the plate, then moved it over just a bit. "I thought for a while that I might learn to like carrots, but it never happened. Every time I saw them, my heart would sink a little."

"All those years you hated my cooking."

"No, just the carrots."

"But I put carrots in everything!"

"Yes," Harry said with another sigh, "you did."

"Why didn't you *tell* me?"

"I didn't want to hurt your feelings." He went over and put his arms around his wife. "If it was going to make you happy, I was going to eat carrots everyday for the rest of my life. I would have done anything for you, what were a few carrots, if it made you happy?" He gently brushed the tears away from Mildred's face.

"I don't like carrots either," she whispered. "Mom used to have huge fights with me over them. I never ate carrots until after that first dinner at our house." Harry realized that the shaking in her shoulders wasn't crying but laughter.

"Aren't we a pair of fools," he said. "All those years pretending to like carrots to make the other happy."

"But think of what we would have missed."

"Besides a hundred ton of carrots?"

"How many of our stories are about those awful orange roots?"

"Billy painting the kitchen table with pureed carrot."

"Sally's science fair project on rabbits and carrots."

"James' prize winning carrot at the fair."

Mildred hugged Harry tight.

"Knowing you hated carrots, but ate them for me..." She brushed the grey hair from his face. "I can't tell you how special it makes me feel."

"Knowing that you cooked carrots, just for me, for all those years when you didn't like them..." He kissed her forehead.

"But you don't like carrots."

"That doesn't matter. What mattered was that you were cooking them because you loved me."

"All those years..."

"All those years."

"It's almost better this way," she said, "We get to discover again how much we love each other."

"Mmmm," he said holding her tight. He heard the front door open and close, but wasn't about to move.

"Hey, folks," James said, "Get a room." He hugged his parents for a moment. "What's got you all lovey-dovey today?" He put a box on the table. "I brought a treat for you lovebirds."

Mildred and Harry looked at each other and smiled.

"It's carrot cake!" James said with a flourish.

"That *is* a treat," Harry winked at the love of his life.

"I'll get the plates and forks." Mildred winked back.

74

FIRST BOY

The place smelled like a dozen dogs had peed in the corners; about right for a dog pound. Nicer than some places I've stayed. When you're a pit bull you see a lot bad spots. The yard had real grass even. I was alone when they brought in a litter from a puppy mill. Sad cases every one of them. Breaks my heart how people abuse us in the name of having a pet.

One pup broke loose from the squirming mound drinking from their mom, and staggered over to the cage that divided us.

"Hello," he said.

"Hey," I said and eyeballed him from where I lay on my mat. The rest of the pups were black, but this one had black blotches on grey fur. Reminded me of this Aussie I once met. The kid had these crazy blue eyes. All pups have blue eyes, but I wondered if his wouldn't glow a little when the humans turned off the lights.

"What are you doing?" He tried pushing his nose through the mesh, but the humans were onto that and it was too small for even his nose. I crawled over to put my nose against the mesh and we breathed each other in.

"Sleeping, kid." I said after we'd done sniffing each other.

"Where are we?" He shook himself and peed on the floor.

"This is the pound," I said, "The beginning for some, end for others. You might want to pee over on the paper there," I pointed with my nose. "Humans are funny that way."

"So what about the humans?" he said. "I don't need 'em"

"Yeah, kid," I said, "you do. I was only a little older than you when I got my first human. Boy came in and didn't know a pit bull from a poodle, He wanted me on account of the black patch on my eye. It reminded him of some movie he'd just seen. I was going to be his very first pet."

"What's a movie?"

"Beats me, kid. Never seen one. Anyway they put a collar on me and he led me away on a leash. He named me Patch; proudest day of my life. I had no clue. The boy put out some of that paper in a box and a bowl of food and left me there. All night I howled in terror. I had no idea where I was or what was going on, and I missed my mom and my litter mates. The mom came and shushed me, then the dad came and yelled at me. The boy came after them and carried me up to his room. *Don't tell Mom.* He whispered to me. I slept on his pillow. He took me outside in the morning to do my business on the grass."

"I thought you said to do it on the paper?"

"On the paper when you're inside and a pup, but outside the rest of the time. Nothing makes a human happier than a dog peeing on the grass."

"Oh."

I could see the wheels turning in the kid's head. This pup was a smart one. He stumbled back to the pile and attached himself to his mother. She hardly had the energy to look at me. Poor girl was worn out, but then I was pretty worn out myself.

Woke up next morning to the sound of pee on paper and opened my eye to see the kid whizzing like a pro on the paper. He pranced over to me.

"Tell me more about humans, Patch."

"Sure, kid." I got up and stretched, then shook the cobwebs out of my head. Enough exercise for the day. I lay down on my mat. "Well, soon as I learned to pee on the grass, the boy started teaching me tricks."

"What's that?"

"That's when a human tells you to do something silly, then gives you a treat, food usually, but I'd do tricks just to get him to scratch behind my ears. The boy, his name was

Sam, taught me to sit, and stay, and rollover, simple stuff really. When I got good at those he started teaching me to shake a paw or play dead. We had this game where he'd put a biscuit on my nose and I'd balance it until he said *Go* then I'd throw it in the air and catch it. That game was my favourite thing in the world. Most of the time we just ran around and wrestled."

"Wow," The kid panted at me, a natural. "So, then what happened?"

"Sam went back to school. That's some place all humans have to go. It's like peeing on the grass. Doesn't make sense, but they do it anyway. I waited by the door for him to come home and we'd go play in the yard or he'd take me for a walk. Every night I slept on his bed."

Thinking about those days made me want to howl like a puppy. You can't go back, you just can't go back. The kid wandered off and piled into his litter mates, and left me with my thoughts. If I could only do that one thing over again. I closed my eye and snoozed a while. To be honest, just watching that much energy made me tired. Hadn't thought about Sam in ages. Even if humans didn't grow as fast as us, he'd be a lot older; maybe even finished with that school thing.

The door opened, and some humans came in. A little girl ran over to the cage with the puppies.

Look, aren't they cute?

The kid pulled himself out of the pile and wobbled over to her.

He's an unusual colour, looks like a seal.

He's a catahoula.

Well, wouldn't you know, the kid's something more than an odd looking mutt.

Can I pick him up? Please?

The pound human opened the door of the cage and put the pup in the girl's arms.

"Remember, pee only on the paper!" I said to him. I know what pups are like when their excited. Sure enough he wriggled away from her and went to pee on the paper like a champ. She picked him up again when he came back.

"Lick her face, kid," I said. "They can't resist that."

He did what I said, and the girl laughed. Sam used to laugh like that. I put my head on my paws and watched them.

I want this one, Mom.

Are you sure? We haven't looked anywhere else.

Please, Mom? I want this one. I'll call him Patches.

Ok, Sue, if you want.

You'll have to wait a week for him to be weaned and get his first shots...

The adult humans walked away while the girl cuddled the pup. A little while later they came back. They put a collar on the Patches, then left. The girl walked backwards out the door waving at him.

The pup came running over to me.

"Did you see that?" he said. "This thing feels funny." He scratched at the collar.

"Wear it with pride, Patches," I said. "The collar tells the humans that you belong."

"Wow."

"Listen, Patches," I said. "I have to tell you something, so you don't make the mistake I did."

He sat down and wagged his tail at me.

"Sam took me for a walk one day. I was grown by then. Humans grow slower than we do, so Sam wasn't much bigger. We met another kid. He was bigger than Sam. I could tell Sam was afraid of him. The other kid came over with his friends. They yelled at Sam and pushed him around. I growled at the kids. Sam told me to stop. One kid laughed at Sam and punched him in the face. I bit the kid."

"That's brave," Patches said.

"No," I said, "It was bad. We mustn't bite a human. We can growl or bark, but we can never, never bite, especially a young human.

"The kids ran away screaming and Sam took me home. Later that night a human came and took me away from Sam. They brought me to a place like this one. I went off with another human. He liked me cause I was a pit bull. He tied me on a chain and left me in his yard. I think I went a little crazy. Another human bought me and put in a worse place. I don't want to tell you, or I'll give you nightmares."

"Is that when you lost your eye?"

"Yeah," I said, "my eye and more than a little of my soul."

"So pee on the grass and don't bite,' Patches said and panted happily.

"That about sums it up," I said. "Just make your human happy."

The week went by in a flash. Patches went off with his girl and the rest of the pups went too. Even the old girl went to a new home. I ate my meals, did my business on the grass though the humans had to help me out there. The place stank of pee, but I didn't care. There were worse places. I'd been to most of them.

I dreamed Sam put a biscuit on my nose. We stared at each other. All the horrible things melted away. Every part of me waited for that magic word. The one that would make everything right.

Go!

OLD SUPERHEROES NEVER DIE

"Superman has Clark Kent when he wants to kick back and just not go out to fight the bad guys. I've wearing this costume for so long I can't remember what name my mother called me. It gets tiring sometimes. There are days I could use an extra hand, but who offers to carry groceries for a guy in a superhero costume? Even if the guy qualifies for his old age security."

The old man sat in the chair in my office and glowered at me. The blue spandex might have been a good choice when he was younger and in better shape, but now it showed off the softness of his old body. Not that he was soft, that gun was real enough, and his eyes held the same steel as the gun.

"What do you want me to do?" I asked and looked at the blank page where I would normally have reams of notes.

"I need a retirement home," the old man said, "somewhere where the bad guys can't find me and where everyone else will leave me alone."

"I need a name, a social security number, an address," I said, "I understand you wanting a rest, but I can't place a nameless stranger in a home. You have to give me something."

He pushed himself to his feet. The sound of joints popping and cracking made me wince. His fingers were swollen, super-arthritis? Was surgery even possible on him?

"Come with me," he said, "see for yourself. Don't get too close and don't get in my way." I followed him out of my office and watched him walk along the street. Nobody paid the slightest attention to him. A flock of pigeons flew over him and left their mark on his blue costume. His shoulders sagged a little as he kept walking, though I noticed his hand brush against that gun at his side. I don't know if he walked slowly so I could keep up, but if so he over did it. Several times I had to stop to tie my shoe or look in a window to give him the space he needed.

We turned down a ramp into a parking garage. Shouts echoed through the empty space as men in black ninja costumes jumped out to surround him. None of them saw me as I ducked between two cars and pulled out my cell phone. No signal.

My debate as to whether I should go out on the street to call for help ended when the ninjas leaped to the attack. In the movies, they'd charge one by one and allow him to defeat one before the next moved in. This wasn't the movies. They moved as a coordinated team to pummel the old man.

Only he didn't move like an old man now. One opponent moved a little too fast. The man in spandex grabbed him by the throat and tossed him at those attacking from the rear. The smack of a fist hitting flesh reached my hiding place, but the hero used the arm to pull the ninja off balance and drop him with a quick jab. He spun out of the attempted headlock by another opponent and threw that man on top of the first hard enough to bounce.

One by one then ninjas joined the pile of unconscious thugs until it was taller than the old man. The last one he dispatched with a jump kick I couldn't imagine trying, though I was sure he had thirty years on me. As I came out of my hiding place the energy left him and he puffed like I did if I walked up a hill too fast. He waved at me and I waited for him to catch his breath.

"Why didn't you use that?" I pointed at the gun at his side.

"Do you know... how much... ammunition costs?" he said between wheezes. "Nobody pays me for this." He walked to the back of the garage and pulled the cover off a classic muscle car. Well, it would have been a classic if it weren't for the fifty caliber machine guns mounted on each door.

"You may as well get in." He waved me over to the passenger side and climbed into his seat.

"Where are the seatbelts?"

"Never needed them." He pushed a button and the engine roared to life. Tires squealed as smoke filled the garage, then he popped the brake and we took off. He weaved through the garage slowing only slightly to bump a reviving ninja back onto the pile with a rear fender. We erupted out of the garage and onto the street, where he had to slam on the brakes to fit into the bumper to bumper traffic.

"We'd be faster walking," I said.

"Tell me about it," the old man thumped the steering wheel and glared up at the flock of pigeons that left white gooey marks across the windshield. "Flying's better, but everyone's so uptight now I'm afraid they'd try to shoot me down. Got some nice pictures the first time they scrambled on me, but now it's just a nuisance."

He pulled off the road and sped away through an alley making one turn after another into spaces I was sure we'd never fit. Even with the extra width of the guns we didn't leave a scratch on the wall.

"Here we are," he said and whipped the car through an open loading door. The car rocked and creaked as the elevator lifted us up to the top floor.

We stopped and he climbed out of the car. I had to climb across the car to get out.

"Don't hit any buttons," he said.

The words *rocket launcher* peeked out from beneath my hand. I moved it away and made sure to watch what I did until I stood safe outside the car.

The penthouse was sparsely furnished, almost barren. I shivered, it might be a great hero's lair, but I wouldn't want to live here.

82

"Tea, coffee?" the old man said, "I'd offer you biscuits and jam, but jam jars are my one weakness."

"How can a jam jar be your weakness?"

"Can't open them," he said, "never could." He poured boiling water into a pot and swirled it. Then made tea.

"Was a time I didn't mind it up here," he said, "I needed a quiet place to get away from the rush; being a super hero is addictive. Then like any addiction it takes over and you lose yourself. Those guys with their secret identities had it right. You've got to step back and let it go once in a while."

"So why not take off the mask and retire?" I watched him make tea in the window's reflection.

"I'm not sure who's under there anymore." He came over and handed me a cup. I sipped at it. I hate tea, but its bitterness seemed appropriate. He stared through the window at the city. From up here it looked quiet and peaceful.

"They'd find you anywhere I placed you," I said, "Unless you take off the mask and become just another old man."

He sipped his tea and I waited. When I finished my tea, I left him there, still looking out the window. I saw him wave once before I closed the door behind me.

JACK'S APOCALYPSE

First published in Inkspots by Polar Expressions
Publishing 2011

"Say something, blast you!" Jack yelled at the
mannequin. He knew he was losing it, but why should he
always be the one to carry the conversation? "You cheap
bit of plastic," he said, "We're through." He pushed her
over onto the pile of clothes and walked away.

It hadn't taken long after the apocalypse had been
inconsiderate enough to leave him behind for him to start
losing what used to be referred to as sanity. Now that he
was the only one left the whole question of what was and
wasn't sane was up for grabs. Jack peeked back at the
mannequin but she had her hand up in what clearly meant
to be a rude gesture. Let her stew for a while.

Yap trotted after him growling at his ankles. In all the
movies he'd watched the lone survivors were accompanied
by loyal and intelligent dogs, big ones. Yap was an
irascible little mutt who would have a hard time protecting
him from a squirrel. The dog stopped and lifted his leg.
"Yap," Jack said, "how many times have I told you. Don't
pee on the canned goods?" He walked over to the
telephone. "Clean up on aisle four. Clean up on aisle four."
He waited but nobody came, so he went to the back of the
store for the mop and bucket. He put on the blue vest and
mopped up the puddle. Then he carefully hung up the vest
and went back to his shopping.
"We don't have much of a choice today, boy." Jack pulled
his can opener from its leash and opened a couple of tins.
He put one on the floor for the dog and spooned the cold
beans into his mouth. He hated beans, especially cold, but
he hated moving even more. But the shelves were
dangerously empty.

84

"Well, Yap," he said, "It's time we found another place to hang out." The dog barked then trotted over to a shelf and lifted his leg. "OK, OK, I'll pack the cart."

Jack put the last of the tins of food in the shopping cart along with a tent and sleeping bag from camping supplies. The final item was the shotgun and box of shells. There were predators out there. This was going to be a big move. He had cleaned out all the stores in this town. The next town was at least a week's walk to the south. There would be stores there with shelves full of food. His mouth watered at the thought of eating something other than beans.

They started out in the early morning. Yap was on a leash tied to the cart. The dog hated the leash, but it was safer to keep him close. Jack pushed the cart along the road and basked in the warmth of the sun. He let Yap ride in the cart when he got tired.

"Leave the leash alone," Jack said tapping the dog on the nose. "I don't want you chewing at it."

They made good time and he found himself enjoying the walk. Other than the faint squeak of the wheels the only sounds he could hear were the birds and the squirrels.

Then Yap took off after a squirrel that crossed right in front of him and the leash broke.

"Come here you stupid dog! That squirrel will eat you alive." The dog ignored him and ran around the base of the tree barking. Jack didn't see the eagle until it swooped down and snatched Yap from the ground. Picking up the shotgun he shot at the eagle but it was long gone.

Jack wiped at the tears that poured down his face. Here he was Jack, Survivor of the Apocalypse, crying over a stupid little dog. He looked at the shotgun in his hand. Maybe it was time to just end it. He was no heroic survivor; he was just a freak. There was no reason he could think of why he was left behind.

He put the gun back in the cart.

"Sorry, Yap, but I'm just not ready to let go." He untied the end of the leash from the cart and dropped it to the asphalt then started pushing the cart down the road.

ADVENTURES IN A NORTHERN WONDERLAND

First published in 'Canadian Creatures' Schreyer Ink Publishing 2018

Alice didn't like her name, she'd have preferred something from her parents' homeland in Somolia, but they didn't want to remember those frantic days, and Alice couldn't. She tried, but a wall of opaque glass stopped her memories of anything before they stepped off the plane in Winnipeg and the icy wind wrapped bitter arms around her.

She'd thought Winnipeg the coldest place on earth until they moved to Flin Flon. The white extended as far as she could see from the airplane which dropped them into the middle of it. Dark green trees were the sole relief from the white.

The snow had been exciting for a week, tolerable for another, then excruciating after that. Her classmates didn't make fun of her, but made sure she dressed for the weather, then ignored her to follow their own interests-- snowmobiling, ice fishing, skiing, hockey.

Alice stared out the window into the blowing white dance, and sighed deeply. Her mother and father were working at the hospital tonight, so it was her and her older brother and his video games. Really just her.

Something moved outside. Not a person, but not a dog either. It bounded along Church St, huge furry feet sticking out from under a green parka. Immense ears flapped in the wind.

Alice ran to the door and put on her snowpants, boots, parka, hat, mitts, scarf, a second scarf. Surely by the time she'd finished the creature would be gone, yet here she was, dressed for the outdoors, so out she went.

Whatever it was turned and headed up Fourth Ave, past the new hospital toward the mine. Alice ran through the snow after it. Just before it reached the fence the thing dove into a hole under a rock. Without giving herself time to think, Alice crawled in after, then the ground disappeared from beneath her hands and she fell screaming into the dark.

After a bit, she ran out of breath and had to stop.

"Thank goodness, you were giving me a headache with that racket, and I detest willow bark."

"Doesn't this hole have a bottom?"

"Oh yes of course."

"But I can't see it."

"Neither can I. It's dark."

"But--"

Alice hit something soft and cold. It slowed her, then stopped her. Far, far, far above, like a single twinkling star shone the entrance to the hole.

"Where are we?" Alice floundered to her feet. Nobody answered, but tracks led away, so she followed them to a tent.

A lantern hung from the ridgepole of the tent. On a table sat a steaming cup of tea and a bowl of ice cream. Alice picked up the tea and took a sip.

"Now you've done it. Can't you read?"

Alice looked around for the speaker, but she started shivering so hard she was afraid her teeth would break from the chattering. On a card beside the tea cup, she saw the words Don't drink me. The card next to the ice cream read Don't eat me. She reached for the ice cream, but her hands had frozen to her side. Alice bent at the waist and took a big bite from the bowl.

Immediately she felt warmer, then warmer still. Water melted around her and dripped from icicles above her. Steam rose off her coat. She threw off her coat and ski pants, mitts, hat, scarves. Hotter and hotter until Alice feared she'd burst into flame. She picked up the tea cup and

88

took a tiny sip. The fire in her receded. A few more tiny sips and she was almost comfortable.

"Strange." She put the tea cup down and looked around.

"What's strange is you not following instructions." The voice came from above her. "You'd have found it so much easier not to drink or eat the right amount." A tiny spider hung from a web.

"What are you doing here? I thought spiders didn't like the winter?"

"I made the winter, of course I like it." The spider lowered herself. "Let me take a look at you."

"If you made the winter, couldn't you have made it a little less cold?"

"It would hardly be winter then, would it? I made everything to be the way it is."

"But you're too small to have made everything."

"Pfah." The spider hung before Alice's face. "What is big? What is small?" She scurried up the thread. "You'd better get along now."

"But I don't know where I'm going." Alice looked around, but the tent had vanished.

"Then it shouldn't take you long to get there." The spider said.

Alice looked up to find the spider, only to catch a glimpse of a shadow slip across the green and blue lights dancing in the sky.

She walked through the forest of spruce trees, craning her neck to watch in every direction. She tripped over something and fell into the snow.

"Watch where you're going." The voice from the hole sounded cross.

"But I can't see you." Alice turned in a circle. "Are you big or small?"

"It really depends on who's asking." A white rabbit hopped out of the snow.

"That's why I couldn't see you." Alice said. "You blend right into the snow."

"Of course, it's winter. I'd have thought you'd have changed by now too."

"I don't change." Alice looked at her ebony skin. "I'm always this colour."

"Well each to their own. Watch where you're going next time."

"But if you're white, I can't see you." Alice looked around but the rabbit had vanished. She walked over to a log and wiped the snow off it. "Now I'll never get to where I'm going."

"You could ask." A different voice said.

"Where are you? Are you white too?"

"Hardly." Something shook itself from under the snow she'd brushed off the log.

"You're a bug!" Alice backed up.

"I'm a caterpillar." The tiny creature straightened the funny hat it wore.

"What are you doing here?"

"Smoking." The caterpillar reached around under the snow until it retrieved an odd shaped pipe.

"I smoked when I ate too much of the ice cream."

"You're supposed to not eat it."

"That's what the spider said."

"Well, she would know." The caterpillar sucked on the pipe until Alice feared he'd be pulled inside it. Then he blew out a long stream of smoke.

"Oh that kind of smoking. It's bad for your health."

"This is medicine. I came to help grow it underground, but they gave it up."

"Then why are you still here?"

"I haven't smoked it all yet."

"Do you know where I should go?" Alice looked around. Even her brother might have missed her by now.

"No." The caterpillar blew a smoke ring.

90

"Do you know how I can get home?"

"No."

"Don't you know anything?"

"I know the square root of 1369 is 37."

"That's not much help."

The caterpillar shrugged and went back to his pipe.

Alice kicked her way through the snow, trying to spot the white rabbit again. She arrived at an enormous tree which shook with loud snoring floating out of a crack in the trunk.

She peeked through the crack and squeaked. A bear huddled in a ball sleeping.

"Excuse me," Alice said from a safe distance. "Do you know how to get home?"

"mmm I am home." The bear rolled into a different position.

"I mean my home."

"Is it Spring?" Bleary eyed, the bear looked at her.

"No."

"I don't know anything until spring." It curled back up and started snoring again.

Alice humphed and put her hands on her hips.

"That won't help, you know."

"Where are you?" Alice turned in a circle, looking for a spider or white rabbit.

"Here." A gigantic cat appeared on a branch in front of her. Its fur was grey and spotted and it had pointy ears.

Alice squeaked and fell back into the snow.

"Are you a mouse?" The cat licked its lips.

"No, I'm not."

"You squeak like a mouse." The cat smiled toothily.

"So does a rubber duck."

"You don't look like a rubber duck."

"I don't look like a mouse either."

"Do you taste like a mouse?"

"I wouldn't think so."

"Oh well." The cat started to fade.

"Wait." Alice got up. "What do I call you?"

"I'm a Cheshire Lynx."

"What's that?"

"Like a Cheshire Cat, only better, or maybe the Cheshire Cat is like me only not as good."

"Is everyone in this place irritating?" Alice threw her hands in the air.

"You must be irritable." The lynx faded again until only its toothy smile remained. A massive paw materialized for a moment. "Go that way."

"Why, is my home that way?" Alice's heart leaped with hope.

"I don't know where your home is, so I couldn't really say." The smile vanished.

"Then why did you tell me to go that way?"

"It's my favourite direction." The Lynx's voice said behind her.

Alice picked up a cone and threw it toward the voice.

"Missed me." The Lynx said behind her.

Alice turned, the Lynx's smile hung in front of her face. She squeaked and fell into the snow again.

"Will you stop <u>doing</u> that?"

Her only answer was a deep chuckle.

The direction the Lynx pointed looked as good as any other, and he did say it was his favourite. Alice set off through the snow. The lights in the sky had given way to an almost full moon creating an ethereal glow through the forest. She wandered in a trance until shouting distracted her.

"Stop that, you look ridiculous." The speaker wore a coat covered with black paper feathers. An black beak was held on his nose by an elastic band.

In the middle of a small clearing a woman wearing an identical outfit ran about laughing, flapping her arms.

"Caw, caw."

"She looks like she's having fun." Alice stopped beside the man.

"Oh sure, fun now, but what happens when her feathers fall off and she plummets to the earth? See there's another one."

Sure enough, a black feather came off the woman's coat and wafted down into the snow in front of Alice. She leaned over and picked it up.

"But this is real!" Alice stroked the soft black feather.

"Of course it's real, you aren't imagining it."

"But it's not paper." She held it up for the man to see.

"Real is real." The man shook his head sadly. "But that is just silly. Come down here. Come down at once. We have a guest."

The woman flapped her way over to them and looked at Alice with her head tilted.

"Caw."

"She means 'hello'," the man said.

"Caw."

"Now she's asking your name."

"Alice. But she just said the same thing."

"Caw."

"She said 'don't be ridiculous, the words are completely different, anyone with half a brain could hear the difference.'"

"I have more than half a brain, and I heard exactly the same word."

"Caw." The woman said yet again.

"She said 'That's strange. She's sure you are one of us.'"

"Why would she think that?" Alice looked at her coat. "I have no feathers."

"But you're so beautifully black, like a raven." The man stroked his hand across hers.

"Caw!"

The man hung his head.

"She said I'm being rude, I shouldn't say things like that."

"I don't mind. I am black, and it's nice you think I'm beautiful."

"See, you silly goose? She doesn't mind."

"Caw." The woman huffed and flapped back out into the clearing. She ran about flapping her arms, but not laughing.

Big tears ran down the man's face.

"Oh dear, I've done it now. Ravens are so much more intelligent than geese, but the second cousin of her mother's uncle's second wife has a bit of goose in her."

"Why don't you go over and apologize?" Alice patted the man on his shoulder. "I'm sure she'd forgive you."

"I can't fly." The man looked at her wide-eyed. "My feathers might come off and I'd plummet to the ground."

"Here, take this one just in case."

"Really?" The man took the black feather from her hand.

"Caw," The man said, "that means--"

"Thank you." Alice said.

"See, you do speak raven."

"Caw." He ran out into the clearing flapping his arms.

"Goodbye." Alice watched as the two circled the clearing cawing at each other. Then the ravens took off and flew away through the forest.

A feather drifted down to her.

"He dropped his feather."

"No, she gave you another one."

Alice turned to look at the Cheshire Lynx.

"They are silly though, ravens don't fly at night," the Lynx said.

"Hush, they might hear you."

"It's OK, I don't speak raven." The Lynx grinned and faded away leaving the teeth to disappear last.

Alice stuck the feather through her hair above her left ear and started out again.

"This is a very strange place."

Far ahead light flickered between the trees. She headed in that direction. A man sat by a fire, shaking a tin teapot.

"The tea is frozen, again."

"Why don't you put it back over the fire?"

"Sorry, dear. I don't speak raven."

"I'm not a raven."

"You have a raven feather."

Alice pulled it out of her hair.

"Only one."

"For some people that's enough to make them a raven."

"But I don't want to be a raven." Alice stared at the feather in her hand.

"Then you probably won't be."

Alice stepped forward to warm herself by the fire. But the man sat between her and the fire. She moved over and tried again.

"When I'm all alone in the woods, I have to keep myself company." The man said. "It doesn't leave much space around the fire."

"You're being rude." The man blinked to the other side of the fire.

"Oh, of course. I'm Cornelius John Joseph Ivan Harold Isn't-he-a-precious-thing. The Third."

He appeared across the fire.

"Mother wasn't good with decisions." He said from another place.

"How do you keep track of who you are?"

"I'm"

"the"

"one"

"talking." Cornelius appeared at a different place in the circle with each word.

"May I join you?"

"The tea's frozen." Cornelius shook the pot.

"You could warm it up over the fire."

"That's crazy talk," Cornelius said from across the fire.

"One boils the water," he said from her right.

"Then makes the tea," he said from the left.

"You can't make the tea," he said with his back to her.

"Then boil it." Cornelius appeared across from her again.

"Can't you stay in one place; you're making me dizzy."

"Better sit down then." He appeared on her left.

"Say 'disestablishmentarianism."

"Why would I"

"want to say"

"disestablishmentarianism?"

Alice jumped into the circle while he stumbled through the long word.

"Sneaky thing," Cornelius said beside her on the right.

"I admire that," he said from her left.

"Now that you're here, we'd better have a conversation." Cornelius appeared across from her. "What's the square root of 1369?"

"37" Alice popped over to the left of where she'd been.

"What's the capital of Winnipeg?" Cornelius appeared on her right.

"Winnipeg is a city, it doesn't have a capital," Alice answered from across the fire.

"Then it would be winnipeg, which is not the same thing." Cornelius appeared and disappeared. Alice stopped trying to follow him and stared into the fire.

"I suppose it's 'W' then."

"What the capital of Canada?"

"'C'?"

"No, it's Ottawa? Didn't you pay attention in school?"

"I don't want to talk about school." Alice crossed her arms across her chest.

"Well if you're going to be like that, Young Lady, you can keep yourself company." Cornelius vanished along with the fire.

"Now what am I going to do?" Alice asked herself.

"You could go that way," she answered from the other side of the clearing pointing into the trees.

"It is the Lynx's favourite direction." She shrugged on her right.

Alice stood up and shook off the snow.

"This place just gets stranger and stranger."

She started walking again.

A wolf stepped out of the woods and stared at her. It was huge, almost looking her in the eye, but also beautiful.

"Hello?" Alice's knees shook.

"Hello, yourself." The wolf walked around her. "Should I eat you or not?"

"I'd rather you didn't." The hand holding the feather trembled.

"Is that a raven feather?" The wolf sniffed at her.

"Yes."

"Are you a raven? I couldn't possibly eat a raven."

"Yes, I'm a raven."

"It's only one feather." The wolf grinned, showing huge teeth.

"Sometimes it only takes one feather to make a raven." She stuck the feather in her hair.

"So fly, little raven." It sat on its haunches.

Alice ran in a circle around the wolf.

"Caw, caw." Suddenly she was flying above the trees.

"Not bad, but your accent needs work." The Lynx's smile floated along beside her.

"I thought you didn't speak Raven?"

"I don't, but I recognize the accent." He vanished again.

"The world was dark and cold," the spider said from behind Alice's head, "and the humans were hungry and shivered in the snow. The raven flew high into the sky until it reached the sun and brought a tiny bit of fire down to the earth to give to the humans who couldn't sleep like a bear; didn't have a fur coat like the wolf. With fire, they could stay warm until spring."

Alice flew higher and higher until her wings ached and the world looked tiny below her. Far away light edged its way around the earth.

"His favourite direction. East, where the sun rises." Alice flew toward the sun. She got warmer and warmer, finally getting away from the cold snow of that strange place. Her eyes grew heavy as she flew.

"Alice, what are you doing sleeping in your snowpants and parka?" Her brother poked her in the shoulder.

"It's warm?" She sat up and stretched. "I had the strangest dream." Alice took off all her winter clothes, when she pulled off her hat a black feather fell to the floor.

"Where did you get that?" Her brother reached out and ran his finger along the feather. "It's cool." He shrugged. "I'm going back to my game."

Alice turned the feather around in her fingers. Did it mean...?

"Caw." She said from the top of the freezer and winked.

A WEEK AFTER MIDNIGHT

First published in 'Tales of Ever After' The
Fellowship of Fantasy

The shoe fit. Prince Charming smiled at the woman
with a bemused and somewhat pink face sitting in an
unornamented wooden chair. He took the glass slipper off
her foot and handed it to a servant.

"I would be most happy to have you come to live in
my palace as my wife." He'd been practicing the line in his
head for six days; the relief of finally speaking it out loud
gave him a silly grin. Ella's mouth crooked into a wide
smile, and the twinkle in her eyes confirmed she was
indeed the one.

"I have no experience of living in a palace."

Prince Charming glanced around at the room,
comfortable, worn; not a hovel, but no mansion either. He
wasn't marrying the house.

"It isn't any different than living here. Just larger, I
guess." The prince debated getting off his knee, but
standing too quickly might imply he didn't take her answer
seriously.

"Well, then, I will come and give it a try." Ella put
her hand on Prince Charming's shoulder. "As for wife, we
will see. You may grow tired of this farmer's daughter."

Prince Charming took her hand and kissed her
fingers, then stood and pulled her to her feet.

"Shall we go?"

***

"Good morning, Your Highness." Robert, Prince
Charming's valet, pulled the curtains on the bed open.
Light streamed into his room from the window.

"Ah." Prince Charming sat up and grinned; for the
first time in a week, he wouldn't be traipsing all over the
kingdom handling maiden's feet. It had been excruciating,

and he could never think of what to say to those who didn't fit.

"Perhaps you could invite Princess Ella to join me for breakfast on the veranda."

"Your Highness." Robert laid out the prince's clothes for the day. "I was informed the princess was up and dressed before dawn."

"Really?" The prince dressed quickly then allowed Robert to check the fit. "Whatever for?"

"You would need to ask the princess, Your Highness."

Prince Charming's stomach knotted. Whatever magic had overcome his usual lack of social graces had vanished. The reality that he'd not only invited a woman he'd only met twice to the castle but asked her to marry him sank in. For a brief moment, he considered returning to bed and hiding under the covers.

But that was the very kind of reaction which had resulted in the need for the Ball in the first place and thus for Ella's presence in the palace and his life.

Prince Charming gathered his courage and headed over to the wing where his mother had given Ella a suite of rooms. He knocked on the door and a maid answered, curtseying.

"Good morning, Your Highness. If you are looking for Princess Ella, she's not here."

He'd been planning a leisurely breakfast and a chat, assuming his tongue didn't get tied up. It still astonished him that it hadn't been an issue at the Ball, perhaps related to whatever created a slipper which only fit one foot in the kingdom, however average-sized.

"Can I help you, Your Highness?" The maid curtseyed again.

Over the girl's shoulder, the prince could see another girl bustling about pulling sheets off the bed.

"Weren't the linens fine enough for the princess?"
Prince Charming winced internally.

"She said they were the softest she'd ever slept on
but were a little musty. After we had tea, the princess
headed off to chat with the laundry maids."

"Laundry maids?" Prince Charming felt his face
grow warm. "I have to admit; I have no idea how to find
the laundry."

"We're just about to take the linens there now,
Your Highness."

The two girls carried a basket full of sheets and
blankets between them, and the prince followed. He had
the feeling they normally would have chattered about
something if he weren't present.

"Do you like working here?"

The girl who'd answered the door nodded, and the
other blushed.

"We're treated well, and the wages help our family.
Father has a business making furniture, but living in the
capital is expensive."

"I see."

The girls turned down a plain hallway he didn't
recall paying attention to before then knocked on a door
before pushing it open and walking in. Steam poured out
the door, and the prince started sweating at the heat. Huge
tubs held immense amounts of hot water and cloth; they
were the source of the steam. Several women sat in a
corner chatting, holding teacups. They ranged in age from
hardly older than the maids to one with gray hair. They all
wore the same white dress, sleeves pushed up to their
elbows. The oldest waved the girls over, then she saw the
prince and shot to her feet before going into a deep curtsey.

"Your Highness." Her voice trembled. "The
princess told us we should take a break. We'll get back to
work immediately."

"No need." Prince Charming resisted the urge to wipe his face. "Finish your tea. If the princess gave permission for you to have tea, I'll not stop you. You wouldn't happen to have a spare cup? I haven't had any yet this morning." He needed something to get him through this strange morning.

The women stared at him, then the one who'd spoken straightened. "Happens we do, Your Highness." She poured a cup and handed it to him with another curtsey. The others stood with their cups.

"Sit down." Prince Charming waved at them. "No need to be formal here." They sat uncertainly, as if their chairs might burn them. "Tell me about the princess's visit."

"She come by to chat about the sheets, Your Highness. She weren't complaining, but the bed did smell musty. Comes from drying the linens indoors 'cause of the rain yesterday. Told us to try a bit more vinegar in the rinse water as that's what she did. Went off to the kitchen to find us some vinegar. Said we was to take a break too as working all day without one ain't good for a soul. A lad from the kitchen brought the vinegar and some old cups."

Prince Charming sipped at the tea, strong and black.

"Ah, reminds me of training with the army." He smiled and took another sip. "What the cook called an honest cup of tea." He missed the structure of the army, though not the skirmishes with bandits. No need to embarrass himself stumbling over words while talking to women. At least these laundry maids didn't expect him to make conversation.

When he'd finished the tea, Prince Charming stood and nodded to the women.

"Thank you for your time and the tea." He found his way back to the hall and breathed deeply of the cool, dry air. *At least I know where the kitchen is.*

102

The kitchen too was hot, though not as steamy as the laundry. The clatter of knives and pots came to an abrupt stop as he stepped into the room.

"Your Highness." The chef bowed, and the rest of the staff bowed or curtsied with him. "Was there a problem with your breakfast?"

"No, no." Prince Charming put his hands up. "Though I have yet to eat it. I'm looking for the princess, the maids at the laundry said she came here."

More than one set of eyebrows lifted when he mentioned the laundry, but the chef waved everyone back to work.

"Aye, she dropped in, sent some vinegar and old dishes for the women to have tea. Said you'd approve."

"The women were very appreciative." Prince Charming took a deep breath. "What are you cooking?"

To his surprise, the chef turned red and looked down.

"Chicken stew, Your Highness. The princess was upset at the amount of leftovers."

"Leftovers?"

"Aye, we only send the best meat to the royal table, so even after the staff eat, there's plenty left on the platters. We normally send it out to the trash heap, but the princess told me to make stew with it. One of the lads said there's always folks at the palace gate hoping for a bit to eat. Already sent one big pot out along with ends and bits of bread. 'Nother one's about ready to go. She said if we were throwing it out, it might as well feed someone."

"Very true." Prince Charming took another breath; his stomach reminded him of the missed breakfast. "How about you bring a bowl, then I'll go with you to the gate?"

One of the boys dipped a bowl from a pot hanging to the side of the fire, put a chunk of bread on the side, and brought it to the prince.

Prince Charming stood in a corner out of the way and worked his way through the hearty stew while he watched the kitchen staff work. Like the maids, he had the feeling they would have been talking and joking if he weren't there.

"Excellent stew." Prince Charming handed the bowl to a young girl who added it to her pile of dirty dishes. "Please continue using leftovers in this way."

"Aye, Your Highness, the princess said you'd approve."

Prince Charming picked up a basket of bread pieces, two men carried the huge pot of stew, and they headed toward the palace gate. A crowd had gathered, and they cheered when they saw the prince. He was used to the cheers on the occasions he'd paraded through the city, but these were more heartfelt. There was no table, so he stood holding the basket as two boys in kitchen whites served stew.

The people bowed or curtsied as they took bread, but they also grinned at him and murmured thanks. One man limped painfully as he came forward.

"How did you get injured?" Prince Charming asked.

"Took an arrow to the leg rousting out some bandits. Never healed quite right." The man shrugged. "Was a stone mason before being a soldier, but can't do that neither."

"How do you live?"

"Get a bit of pension from the army, my son's training for the guard." The man lifted his bowl slightly. "This will mean he can eat proper tonight. Can't train hungry."

Handing out bread made talking to people easier, and these people didn't expect him to be witty. The prince stayed until his basket had emptied and heard a wide variety of stories.

"I've been looking for the princess," he said to one of the boys as he put the basket down. "Do you know where she went from here?"

"She were handing out bread like you, Your Highness, then an old woman come with a sore on her leg. The princess headed off to the herb garden to make a poultice."

"We have an herb garden?" The prince shook his head. *Sounding the fool again.* "Of course we do, please tell me how to find it."

The boy's directions sent Prince Charming around the back of the palace where he rarely had any reason to go. A man worked in a large garden planted in neat rows. Another smaller plot to the side grew green plants the prince guessed might be herbs. He walked over to investigate, and the man joined him.

"Here's where we grow greens for the kitchen, but also plants the doctor uses for healing." The gardener picked a sprig and handed it to the prince. "Basil, Your Highness. Goes well with a lot of dishes."

Footsteps behind him on the stone walk made the prince turn around.

"Ah, found you." Robert smiled ruefully at the prince. "Your morning schedule is in disarray. I'd suggest you go to your training now, and I'll reschedule the meetings with the Secretary of Accounts. The queen wishes to remind you of supper tonight. Your brother is back from the border, and your sister has yet to return to her husband after the ball. There will not be another chance for all of you to eat together in some time."

"I'll put myself in your hands. Let me know where I need to be next after I've done training."

Prince Charming went to change into his sturdy clothes and padded jacket for his training then strode to the practice yard. A plain stone-walled square enclosed the sandy floor. Large enough to work on fighting in lines and groups, it was empty save for Sir Trevor, waiting. The tall knight tossed the prince a wooden sword, his face impassive. Prince Charming caught it and saluted.

After his warm up, training, and a couple of bouts, Prince Charming poured water from a pitcher on a small table in the corner of the yard.

"How many of our soldiers end up so injured they can't work?"

"What brings this up, Your Highness?" Sir Trevor stood relaxed as if he'd only just arrived and not spent an hour chasing the prince around the yard with a sword.

"I met a fellow at the gate, said he'd taken an arrow in the leg while fighting bandits."

"It does happen." Sir Trevor helped himself to water. "Fortunately, most recover from their wounds or find other work."

"Please find out how many are completely dependent on the pension we give them."

"The pension isn't much, Your Highness." Sir Trevor drank another cup of water and nodded. "I will look into it."

They trained for another hour before Robert showed up.

"Your Highness," Sir Trevor said, "it might be useful for you to train with the men on occasion. At the least, it will teach them not to be distracted by your presence."

"Very good, I will leave it up to you."

"Thank you, Your Highness." Sir Trevor bowed and left the yard.

"Your bath is waiting in your room. You have half an hour before meeting with the secretary."

"Great." Prince Charming led the way to his rooms. "Any word on the princess?"

"Last I heard, the queen's lady-in-waiting invited her to join them for needlepoint."

"And Grace will be there too." The prince shuddered. "Better her than me."

Robert laughed and left Prince Charming to his bath.

***

The Secretary of Accounts spread ledgers and scrolls over his desk and gave Prince Charming a weary look. Ink stained his fingers, and his hair looked more white than gray, but his eyes were sharp, if a little wary.

"What questions do you have for me today, Your Highness?"

"Am I truly that tiresome?" Prince Charming put a smile on his face to lighten his words.

"Ah, no, but your enthusiasm for tracking numbers has on occasion been a challenge."

"More than a challenge, I'm sure." The prince sat back and thought. He stifled a grin as the secretary's fingers began to tap on the desk. "Let's start with food."

The secretary sat up straight. "Food, Your Highness?"

"Yes, is all the food for the palace purchased together, or do we have separate accounts for the royal family and the staff?"

"Most times, the royal family is served the choice cuts and best vegetables, the staff eat from what is left." The secretary flipped through a ledger.

"And what is left is thrown away."

"Usually; I heard about the stew at the palace gates."

"You don't approve?" Prince Charming frowned.

"It is more orderly than people rummaging through the palace trash, healthier too. As it depends on what is uneaten, there is no cost, but some gain in people's trust. You might want to consider an easier way of serving."

"One of Ella's maids has a father who builds furniture. A couple of trestle tables." Prince Charming caught the secretary's eye. "I could purchase them myself. But give me an example of where giving something away would be harmful."

"I heard you visited the laundry." The secretary flipped through the ledger. "We replace the sheets on the palace suites every season. Some of those old linens may get cut down for servants' use, but most are thrown away. If we were to give them away at the palace gates, the people would buy fewer linens from the merchants in the city. The ones who sell linen to the palace would be fine, but the stores which supply the general populace would be in trouble. Dumping that much into the economy without consideration can do a great deal of harm."

"It seems a waste."

"It is, but unless we can find another way to dispose of them without hurting our people, it is a necessary waste."

"Hmmm." Prince Charming stared up at the ceiling. "I think I understand; we have to think of the people behind the numbers in the ledgers."

"Exactly, Your Highness." The secretary opened a different ledger. "For instance, look at this tax ledger…"

***

At supper, Prince Charming arrived just in time to escort Ella to her place at the table. Her hand on his arm sent warmth through his sleeve. Her gown wasn't as fancy as Grace's, but it suited her. *When did she have time to find a gown?* He pushed the question aside and pulled out her chair for her to sit.

"I am Prince Juste, this is my sister, Princess Grace." Juste smiled broadly at Ella and waved his hand in Grace's direction. "My parents named us for the qualities they wished us to have." He toasted Prince Charming with his wineglass. "Two out of three isn't bad."

"I'm not complaining." Princess Grace nodded at the servant who placed soup in front of her. "The Ball gave me a lovely excuse to come home for a visit. I'm even more happy to look forward to the next visit. Have you set a date yet?"

Ella turned a wonderful pink. "We haven't discussed dates."

"Make an appointment with the Secretary of Accounts to visit Char. It is the only sure way to see him." Juste attacked a roll with his knife and sent a wicked look at the prince.

"Accounts are important." Prince Charming bit back the rest of his retort and sipped his wine. He marshalled his thoughts so he wouldn't stumble over them. Funny how he had no problem talking to Sir Trevor or the secretary, but put him at a dinner table… "But I'm learning they are even more fascinating when I imagine the people behind the numbers."

"Oh, really?" Juste spooned up his soup and wiggled his eyebrows at Prince Charming. The queen had the pained look on her face which had long been normal at their meals. The king ate, watching with the same fascination he did the jousting at tournaments.

"For example, the farmers in Southern Frankland who are petitioning for tax relief." Prince Charming suppressed his grin at the glare Grace sent his way. Her husband, Rudolph, wouldn't let the opportunity pass to send a message direct to the king's ear, but Grace hated to look like she was working. "They are arguing that with the drought lowering their yields, they don't have as much income and not as much ability to pay taxes." He rewarded himself with another sip of wine.

"Those same farmers want to raise the price of their crops." Grace put her wineglass down and clenched her hands. "Higher prices for grains will mean more costly food and everyone else will want reduction of their taxes too."

"Let them tough it out." Juste waved his hand before starting into his fish. "Use the grain in the Royal barns to lower the price."

"If you force the price low." Ella tasted the fish before pointing her fork at Juste. "How will the farmers have anything to invest in next year's crop? They'll have to sell their seed grain to pay their bills, so less land will be planted next year and the situation will only get worse. Yet, if prices are too high, they can't sell anyway."

The others at the table stared at Ella, and she turned pink again. Prince Charming rather liked it. At the Ball, she'd blushed too, the first time he'd asked her to dance.

"What would you do?" the king asked.

"Let the farmers sell the grain from the Royal barns, but in return they don't get help with their taxes. I'd not use the whole store, maybe a third since you don't know what next year will bring. I'm sure you have a way to compare this year's and last year's harvests to know who needs help. Pay the farmers commission on what Royal grain gets sold. Prices stay low, taxes stay as they are, and everyone is happy. Well, everyone except those who are speculating on a grain shortage."

"Why should the kingdom get that involved?" Juste tilted his head.

"Isn't that the government's job?" Prince Charming grinned. "We're supposed to even out risk across the country to make everyone's lives a bit better."

"I like her," Grace said. "You can keep her. Father, do you think her notion would work?"

"You and Charming work out the details, and I'll sell it to the Privy Council."

***

Prince Charming wiped at his eyes and tried to make the numbers on the pages in front of him to stop dancing.

A knock at the door made him sigh.

110

"Just a bit longer, Robert, I promise." The door creaked open; Prince Charming refused to have the hinges oiled.

"Sorry, not Robert." Ella put a wineglass down beside Prince Charming and filled it. Then she poured one for herself and perched on the edge of the desk. "He asked me to convince you to get some sleep."

"But—"

Ella put a finger on his lips.

"If you take a day or two, or even a week, it will be fine." She sipped at her wine. "I wanted a chance to talk to you anyway."

Prince Charming's mouth went dry as his stomach clenched, so he drank from his glass. "Talk?"

"Yes. It's what couples do."

"We're a couple?" Prince Charming's heart skipped a beat. He took another drink and choked on it. *Great, now she knows I'm an idiot.* Ella thumped on his back and laughed.

"Princess Grace gave you permission to keep me." She smiled at him and tilted her head.

His stomach unknotted, and Prince Charming laughed as he reached out to take her hand. "You captured my heart at that ball, but I don't want to pressure you—"

Ella stopped his words with a kiss this time. Her lips tasted much sweeter than the wine.

"Every love starts with a first meeting. If I hadn't wanted this, I would have found some way not to fit into that slipper. I only have one serious concern."

"What's that?" Prince Charming wrapped his arm around her and pulled her onto his lap.

"What am I going to call you? Prince sounds like I'm training a dog, Charming comes out sarcastic no matter how I try. Your brother called you Char, but that isn't quite right either."

Prince Charming tilted his head down a little and kissed her. Definitely sweeter than the wine.

"That is a conundrum." He nibbled at her ear and set her giggling. "I suppose we'll have to meet every night and talk about it."

"I guess you're right." Ella leaned against him, and he could feel their hearts beating in time. This was much easier than talking.

The clock on the mantle chimed.

"Midnight." Prince Charming sighed. "Don't go."

"I must." Ella sighed too and stood up. "Tonight, and each night until I no longer must."

"Very well." Prince Charming escorted her to the door. "Goodnight, my princess."

He watched her slip away down the hall then went to his bedroom where Robert waited for him.

"Robert." Prince Charming hung up his jackets and pants as his valet turned down the covers on the bed. "Just how quickly do you think Mother and Grace could plan a wedding?"

"You had a good day, Your Highness?"

"Oh, yes." He climbed into bed and grinned up at the shadows. "Magical."

STEEL

This story was previously published in 'Song of the Axe Slave' Schreyer Ink Press. 2018

Yuki's kendo sword in its case thumped on her back. She shouldn't have stayed back to work with sensei even if her testing was coming up all too quickly. Now the train would leave without her. Most days she'd run home, but the cold downpour sapped her will. Vaulting the stone fence around the park, Yuki dashed through the woods. If she pushed herself, she'd make the station for the alternate route.

She'd actually get home faster this way but hadn't travelled it since the day she'd seen the broken guardrail from the train window, then arrived home to discover a sorrowful police officer on her doorstep to tell her she was suddenly alone in the world.

The concentration needed to keep her footing on the dim path, dodging roots and slippery rocks kept her from heeding the noise of the creek until she broke out on the bank. The water roiled up the edge of the bank. Yuki tried to stop, but her feet slipped on the grass sending her sliding toward the water. She snatched at a bush and somehow held on as water slammed into her.

The roots on the bush were pulling out of the ground. Current hitting her case twisted her, almost breaking her grip then a hand in a grimy glove grabbed her wrist. The dirtiest face she'd ever seen stared at her from close enough she could see the man's every wrinkle.

"Hang on, I've got you."

The creek's roar shifted to a monstrous howl and a wall of muddy water hit them sucking them both under the thick liquid. The grip on her wrist held. Ice ran through her as muck filled her mouth and nose, the sound vanishing as her ears filled with mud.

***

Bright light banished the darkness of the creek, and Yuki dropped onto rough stone, vomiting mud and gasping for air.

"Praise Dei, you made it." A tenor voice quavered behind her.

Yuki shook her head and looked around for the owner of the words. She smeared muck away from her eyes and saw a bleary vision of a man in a dirty white robe. Others stood behind him, but her stomach rebelled again before she could focus on them.

"The other one, he tried to help me." Yuki forced her words out past the spasms. "Is he--"

"Only you." A different voice, deep and strong as the first was high and weak. "A pity, we could use more brave warriors, but it is you we called. Magus Peginus pulled you from the moment of your death to this world."

Hands lifted Yuki and soft cloth wiped her face. Though the shortest in her class, she stood a head taller than the broad man beside her. He held her gently but firmly as she gazed out over a canyon. Far below a brown thread gleamed.

"Called?" Yuki struggled to breathe, this was no place she knew.

"A hand from a different world to wield steel of another world." The Magus' tenor voice lost some of its shake. Yuki turned to stare at the tall man in the robe. Some of the newbies at the dojo got that look after trying to keep up with the class; pasty white, he leaned on another man who stood like a rock, expressionless. He wore leather with a sword hanging from his belt and a bow on his back.

"What's done is done." The short man led Yuki toward the others. "We must return to the others and let them know we've succeeded."

"But—" Yuki looked over her shoulder. Her guide didn't slow so she sighed and followed. It was too bad, but not like she knew the man.

114

They met up with a woman holding several horses' halters. Yuki's eyes insisted the woman's ears were pointed, but the world swam about her and she didn't trust her senses.

"Thou wert successful." The soft alto caressed Yuki's ears. "Yet, we mustn't tarry. Our guest needs soul care."

"It took more out of me than I expected." The Magus clambered onto the tallest horse. The one in leather mounted a solid grey horse beside him.

"Thou shalt ride with me." The woman leaped, impossibly graceful, onto a sand coloured horse. "Bothurn, if thou wilt?"

The short man lifted Yuki and tossed her up. The woman caught her with a surprisingly strong grip and settled Yuki in front of her. A brush of cool fingers across her brow settled the world in place.

"Thou shalt tarry now until we arrive at camp. Rest gentle."

Yuki tried to answer, but her eyes closed and the movement of the horse rocked her to sleep.

***

Lance crawled out of the river, spitting mud and gasping.

"So, they've called a champion." The most beautiful voice Lance had ever heard spoke, like bells ringing from a church spire. "You must have been touching the one, but released your grip in this world."

He rolled onto his back to see the owner of the voice. The man wore clothes which shimmered between black and silver. They looked like costumes Lance had seen in a play in the park once.

"What, who?" Lance struggled to make his mind work.

"My enemies dragged you into this world and abandoned you as trash. They have what they want. You are nothing." The man's eyes gleamed as his mouth twisted in contempt. "They think a foolish saying will be my end. I will crush them." He pointed toward figures in the shadows. "Bring him along. He'll be amusing while I wait for the moment of my victory."

Misshapen beings scampered out. One slung Lance over a shoulder, then followed the man back into the gloom. Lance tried to fight, but his head spun like he was in the middle of a three-day bender.

***

Yuki woke to the clattering of wood. She rolled out of bed, then stared at her surroundings as the events of the day before returned. A Magus had yanked her from her world, she was dead there. Shaking her head, Yuki pulled on the clothes which lay at the foot of the bed. If she started thinking about magic and different worlds, she'd never stop. Better to go find out who was making all the noise outside the tent.

Men and women trained with wooden swords, a little shorter than her kendo sword, but the movements were familiar. She picked one off the rack and ran through her basic forms to warm up, then practiced the katas for her testing. As she made her final salute and returned to rest, Yuki became aware of the crowd watching.

"Impressive." The man the Magus had leaned on picked up a weapon from the rack, shook his head and chose a different one. He went to the ready stance and nodded at her. Yuki bowed and attacked before she was fully upright. Katas were fun, but sparring made her heart sing.

He parried and dodged easily, frowning slightly. She plastered a look of concentration on her face and kept up her lunges and slashes. The shift in his footwork warned her when he decided to return the attack. He held nothing back and the sheer strength of his blows would have numbed her arms if she'd parried but she pushed them aside and danced away.

116

Blood rushed through her, giving her feet wings. As the swords became blurs, Yuki stopped holding back the grin she'd been told gave her opponents the chills. He overreached slightly and she went back on the offensive, chasing him with lightning slashes and lunges. To her delight he took everything she threw at him and gave it back in full measure. His smile matched hers.

The high began to fade, the bout would end very soon. She put everything into one roll of the die. Feinting a low slash, she deliberately set her foot wrong. He whipped his blade in a vicious circle cut at her neck. Yuki dove under, feeling the draft tug at her hair. As she rolled, the sword in her left hand dragged across his ribs. When she came to her feet, he'd already reversed his swing and she laid her sword on his shoulder, edge to his throat.

He roared and pointed his sword straight up. She lifted hers and stepped back, unsure about the etiquette in this new place. He turned and saluted her, sheer joy across his face. Yuki saluted in return, then went to rest position.

"Harin Galeson." He went to his knee. "I have never been so happy to lose a match."

With a rustle, the surrounding warriors went to their knee holding their swords up in salute.

"Can't remember you ever losing with a sword." Bothurn leaned on a long axe. "I'll have to give her a try with my axe later."

"That would be interesting." Yuki grinned at Bothurn. "I am Yuki Nakamoto."

"Well met, Yuki. Let's go find something to eat, then get the Magus to explain just what is going on." Harin stood and spun to glare at the onlookers. "Back to work, now that you know how far you have to go."

***

"The Bloodmancer," Magus Peginus slurped at a cup of steaming liquid. "should be a minor god, only his attachment to this world is too strong. He'd be less trouble

117

as a god. The only chance to hurt him is a phrase in an old prophecy, 'A hand from a different world to wield steel of another world.'"

"Prophecy?" Yuki sniffed at her cup and took a reluctant sip. It wasn't coffee, but maybe it had caffeine. "They never mean whatever people think they mean."

"The cant harkens from a time before even my memory." Nymedhiel, the woman who'd held the horses, nibbled at a chunk of bread. Her ears weren't Yuki's imagination. "Scholars translated it from an inscription on a cave wall into Elvish, later from Elvish into the human languages."

"How did they know what the inscription said?" Yuki drank more of the tea, the stuff was growing on her.

"It's still there. The dwarves guard it as part of their doom. You want to go read it for yourself? The trip would only take a few months, there might be a few scattered survivors on our return." Peginus put his cup down hard, slopping hot liquid over the table.

"Quiet yourself." Nymedhiel smiled at the Magus. "She is not questioning your work." She offered the loaf to Yuki. "The exact wording isn't essential as Magus Peginus created the calling to bring who was needed for the task."

"Your demonstration this morning," Harin said, "proves you are the one to wield Cylk."

"Cylk?"

"The steel of another world." Harin grinned and saluted Yuki with his cup. "A sword almost as old as the prophecy, made from a rock which fell from the heavens."

Yuki chewed on the bread and washed it down with the tea. It tasted familiar, the faces around her friendly. Neither Nymedhiel's ears, nor the green-skinned man at another table felt unusual.

"Why aren't I weirded out by all this?"

"The soul bonding the Magus and I did while thou were sleeping." Nymedhiel put her hand briefly on Yuki's.

118

"It works to make thy heart feel at home in this world, or else thou wouldst fade away from sorrow."

"And I'm guessing, the language too? Well, soul bonding or not. I'm here, and I will do whatever I can to help." Yuki finished her bread. "I'd like to see this sword."

The others stood and followed the Magus out over to a tent to one side of the practice ground. The interior surprised Yuki. She'd expected a cluttered mess, but instead found an ordered, almost monastic simplicity.

"Magus," a young woman stood from behind a low table and bowed.

"My apprentice, Krythin." Peginus smiled.

"Krythin." Yuki bowed to the apprentice. "I am pleased to meet you. My name is Yuki Nakamoto, you may call me Yuki."

The apprentice blushed slightly and smiled, then sat and returned to work. The Magus lifted a corner of a carpet and pulled out a long thin box. He waved his hands over it and the lid swung open.

Yuki wasn't sure what she'd expected. Maybe a hilt encrusted with gems, or a blade covered in runes, but it could have been a practice sword with its plain, functional hilt and scabbard. She picked it out of the case, drew a few inches of the blade and admired the gleam of the steel.

"Ahem." Peginus closed the case and Yuki caught wide-eyed looks on the others in the tent.

"Did I do something wrong?" Yuki's hand gripped the sword tighter.

"Cylk is very particular about who carries her." Harin bowed slightly. "Usually some ceremony is needed to placate her."

"If you want..."

"No need, the sword has made her choice." Peginus put the case away under the carpet. "Go get used to each other, we'll talk more tomorrow."

A larger crowd gathered as Yuki warmed up, then sparred with Harin. Bothurn showed up and demanded a chance to test her out with his axe. He had a padded leather cover on the head.

The axe had a longer reach than her sword, and with his broad shoulders it whistled through the air. Yuki danced out of the way and watched how it moved. Even with the dwarf's strength, he couldn't shift from attack to defense as quickly as a sword. Yuki tried lunging in after the blade passed only to have her blow blocked by the steel banded shaft.

They circled the grounds, voices calling out what Yuki guessed were bets on the outcome. Her breathing was steady, but hard. Bothurn looked like he'd been out on a stroll. Wearing him down wasn't going to be an option.

When he tried a hard swing at her head, Yuki lunged in low forcing the dwarf to jump over her sword. She flipped back out of reach as he brought the axe down in a cut which drew a line on the ground.

After another turn of the grounds, Yuki allowed her breathing to get ragged. Then she dropped her guard, prompting a chop at her head. Bothurn anticipated the slash at his legs, but not the jump which landed her on the shaft and drove the axe into the ground. She ran up the shaft to land two quick blows, one on either side of his neck.

"Well fought." Bothurn bowed. "I've never seen anyone but an elf pull that attack off."

"I wasn't sure how else to attack."

"Most try cuts at the hands and arms." Bothurn lifted his hand to show the armoured gloves he wore. "Hard to swing an axe with one hand."

"I'll remember that."

At breakfast the man with the green skin paused beside Yuki.

120

"You won me a very nice purse. My family will be very pleased. Call me Gloth." He dropped a ring on the table beside her and spread his fingers to show the webbing between them. "We don't wear rings, so please accept this."

"I will." Yuki slid it into her pouch. Others from the training yard congratulated her or nodded as they passed. All through the mess tent, men and woman chattered as they ate. If she hadn't been told this world was in dire peril, she'd have been perfectly content.

***

The stench in the chamber made it hard for Lance to think. Even the cattle yards weren't this bad. The Master had left him with orders to feed the prisoners and not step foot outside the room. As much as Lance wanted to escape the stink, it followed him, twining about his throat, choking him if he looked too long at the gaping black openings which promised escape from this hell.

The prisoners weren't chained, but their bodies clung to the walls as if glued. Lance used the tiny knife he hid in his boot to cut up the hard bread to stuff in the mouths of the men and other things hanging on the stone. They cursed him, wanting to die, but Lance couldn't ignore the Master's command any more than he could gravity.

He caught a rat and planned to cook it over the smoky flames of the torches. Whatever the Master said, it couldn't stop Lance's hands from shaking from lack of drink. The knife slipped as he skinned the beast. As blood poured from Lance's thumb, the stench of the room weakened and he could think a little.

Lance sucked at his wound and started planning. Life on the streets had taught him the value of careful thought, at least when he wasn't drinking away his ability to remember.

"Slave." The Master stalked into the chamber followed by huge grey, vaguely man-shaped things dragging struggling prisoners. The stink bit Lance and stole his mind. Neither the sight of trolls nor the bloodied men, could force thought past the absolute obedience commanded of him.

"We'll never tell you anything." The speaker had long pointed ears, and even in this place shone.

"You aren't here to talk." The Master put a long black dagger against the speaker's throat. "You're here to bleed." He cut lightly and red glistened against the shining skin. A wave of his hand and the new prisoner slammed against the wall, unable to move. Each one was treated the same, then the Master left Lance alone with the moans and curses.

Lance picked up the rat and turned it over in his hands. Right, he was going to cook it. He pulled his knife out and finished cleaning it before skewering it on a long poker. As he returned his blade to his boot, Lance nicked his finger. The stench retreated, leaving him as able to think as he ever was. What he wanted was a drink.

After feeding the prisoners on rat and hard bread, Lance hunched in the corner and gnawed on his own meal. Blood was keeping them prisoner, but it was going to set him free.

***

Shouting outside the mess tent interrupted Yuki's breakfast. She'd worked up an appetite using Cylk for her training so the sword hung on her back as she ate. Harin cursed and headed to the door along with half the people in the tent. Yuki drew Cylk as she ran and urgency flowed from the sword. She sliced through the heavy canvass walls and landed in the midst of chaos.

A phalanx of six huge grey humanoid creatures were stomping and clubbing their way through the army. Wooden swords shattered against the trolls. The closest one looked ready to smash Gloth, her friend with the green skin. Yuki dashed forward swinging up hard at the

122

enemy's wrists. To her shock, the sword sliced through with little resistance. Club and hands flew away as she hacked at the back of the troll's knee. She didn't slow down to see how effective the blow was.

The next closest had an elf, who looked like male version of Nymedhiel, clutched in its fist. Yuki freed the elf, continuing her swing to cut through most of the troll's neck. With a roar, another troll raised a massive hammer and charged at her. Yuki ran towards it staying low, then as the creature swung at her jumped onto the troll running it through the heart, splitting it open as she flipped her sword free.

She jumped and rolled as the troll fell backwards, but had to brake hard as the one in front of her dropped its weapon and put its hands up in surrender.

"Face down, hands behind you." Yuki kept her sword ready to slash if needed, but the troll dropped with a thump and lay quivering. Soldiers surrounded it with spears, so she looked around for the other enemies. One was being pushed back by men with long spears. The other collapsed with Bothurn's axe buried in its chest. The spear wielders cheered and the last one went down looking like a giant pincushion.

"Why would they send so few to attack?" Yuki wiped Cylk carefully before returned the sword to its scabbard.

"Six trolls can do serious damage." Harin stalked over to the prisoner. "I've never seen anyone cut through them like you did."

"Must be the new training regime." Yuki said. The troll on the ground shook violently.

"Bind this one and guard it. If the ropes break, it dies." Harin wiped his sword and put it away as he led the way back to the tent.

"According to my scrying, the armies are three days away." Magus Peginus slurped at his tea. "Unfortunately there is a large horde heading this way from the mountains.

123

They'll be here in three days as well. Hard to fight a siege and a set battle at the same time."

"Can we get messages to the armies?"

"The elven army has been in regular communication with me. They will be simple enough to reach, but they are furthest from the mountains. The dwarves are closest, but the task will be to get a bird to them without it ending up in the soup."

"Tie a green band on its leg. They'll wait to read the message. I'll write the orders in my own hand." Bothurn grinned.

"The humans are closest to us, but the slowest moving." Harin sighed. "If we can't get word to them any other way, we'll send riders out."

"So in three days there will be four armies between us and the guy you brought me here to defeat." Yuki rubbed Cylk's hilt absently. "It may be easier to get to him before the party starts."

"True." Harin shook his head and looked through the cut in the tent to where their prisoner was tied to a massive tree. "I'll bet that troll knows a back way into the Bloodmancer's warren."

"Perhaps we can burden it with the heads of its companions and send it to meet that horde. They might be less eager for battle if they knew they were fighting warriors who cut trolls down like weeds." Bothurn grinned maliciously. "A little confusion among our enemies would buy us time."

Peginus muttered behind her as Yuke questioned the troll about how to get into the Bloodmancer's lair. Then she sent it off with a bag of troll heads to discourage the horde from the mountains. By the time they'd finished, Peginus had to lean heavily on his staff.

A dozen men and women readied themselves to escort her to the entry while the rest of the camp went to work striking camp and preparing to move. The sun had hardly

124

slipped toward afternoon when Yuki, Harin and her escort marched away.

The troll's instructions were easy enough to follow, but avoiding patrols of orcs and goblins took time. Fortunately, the enemy didn't try to keep silent, one group came too close and were cut down in seconds. Yuki claimed the leader's black tunic for later.

At the entrance, Harin unwrapped a stone Peginus had given him to provide light.

"You remember the directions?" He handed her the stone reluctantly.

"I do." Yuki donned the tunic, then adjusted how Cylk hung from her waist. "I should be more nervous."

"I expect it is the soul work and the call." Harin frowned. "This is why you've been brought here, but don't let your guard down. Your task will not be easy."

"That's why some nerves would be helpful." Yuki grinned and shrugged. "I'll have to make do without them. If I can't get out after, I'll hole up somewhere and wait."

"Be safe."

Yuki snorted. "In there? Unlikely, but given the chance, we'll meet again." She slipped into the tunnel and headed toward the first of the troll's landmarks. It didn't take long for her to figure out the troll had no idea how to get through the labyrinth of tunnels, probably followed whoever was in front.

The foetid air barely moved and she wasn't sure of the way out. When faced with a choice of paths, Yuki chose the one with the worst stench and pushed on. She had to stop and cut a strip from the tunic to make a mask for her face. It didn't do much, but the annoyance distracted her from the smell.

The slap of feet on stone warned her something was approaching.

"I want to go fishing." A nasal voice said.

"We ain't going out for fun." That one sounded like her sensei with a head cold.

"If we just happen to go past a creek—"

"You want to explain to the Tribune how you happen to stink of fish?"

From the voices, Yuki had expected a pair, but six orcs walked around a corner and stopped to stare at her.

"Take me to the Bloodmancer." Yuki drew Cylk. She expected them to attack, or possibly run to raise an alarm. Their laughter made her face grow hot and her grip on her sword tightened.

"This could be more fun than fishing," sensei with a cold said. Yuki thought he was leering, but the tusks made it hard to tell. The others laughed louder. "Wrong kind of sword for tunnel fighting, unless you like breaking rocks." The orc drew his sword, not much longer than a dagger, and charged.

Yuki flicked her sword cutting the orc's hand off, then his head. The others yelled and ran at her waving their swords. Cylk's length *was* a challenge. She couldn't use a full slash, so ended up lunging and fighting with her wrist movement. The advantage of the tunnel was they couldn't get past her. She gave ground until one more eager than the rest got too close, then Cylk cut through arm, leg or neck like they were butter.

The second to last orc impaled himself on her sword, and if the last had attacked then, Yuki would have been in trouble. Instead it turned and ran yelling as it went.

"I guess that will do for now." Yuki pulled her sword free, picked her way passed the bodies and followed the fading cries of the orc. She entered a larger tunnel and loped along it hugging the wall. A slight echo came from an opening, so Yuki waited with her back to the rock. The sounds grew louder. She hardly had time to ready herself before a squad of goblins burst out of the tunnel. None of them lived long enough to see her attack.

126

A shield from one of the fallen in her left hand made her a little less concerned about bolts or arrows. Yuki took off along the tunnel again. There would be more coming from behind. She needed to get going.

A huge troll stood in the centre of the tunnel taking so much space, Yuki didn't think it could swing its club properly. It must have agreed since it fired the massive chunk of wood at her. She dove to the side and rolled to her feet as the club clattered on the stone. The creature took up what looked like a wrestling stance. All it needed was to land one blow, even a glancing blow, and she'd have failed.

Yuki picked up speed and raised her sword for a thrust to the heart. The troll clapped its hands in front. If she hadn't stopped and pulled back at the last instant, Cylk would have been trapped. She spun and slashed, leaving the creature's arms falling to the floor, then on the return cut through the neck, taking off running again before the head hit the floor.

Ten minutes later, on a spiral ramp, Yuki leaned against the wall gasping for breath. In movies and books the hero could run and fight endlessly. Even going down the slope she staggered as much as ran, wielding her sword in desperate swipes. Blood trickled from scratches and cuts she didn't remember getting.

Feet on stone echoed from above and below her.

Might as well rest a minute.

The sounds grew louder, but Yuki got her breathing under control and most of the shake out of her arms. Moving as quietly as she could down the ramp, she prepared herself to deal with whatever came around the bend.

What she faced was a wall of spears. Countering her first instinct to slash at them, Yuki used the flat of her blade to push the centre few up and crouch under them. She dropped into a low attack position and lunged forward slashing at the legs of the enemy. The closest dropped screaming to the floor while the other either backed away to try to bring their weapons into play or dropped the spears and snatched at swords. Yuki cut through them all.

Behind them stood a man in immaculate black robes. He held a sword and dagger, both jet black to match his clothes.

"Well, well." He smiled and lifted his sword. "If you'd let me know you were coming, I'd have prepared something more appropriate."

Yuki moved to ready, then attacked.

He moved blindingly fast, but sloppy, like someone who'd learned swordplay from watching the wrong movies. If she'd met him first, he'd have been easy, but now, heart banging painfully and every muscle trembling, Yuki was hard put to hold him off.

She slipped on the rock, slick with blood and went to one knee. Her opponent lunged to the attack. Yuki pushed his sword to the left and simultaneously blocked him from using the dagger. That gave her a fraction of a second's opening to cut with all the strength remaining in her. Cylk flashed at the man's throat, then rang like a bell. Her numbed hands dropped the sword to clang on the stone. Rough hands grabbed her from behind and held her immobile.

"Bring her." The man picked up Cylk and peered at it, then walked away. The orcs dragged Yuki after him.

***

The Master sauntered into the room followed by orcs dragging a woman in torn and bloody clothes. Something about her tried to reach Lance through the stench, but he couldn't concentrate.

"Take the scabbard from her, slave." The Master didn't even glance at Lance.

Lance took the sword belt off her, surprised to catch her deep brown eyes looking at him, tears leaking across her cheeks.

"Now, now." The Master scratched her cheek with the sword in his hand, then as with all the others, flung her against the wall with his magic. "Someone who came this far to give me victory can't be so weak as to cry." He put his hand out and Lance passed him the scabbard. The Master put the sword away, then hung it over his shoulder. "In three days, the armies will arrive, and the blood of the one they put all their hope in will destroy them. Until then, my slave will keep you alive. Enjoy your despair."

Lance waited until the last echoes of the orcs' footsteps faded before he slipped his knife from his boot and cut his arm. On impulse, he scratched the woman to draw blood. Her eyes cleared as she glared at him.

"Blood, stink." His voice grated, even with the blood he couldn't get words past the smell. Lance shrugged and turned to hunt for a rat.

***

Yuki hung on the wall and watched the man meander through the room. He never put so much as a toe through the open doorway. To her disgust he caught rats and semi-cooked them over the smoky torches before forcing her and the other prisoners to eat.

This was the man who tried to save her, and she'd abandoned him to this place. No wonder he tortured her. Every time he fed here, and at other random times, the man would cut her with a tiny knife he kept in his boot. She'd heard in books and movies of the death by a thousand cuts, but never believed in it until now. The scratches hurt worse than her other wounds. Each one dug into her soul reminding her of her failure. She didn't even try to find him, just took their word for his death. If it weren't for her, he wouldn't be here, mumbling about blood and stink.

As the days passed her hatred of him began to match his. What did he expect? How could she have known? It was his own choice to try to save her. All she wanted was a second free from her invisible bonds and she'd repay him for the torture. Then she'd die, but she'd die anyway, this whole world balanced on the brink of death, one more didn't matter. Too bad she didn't turn out to be worth the trust Harin and the others gave her.

The torch never stopped burning, the slave fed them whenever he found prey, or a guard tossed hard bread into the room. Yuki had no way to tell how much time had passed. Footsteps sounded faintly, then grew louder. The Bloodmancer strolled into the room, a feral grin on his face.

"The time has come for you to give me victory."

"I won't help you." Yuki fought against the invisible chains.

"I don't need your help, just your blood. The fool Peginus bound the fate of this world to your blood when he called you. The elf strengthened the bond when she wove your soul into destiny. When I bleed you dry, there will be gods not as powerful as I."

"Why not be a god then?"

"The gods have rules, conditions. Some may envy the gods, but I want to live where red, hot blood can run across my hands."

Black despair filled Yuki, even if she were free with Cylk in her hands, she could do nothing.

"Slave, bring her to me." The Bloodmancer drew Cylk and tossed the scabbard into the corner. He slashed his hand and let the flowing blood draw a pattern on the floor.

Yuki fell from the wall and the slave dragged her to her feet. Fire burned in her. If she were to die, she'd not let this torturer go unpunished. She grabbed his throat and squeezed. The man's face didn't look fearful, or angry. Why would he be sad? Then pain tore through her leg.

130

Yuki screamed and pushed him aside as the agony consumed her despair, her hate, her fear.

"Come." The Bloodmancer frowned at her when Yuki didn't move. "Come!" This time he pointed at her then made a pulling motion.

She took a couple of steps, then stopped.

"No." Yuki gasped for air as if she'd been running all day. Bending to rest her hands on her knees, she touched the hilt of the slave's knife sticking out of her thigh.

"Then I will kill you where you stand." The Bloodmancer lifted Cylk and pointed it at her.

Yuki lifted her face and laughed. This was ridiculous. Here she was, the heroine, facing death by her own sword. It went beyond failure to the absurd. She had no weapon, no strength, but laughter poured out of her.

The Bloodmancer lunged at her, but had to overextend to reach. Yuki twisted to the side as Cylk sliced across her ribs. She grabbed the hilt with her right hand, but he'd pull it free easily enough. Her left hand brushed against the knife in her leg. If being stabbed hurt, pulling the knife free was worse. Yuki shrieked and slashed at her enemy's face with the tiny blade.

A faint red line marked his cheek. Yuki brought the knife back to cut him again, but he let go of Cylk and staggered back. A red drop appeared from the scratch and dripped down the Bloodmancer's face.

Yuki whipped Cylk around to attack, and when he flinched to the side, she stabbed him with the knife in her left hand. The Bloodmancer's scream cracked the stone floor. He pulled the knife from his side, but instead of blood, darkness leaked from between his fingers.

Yuki attacked with Cylk, each wound opened to emptiness, the shell of his body falling to dust.

A scuffle at the door warned her of someone's approach. A troll followed by a squad of orcs stood staring at her. Yuki lifted Cylk and grinned, and all of them fled.

After she found Cylk's scabbard, cleaned and put away the sword, Yuki picked up the knife and went over to the old man still huddled in the corner.

"You OK?"

"Blood, stink gone."

"Yes, it's gone." Yuki looked around. The other prisoners had fallen from the wall. Some were helping others. They didn't look to need her. She sat beside the man. "My name's Yuki."

"Lance." He peered at his feet. "Could use a drink."

"Me too." Yuki held out Lance's knife. "This is yours."

"Keep it."

Yuki nodded, then leaned her head back to rest.

* * *

"So you are going to care for him?" Harin peered down the table at where the old man, Lance, was wolfing down food, a wineskin clutched in one hand.

"Someone needs to. He won't be any trouble. I'll still be able to help you with your plans to open a training academy."

"Are you sure about this?"

"I owe him. He saved my life, twice." Yuki swirled the wine in her cup. "Magus Peginus brought me here. Nymedhiel bonded my soul to this world so I wouldn't fall into grief. You and Bothurn trained with me and gave me a place to belong. Lance was dragged here and dropped alone somewhere. He was taken by the Bloodmancer and with no help, fought for his soul and gave me the weapon to defeat the enemy."

"Cylk—"

"Cylk bounced off the Bloodmancer." Yuki put Lance's knife on the table in front of Harin. No longer than the width of her hand. "This is what killed him. You called me and made me a hero, the one from another world. He," Yuki nodded at Lance as he took a long drink from the wineskin. "gave me the steel."

RUNNING WOMAN AND DOG MAN

Winner of the Cisco Writers Club Short Story Contest 2018

Simon waved at the woman in the pink shorts as she ran past. She never acknowledged him; focused only on putting one foot in front of the other, white wires feeding music into her ears.

When he'd first seen her, the running woman had been more of a shuffling woman. Over the course of the year, she'd moved from shuffling to jogging, to running. Now she sprang like a gazelle through his mornings, not knowing she saved his life every morning. Each day he'd stare out over the eleventh-floor balcony, contemplating the three-second trip to the pavement. He'd consider the sadness of not seeing Running Woman, then he'd put the leashes on his two dogs and walk out the door to their daily meeting.

He called the pair Beer and Brandy after what he didn't drink anymore. They followed him into the elevator, noses leaving prints on the stainless-steel as they sniffed each floor as it passed, until they could drag him out and out onto the street.

Simon could have walked the route with his eyes closed. There was the tree where the squirrel chattered at them. Here the bush they had to mark every time. A little further on they'd hear the terrier on the second floor. Then the vision in pink shorts striding gracefully past. Each day a different tee shirt, sweater, even a parka, but always those pink shorts. He'd get to the leash free park and turn the boys loose to run and play – their reward for reminding him to walk.

The morning the world changed started like any other, the view, the dogs tugging him, putting on the vests, the leashes, then the squirrels, the terrier. No woman in pink shorts. He kept walking. Maybe he'd walked too fast, it had happened before.

He turned the corner toward the park.

She lay on the grass weeping, pounding the ground with her fists. White wires tangled under her hand. Simon's heart raced, his breath came fast and shallow until he came close to falling beside her.

Beer saved him. A dog with no restraint, he pranced up to the woman, crouched down and licked her face. Simon closed his eyes and assembled the words, lining them up like dominoes, then tipped the first one. He could no longer remember the days when words had been easy.

"M, may I -- help you?" He pulled tentatively on Beer's leash, nothing doing. The dogs walked him. It was their work after all.

"Twisted my ankle." She wrapped her arms around the dog and hugged him. Simon stopped pulling on the leash. Brandy edged toward the woman, as nervous as Beer was outgoing. Her lifted hand encouraged him to a careful taste of her fingers, tail wagging faster.

"May I help you?" Easier to repeat words than make a new line of dominoes.

She looked up at him, then reached out her hand. He gripped it, strong, warm, sweaty. The woman pulled herself up. Simon stood frozen by the touch.

"You have a cell phone?" Running Woman balanced on one leg, keeping contact with Simon's hand.

"I…" Simon tried to find the words, but they scattered and fell. The pain started behind his left eye, forcing its way out like a crystal growing in his head, making his body shake. Closing his eyes helped a little. "…here." He unlocked his phone and passed it to her.

The woman's words flowed like her running; fast, graceful, beyond his comprehension.

"Blast." Tears squeezed out to join her already wet cheek. "He can't come right away. I'll have to wait."

Simon pointed to the bench by a bus stop, almost invisible to him since the dogs ignored it. She let go of his hand to wrap her arm around his shoulder. In a painful hop the running woman made her way toward the bench with a realtor ad on the back. He found his arm had gone around her waist. Under the loose t-shirt she was soft. He'd expected hard muscle, an athlete's body.

Beer and Brandy flanked them as if to guide and protect. Running Woman sat abruptly pulling Simon down beside her. Their shoulders brushed. Beer jumped up beside her. Brandy sat at Simon's feet.

"Marcie." The woman spoke her name out into the traffic as she wound up the wires and tucked them into her shorts. Marcie stiffened and sucked in her breath, tightened her hand on his leg.

"S…" Even his name had left him, he held his head in his hands trying to squeeze out words, even one. Brandy nudged him with his nose. Licked his hand. Warm fur, soft ears. "Brandy – the dog." He tilted his head at Beer lying with his head on her leg. "Beer."

"Good names." Marcie laughed, then hissed.

Simon untied Brandy's bandana, kneeling to wrap it around her ankle, Beer lifted his head and stuck his tongue out. Simon took Beer's bandana and tied it over Brandy's.

"Thanks, that helps." Marcie patted the seat beside her. When he'd sat; she swiveled to put her foot on the bench and lean against him. She let her head tilt back. Her hair tickled his nose. teasing him with an indefinable scent. "Sorry, I shouldn't assume, your girlfriend would be jealous." But she didn't move. Marcie played with Beer's ears. "So soft." Her breath evened out and she slumped more against him. He had to put his arm around her to hold her in place.

Cars rushed past, buses stopped to open their door. Simon would shake his head and they'd drive on. The sun moved through the sky, and the bench fell into shade.

136

Marcie shivered in her sleep. Simon snapped his fingers and Brandy jumped up to lie against her, Beer snuggled closer on the other side.

People walked past eyeing them. Simon tried to line up the words, but they fell too soon or the wrong direction. The pain returned and he gave up.

He moved from the simple desire to help, to a little embarrassment at sitting holding a woman sleeping on a bench. His backside hurt, his back ached. He sweated where she leaned against him, chilled on the other side.

Simon couldn't point to the moment when the embarrassment and discomfort shifted to tenderness. He wanted to protect her.

His heart thumped painfully, agony exploded in his head. Brandy turned his head to lick Simon's face; Beer whined, looking anxious.

"OK." Simon stroked Brandy with his free hand. "OK."

A car pulled up in front of them, and a man with grey hair ran around to kneel by Marcie.

"Are you all right? I should have been faster, to heck with business."

"Dad?" Marcie swiveled back to a sitting position, scattering the dogs. Simon let his arm drop. "What time is it?" She turned as pink as her shorts. "I'm sorry, I slept on you all day."

Words dropped like a gift from heaven.

"I don't mind, Marcie." Then they were gone again, but the pink faded from her face. She let her dad lift her into the car like a toddler. Running Woman's dad nodded at Simon before climbing into the car and driving away.

Simon swore as he forced stiff limbs to move. Cursing was easy as words were hard. "Home." He faced back toward his apartment, but the dogs dragged him to the dog park as if spending most of the day on the bench were only a brief interruption. After the appointed time of freedom, they trotted back to him. Simon clipped their leashes on and walked home.

***

He stood on the balcony. There'd be no Running Woman today. Simon couldn't call her Marcie - it hurt too much.

Beer tugged at his pant-leg. Simon followed to where Brandy waited. He put their vests and leashes on, and they went for their walk. The dogs pranced unconcerned, but Simon's gut churned. She wouldn't be there, then what would call him from the precipice tomorrow? He tried to turn back, if he didn't meet her absence, maybe it would be all right.

The boys refused to budge. Simon kept his eyes down but turning the corner he caught a flash of pink on the bench. Beer and Brandy perked up their ears and walked over to her. They jumped up and lay on her as if they'd always done this. Marcie had her foot up on the seat, a pair of crutches on the pavement in front of her. Simon sat beside her.

"I had to come, to thank Beer and Brandy, and you." Marcie leaned against him and pulled his arm around her. She sighed, her ribs moving against him. "I took up running because I wanted to die having made a difference in the world." Marcie spoke to Beer lying beside her raised leg, his head on her other. "I have this thing eating me. The doctor calls it cancer. I refuse to give it a name, but it's killing me. The day he told me, I looked in the mirror, and I didn't matter. I decided to enter the first 5k I could. Stupid, but I had to leave some accomplishment behind. So, I started running – away from death, away from hating myself." She played with Beer's fur, and he panted at her in pleasure. "The first day thought I'd killed myself early, but next day I went out again, and the day after that. But you know all that." She laid her head back and Simon thought she'd gone to sleep again. He planned how he'd get his phone out, but couldn't imagine talking through it. Phones were impossible.

"The more I ran," Marcie's voice was barely a whisper. "the weaker I got. But I'd paid my fee I was almost ready…" Her words faded out and this time, she slept.

Simon closed his eyes against the ache, not his head today, his heart. How could she be so brave?

"Hey." Marcie's dad pulled up. He climbed out of the car, picked Marcie up and placed her in the car. "I didn't catch your name yesterday."

"Sss…" Simon's head filled with a deep void, swallowing his words.

"She talks about you as the Dog Man, said you don't talk much. These must be Beer and Brandy." The dad scratched their heads. Simon nodded. "I have no right to ask you this, but can you come tomorrow? Seeing as you might be the only thing keeping her alive." The dad's eyes glistened.

Simon nodded, then watched them drive away. He stood and followed the dogs to the park.

The next day he joined her on the bench, and the day after that. Then it poured for three days, but Marcie still sat with him on the bench. Some days she talked; most times she played with the dogs until she fell asleep.

The day the rain stopped, Simon wrote a note.

I picked up my wife at the doctors. Her face glowed with excitement. We drove through the city looking at gardens and trees.

The pain almost knocked him to his knees. He put the vests and leashes on the dogs then went for their walk.

Marcie waited, no crutches now. She curled up against him and slept before her hand found Beer's head. The dog pushed his nose under her hand and sighed. When the dad came to pick her up, Simon tucked the note in her hand.

Through the following days he put more notes into her hand.

For nine months, we waited, laughed, celebrated. We brought our daughter home, but something was wrong.

The dad met Simon at the bench now, putting Marcie in his arms to hold like a child.

I woke to find the baby silent, my wife gone. Then the screams from below started.

The dogs lay curled up beside them, watching, keeping guard.

I could find no words to describe my feelings, so I gave up on words, then they gave up on me.

Simon cradled Marcie, tears running down his cheeks. Fear burned in his heart.

I drank to dull the pain, to fill the hole the words left behind. I hated myself. A neighbour left me his dogs when he moved out.

He breathed in the scent of her hair; it eased the tightness in his chest

The morning I went to follow my family, the dogs stopped me, and took me for a walk.

The dad waited in the car after he put his daughter in Simon's arms his tears flowing like rain. Simon's heart cracked in two. Her eyes captured his. He kissed her hair and held her tight.

Like a miracle, words came.

"You saved my life, Marcie."

She smiled, sighed and stopped breathing. Simon held her until his sobs had run their course. The dad sat beside him, then buried his face in Simon's shoulder and wept. When Marcie's dad lifted her away one last time, he looked at Simon through wet eyes.

"At the end, all she wanted was to die in your arms." He tried to speak again but failed. Simon knew the feeling. He handed Marcie's dad the final note.

Every morning since, I chose to stay alive, to see you.

140

***

Simon stopped going out on the balcony. He walked the dogs who marked the bush and barked at the squirrel. Each day they'd stop at the bench and sit curled up beside Simon for a while.

The air grew colder. Snow fell. They missed the squirrel, but a crow a couple of trees over, took up the friendship.

One day they arrived at the bench to find an envelope addressed to the Dog Man.

I don't know how to thank you. I don't have the words. I think you know about that. Marcie would have wanted you to have this.

In the envelope was her music player and white cords. He put the earbuds in and touched play. What music did she listen to?

There's the park, one, two, three... Marcie's voice counted to where she turned the corner, then counted again. *One, two, three... there's the Dog Man; he looks so sad, but he always waves. One, two, three...* Her voice carried her through her run, naming landmarks; counting the steps between them until she reached the end of her run.

See you tomorrow, Dog Man.

Simon had no idea how long he sat holding the player. Beer and Brandy woke him from his daze licking the tears off his cheeks.

"OK." Simon stood up and they went to the park. On the way home, they passed an obese man bent over, red faced and gasping.

"Why am I doing this?" Anger choked the man's words.

Simon tapped him on the shoulder. The man looked up glaring at Simon. Then Beer walked under the man's hand. His fingers twitched, then briefly caressed the dog.

"See you tomorrow," Simon said.

SAL'KY

First published in 'Young Explorer's Guide Volume 6' 2019

Edith followed her mother down the ramp from the space ship. Her heart wanted to skip down the steps and spin in excitement, but her wheelchair might have been made of lead. Her dad warned her the gravity was five percent stronger than Earth's. She'd never imagined such a small difference would make her instantly tired.

"Your father said he couldn't get away to meet us, so we'll spend the night in town and take a boat to the station tomorrow."

They joined the line for customs.

"So, you're Edith? Says here you're eleven." The man in the blue uniform leaned over to look at her. His expression looked friendly, so Edith smiled.

"My friends call me Edi."

"Well if we meet again, perhaps you'll let me call you Edi." The man stamped her papers. "Welcome to Poseidia. If you know how to swim, you'll find it the fastest way to adjust to the gravity."

"Thanks." Edi smiled and took the papers back from him as he turned to talk to her mother. She liked people who talked to her, not her chair.

The hotel stood just across the street from the spaceport. Edi dragged her suitcase behind her. Up in their room, she pulled out a bathing suit.

"I'm going to go for a swim."

"I don't know where you get the energy." Her mother waved at her from where she lay on the bed.

Edi showered and rolled to the edge of the pool. The gravity made her hit the deck harder than she'd planned, but once in the water it vanished. She floated blissfully.

"You new here?" A boy sat on the edge of the pool, peering at her stick-thin legs.

142

"We just came in to join my dad at the Southern Shelf Station."

"You poor kid—there's nothing to do at the stations." The boy looked down his nose at her.

"I can always swim."

"Only if you don't mind being eaten." The boy's mouth twisted in a sneer. "We're poisonous to the creatures here, but they haven't figured it out yet."

Edi floated away from him, just a while longer; then she'd have to figure out how to get back into her chair.

***

In the morning, they boarded the boat. Edi had expected a huge ship, but it wasn't much bigger than the yachts she used to see from her room overlooking the ocean.

Her mother found a seat and closed her eyes. She got seasick standing on shore, just looking at the water. Edi must have got her water-loving genes from her dad.

Edi rolled up to the front of the boat and set her brakes. The ocean looked a little greener than the water at home, but waves were waves.

"Not much to see, unfortunately." A young man leaned against the railing beside her. "There's lots of life in the water, some of it as big as your whales on earth, but they don't like the boats and stay away."

"Do you know why?

"Nobody's sure, and since some of the things that stay away are pretty scary, no one's trying to find out."

"I saw some pictures in the books my dad sent me. The one called Cthulhu gave me nightmares."

"No kidding! Fortunately, they live in the deeps, so no one sees them much. There are some kraken near the edge of the shelf, but the station is set far enough from the edge to be safe."

They watched the ocean for a while, then Edi licked water from her fingers.

"It tastes different."

"Tastes?"

"From the ocean at home."

"I wouldn't know, never left Poseidia, but we are told not to swallow the water."

"You shouldn't swallow the salt water at home either. I'll have to ask my dad."

"You're Dr. McKaily's daughter."

"Edi." She turned and held out her hand to the young man.

"Ribert." His hand held her firmly before releasing it. "Your dad is a cool guy. He doesn't mind talking to the cabin boy."

"Cabin boy?"

"Youngest hand on the ship." Ribert rolled his eyes. "I could be twenty-five, and they'd still call me cabin boy."

Edi giggled. Ribert punched her arm gently, but he smiled at her.

"You need anything, ask for me." He wandered away, leaving her at the rail by herself.

The extra gravity started making her tired again. Edi went back and lay down near her mom.

***

"Hey, Edi." Someone shook her shoulder. "You want to see the station? Now's your chance."

She opened her eyes to see Ribert leaning over her.

"Thanks." Edi pushed herself up. "Did someone turn the gravity up again?"

Ribert laughed.

"I've heard people say you get used to it. You want a hand?"

Edi put her arm around his shoulder, and he helped into her wheelchair. They went out to the deck. Something broke the monotony of the water. To Edi's surprise, it approached rapidly.

"I thought it would be bigger."

144

"It is, but most of it is underwater. Some months this area gets nasty storms. During those, they lower the pier and the whole thing is below the surface."

Edi opened her mouth to ask a question, then spotted someone on the deck of the station. She waved until he waved back.

"Your dad always meets the boat."

The boat pulled up to the pier and Edi watched as her dad caught the rope and helped the boat to tie up. As soon as the ramp was lower and the sleeping man from the mess moved the chain, Edi wheeled to her dad and wrapped her arms tight around him.

"Hello, Urchin." Her dad squeezed her back until she could no longer breathe normally. He finally stepped back a bit. "You're looking good." His eyes were suspiciously wet, but he smiled broadly at her.

Edi's mother appeared at the top of the ramp, then walked slowly down. Her dad stood at the bottom with a strange look on his face. He reached up to touch Edi's mom's face, then wrapped her in a tight hug. His shoulders shook, and a lump formed in Edi's throat. When her mother tilted her head up to kiss her dad, Edi wandered to the edge of the platform and leaned over to peer into the water. Odd things floated on the surface and deeper. A tentacle slapped onto the deck, brushing her hand. Edi squeaked and pushed the wheelchair away. For a brief instant, an eye the size of her fist lifted above the steel deck and peered into Edi's eyes.

It vanished as she gasped in air to scream, and choked instead.

"You OK?" Ribert squatted down beside her and waited for her to get her breathing under control.

Heat travelled up her face.

"You should have seen me the first I saw Sally." Ribert sat beside her and leaned against the bulkhead. "Just about jumped out of my skin. Captain says I squealed like a girl, but I don't know. You didn't squeal did you?"

"Sally?" Edi looked back at the ocean, half hoping to see the tentacle again.

"Don't know who gave her the name, was before my time. She welcomes everyone the same way. That's the only place to look down into the water without being in the way. I think she lies in wait."

"Octopuses on Earth are surprisingly intelligent— what if the ones here are too?"

"That's part of what your dad is doing here. We don't want to make the same mistakes the people on Earth made."

"Ready to head down under, Urchin?" Her father stood in front of her, holding her mother's hand.

"You're sweet." Edi released her brakes and rolled along beside him. "But you're going to have a hard time working with one hand." She giggled when her father blushed.

He led them to big steel doors which stood open to show a short hallway to more steel doors at the other end.

"We get the next ride down." Her dad squeezed her hand. "I like to make sure the cargo all arrives in good condition."

"Score one for Dad." Edi's mom peeked around and grinned at Edi.

"See you next time, Dr. McKaily," Ribert called to them, gave Edi a thumbs-up, then pushed the big door shut with a clang.

The other doors opened into a large elevator. They got in, and Edi snorted when she saw it had only two buttons. Her dad pushed the down button and grinned at her.

"How deep do we go?" Edi leaned against the wall and crossed her arms over her front; the air suddenly felt cold.

"We're down two hundred feet. It's one of the deeper spots of the shelf and still looks barren after months of study." Her dad looked up into a corner of the elevator. "There are presently 237 people down below, most are involved in the greenhouses or the aquaculture. My team is only five people."

"I thought this station was all about research."

"It is, but some of the research is about greenhouse and aquaculture in the below. Other people are studying the community itself to try to figure out how to make us more self-sufficient."

"A boy at the hotel said the things in the ocean can't eat us, we're poison to them or something, so we can't eat them either?"

"That's right, we have a plant to take all the salt out of the seawater before we use it."

"It tasted different."

"A little bit won't hurt you, but don't be doing a lot of tasting." Her dad glanced at her briefly before his eyes found the upper corner again. "The salts in the water are different. I think that's why we're mutually toxic."

Edi sighed; her dad hadn't changed at all. He still stared into space to talk science. "Reading the teleprompter," he'd told her.

When the doors opened, a family stood waiting for them—a man, a woman, and a boy about Edi's age.

"Welcome," the woman said. "I'm Katrin, the Reeve for South Below. If you have any problems or you need something, ask anyone and they'll point you toward me." She turned and walked away. Edi followed her mom and dad as they walked beside the woman.

"So you're from Earth?" the boy said.

"Yes." Edi puffed, trying to keep up.

"I thought they had electric wheelchairs."

"Too heavy to bring on the ship. One's being made for me at the port. Pushing this antique will make me stronger anyway."

He put out his hand. Edi took it, apparently having passed a test.

"I'm Piotr." The grin on his face transformed him.

"Edi."

"Did you bring any chocolate?"

"Now don't be harassing her already for treats, you know how expensive they are." Katrin spoke without turning around. Piotr hunched his shoulders.

"Chocolate was too heavy to bring as much as I wanted." Edi elbowed him. "So I brought the biggest can of cocoa I could fit in my bag. Just wait 'til you taste my brownies." She didn't mind using some of her precious store if it helped her make a friend.

Piotr rolled his eyes deliriously and Edi laughed. He moved around behind her and pushed her along.

"We have school tomorrow. There are twenty of us, counting you. First thing you'll learn is all the safety rules."

"Dad sent me a copy of the manual and told me to memorize it." Edi groaned. "I could have been reading good books. I have this really interesting one about space squids."

"You're weird." Piotr said. "We could use some weird around here."

"Piotr." Katrin's voice floated back. "Don't be rude."

***

With Piotr's endorsement and the help of a plate of brownies, Edi was immediately absorbed into the group of pre-teen school children. They roved through the station, pointing out the odd nooks and crannies, taking turns being her "motor" when she got tired. Her friends talked with pride about parents who worked hard at keeping the station fed, safe, and clean.

148

Sometimes she had horrible nightmares. She'd wake up struggling for breath, face drenched with tears. All she could recall was panic at being trapped. Other kids shrugged and said it came with being a newcomer. Edi pushed the nightmares aside and concentrated on her new friends and spending time with her dad.

In the evenings, she'd finish her homework in the lab then help her dad. It had to be one of the creepiest places she'd ever seen. She loved it. The square room was twenty feet a side with one wall covered floor to ceiling with large glass tanks. Each held a cephalopoid from the surrounding ocean. Her job was to keep the glass on her side clean.

"Don't lift any of the lids." Henry, her father's assistant, pointed to a scar on his hand. "Some of them can burn you badly."

"Sally's tentacle touched me, and I didn't get burned." Edi looked at her hand and shivered.

"Sally, huh?" Henry said. "I haven't seen enough of her to say what species she is. I'll make a note she didn't burn when she touched you." He patted her shoulder. "Every bit of information is useful."

Edi resisted the temptation to roll her eyes.

Along the wall to the left of the tanks was one large tank that took up the entire wall. The creature in it looked like a mixture of shark and octopus. It followed her with its enormous eyes.

"I've got a meeting." Her dad saved his work. "You OK to finish up here?" He looked at her with a few wrinkles on his forehead. They'd been together long enough for him to remember to worry about her.

"Sure, I'm almost done anyway." Edi waved at him then turned back to her book. This was her favourite course, which tried to teach everything humans knew about Poseidia.

She closed the book, resisting the temptation to read ahead. Her mom told her absorbing information worked better if she didn't rush. Her mom taught the teens, and from her stories, they were a challenge.

"Time to clean up." Edi said to the cephalopoids. She used a cloth with no soap and scrubbed at the front of each tank she could reach. The inhabitants hid, peering out from under a rock or whatever shelter they had in the tank. Edi checked each tank for activity. After she'd found one dead, Henry told her their lifespan appeared to be very short.

She started on the big tank. The creature floated out from its hiding place and rested by the glass, its tentacles following her hand. Edi almost stopped and left the lab. Washing the tanks was probably just an excuse for her dad to keep an eye on her; she'd never seen the slightest speck on her side of the glass.

Every bit of information is useful. Henry would want to know about this new behaviour—maybe they could set up a camera to record it.

Edi focused on her task again and came face to face with the cephalopoid's eye. Big as her fist, it glowed slightly. She'd read about people getting lost in someone's eyes, but this was the first time she knew what it meant. Her hand slowed, and she brought her face closer to the glass until her nose squished against it.

Help.

Pain shot through Edi's head. She screamed and fell back, then crashed to the floor. Red shot through her mind, and she held her hands in front of her. The pain stopped, leaving a ghostly ache behind her eyes. The cephalopoid had hidden again.

Did it really talk to me? Edi pushed herself to a sitting position. Now that she considered it, Edi wasn't sure she'd heard a word, more like a desire.

Edi set her chair on its wheels and lifted herself in. Her arms shook with the effort, but she pushed herself out of the lab. As she was closing the door her nightmare hit her. *Fear, despair, locked away. She was dying.*

Edi slammed the door and the feelings cut off, leaving her shaking and wiping tears from her eyes.

***

"For some reason, all the kids who come here from off planet get headaches." Edi's dad changed the cloth on her head for a cool, fresh one. "It may be a trace element in the water. Since it always fades within a week, the doctors haven't figured it out."

"You just rest then." Her mom sat beside her and took her hand until Edi fell asleep.

Edi woke up screaming; her parents ran into her room.

"Is it your head, is it worse?" Her mom looked frantic, and her dad had a phone in his hand. Edi couldn't speak past the gasping echoes of the scream, so she shook her head. Tears soaked the front of her pajamas.

"Just a really bad dream." Edi struggled for each word as if she'd forgotten her own language. "I'll change my PJs and go back to sleep." When neither of her parents moved, she rolled her eyes and pointed to the door.

"Now I know she's fine." Her dad pulled her mom out of the room and closed the door behind him.

After school, Edi returned to the lab, forcing her hands to push her over the threshold. Henry pointed to the big tank.

"Is that a nose print?" His lips twitched at the corners.

"The big cephalopoid started following my hand, and I wanted to get a closer look." She looked down. "Sorry, I should have wiped it away."

"No harm done." Henry walked over to the tank and peered into it. "I never heard of them reacting to humans, other than to hide."

"Maybe set up a camera and see if it does it again?" Edi rubbed her head. A ghost of a headache swam behind her eyes. "It was the first time I was alone in the lab."

"Are you up for it?" Henry examined her. "Dr. McKaily said you had the newcomers' headache and a bad dream."

"I'm fine." Edi slammed her books down and started her homework.

"I'll set up the camera before I leave."

She tried to concentrate, but her brain felt full of mud.

"I've set up cameras to cover several angles." Henry stood beside her. *How long have I been staring at the same page?* "I've let Dr. McKaily know what we're doing. He will check on you in half an hour."

"OK." Edi closed her books and resisted the temptation to shake her head to clear the fog. The door clicked behind Henry. The three tiny cameras had red lights showing they were recording. Half an hour wasn't that long, and there was no guarantee her dad would wait that long.

The cephalopoids in the small tanks hid as usual. She washed them more quickly, wanting and dreading the moment she reached the big tank.

As if it were as eager as Edi, the large cephalopoid swam out to meet her, again matching her hand motions. Edi kept her eyes closed. Tears leaked out as inexpressible sorrow tore at her heart. *Why am I so sad?* She opened her eyes. *It isn't my feeling.*

The huge eye stared into hers. Pain lanced through her head, but Edi tried to understand what went on in the creature's mind.

Help.

"I don't know how, I'm just a kid." Edi forced the words out. The sorrow grew deeper and Edi shook with sobs. "I can ask my dad." Fear overwhelmed the sadness. Her heart raced and her body shook, she tried to push away from the tank and fell to the floor.

"Edi!" Her father rushed in and picked her up. The cephalopoid had vanished when the door opened.

"It's so sad, and scared." Edi rasped into her father's shoulder.

"What is, Urchin?"

She pointed toward the tank, her hand shaking in a terror that wasn't hers.

Her dad carried her out of the lab. When the door closed, the feelings cut off. Edi gasped, then burrowed in closer to her dad. Whatever the creature thought, she was safe with him.

***

Katrin sat across from Edi's dad in their apartment. Edi sat beside her dad, unwilling to break contact. Her mom made tea in the kitchen and raided Edi's store of brownies.

"Thank you Ms. McKaily." Katrin took a cup of tea and a brownie. Her eyebrows rose when she took a bite. "I see why Piotr raved about these."

"They're Edi's specialty." Her mom handed tea to Edi's dad, and milk to Edi, and both took brownies. Then she sat on Edi's other side. They sipped and munched in silence.

Katrin set down her cup and sighed.

"As pleasant as this is, there must be a reason you've insisted I come immediately."

"Edi has communicated with the large cephalopoid." Her dad said it as calmly as if he were saying she'd walked through the door.

Katrin's eyebrows lifted.

"I'll show you the video later, but Henry and agree the behaviour is consistent with communication. The cameras also caught Edi's expressions; that alone is convincing."

"What did it say?" Katrin looked down at Edi.

"More feelings than words." Edi forced herself to put distance between her and the memories of those intense emotions. "Sorrow, fear. The only thing that might have been a word was *help.*"

"Help?" Katrin moved her hand before putting them back on her knees.

"I heard that both times."

"The reason we had cameras set up was at Edi's request. Though she didn't mention communicating then." Her dad looked sharply at her.

"I see." Katrin closed her eyes and bent her head. "We need to be sure before we institute a Section 1."

"Section 1?" Edi's heart pounded. What could upset Katrin and her parents so much?

"If there is intelligent life, we must stop all development and negotiate permission to remain here. If we can't prove we've made an agreement, then we have to leave." Katrin let out a sob. "We'll lose our homes, everything."

"How long do we have?" Edi's stomach twisted into a knot.

"One year from the time we set Section 1 in motion." Edi's dad said beside her. "I don't understand. None of them tested for any intelligence at all. We should have seen some indication."

"What if they were lying?" Edi felt heat rise into her face as Katrin stared at her, and her dad's hand landed feather-light on her shoulder. She covered her face with her hands.

"You said it reacted with fear when you thought about telling me?" Her dad squeezed her shoulder. "Lying might be a reasonable hypothesis."

"So what do we do?" Edi's mom asked.

Edi's stomach hurt. There was only one answer.

"I need to talk to it more."

"No, not if it hurts you that much. What if it's damaging you...?" Her dad trailed off.

"I'll get them to bring in a scanner from the port." Katrin clenched her jaw. "They'll have no choice if we call a Section 1. That way we can monitor any change in Edi."

154

"We'll wait until the scanner gets here before we proceed," Edi's dad said. She leaned her head against him.

"I don't think we should." Edi's hands clenched; she wanted to climb onto his lap and bury her face in his shirt, for once not hating his protectiveness. "One of the things I felt the first time was that it's dying. We might not have time."

Her dad swore, and no one said anything about it. This *was* serious.

"I'll put a rush on it." Katrin stood then came over to crouch in front of Edi. "I know you feel like this is all on your shoulders, but I will do everything I can to help." She straightened up, nodded at Edi's parents, then left.

Her dad lifted her onto his lap.

"I know you're too old for this, but ..." Her dad wrapped his arms around her and held her tight.

"No, I'm not." Edi buried her face in his shirt. Her mother's arm came around to hold Edi too.

It was almost enough to make her stop shaking.

***

"Nothing." Henry paced the lab while Edi's dad and Katrin watched. "We've been at this two days and nothing."

"I *told* you." Edi spun in her chair. "I need to be alone. Set up a remote camera to watch if you want, but don't interrupt."

"If you collapse, I'm coming in." Edi's dad stopped her spinning to look in her eyes.

"OK." She sighed and nodded.

Henry set up a couple of cameras, synced them with his tablet, and then the grownups left the lab.

Edi pushed herself over to the large tank. She put her forehead against the glass.

"Let's get this done."

The cephalopoid pushed out from under the rocks and tears streamed down Edi's face. It looked sick, only a faint glow in its eyes.

"I'm sorry. I'm too late."

A caress brushed across her mind under the pain of communication. Edi laughed through her tears.

"How much time do you have?"

?

"What do you need?" Edi steeled herself against the pain.

Longing, regret, peace. Floating in a huge ocean. Currents connecting to the world. An immensity far away, but tugging.

The connection broke as the last light faded from the cephalopoid's eye, and it dropped to the bottom of the tank.

Thank you. A faint thought brushed against her mind as Edi slumped in her chair sobbing, holding her head.

She didn't know the grownups had returned until her dad picked her up and held her tight.

"Blast." Henry looked at the tank. "Now what do we do?"

"I don't know," Edi's dad said, his words vibrating against Edi's forehead. "I really don't know."

***

The scanner arrived, and they ran Edi through it several times.

"It's hard to say without a baseline." The technician pointed the image on the screen. "That could be a bit of bleeding in these areas of her brain. They are connected to emotion and language. At this level, it isn't something to worry about. We'll monitor her on a weekly basis. That will tell us if it is healing or getting worse."

"Thank you," Edi's mom put her hand on Edi's shoulder. "You OK?"

156

"I guess." Edi peered at the spots where the tech had pointed. She couldn't see anything.

She followed her mom out of the doctor's office and back to their apartment. Her dad had flown to the port to talk to the Governing Council. Rumours swirled through the station with people gathered in bunches, peering around as they whispered.

Edi avoided their looks, feeling unreasonably guilty.

***

The horn sounded in the middle of math. Every head snapped up, then the teacher led them to the gym, which doubled as a town hall—the only place where every man, woman, and child could fit at one time.

"Sorry to call you away from your work." Katrin stood at the podium, pale and shaking a little. Edi's heart sank. "Some of you know there is some evidence that some of the cephalopoids show intelligence, and one tried to communicate with one of our citizens." The crowd murmured, some looking shocked while others nodded their heads. "I would have explained about this earlier, but the Council didn't want to start a panic." She bowed her head and gripped the podium tightly.

"Why tell us now?" someone yelled out of the crowd.

"The Governing Council asked Earth for advice, as the evidence was slim and work just beginning. The answer from Earth came back today." She held up her tablet. "I will send you the text after the meeting. Everyone on Poseidia will have a copy by the end of the day. The short version is this: The Congress of Earth understands the hardship their decision will cause; they also understand there is no precedent in our history. In every other case, the evidence was incontrovertible, but they feel it is necessary to err on the side of caution. That is why they are declaring Section 1 to be active upon receipt of this communication." Katrin looked around the room, making no effort to hide her tears. "We have one year to learn to communicate with the cephalopoids and gain agreement for us to remain and under what conditions. If we fail at this task, we must vacate Poseidia, and it will be declared off limits to all human activity."

The room broke into groups of people shouting at each other. Edi put her hands over her ears and closed her eyes. Her mom pushed her out of the gym and back to the apartment.

"This is all my fault." Edi hung her head.

"No." her mother knelt beside Edi and hugged her. "It is better we do the right thing even if it hurts. Every human who goes to another planet signs an agreement to abide by Section 1."

"What happens if someone doesn't sign?"

"They return to Earth and will never be allowed to travel to another planet again."

"I think I understand. I was so sad when the cephalopoid died. I can't imagine how I'd feel if they all vanished." Her dream of an empty ocean came to her, and she gasped and hunched.

"What's wrong?"

"My dreams—they're about an empty ocean." Edi looked at her mom wide-eyed. "We must be doing something that hurts the cephalopoids. It wasn't just that one dying. It was *all* of them." She wheeled in circles through the apartment. "We have to do something now."

"Maybe your father will have an idea, but we aren't allowed to capture any more cephalopoids. Even the small ones are going to be released back where they were caught."

"Maybe I need to go to where the cephalopoids are, talk to them there."

"There's a reason no one goes down into the water without being in an enclosed capsule. The cephalopoids attack swimmers."

158

"The enclosed capsule would be no good, the cephalopoids won't come near a boat."

"We have a year, Edi. We'll figure something out."

"I don't think we have a year, Mom. My gut tells me something is drastically wrong."

"Talk to your father."

The discussion with her father didn't go much better than it had with her mother.

"We have a process, Urchin." He waved his tablet. "We'll follow the process carefully. And we don't know what damage it may have done to you."

"But we don't have time!" Edi's breath came short, and her heart pounded. Her dream meshed with the present moment.

"We don't know where any cephalopoids live."

"Yes, we do." Edi thumped the arm of her chair. "Sally. She always comes after the boat docks and the engines shut down."

"How are you going to talk to her? I won't let you go in the water." Her father frowned at her.

"What about a tank? Put the tank in the water and I talk through the glass, same as in the lab."

He looked at her and took a breath.

"I know you think I can't do anything, but I have to do this."

Her father looked like she'd slapped him, then put his hand on hers.

"OK."

***

Up on the deck with waves splashing salt spray over her, Edi's stomach quivered. The tank had been fitted with a lid to seal it. Her dad gave her an air bottle with a mask on it.

"Katrin insisted you have this along."

Edi took the air bottle, and her dad lifted her into the tank. She'd dressed warmly at his insistence.

Two men sealed the lid, then checked it before winching it, and her, over the side and into the water.

Edi almost panicked when the water closed over the top of the tank. She waved at the men, and they lowered her farther into the depths. Forehead against the floor of the tank, she called out into the ocean.

"Sally, please. I need to talk to you." Her head ached with the effort.

Then suddenly Sally was on the other side of the glass, more than twice the size of the cephalopoid in the lab.

Sal'ky.

"Edi." She gazed into Sal'ky's eye. "Please tell me what to do. How are we hurting you?"

Sal'ky wrapped her arms around the tank and wrenched opened the top. Edi screamed and snatched the air bottle as tentacles fished her out of her safe container.

Safe.

Edi forced herself to relax. *I can do this.* The air bottle would give her more time. As Sal'ky pulled her down into the depths, she hoped it would be enough.

The water grew cold and dark, but Sal'ky sent reassuring waves of thought to Edi. It didn't hurt near as much as in the lab—maybe the glass had made it harder? Or she was so cold the pain didn't reach her. The air bottle slipped from her numb fingers. Sal'ky caught it and held it. When Edi reached for it, Sal'ky held the mask against her face.

She popped her eardrums a couple of times, then they floated still in the water. Edi recognized her dream. She stretched her mind but couldn't find any life but Sal'ky beside her.

Help. Sal'ky put tentacles on either side of Edi's head. This time it hurt, worse than ever before, but Edi listened through the agony. Far, far away a thought reached out to her. *The ocean filled with a network of messages, songs, memories. A living being, the entire world! Then things on*

*the surface causing pain, breaking the network. The ocean
began to lose itself.*

"I understand." Edi said. "I'll tell them."

Sal'ky shot upwards, pushing the bottle at Edi for her
to breathe, then one time it didn't work. Edi could see the
light coming from above. It wavered and turned black.
Something slammed against her. Edi gasped in shock.

Air.

She lay on the deck of the station with her father
kneeling beside her, weeping. Edi turned to see Sal'ky's
tentacle wave one last time and vanish.

"We've got to get you inside." The doctor mercilessly
cut her clothes off and wrapped her in a warm blanket.

"The boats, the engines." Edi whispered. "We have to
stop them. All of them. They are disrupting the ocean's
dreams. Stop them, Dad."

"Dreams?"

"The cephalopoids are parts of a single being. The
ocean is like its brain. The motors disrupt its thoughts."

Her dad gathered her in his arms and the salt of their
shared tears blended with Poseidia's water on her face.

***

Eight months later, Edi sat on the deck of a sailing
catamaran, holding onto a rope with one hand. She wore a
skin-tight suit and two tanks of air on her back. The water
around the ship boiled with huge tentacles.

"Remind him you can't go safely below one hundred
feet." Her dad tapped the depth gauge on her wrist.

"It's OK, Dad. I've got this." She put her face mask
and mouthpiece in place, then leaned forward to fall into
the water to begin negotiations for her people to live on
Sal'ky's home.

ENOUGH

Xantipe walked into Haleston through the open gates; hood up to shelter her from the exuberant crowd packing the market as the royal crier read the proclamation of victory. "…the invaders have been pushed back behind the mountain passes; their sorcerous king is destroyed. The kingdom and its people are safe again."

She didn't fault them for their joy, she wished she could share it.

As she walked around the outside of the square, her breath came harder and faster, pulse racing until her whole body shook.

***

Figures in black robes sent flames to sear women and children. Xantipe desperately threw up a shield. Screams of those outside her shield assaulted her. A tiny blond boy put his hands against her shield as he fell to ash.

***

Xantipe bolted from the market, unnoticed by those around her. She found a deserted alley to empty her stomach, then lurched her way to her room over her sister's apothecary.

"You don't look good." Correin came around the counter to greet Xantipe.

Xantipe flinched away from the offered hug, then fled up the stairs to lock herself in her room. She threw her cloak into the corner, followed by her pack. Standing rigid in the center of the room her fists banged her head, face fixed in a grimace. Pain was her only weapon against the overwhelming flood of fearful memories.

When the moment passed, she collapsed on her bed too exhausted to weep.

***

'Come, Xan,' Mirio tugged on Xantipe's hand, 'you should get out some. We head out tomorrow.'

162

Xantipe shook her head and scuttled back against the wall. Mirio sighed then the setting changed to a charred village, his outstretched hand turned to stone followed by the rest of him, leaving his accusing eyes to last.

'Weak, you'll always be—' The words stabbed into her flesh painful as the first time she'd heard them.

***

Xantipe woke, her pillow soaked with tears. She only wept while she dreamed. A glass of rose water stood on the table beside the bed. The cloak hung on its peg. The pack leaned against the wall.

She huddled against the wall, bile in the back of her throat. Even here in her room she wasn't safe. A gentle knock on the door made Xantipe scream, hands glowing blue.

"Tipe, what's wrong?" Correin stood in the open door, concern on her face.

"I-I...sorry." Xantipe wanted to explain, but the pounding of her heart stole her words. The blue faded from her hands as they dropped to hug her knees. She hid her face until the shaking stopped. When she looked up, Correin had gone.

For the next week, Xantipe ate the rations in her pack. She snuck out in the middle of the night to refill her water skin. Used the pot under the bed.

Each morning a glass would be beside her bed until a rainbow of concoctions covered the table, untouched for fear of what they might contain. The chamberpot would be empty, and a tray with bread, cheese and sausage *waited* outside the door.

When her rations ran out, Xantipe tried to nibble on the bread, but it tasted wrong, deceptive, too soft, too flavourful. A trap. She didn't even try to taste the cheese or sausage.

By the end of the next week, Xantipe's stomach had stopped complaining. It wasn't the first time she'd been on short rations. Her hair hung around her face, an indeterminate colour. Even to her own nose the fug in the room was thick. But just thinking of opening the window made her body tremble and retreat to the corner of the bed, hiding behind her knees.

She stopped leaving her bed. If she died here, the fear would end. The smell grew worse until she disgusted herself, but hatred of her weakness wasn't enough to allow her to move.

Arms cradled her, Xantipe tried to lift her head to see, but couldn't move.

"Carry her down to the back room, Endre, then leave us."

"You sure?" The deep voice rumbled against Xantipe.

She tried to fight free, but her hands wouldn't move, the magic refused to come. The wail of fear came out as a whimper.

"Don't talk." A familiar voice, a familiar order.

Hands peeled her soiled clothes away sending Xantipe's lungs pumping frantically to get enough air. Her chest hurt.

***

The enemy soldier, face snarling, pushed her spear into Xantipe. She tried to scream, but had no air. Her guard surged forward. Helpless, Xantipe watched them die, one by one, until other soldiers lifted her, sealed the wound with rough magic, then carried her away from the men and women she'd killed with her frailty.

***

Warm water surrounded her, buoyed her up. Hands washed her skin, cleansing away filth. More water poured over her head.

"Up." The hands lifted and steadied her as she stepped out of the tub, then into another filled with warmer water.

Mother bathed me when I was a child. Comforted me when I ran home, unable to live in the world outside our house. When she died, Correin took over being...

Xantipe opened her eyes to meet the gentle brown gaze of her younger sister; tears glistened on her cheeks.

"Welcome back, Tipe."

Xantipe tried to talk, but her throat closed on her words, blood beat in her head.

"Shhhh." Correin cupped her hand on Xantipe's face. "It's all right. I know." She rubbed soap into Xantipe's hair. Xantipe tried to stop her, but barely had strength to lift her arms from the water. As months of grime washed away, the bright red of a mage's hair shone again. The badge of her failure to protect those around her.

Correin helped her from the water. Xantipe looked down. Ribs stuck out like a starving dog's, scars crisscrossed her skin. She was a stranger to herself. Correin wrapped a soft robe around that pitiful body, and Xantipe breathed a sigh of relief.

"Sit." Correin led her to chair by a fire. Why would she have a fire in the summer? Xantipe stretched her hands out to absorb the heat.

"Drink this slowly." Correin put a cup in Xantipe's hand but held both hand and cup. "It's broth, like Mama used to make."

The familiar scent set Xantipe's mouth to watering. She sipped at it, and tears leaked from her eyes. For the first time in years, she almost felt safe.

***

"Good morning." Correin smiled at Xantipe. After a month of her sister's careful ministrations, Xantipe had the strength to walk down the stairs on her own. More, leaving her room didn't cause immediate panic. Her world expanded to take in Correin and Endre's sitting room behind the shop.

Xantipe's clothes hung on her like when she'd dressed up in her mother's clothes as a child. Correin didn't mention it, nor did she talk about the overwhelming fear never far beneath the surface of Xantipe's mind.

Xantipe smiled slightly and ducked her head before sitting in the chair by the fire. The room had to be torturously warm for Correin and her husband, but neither spoke a word of complaint.

Tea and toast waited for her on a tiny table beside the chair. She sipped and nibbled through the morning as Correin worked in her shop out front.

Her cheery voice floated back to Xantipe. This powder to ease pain, that one to settle a stomach. Correin had a balm for every ailment. Words in hushed voice meant she was selling the herb to prevent children. Not all husbands liked that.

"What are you doing selling, nightbalm to my wife?" The loud voice made Xantipe start and drop her cup. It smashed on the floor by the hearth. She pulled her knees up and put her hands over her ears, but they couldn't block out the anger.

"It is not illegal." Correin didn't raise her voice. "And it is your wife's choice. You aren't the one who will die with another pregnancy. Be happy with the four children you have."

"Daughters," the voice grated, "I need a son to carry on my name."

"Are you truly willing to sacrifice your wife for your pride?" Correin's voice took on an edge, and Xantipe shook harder.

"Time to leave." Endre's basso voice never raised above a soft rumble, but no one ever argued. It had a lot to do with him being a head taller than anyone else in Haleston. The door slammed.

166

"Better alert the constable." Correin's voice shook. "That man must learn his outdated ideas are no longer acceptable."

"He's the constable's brother." Endre rumbled. "I will have a chat with the constable anyway. The law is the law."

Correin came into the back and put water on the stove for tea, then swept up the pieces of the broken cup.

"S-S-or-" Xantipe stammered. Correin put a hand on Xantipe's shoulder.

"Don't worry, Tipe. They are easy to replace." She bustled about the room putting leaves in the pot, pouring the water, adding honey to the cups. Her hands trembled as she handed Xantipe her tea.

Xantipe held her sister's hand until it stopped shaking. They drank their tea, then Correin sighed and went back into her shop.

Xantipe stared into the fire. Correin afraid? She was always the calm one, the strong one. The room felt cold, the sun might as well have risen black.

***

Not black, but red, blood red. It hung over the battlefield, tinging the ravens and wolves. Men shrieked and moaned. Others scrambled through the wounded finding those who could be helped giving mercy to those who could not.

This battle they'd won, if you could call such devastation winning. Xantipe watched from her post on the wall. Even if she'd been close enough to the fight to get blood on her hands, the blue fire of her magic would have burned it away, but the sun coloured them bloody. Great swaths of ash drifted on the wind, neither friend nor foe survived near them. Magic didn't distinguish, Xantipe didn't distinguish. The need for victory made morality irrelevant. At least until the dreams tortured her at night.

***

Xantipe didn't know she sobbed, her body wracked by grief, until Correin knelt to wrap arms around Xantipe's shoulders. When the spasms passed, Xantipe opened her eyes, the room distorted by her tears.

"W-w-wea—weak."

"Aren't we all?" Correin sighed and wiped Xantipe's face with a cloth before drying her own.

"A-all?"

Correin sat down and gazed at Xantipe until she hid her face behind her knees.

"Sorry, sister."

Xantipe peeked out to see Correin run fingers through her hair.

"Do you remember mother ever leaving the house?" Correin leaned forward as if the question had an inner urgency. Xantipe furrowed her forehead as she rummaged through her memories. Mama had always been present in the kitchen, the goddess of the household. Tucking the sisters in at night, welcoming them in the morning, smiling when they came home from their chores.

No memory of her ever being outside the house, not even stepping onto the porch where Xantipe and Correin would watch fire bugs in the summer dusk.

Xantipe shook her head.

"Mother couldn't go outside. Even thinking about it made her break into a panic. She prayed every night that we would be spared her anxiety. Her prayers were mostly answered. I have little trouble going out to shop for what I need, but confrontations – they cause uncontrollable shaking. You went off to be a mage, then fought for the kingdom. I'd hoped you had shaken the anxieties which haunted you as a child."

Xantipe nodded, then sighed and lowered her head.

"I would like you to try something." Correin went to the cupboard and took out a vial. She put a few drops in a cup, then filled it with water and swished around to mix it.

168

"My master taught me to make this. He called it soul-ease." Correin handed the cup to Xantipe.

She sniffed it, her nose detecting a hint of herbs. Tasting it made her mouth dry up and she made a face.

"I should have warned you it tastes awful. He said I could hide it syrup, or even wine, but I wanted to know it was medicine I drank."

Xantipe put the cup to her lips and drained it to the bottom. She didn't feel any different.

"It isn't magic." Correin put the vial away in the cupboard. "It's a plant which eases what my master called excess anxiety. As humans we are weak, we'll always be..."

Xantipe put her hands over her eyes and whimpered.

Mirio turned to stone slowly, unstoppably. Correin's words were an echo of his last complaint, the stone reaching his lips before he could finish...

Correin's hands pulled hers from her eyes. Her sister's eyes met hers, filled with compassion. For an instant, Mirio's sapphire blue eyes overlaid hers, but they didn't accuse. That was her own mind. Blue and brown eyes together, meeting hers as if they were giving her a gift.

"W-weak?" Xantipe forced the word out past her fear.

Correin nodded, still holding Xantipe's hands.

"We are all weak. We're human. That's why we need each other."

"Need?"

***

Standing on a wall. Hand outstretched in battle. Watching others die. Facing HIM at the end as his magic flailed her soul. Always alone. She'd thought her anger had defeated HIM in the end, but how many had stood behind her to get her there, in that place, in that time? Had she ever truly been alone?

***

Pressure welled up in her chest until Xantipe couldn't hold it anymore. A wail burst out and she threw herself into Correin's arms. Her sister held her as hope crashed painfully into Xantipe's heart.

***

Xantipe came downstairs and put the kettle on the stove. She took the drops of soul-ease as Correin had shown her. Standing in the door to the shop, her heart pounded.

'Do you remember mother ever leaving the house?'

"Not Mama." Xantipe whispered and wiped her hands on her trousers. She took a step into the front room of the store, then another. Her heart didn't burst; the walls didn't collapse on her. The bell over the door rang and Xantipe put her hand over her mouth.

"Good morning." The woman held a basket filled with a selection of vegetables.

"M-m-morning." Xantipe forced herself to meet the woman's eyes, though she couldn't make her lips smile.

"You must be Xantipe." The woman put the basket on the counter. "Correin is so proud of you. I'm glad to see you up and about. Just tell her Nan Hlochet left her a little something from the garden."

"Thanks." A whisper, but no stammer. Nan Hlochet left, then a man left a jar of butter, another a small ham. All talked to her, but none showed any concern that Xantipe responded in single words if at all.

"Tipe?" Correin stood in the door her eyes wide.

"This." Xantipe waved at the counter. "People you h-help?"

"Not everyone can pay in coin." Correin came in and took Xantipe's hand. "How long have you been here?"

Xantipe shrugged, it felt like forever and an instant of time. She sat in the chair in the corner behind the counter as Correin met and chatted with her customers. Some waved at Xantipe, some acted like she wasn't there.

170

Sitting in the shop became part of her routine. She basked in watching people who had no expectations of her.

A man in uniform sauntered into the shop. He looked around peering at jars of herbs.

"I have heard that you have been selling illegal tinctures." The uniformed man crossed his arms. "I will have to inspect your medicines."

Correin paled and shook her head. "I have done no such thing."

"Your face tells me you're lying."

Anger sparked deep inside Xantipe, hot and painful. She stood up and walked over to the officious man.

"Ap-p-pothec-cary?" She pointed at him.

"What? Of course not." The man glared at her.

Xantipe picked a jar at random from the shelves.

"W-what's th-this?"

"I have no idea? Why are you wasting my time? Let me do my work."

"How?" Xantipe stared him in the eyes. "Ig-g...ignorant."

His face reddened and his hand fell to his club. "Just who do you think you are?"

"Xantipe, m-mage." She held up a finger with blue flames running up and down it. "F-fetch s-sargent, or I w-will."

The man ran out of the shop. Correin sighed and thumped down on Xantipe's chair, shaking violently. Xantipe put her hand on Correin's shoulder, then fixed a glass of the tincture for her sister. She took one herself, then returned to the shop to wait.

In time the uniformed man returned with another with stripes on his sleeve.

"See, Sarge, she can't even talk properly." The first man pointed at Xantipe.

"Go outside and stand at attention. You will not speak or move until I say so." The sargent's voice ground like rocks. The constable frowned but did what he was told. "Xantipe, you won't remember me, I saw you at the battle of Murliem."

"Second b-bata…batal f-first c-col-lumn, f-fifth p-position."

"I am honoured." The sargent held himself straighter. "I was injured out and came home." Xantipe nodded, not trusting her mouth to give her words.

"I run a good shop, as anyone will tell you." Correin stood white faced. Xantipe put her hand on her sister's back. "His brother is angry that I sell nightbalm to his wife."

"The accusation has been made and must be addressed, for your sake as much as anybody's."

"Do you know apothecary medicine?"

"Can't say I do." The sargent rubbed his chin. "I see your point. Need to be judged by one's own." He stuck his head out the door. "Go fetch a master apothecary, better yet, get Guildmaster Stantus. Hop to it."

"Bu-but that's on the far side of town." The constable's eyes widened.

"Then I suggest you run." The sargent came back into the shop. "Blast, and I was about set for tea."

Xantipe went to the back room and put the kettle on for tea. She sliced bread and put it and the jar of butter on a tray. When the tea was ready, she carried it out to the shop. Correin and the sargent were laughing at some story he was telling. Xantipe poured the tea, then remembered she'd forgot the honey.

"H-honey." She stood up to fetch it.

"I don't need it." The sargent tasted the tea and sighed. "Ah, this is my wife's favourite leaf. Haven't tasted it since the war started." He buttered bread and ate it thoughtfully. "Wife gets it from the same baker. Have you tried his raisin cakes?"

"I'm not big on raisins." Correin laughed and pointed at Xantipe, "but she could never get enough of them."

"I'll get him to send some over to you. Mage Xantipe deserves a treat. None of us would have made it out of Murliem without her." The sargent's face stared at some horror only he could see, then shook himself.

A coach pulled up in front of the shop and an old man climbed out with a dexterity putting the lie to his white hair. He walked into the shop, peered up at the wall and grunted.

"No problems here." The guildmaster would have left if the sargent hadn't stopped him.

"So I don't need to bother you again, Guildmaster. How do I see for myself what you just saw?"

The old man harrumphed.

"No reason you'd know, but it's not a guild secret." He pointed to the medallion hanging on the wall behind the desk. "That's her guild license, it isn't tarnished. No tarnish, no problems. I will send you my bill."

"Thank you for your time." The sargent bowed and left the shop.

"Guildmaster," Correin said, reddening slightly, "I would ask for a consultation while you are here."

The old man picked up a slice of bread and spread a thick layer of butter on it.

"I've been getting soul-ease from Master Vislic."

"Smart, not to mix for yourself." The Guildmaster took an enormous bite and raised his eyebrows.

"My question is about my sister. I've given her soul-ease, and it has helped, some."

"Ah…" He glanced over at Xantipe. "A mage, that makes a bit of difference in the concocting as you need to take the balancing of medicine and magic into account." They dove into discussion of herbs and preparations. Xantipe cleared the cups and dishes away, leaving the plate with the last slice of bread and the jar of butter on the desk.

She cleaned up in the kitchen, her gut buzzing at her. That was her life they were talking about. She trusted Correin but…

"Tipe." Correin called from the shop. Xantipe put the washcloth down and took a breath before going back out to the shop.

"Let me look in your eyes." The guildmaster waited, as patient now as he'd been brusque with the sargent. Xantipe pushed herself one step after another until she stood in front of him and fixed her gaze on his vest buttons. "When I was young," the guildmaster said, "I joined the army for a campaign in the south; thought it would be an adventure. Saw things that still haunt me, did some things which would have turned my licence to rust if they'd had such a thing then. One reason I pushed for them, to save young apothecaries from my folly."

Xantipe lifted her head. His eyes were clear and grey. They bored into her head, not reading her thoughts, but seeing the cost of them.

"Use the mix we talked about, but I'm going to send you some valour root. Use two grains in the tincture. No more." He held up a finger. "Better to be weak than strong."

Correin bowed. "Guildmaster, I'm not licensed for valour root."

"You'll make the third in Haleston. I'm one, Master Tharinke, serving the Duke is the second. I've been looking for another. Master Vislic has nothing but good to say about you. Says you're compassionate, but not one to bend the rules for any reason." He pointed up at her medallion. It had a tiny red jewel glowing in the center. "Master Brovost, you will have to ask for larger hams."

He grinned and it changed his face completely, then helped himself to the final slice of bread with a nod to Xantipe. "Mage Xantipe, you and your sister are indeed fortunate to have each other." Guildmaster Stantus nodded to them, ate the last bite of bread on the way out the door.

"Master?" Correin sat bonelessly in the chair. She stared at the medallion as if she feared the jewel would vanish.

"D-don't under…under…" Xantipe shook her head in frustration.

Correin took her hands. "There are five Master Apothecaries in Haleston, plus the Guildmaster. The rest of us are Journeymen. I never planned to try for Master. I attended the lectures because I wanted to learn more. Master Vislic made me write the exam because he said that was part of the course, but he never told me he marked it." Correin paled. "I wrote a couple of radical formulations, things I'd never have a chance to use. One of them used valour root."

"Va-valour root?"

"When we are anxious, scared, angry, our bodies react to help us survive whatever is causing our feelings. But sometimes there is no cause. Valour root cancels the reaction. Some have used to make themselves, or their soldiers impervious to pain and fear in battle. But there is a terrible price. Too much valour root will destroy all ability to feel. It is our feelings which keep us human."

"He…" Xantipe closed her eyes.

***

She stood on a field of ash, tears on her face, knees barely holding her upright.

"You can't win." HE'd mocked her. "Already you weep for your death."

"Not mine." Xantipe's voice broke, and HE laughed at her, then sent an attack, and other. Each time she knew she'd die, but somehow, she didn't. Where other mages had thrown their own spells in return, she held her hands up and defended herself. To let HIM pass her would be to waste all she'd done, all the people who'd died.

The battle, if one could call it so, lasted too long for her to count the hours. Wounds dripped blood onto the ash, but Xantipe held on though it wasn't possible.

The first spell she'd ever cast, the one which turned her hair red and sent her to the Academy, had been to put a boy in a shield to stop him from hitting Correin, who'd stepped between them to protect Xantipe.

Her hands moved in the simple casting. It reflected the person's attack back on them. Such a silly thing to throw against the greatest black mage in history. Only HE didn't believe he couldn't break it. The bully had stopped after two punches. HE kept going, fearless, certain of victory, until he cast a spell beyond anything anyone had imagined. The bubble of the shield turned pitch-black and lightning flickered through it. Some leaked out setting her nerves on fire.

Xantipe screamed but the storm vanished before her shield failed. She'd been told they'd found her on her knees, hands reached out holding the shield around a tiny pile of ash.

***

"What is it?" Correin shook her gently. "Come back, Tipe, you're scaring me.

"I d-didn't b-beat HIM." Xantipe's legs gave out and Correin lowered her to the floor. "HE d-des...troyed himself b-because HE c-couldn't l-lose. I d-d-don't have t-to be s-st-trong." She laughed until she cried. Endre came in and carried her up to her room.

***

The new tincture tasted worse. When Xantipe took it, chills ran through her body, but for an hour or two she could talk without stammering.

A week after starting on the new tincture, Xantipe brought her cloak down to the shop. She put it on and tried to walk through the door out onto the street, but there

176

might as well have been a mage shield stopping her. Even with the tincture, her body refused her.

"Give it time." Correin said when she discovered Xantipe frozen in the doorway. "It isn't something you can force. Wait until you have reason."

The shop became busier as the word spread of Correin's new status. She refused to change the way she did business, some of the customers in fine clothes complained when they weren't served immediately. Xantipe stared at them until they shuffled their feet and fell into silence or left.

The regular customers called Xantipe 'their mage'.

***

The storm woke Xantipe from a nightmare where she faced HIM again on the ash plain. The people she'd watch die mocked her along with HIM. Mirio, the golden-haired boy, people falling to ash as they jeered. Xantipe tried to explain, to beg. The crack of thunder woke her as HE broke loose of her shield.

Xantipe lay gasping in her bed until slowly her heart slowed and she could breathe normally.

"Tipe." Correin stood in the door. "Are you all right? The lighting hit the house across the street. It's on fire. Endre's run for the brigade. We have to leave before it spreads."

Xantipe stood and ran down the stairs after her sister. She threw her cloak on, then hit the barrier at the door like it was a wall. Correin tried to pull her through, but her body wouldn't budge.

Then the scream came from the street. Three men were holding back a woman. Xantipe recognized her from the shop. She bought tinctures for her son who had weak lungs. The boy's father had never returned from the war.

Xantipe didn't know she'd left the shop until the rain slashed into her face. The wood of the building flared up even in the downpour. Endre returned and the brigade worked on saving the buildings beside the fire.

A golden-haired boy screamed as he fell into ash.

She walked across the street. Men tried to stop her, but their hands slipped off her. Xantipe closed her eyes. Fear came from upstairs where the boy huddled in a room rapidly filling with smoke. The stairs burned, but the flames couldn't reach her through her shield. Blue flames supported her as the wood failed. Upstairs, the air was black, but the boy's fear called her. With a wave of her hand she put a shield around him, then cooled the air and forced the smoke out. The room exploded when she opened the door. Flame erupted through the ceiling. Xantipe walked through to pick the boy up from where he hid in the closet, merging their shields.

"Y-you're g-g-going to be all r-right." Xantipe whispered, then put a barrier up around the entire house. No matter how the fire raged, it couldn't break free. As it used up the air the flames died, Xantipe let the rain fall through the barrier until the wood was sodden. The house collapsed inside the shield, then she walked downstairs made of blue fire, until she stood on the street, all the people staring at her.

"I-I c-c-couldn't let him d-die." Xantipe put the boy in his mother's arms. Endre caught her as her legs gave out and carried her into the shop. Correin brought the mother and her son in after them. They sat in the back room as Endre made tea.

Correin made a tincture for the boy.

"Give this to him once a day until it's gone. Seven drops. It will help counteract the smoke."

"I never imagined someone so powerful." The mother caressed her son's hair, brown like a mouse as he curled up and slept.

"N-not p-power-f-ful." Xantipe put her hands on her head and fought for the words. "Weak, b-but w-weak is

178

enough." She accepted a cup, the handle broken off, the rim chipped. "D-damaged, n-not b-broken. I..." The words fled her. Visions of what might have happened fought in her mind.

Xantipe drank the tea, its sweetness coating her throat. She gazed at the sleeping boy, and let his quiet breathing drive out everything but the knowledge that this time she'd been enough.

Tomorrow would come. She'd take her medicine; maybe go for a walk, maybe not. Xantipe sighed and drank more of the honeyed drink.

She was fine with that.

THE SILENCE

The trembling started in my hands. I forced them to complete the motions. The slightest variation could be fatal. The spell continued flawlessly. A mage who couldn't discipline his body was a dead one.

The knees were next, locking them kept me standing, but only just. Sweat poured down my face. The casting space wasn't hot, but fire burned in my bones. I was going to die as one more mage who took on more than he could manage. But I'd done this spell more times than I could count.

Indigo opened their mouth, but thankfully didn't speak. Only my words were permitted in this time, in this place.

My mouth struggled with words which usually flowed from my lips. I called them up and spit them out like glass. Was that blood in my mouth? No way to stop without dying, maybe killing everyone in the room.

My vision went black, my heart pounded thinking I'd gone blind, but it was just my eyes had closed themselves. I didn't need sight. The words crashed forward, my hand moved as if time itself slowed and fought me. Every part of me screamed, rebelled, betrayal.

The spell came to a conclusion.

"...my words make it so."

The spear of pain in my heart made me scream the final syllable. I fell back from the circle scribed on the floor. Now I'd breathe my last; never thought it would hurt so much. The pounding in my chest grew faster and faster until the beats blurred together. Red bloomed behind my eyes and agony shot through my skull.

A tiny part of myself listened to the animal noises coming from the sad figure curled in a fetal position on the floor. It shook its head, not in disgust at the scene, but in sadness. Then the last of my consciousness fled gibbering.

180

Waking into darkness, I expected pain, but nothing felt out of place. I opened my mouth to call out to Indigo and my heart rushed like I faced a charging dragon. No sound came out. When I gave up on speaking, the pain in my chest eased.

"Mater," Indigo spoke quietly, "We were worried." The kryrin's blue eyes stared into mine.

I tried to answer, and anxiety shook me, as if my dislike of conversation was multiplied. They touched me gently and wiped my face with a soft cloth.

"It's OK,' one of their childish voices lisped and a hand patted my head.

I lay in darkness comforted by Indigo's voices. Whenever I grew restless, they talked to me in the voice I needed to hear.

I must have slept because faint light woke me. Indigo slept in a chair, curled up like a cat. Even in repose, lines of exhaustion and worry ran across their face. A blanket from my bed did well enough to cover them. I wanted to brush the black hair back from their face, but it would wake them. They were the closest thing to a child I could expect to have.

Instead, I headed for the public room to satisfy the growling in my stomach.

As an itinerant mage, I never knew what to say to people who were as rooted as I was homeless, words directed to people had always trouble me. Indigo did most of my talking for me. I saved my voice for magic – or I used to.

"What would you like to eat, sir?" The serving woman stood hardly as tall as my shoulder though I sat at a table. A kryrin like Indigo but not a broken one.

Opening my mouth to ask for porridge and tea caused my throat to close and my hands to sweat. Closing my mouth put it to rest. Clearly something in me didn't want me speaking. I pointed at my lips and shook my head, then pointed at a neighbouring table where a man tucked into a meal which made my mouth water.

She nodded and returned quickly with my meal and hot tea. She held a honey pot and creamer for me to fix my tea, but I waved them away. Years of travel in the wilderness had made me prefer it black and strong. Years? Who was I kidding, decades.

This village was one of countless places I visited, pulled by the magic to answer the need. I would probably have forgotten it within a day of leaving if it hadn't been for this silence imposed on me. The spell which had left me a whimpering wreck on the floor was a simple enough dispersal of ill will. A feud between neighbours which carried on across generations until it became a living thing itself wreaking havoc.

A silver coin paid for the meal, and I headed out to stretch my legs and get clean air to breathe. Villagers nodded at me, but no one spoke, so I had no requirement to test my own speech. Odd, but comfortable; in most places, I would be inundated with chatter. Easy enough to filter, like when Indigo's child voices spoke of rocks and flowers and whatever else had caught their attention.

At the edge of town, I found a rock to sit on and absorb the sunlight while I took stock of my being. Physically, I could detect nothing out of the ordinary. No fever or lingering pain, neither my hands nor knees trembled. I moved my fingers through a blessing, and they flowed exactly as I intended.

The only thing which I could not do was speak. For all the knowledge in my head, the feel of magic moving about me, as a Mage I was now as useful as the rock I sat on. My hands trembled when I considered remaining with people. I loved the quiet forest.

A chill breeze made me shiver and another subtle change came to my mind. I felt no call to a new village. No

182

imbalance in the magic needed me. For decades those calls were my life. I didn't know what to do without it. Tears sprung in my eyes and unbidden deep sorrow filled my soul. Indigo found me sobbing like a child on my rock.

They climbed into my lap and wrapping arms about my neck, held me tight until the grief eased.

"All better?" Indigo gazed into my eyes with their magical eyes. No other Kryrin to my knowledge, nor any other being I'd met had eyes of that deep blue. Looking into them was to peer into a bottomless well.

I nodded, not trying to talk.

"Mater, Lisbeth, the serving woman said you'd taken a vow of silence." Indigo settled on the rock beside me. That was a reasonable interpretation of my sign as any. She'd have spread the word out of respect for the visiting mage.

I put my fingers to my lips and shook my head.

"Are you OK with that?" Indigo tilted their head. Concern in those eyes which missed nothing.

I shrugged, then had to wipe more tears away. Desperate for communication I put my fingers on Indigo's temples and thought at them.

Pain spiked in my head as if I'd been struck. Opening my mouth to scream made my heart race. Red light danced at the edges of my vision. Indigo gripped my hands until the world returned somewhat to normal.

"Master Mage." A man in rough clothes stood in front of us. "May I aid you?" He ducked his head, turning red. Even thinking of replying caused my mind to tilt dangerously.

Indigo gripped me tightly.

"We would appreciate your aide."

I mimed a staff as best I could. The man ran off and came back with a branch, freshly cut, and the bark scraped from the place where I would grip it.

The three of us made a sight walking through the village. I with my staff feeling ahead as if blind, Indigo holding my hand and never taking their eyes from my face. The man came last, as if not sure where he fit, but unwilling to abandon us.

At the inn, Lisbeth ran out, took in our parade, and guided us to a table. I signed to the man for him to join us. Face bright red, he sat gingerly across from us. Indigo kept their grip until Lisbeth brought tea.

"Whatever happened, Thoms?"

The fragrance of the tea soothed my jangled soul, and since she didn't address me, I had no concern but enjoying the simple pleasure. Indigo went still as they held an internal debate, then they reached for the honey and cream, a wide smile on their face.

"Twas coming in from cutting in the forest and saw the mage pale and shaking on that big rock the kids like to play on." He lowered his face. "I know you said not to speak with him, but I worried so."

Indigo reached over and patted Thom's hand. "You did well, friend. We were worried for Mater. Help was welcome."

"That's all fine then." Lisbeth smiled at the man. "I will add my thanks."

Thoms turned even redder. This man communicated with blushes as I once did with words. I lifted my mug and saluted him before sipping, then worried I had melted him completely. He picked up his own tea and hid behind the mug.

We three sat in silent company, one by misfortune and two by choice. Conversations around us were muted and I smiled. In all my time of travel I'd always arrived knowing I would leave. Staying in one place for a while would be a new experience. I prayed I'd learn to enjoy it.

***

Thoms waved as he passed. I waved back with the hand holding my carving. The village had repaired the little shed and furnished it for me. They'd wanted to give

184

me an entire house. With hands waving and Indigo's help they were convinced to fix up something less grand. For someone who'd slept under the stars more than under roofs, the hut was perfect.

"Mater, you are well?" Indigo came out of the hut holding a woven bag someone had given them.

I nodded and smiled. In the months since my collapse the fields had grown up and turned to gold. If I refrained from speaking or trying to use magic in anyway, I'd never felt better. They'd be harvesting soon. No one spoke of it, but the village clearly intended on keeping me like a pet through the winter. I've seen villages like this in the cold season, faces stretched by hunger. If I thought I'd become a burden, I'd be off into the forest.

Calls came from all directions now, as if they were echoes. Over the months they'd grown clearer, but not compelling. Something far away, but I learned to push it aside until I hardly noticed.

"Mater." A little girl curtseyed to me. They all called me Mater now, as Indigo did. Julia, I think this girl was, Thoms' daughter. I smiled at her and she sat at my feet taking out pencil and paper. She worked through her letters with her tongue sticking out. Other children of various ages appeared as their chores were completed.

Julia presented her page to me, and I gave it my solemn attention. Her letters were well constructed and even. With a grin, I handed it back, reached back for my journal and wrote her name out. I pointed at the word, then at her. The first word each of them learned to write was their name.

Her face lit up before she meticulously copied her name on the top of the reverse side of the paper. She'd fill every available space with her name.

Another child presented a paper, and so it went. In between instruction, I whittled, making a chunk of wood into a fearsome beast. This one was the Fenris wolf. I'd seen it once long ago on the northern edge of the world. It sneered at me and trotted away into its icy land.

I'd already created dragons and griffins, trolls, and faeries. The carvings got handed out by Indigo according to some system they'd devised. No child had ever argued with them.

So, the afternoon passed, my pupils vanishing as they came, mostly in silence, but with their boundless energy only loosely held in rein. Honestly, I can't recall how it started, but I'd miss their presence if they stopped coming. Their presence made no demands, my nerves stayed quiet.

Indigo returned. It was their turn to cook on the little stove tonight, so I stayed at my whittling until the light grew too poor. That was another oddity in my life. They'd joined me maybe fifteen years ago. I'd found them huddled in the snow outside the Kryrin village. They'd spoken then in a babble of voices – a broken one I learned later - the internal voices separate. The broken ones were feared as they'd been known to be violent, though I never experienced Indigo as anything but gentle.

In ignorance, I'd picked up the young one, and when they couldn't tell me their name called them Indigo, only to learn I would be forever responsible for them. To be truthful, Indigo was more responsible for me than I for them. The clatter of dishes and the even drumming of a knife chopping added music to the evening.

A woman walked along the road, her entire life strapped to her back. I admired her kit. Complete, but not heavy and no thing which didn't do at least two jobs. Her head swivelled to look at me as if I'd shouted to her. I waved a hand and she turned toward me, dropping her bag beside the steps and taking a seat with a sigh.

"I felt a call to come here only to learn there was nothing for me to do." The woman spoke without looking at me.

186

I knocked on the deck, when Indigo came out from the kitchen knife carefully held non-aggressively, I held up three fingers.

"Yes, Mater." They ducked back into the hut.

"Fascinating." The woman stretched until her joints popped. "A broken one and a silenced mage."

If she'd been looking at me, I'd have raised my eyebrow in interrogation. She sat watching the sun set not saying another word until Indigo called us in for our meal.

On my days, I favoured simple stews of vegetables with maybe a bit of squirrel or rabbit the children brought. Indigo cooked masterpieces. We ate giving their art proper attention.

"Ah me." The woman wiped her plate with a crust of bread. "I haven't eaten that well at King's tables."

Indigo glowed at the praise, and I added my smile and nod. They gathered the dishes and took them to the sink to wash. We usually argued over the washing, both of us finding it soothing in our own way. Tonight, I'd let Indigo win without a challenge.

"I'd forgotten how peaceful it is to sit with a silenced mage." The woman sighed and leaned back, stretching her legs out. Younger than I'd first thought, she still carried an air of confidence. "My master went silent just before I'd finished my apprenticeship. One day he could cast any spell you asked. The next he woke unable to speak a word. Don't try to work magic other ways either. He paid a terrible price for his attempts, but after a year he accepted his new life. I got my first call and walked out, didn't look back and never saw him again."

Tears glistened in her eyes but didn't fall. Indigo came up behind her and put their hand on her shoulder. The woman patted it.

"Thank you, dear." She smiled sadly. "I've met other broken ones. They've been no more violent than any other being I've met. A kryrin I knew made a study of them. As far as she could tell, there was just something in the broken one's mind which didn't connect, leaving the pieces to speak for themselves."

"We've learned to negotiate," Indigo said.

"We take turns," the child Indigo spoke up.

"We all love Mater," a whisper like a chorus brought me close to tears.

"Whatever others may call you, you aren't broken." The woman's eyes glistened again. "Neither are you, silent one. I've thought about it over the years. My master worked constantly never staying still in one place, you know what it's like." She closed her eyes and I thought she'd fallen asleep. "I think the paths on which the magic flows grow weary. Each casting takes its toll. We learn to help the world, but if you are like me, you never asked the price."

Indigo came around and sat by my legs. I put my hand on their shoulder. If this was the price for all those years, it was a light one.

"As far as I have found out, mages don't talk much about silencing. The silent ones because they can't, the rest out of fear, but there are legends. They say the ability to work magic is taken so a mage might enjoy the last part of their life. In no story I've heard has any silenced mage survived continued attempts to regain the magic.

I recalled the pain at the rock and nodded, enough of that and I wouldn't want to wake up. Indigo shook under my hand. I gave them a squeeze.

She looked at Indigo. "Ah me, I didn't mean to make you sad, dear. Your Mater has accepted the silence gracefully. The magic will give him plenty of time to enjoy".

We sat until it grew dark, I tried not to think of those echoes of a call I ignored. It might not be completely done with me, no way to ask without worrying Indigo.

188

"I would be happy to sleep on your porch before I follow my call." The woman spoke quietly. Indigo's even breathing told me they'd fallen to sleep. Though she couldn't see me, I nodded and smiled. "I think the magic brought me here to ease my mind." She sounded far away in another place. "If I live so long, I hope to accept my silence with as much grace as you have."

Rustling told me she'd gone outside. I debated finding my bed, but Indigo's warmth by my leg kept me in my chair. It wouldn't be the first time I'd slept there.

In the morning, the woman had gone. Indigo had crawled into my lap and curled there like an oversized kitten. I ran my fingers over their hair, and they looked up sleepily at me. On impulse, I pointed at my heart, then touched their forehead with the finger. They sat up and clung to me face buried in my shoulder, tears wetting my shirt.

I held them and rocked them. The woman's visit, the notion this was the end part of my life must have unsettled them. Yet, for only the second time in the time I knew them, they'd spoken in chorus, all of them in agreement. The words had been the same then to. We've been together ever since.

When Indigo gasped and shook themselves leaning back away from me, I deliberately this time leaned forward to plant a kiss on their head. Indigo grinned, kissed me on the lips and jumped off my lap.

That was different.

Most of what I know about Kryrin, I know from travelling with Indigo. Kryrin choose their gender when they enter adolescence and start consolidating their personalities. The broken ones never join all their disparate personalities into one, and they never become gendered. I'm certain some of the voices they speak in are female, and some male, some there is no clue. I'm not sure in the fifteen years I've known them that I've heard all their voices.

For Kryrin to kiss me on the lips suggested they were changing as much as I was in this place. I shrugged. This change thing was a part of life. Indigo would let me know what they needed.

The days passed, the children showed up less as the harvest arrived, then more after. One day it was my turn to cook and I didn't have any meat for the stew. I headed into town to see if I could find a little. The inn would be the first place to check, they often had more than they could cook and didn't mind me taking a bit.

As I headed for the kitchen my eye caught a couple of kryrin laughing and joking in the corner. My first thought was they were a visiting couple, rare, but I'd seen a few in the months here. Then I heard Indigo's voice and smiled. Waving at them, I continued on my way. Then a clatter made me turn and Indigo stared at me, first pale as a ghost, then reddening before they bowed their head and slumped at the table.

I went over and sat beside them. Lisbeth shuffled uncertainly, so I smiled at her and pointed for her to stay. Indigo wouldn't let me touch them, and hid their face, so I waited.

Finally, they sat up, and a voice I'd never heard before spoke, definitely male.

"We are sorry."

I raised my eyebrow and waited some more.

"We said we love you, Mater." A new voice took over, this one a girl.

I pointed at my heart, then touched them on the forehead. Their face crumpled and they fell into a heap on the floor crying. Shaking my head, I picked them up and rocked them until they hiccoughed and peered up at me fearfully.

190

We'd always travelled together, just the two of us. They thought I'd be mad at them for making friends. How to tell them with no words I was happy? For the first time in months, I opened my mouth feeling the panic leap up. Indigo, covered my mouth with both hands.

"No, no, no," the voices tumbled over each other.

My arms tight around them, I sighed, and pointed to my heart and their forehead, then took a surprised Lisbeth's hand and put it in Indigo's. Again, I pointed to my heart and my forehead. Indigo's brow wrinkled as Lisbeth giggled. Julia came in with Thoms, and I waved her over. I took her hand and then pointed to my heart and Indigo's forehead.

"He's saying he loves you." Julia poked Indigo in the ribs. "You can love Lisbeth, and he'll love you. He can be my friend and love you. Silly, love is big." She spread her arms as wide as they could go, then wrapped them around Indigo. "You can never run out." From Thoms' grin I suspected it was a routine he used on her.

Julia chattered with Indigo and Lisbeth. Thoms sat and drank tea with me. I never did get meat from the kitchen, but we all ate hearty stew at the inn. Indigo walked home with me, holding my hand. They did this sometimes when the younger ones were out. I liked the small warmth connecting us.

Winter came and I moved my lessons to the inn at Lisbeth's suggestion. She would talk and laugh with Indigo while silent children formed letters and words. I hadn't realized the effect of my silence on others. Indigo and I had always talked while we travelled, it helped keep animals away. The silence had to be hard on them. Now they talked more at home too, as if being friends with Lisbeth and others gave him permission to speak at home.

The snow came deep and hard. Lisbeth assured me the village had plenty. I pushed the call away, the echoes were getting sharper, more insistent. Indigo would have a place to live when the magic forced me to my death.

"The elders get a feeling for these things," she told me as she poured tea. "They made us put away huge amounts this year. We had a great harvest, and good hunting, so we'll be fine.

Thoms had piled firewood higher than our shed, and I was grateful for it. The wind blew chill through the cracks, and we spent most evenings wrapped in blankets, Indigo curled on my lap.

"Broken ones are a mystery." Lisbeth explained to me one day when Indigo was off helping Thoms with something. "I think more to us kryrin than others because we're so afraid of them. I started off afraid of Indigo, but then seeing how dedicated they were when you were sick, I lost all that. I had my reasons for leaving home, and never regretted it. Yet, it's lonely with only a few kryrin coming through in a year. They've been good for me.

"I have no right to any theories, but talking with Indigo, I wonder if the broken ones simply can't decide. To pick one personality, one gender it is a scary thing. I remember lying awake worrying I would lose too much of myself. In the end, it doesn't work that way.

"Indigo has brought all those questions out again, but in a different sense. I can peek down into my soul and find the little girl who liked to watch her grandma knit and learned to knit for herself. Other things too. We're all still there, but not as close to the surface." She drew pictures in the dampness on the tabletop.

"I don't think it's wrong to be a broken one, or to love one." Lisbeth looked at me through her lashes, tears hanging off them. "I know we could never have kids, but..." She slapped at the tears and moved to stand up.

I grabbed her hand, pointed to my heart, then to her, then to her heart and touched her lips. Weird, I hardly even thought in words now.

192

"You want me to tell him?" Lisbeth whispered. "What if they say no?" She lowered her head more. "What if they say yes?"

My finger lifted her chin, then I opened my arms as wide as I could before throwing them around her. She laughed and hugged me back.

Indigo came home a few days later shaking, white as a sheet. I waved them over and they climbed in my lap to huddle while I rocked them.

"Lisbeth said she loved me." Indigo whispered. "I don't know which me. We like her, some us maybe love her, but we love Mater, all of us. What do we do?"

I put my finger on my lips and shook my head. Even if I could talk, what would I say. We sat like that through the night.

"Will you love us if we love Lisbeth?" Indigo's quiet voice woke me. I looked at him, put my hand on my heart, then on their heart, again and again, until they started laughing. I joined in. I all my life, I don't think I've ever been so happy.

Indigo worked at cooking and talked about Lisbeth. The little things they'd spoken about, Lisbeth's jokes, the people who'd come through the inn. It didn't matter I'd been sitting only a few feet away with children scattered about. Their happiness helped me bury the call away.

I smiled as they talked, then they stopped and looked at me wide eyed.

"Is it alright if we kiss her? She wants to be kissed."

I crooked my finger to call them over. Pointed at their heart and made a talking mouth with my hand.

"My heart will talk?" One of their young voices said and giggled. I nodded and ruffled their hair. An older one walked back to the table and started on supper again. Silent.

Magic tugged at me in the middle of the night. I bolted upright, shocked, panicked. Indigo woke and came to hug me until my breathing returned to something close to normal. My heart buzzed within me. I could hardly sit still. I wanted to run away from the call, I wanted to run toward it. Indigo held me all night murmuring in my ear. This was no weak echo.

Morning brought no relief. Before the silence, I'd never ignored a call. Now, I couldn't ignore this one. Slowly I pushed myself upright. I pointed out into the world and made a motion as if a I tugged a string tied to my chest. Indigo paled. They'd lived with me long enough to know exactly what I was saying. I put my hand on their head, then sat them down and put my hands in from of their face. *Stay here.*

When I walked out that door, I'd be moving toward my death. I wanted Indigo to stay and love Lisbeth.

Indigo shook their head vigorously. I signed again, *Stay* and they refused, tears in their eyes.

We might have argued all day if Lisbeth hadn't shown up at the door, white and shaking.

"Thoms didn't come home yesterday. A couple of guys went to look for him, they haven't come back either. What do I do?"

"Mater felt the call." Indigo glared at me; arms crossed.

"The call?" Lisbeth wrinkled her forehead, this didn't answer her question.

"The magic." Indigo shouted. "If Mater goes, he will die. We will go with him." He glared at me.

"I'm coming too." Lisbeth stomped into the hut. Indigo and I stared at her. I though Indigo had perfected the stubborn face. Lisbeth had them beat.

"Pack." Indigo said and pointed out the door. "One hour, we leave."

Lisbeth dashed away through the snow. We packed what we could carry. Nothing more. I struggled to let go of the things I didn't need, but loved because I loved the people who gave them to me.

I didn't look back as we left. The village saw us off, the children crying as they waved. I had never before mattered that much to those I left behind. It hurt worse than leaving the hut.

The pull dragged us into the woods then off the road. Indigo pointed to where feet had travelled ahead of us. We followed the trail in silence. I tried to plan what I could do with no words. I'd tried opening my mouth to feel the familiar fear wash through me. Lisbeth clutched Indigo's hand. When I turned to make sure they followed they wore identical pinched looks. Lisbeth afraid to lose Indigo; they afraid to lose me.

When the night came, I found a spruce with branches hanging to the ground. We crawled underneath. The three of us cuddled under our blankets. Indigo and Lisbeth slept. I lay awake refusing to abandon them to the magic's call, shivering in pain almost equal to what kept me silent.

This wasn't what I knew from my past. This was hungry, demanding. Not the magic, but a thing calling through the magic. A thing of insatiable appetite, I didn't think it would agree to dissolve even if I had the words to cast a spell.

I refused to move until the kryrin woke. We packed up and stumbled out into the cold, white world to follow the agony pulling at me.

The forest ended about midday. The clouds blurred with the horizon reminding me of the time, before I knew Indigo, I'd stood at the edge of the world and seen Fenris wolf.

The thing stood in the middle of the field, sometimes it looked like a person, sometimes like an animal, sometimes a swirl of snow. We walked closer, then Lisbeth gasped and choked when we saw Thoms and the searchers lying grey and still in the snow.

The thing hungered. It wasn't evil. It didn't want to kill; it didn't desire pain or destruction. It needed to be filled. For unimaginable years, it had carried its excruciating emptiness.

How could I, a silenced mage, help it? Even with my voice it might have been beyond me.

"Stay here," Indigo said to Lisbeth. "We love you." The chorus of voices stilled the bitter wind and the thing moaned.

And just like that I knew.

I put Indigo's hand in Lisbeth's. I touched Indigo's heart, then Lisbeth's then Indigo's again. I put my arms wide and hugged them both. Then I made the sign. *Stay.*

They hugged and wept on each other's shoulder as I turned and walked alone toward the hunger. I only needed one word. A little word, both hard and easy to say. I would die when I spoke. The certainty followed me and made me grieve for Indigo who I loved like my own, and Lisbeth who loved who I loved.

The hungry thing waited. It took a human form, that of a young kryrin, not much older than Indigo when I picked him out of the snowbank.

"Hungry." The thing held out its arms.

I opened mine as wide as I could, pulling in the magic until it tingled painfully. Then I threw my arms around the thing and tried to shout the word, to speak it, to whisper it. The one thing in the world which could satiate the void.

"Love."

My heart burst, my mind exploded in white agony. Just before it all faded, I heard an answer from the child, the thing.

We love you, too.

***

I woke in darkness. Every part of me screamed for my attention. Pain raged in ways I hadn't imagined. *Would I have to live with this?* I heard the echo of the child's response, felt the faint strength of its arms hugging me. *If I must, I must.*

A hand touched my face, then a damp face buried itself in my neck.

"We were worried, Mater." Indigo whispered it.

I lifted my arms and wrapped them around them.

***

The snow had melted and spring come before I could wobble outside with my canes. The pain raged, but it was a river I wouldn't let carry me away. The children played in the sunshine, laughing. Julia saw me and ran to hug me tight for a long moment before running back to the game.

Thoms and the other had returned to themselves. Mostly. Without them, Lisbeth and Indigo couldn't have dragged my frozen body through the snow back to the village.

Indigo and Lisbeth came out of the inn hand in hand. Indigo kissed her, then ran to me, stopping at the last second. I wrapped my arms around him, letting the canes fall. The children swarmed about to settle me in a chair. Indigo holding one arm, Lisbeth the other.

I laughed in delight and tried to hug them all. One child I hadn't seen before hung back, eyes green as spring leaves. Then I looked again and turned to Lisbeth.

She grinned.

"You weren't the only one we carried back from the field. They're a broken one. Indigo thinks you brought them back with your magic."

"We named him Ridian." Indigo put a hand on Ridian's shoulder.

"This is Mater." Indigo smiled.

Ridian climbed into my lap and curled up like a kitten.

I pointed to my heart, then touched him on the forehead.

"We love you, too." Ridian spoked in a whispered chorus, then their breathing evened out. Asleep.

I put my hand on their head and watched the children play.

WIRED

First published in 'Places in Between 2019' The Robyn Herrington Memorial Short Story Contest.

Henry checked his vitals before sitting up on the operating table. Everything was green across the board. The surgical robot had retracted against the ceiling like a metal spider. The new Eterna-heart functioned perfectly even after a year. It had been worth every penny to get on that study and become a test subject. Now with the 5T connection and supplementary computer they'd just wired into his brain, he'd swim in the ocean of information like a dolphin in the sea.

Dr. Phinsal came into the operating theatre from the control room. Younger than Henry, he was average in height, weight and every other visual attribute. Fortunately, the man's mind was first rate.

"Thank you, Doctor" Henry concentrated for a brief moment. "I've transferred your fee, and a small bonus to your account."

"Be careful to let your brain acclimatize to the new level of input. The computer will learn what you need, it will flag information you might miss through the 'bubble effect'."

"I've already set the schedule and locked it in." Henry winced and rubbed his temples as the connection turned off. "Knowing my enthusiasm can overturn my good sense. I've sent you an email with the emergency code to control the interface."

"Very good." Dr. Phinsal looked over the checklist on the clipboard before handing it to Henry to sign. "That's everything. Come back in a month for a check-up to monitor your physical response to the unit. You'll find the software will update itself while you sleep. One last thing, be sure to activate the firewall protocol to put a layer of protection between your brain and the world. Even the best security programs have their weaknesses.

Henry closed his eyes and searched the OS for the folder. He activated it, clicked past the End User Legal Agreement and set the firewall in place. On the way out of the office he checked the mirror. His thick black hair hid any scars from the operation. Henry smiled. He'd spent a lot of money to be as non-average as possible – tastefully, of course.

* * *

The following month mixed exaltation with annoyance as the connection turned on and off at what might as well have been random intervals. He'd forgotten to save the schedule and couldn't find it again. Odd that his internal computer had an easier time finding information stored on the web than in his own mindspace. No matter; the shut-downs were growing fewer and he wasn't experiencing any of the symptoms of overload. No headaches, hallucinations or blackouts. The booster computer became transparent, and he didn't need to think about it differently from his own mind. It *was* his mind.

Henry treated himself to a steak dinner and a bottle of very expensive wine after the final involuntary shut down. The visit to the doctor had been a breeze too. Now to use his new technology to conquer the world, or at least try. He grinned and swirled his glass. The computer/brain interfaces weren't that new, but his was cutting edge technology partnered with the fastest connection on the planet. Even now, connection was the bottleneck when communing with the internet.

Information flowed through his mind; he nudged the flow here and there to find nuggets to store for later. He'd signed up for an unlimited cloud service. The rush of data was more intoxicating than the wine. It didn't show up as pictures and text as he was used to with the slower interface. Now it moved, slow or fast, warm or cold, as the

200

potential for information. His mind instinctively pulled out bits for him to look at. Something like the visual filters for sight which only showed what the brain thought was the most vital input.

It took a while for him to control the sensual aspect of the data stream and not visibly react to it caressing him. Trying to negotiate contracts with his eyes rolled back in pleasure didn't go over well. But once he had a handle on it -. . .

"OK." Davidson tugged at his collar. "I can drop another point off the price, but you've left me no more margin." His thinning hair made him look weak. The suit didn't quite hide the belly middle age had given the man.

"You aren't factoring in the warehouse full of parts you'll be clearing out to fill my order. Two more points, and I should get a discount for you using old parts." Henry pulled a couple more tidbits from the flow, but they weren't the kind of thing one used in the board room. He'd arrange drinks after they'd signed the deal and turn the screws a bit tighter.

***

The data stream changed the way Henry visually saw the world. Not as crass as popups identifying people, but names were instantly accessible if he wanted. He'd see a car on the street and know its list price and specs, along with its reviews.

Henry took lunch at the restaurant he always did. The food was good, and the people-watching better. A red-haired woman walked in dressed in an outfit which had cost over ten grand. When he wondered what she'd done to be able to afford that kind of clothing, the outfit vanished, and she walked through the restaurant naked. He blinked and shook his head, but the overlay grew more graphic, showing the many movies she'd been in; what she'd done with who. He instantly knew far more than he ever wanted to about this woman. He closed his eyes and when that didn't stop the flow, he cut the connection.

It felt like a hammer had hit him between the eyes. The world went grey and bleak, two-dimensional without the data flow. Henry staggered out of the restaurant and found an alley where he vomited up the celebratory meal. Back on the street he reconnected to the internet, and the ground spun beneath him sending him sprawling. Tires squealed and horns honked, then a babble of voices broke through the vertigo.

"He's drunk."

"No, a stroke."

The crowd argued the diagnosis while he crawled away, then pushed himself to his feet. His car rolled up in front of him and opened a door. Henry fell more than climbed into the car.

"Home."

In the safety of his car, the vertigo and headache receded. A flag told him he hadn't paid the restaurant bill. Henry sent the money and a healthy tip.

Obviously, he couldn't disconnect quite so abruptly without consequence. He couldn't remember from the forms he'd signed if this was one of the side effects. Trying to find the form threatened to reboot his headache, so he left it for now. He'd call the doctor in the morning. He rode home with his eyes closed to keep from seeing things he'd rather not.

The office pinged him, and he let them know he'd be taking the afternoon off. His underlings could handle his appointments.

At home in his office, Henry investigated the occurrence. His casual thought had tapped into a large amount of information on the woman. He was horrified at how much private information floated in the internet about all kinds of people. The only thing he was interested in was leverage against his competitors. There was a toggle to

202

turn safe search on or off. He turned it on. The flavour of the data changed, becoming a little blander, but that was a small price to pay to avoid another scene. There might be a place or time for him to turn safe search off, but it wasn't in the restaurant, and it wasn't now.

* * *

"Good to see you back, Mr. Cowlin." The receptionist's clothes stayed put, and the only data which flowed into his mind was the long list of excellent efficiency reports in her personnel file. He sighed in relief.

"Thanks, Gina." Henry nodded at her and took the elevator to his top floor office. To his relief the information about each employee stayed businesslike.

Davidson was back to negotiate the next phase of the contract. To Henry's frustration the background information he'd used last time wasn't available. When one of the secretaries came in with coffee, Davidson watched her avidly. Henry closed his eyes and turned off safe search.

Nothing untoward happened to the data stream, though Henry had to restrain a smile at the sensation of the stream becoming more like silk than paper. Numbers and figures filled his head, and Henry knew what he needed to do.

"You're a devil," Davidson straightened his tie after signing the contract. "The bosses are going to take this out of my hide."

"Don't worry, they'll still be making enough money to keep the shareholders happy."

Henry walked the man out of the building. On the way back in he glanced over at Gina. Unwanted images flooded his mind of her in bikinis on the beach, then nudes, nothing as pornographic as the restaurant, but distracting. He looked away at the security guards. One, chubbier than the others, was surrounded by a cloud of images of him with other men. Henry ran for the elevator, then switched to safe search as he rode up.

The data stream scraped at him like sandpaper. He didn't understand how such a simple thing could change the nature of the information flow. Maybe it was that forbidden part of the web which made the experience so delightful. He walked to his office and closed the door. The next meeting wasn't for a good hour. Henry switched off safe search and went looking for answers.

Most of the information on the internet came from the dark web, something most people barely know exists. But data is data and Henry's computer/brain connected to it through the 5T interface. When he turned on safe search, it blocked the dark web, and a huge amount of information.

What he needed was a way to filter the information he didn't want to see, without blocking everything else. He could teach himself over time to ignore it, like his brain already ignored visual cues unneeded for his day-to-day functioning. The downside was it would take time, and he'd be bombarded while he gained control. Each time he acknowledged those images, even to reject them, it made the search algorithms more likely to pull them up.

He found another possibility, a tiny piece of software which would funnel the unwanted data away. Each time something came up he didn't like, it would be marked and kept from him in the future.

Perfect. Henry ran the install, clicking through the EULA. To test the new program, he left the safe search off and wandered through the office. Each time the data veered toward the pornographic, he flicked it away and the program blocked all similar images and knowledge. Somewhere in the file tree there would be a folder holding all the rules he created. He could always reverse a decision later. Maybe there was a way to set the rules for work differently from the rest of his time. He'd look into it.

The interface with the filtering program worked perfectly. The stream ran smooth and warm as skin across his mind, but no unfortunate distractions. He was unstoppable now.

***

To his chagrin, he sat across from another version of Davidson in a dark steakhouse. Henry couldn't understand how people enjoyed eating when they could barely see their plate. The other man took a great deal of pleasure in his steak. Given how much money Henry was going to make off this guy, he could put up with the irritation.

While they ate, Henry idly ran through the information he had on the man and his business. His was a small family firm with one very successful product they kept tweaking. They'd just gone public, but were struggling in the bigger pond. In the hands of his people their product would be expanded and updated with regular versions to keep buyers buying. He'd outsource the manufacturing and add a significant amount to the profit margin.

Before Henry knew what was happening, he'd bought a significant block of shares. The price of the stock started to rise. If he dumped them again, he could be accused of trying to manipulate the value of the company. Better to let it go. At least the buy order had been a couple of steps removed from him, so a casual observer would make no connection to Henry. But unless the stock settled over the next few days, he'd cost his company a few million dollars.

What shook Henry even more was he hadn't given the order to buy. It just . . . happened.

He got through the week and didn't lose as much money as he'd feared.

The next time it happened, Henry found himself sending a memo he couldn't remember creating. He pulled up the sent file and a cold wave ran down his spine. The memo OK'd dumping a division of the company at fire sale prices. True it had been hemorrhaging money, but he needed it for the contract he had with Davidson. Without it, he couldn't control the supply chain on the parts Davidson's company needed to fill their obligations. It loosened the screws on them. Henry had his eye on a hostile takeover, but this could make them too expensive to handle.

Once again it was better to let it go, as much as it enraged him. He had to focus on what was going on. He had no memory of writing the memo, between one thought and another, it appeared on his desktop and had been sent. Henry tried to trace it back, but he was no computer geek. He had an IT department for that, but he could hardly ask them to look through his mind to find the problem. Instead, Henry set a ten-minute delay on anything he sent. If it happened again, he'd be able to kill it.

Over the next few weeks, Henry's brain appeared to be doing its best to destroy his company. He tried turning on safe search, and even tried to make it through a day with the interface off completely. The migraine and nausea made it impossible for him to function.

He had his secretary make an appointment with the doctor. The man would have to fix this.

***

"Sorry, Henry, but you have a software problem. The hardware is functioning perfectly well." Dr. Phinsal wrote a phone number on a prescription pad. "These people are good, and very discreet."

Henry took the page and left the office already calling the number.

"Come in and I'll have a look at your problem." The woman on the other end sounded unreasonably cheerful about the whole thing.

Henry's car dropped him off in front of a strip mall. He followed directions and stomped up the stairs to a dingy office. A woman in jeans and polo shirt waved at him. Her blonde hair in a long ponytail.

206

"Sit down and connect to my server here. It's going to take a while, I have to run a full scan, then determine what needs to be done to deal with the issue."

"You sound like you already know what's going on." Henry pulled up the server and gave the password on the paper the woman handed him.

"Virus, Trojan horse, malware, in short you've been hacked."

"Hacked?" Henry tried to sit up, but his body wouldn't cooperate. He flopped spastically.

"Sorry, should have warned you, the scan might interfere with some functionality."

"Some functionality? I can't move." Henry's concern flowed away. Intellectually he knew he should be enraged, but no emotion bubbled up.

"Yeah, it happens." The woman looked at her screen and shook her head. "Your system is a mess. You've got a nasty bit of malware knocking a hole in your firewall a truck could drive through. I could try to attack it piecemeal, but that could still leave vulnerabilities. I have no way of knowing what files it's hidden in your system." She turned around to face Henry. "The best thing is to do a wipe and a clean install."

"A wipe?" Henry's voice squeaked.

"Won't affect your memory or anything stored in the cloud. It's only the operating system. You won't notice a thing except that queries will execute faster without all the extra processes running."

"How long will it take?" Henry's hands shook slightly.

"No more than an hour to do the install and scan for problems."

"OK, go ahead."

"Read through this form and sign it."

Henry glanced at it and scribbled his signature.

"Don't your lawyers tell you to read everything before you sign?"

"It's all the same stuff about risk and liability."

The woman shrugged and turned back to her keyboard. A couple of clicks and the world went dark.

Henry came back online and immediately felt the difference in the data flow. It moved more directly. He could pull up information and discard it easily.

"Better?"

"Much." Henry smiled and pushed himself to his feet.

"No more unsecured software, everything you need to manage your mind can be done through your settings." She wiggled her finger at him. "Go home and take in the user manual, including the maintenance schedule."

Henry transferred her fee and left the office chastened. He hadn't so much as looked up where the manual could be found. He'd have fired an IT person who was that careless. The car took him back to his office.

"You have a meeting with Mr. Davidson," Gina told him as he walked in. "I was about to call you. Did you forget?"

Henry couldn't remember setting a meeting, but the last month was such a jumble in his mind he could have and forgotten it.

"I'll head upstairs now. Have one of the secretaries bring him coffee. That will keep him happy until I get there."

"Yes, Sir."

Henry walked through the lobby. He looked at the chubby security guard and pulled up the gay porn, then dismissed it. No problem, should have checked with the Doctor earlier instead of panicking and trying to deal with it himself. The connection and computer/brain interface was just another computer, like the one that used to sit on his desk. For computer problems, he needed computer people to deal with them.

208

"Hello." Davidson waved a coffee cup at Henry. "Thought I'd come by and negotiate the buyout."

"Buyout?" Henry sat and picked up his coffee. "I admit I've had my eye on your company, but I'm in no position for a takeover."

Davidson grinned and looked suddenly like a wolf.

"You been feeling a little off the past few days?" He pulled out his cell phone and typed something into it. "You know as soon as they came out with self-driving cars, there were people who set out to hack them."

"What are you talking about?"

"Every new technology is an opportunity. Sure, having a computer running beside your brain and a connection orders of magnitude faster than anything previously available is tempting, but if there is software, there is vulnerability."

"What is going on?"

"Very simply, Henry, you were reprogrammed. The malware opened the door. After a couple of tests, we were able to take over completely when we needed to. You don't have any memory of those times."

"How?"

"Didn't it occur to you to do a background check on the good Doctor? You might have found out a subsidiary of our company funded his work. You should know better than to give out your password." Davidson shook his head. "The Securities Commission will be here soon to investigate your insider trading."

"I'll tell them—"

"What? That your brain was hacked? There's no sign of a problem now is there?"

"That woman will testify—"

"Will she?"

A peremptory knock on the door interrupted their conversation.

"Don't be too upset." Davidson walked over to open the door. "I hear the Wi-Fi in prison is pretty good these days." He opened the door and people in suits flooded the room. One of them handed Henry a search warrant.

HEART OF STONE

First published in 'Shards, A Noblebright Fantasy Anthology' 2018

Baz stomped into the village. At least the trolls called it a village. Baz had never seen any a human village, but he imagined it would be more impressive than this ragged collection of stone huts. What did a being made of stone need with walls and a roof?

"Baz." Mic walked out of his hut followed by Gran and Slat. They towered over Mic; as far as Baz knew, they were the biggest trolls of the Thousand. Mic wanted to be the most important.

"Mic." Baz nodded slightly, the black rock of his neck grinding. The gods hadn't meant for trolls to bend and scrape. "What do you want from me?" He planted his feet and met Mic's eyes. Gran grunted and Mic flapped a hand at him irritably.

"You've been watching the humans again." Mic picked at the sheets of rock on his arm. "We don't need them to be thinking about trolls. Your memories should include what happened last time."

"What difference does it make?" Baz threw his arms up. "We are the Thousand. No matter what the humans do, we will return from the rock."

"Stay away from the humans, Baz. If you want to spend your time thinking, climb a mountain and sit on it."

Baz shifted his feet and made a fist. If trolls had emotions he'd say it was anger, but rocks don't feel.

"I could have you thrown from the Cliff and find out if you return from the rock more amenable to good sense." Mic put up his hand to stop Gran's step forward.

"You could." Baz relaxed his hand. Fighting with Mic would achieve nothing. "But each time we come out of the rock we come out more extreme. A day will come when even trolls won't talk to trolls."

211

"What's there to say?" Mic pointed at Baz. "We are what the gods made us."

"Did it ever occur to you to ask *why* the gods made us?"

"We're trolls." Mic shook his head. "So act like a troll. Stay away from humans."

Baz turned to go, but words snaked out of his mouth. "I may spend time watching the humans, but at least I don't want to be one." Gran and Slat stomped forward, so Baz turned and walked as fast as he could from the village.

"If I ever see you again, you'll go over the cliff." Mic yelled at his back. Baz lifted his hand in a gesture he'd seen the humans use when they were angry. It was appropriate for the situation.

Gran and Slat didn't even walk to the edge of the village. They might be big, but their size made them slow. They'd been Mic's bodyguard for thousands of years. None of the memories in Baz's head showed Mic without them.

He headed down the mountain, the memories arguing with him, calling him a traitor.

"Enough." Baz slapped his head. "Do you want to go grovel at Mic's feet?" The memories went quiet. His own thoughts weren't as easily silenced.

The gods had made trolls from the rock. The oldest legends said the other races were fearful, so the gods decreed there would be a thousand trolls; never more, never less. Only Baz of all the Thousand asked why.

The landscape shifted to meadow and scrubby trees. Baz walked carefully to do as little damage as possible; another one of his oddities. Not that there was anything like a normal troll, they were as different as the rock they came from.

The trees grew taller and farther apart. Baz no longer had to pick his way through the vegetation. Now he placed his feet in slow motion, so as not to make the ground shake

212

and warn whoever camped on the trail leading to the pass. The memories woke and muttered at him, but now they were about the landscape. At one time the trolls used to come down the mountain. *Why?* An ancient memory floated up, a wisp-thin image of long-ago Baz talking with a human. The other memories swirled, of human mages taking trolls to torture; attempting to find the secret to immortality.

Now when trolls climbed out of the rock, they stayed in the mountains.

The memories showed Mic was right about the humans. They had come with armies and magic, and the trolls fought back with rocks and the mountains themselves. The humans left, and the trolls stopped talking with humans.

Am I wrong? Baz froze in the forest. *Will I only start a new war?* The stone in his chest gave him no answer. Rocks didn't feel, didn't change. The only difference between the basalt in the mountains and that in his chest was whatever the gods had done to make him live. He supposed if he were human, he'd be afraid.

Something moved in the dark. The sun had set while he'd been lost in the memories. Baz stayed still. A person in a red hat collected sticks, muttering too quietly for Baz to hear. When the wood gatherer headed away with a bundle as big as himself, Baz followed as slowly as he could. Up ahead, light flickered in a clearing. He crept as close as he dared.

A circle of dwarves huddled around a fire. The one in the red hat sat beside his bundle of wood, feeding the fire. Their breath made fog as they talked.

"I ever tell you 'bout the time I saw a troll come out of the rock?"

If Baz had had a heart, it would have been beating loud enough to alert the gathering. The other dwarves made a mix of groans and expressions of interest. The old dwarf grinned and rubbed his hands together.

"'Twas back when I was a Red Hat."

"Why do all these stories happen when dwarves are Red Hats?" The younger dwarf in the red hat shoved more wood into the fire then adjusted his hat.

"Because when we're Red Hats we do foolish things, and foolery makes for good stories." The old dwarf thumped his foot on the ground, and stared into the fire as if the story he wanted to tell was hidden in the flames. "We were climbing Zareth's Pass, late in the season, but Tompin Wellsdeep had spotted a deposit he wanted to explore, and we'd spent extra days chipping off samples for him. So there we were, sitting around a fire like tonight, and Tompin sent me off to fetch firewood. 'Red Hat fetches the firewood.'"

"Red Hat fetches everything," the dwarf in the red hat said, but he grinned and ducked his head as he spoke. The dwarves on either side elbowed him. The storyteller glared them into silence. Baz silently urged him to continue.

"The path down toward the trees was lit well enough by the moon, but the shadows it cast were stark black. I about jumped out of my skin when a loud crack echoed across the valley. Flakes of rock littered the path where I'd just been. Above them, coming out of the rock was a hand as big as my head." The dwarf shook his head. Baz looked at his hand, clenched it making a slight grinding sound. The crowd around the fire stiffened and looked around, Baz held still until they relaxed and the old dwarf took up the story again.

"I ran back to the fire and told the others, who of course laughed at me, but without anything better to do they followed me back to the rock face where the hand had become an arm waving madly in the night. It knocked my hat off and I scrambled back to grab it. The others shouted at each other, and I thought they were mad at me. I shoved

214

the hat on my head and turned to glare at them, only to see I was alone on the path with the arm reaching from the rock."

"So what did you do then?" The Red Hat threw more wood on the fire.

"I might have been a Red Hat, but I wasn't a complete fool. I chased after the others. Took me all night to catch them too."

"But you could have caught the thing as it came out and taken the immortality stone from its heart."

"There is no immortality stone." Baz's voice surprized him as much as the dwarves. With a crunch of rock, he shrugged and stepped out into the light. "It is just the way we were made. You could kill me here, and try as you might, you'd find nothing but shards of rock. Another me would claw its way out of the rock of my birthplace."

The dwarves huddled on the other side of the fire, the light making their eyes into flame and impossible to read.

"I'd heard trolls hate all other living things and destroy them when they get a chance." The Red Hat stepped forward and looked up at Baz.

"Some of us do." Baz held up his hand and peered at it. "It is wisest when meeting a troll to run first and live to ask your questions of another being."

"What's it like to live forever?" The storyteller stepped forward and put his hand on the Red Hat's shoulder.

"We don't live forever. We die and are reborn as ourselves, but not with all our memories. Each time, something is lost."

"What can a troll die from?" The Red Hat tilted his head.

"What do dwarves die from?" Baz pushed the fire together a little with his hands. "Mostly, we erode, get weary of life, and become lifeless rock to let a new troll come forth." He nodded his head at the group, then pulled a chip of rock from his torso and tossed it across the fire. The Red Hat caught it and stared wide-eyed at Baz. "I thank you for your time and the light of your fire." He stepped back into the shadows and then walked away through the trees, making no effort to hide his footsteps.

There were times Baz envied the soft ones the emotions he saw on their faces. Other times, like now, he was satisfied to be free of the fears and griefs of the flesh. Baz stumbled through the forest until he stepped off the edge of a cliff.

He had no time to curse himself for his stupidity before he hit the water. It slowed him enough that the rocks on the bottom of the lake only knocked chips from his torso and broke off his left foot. Baz pushed himself upright and picked his way through the rocks until he found a place he could climb out.

The memories called him all kinds of a fool, and Baz didn't argue with them. This was what Mic had warned him about.

He looked around to see if anyone was there to watch. The strangest urge to hide came over him and Baz almost returned to the water. The threat of deep mud made him walk away from the lake. Quar had told him about spending a thousand years on the bottom of a lake buried deep in the mud. Of course, for Quar that would have been a perfect place.

The ground sucked at Baz's feet, and at times he sank in as far as his knees.

"Bah," he grunted aloud. He ripped a nearby tree from its roots and stripped it of branches with his hands. Using the makeshift staff to test the ground, he meandered his way onto solid footing.

He'd been walking for days using the tree to compensate for the missing foot, when he heard sounds of fighting coming from the distance. The smart thing would be to head away from the fight. Whoever was trying to kill whom, it made no difference to him. But his feet carried him toward the clash.

A tall human had her back to an immense boulder that towered above the trees. A smaller human lay unmoving beside her. Four other humans faced her, mounted on beasts that might have been either bears or dogs. They roared and batted at an invisible barrier. Two of the humans hammered at the barrier with swords, while the other two held staves in front of them, red light hitting the barrier and sending cracks through it.

"Foolish," one of the sorcerers spoke casually. "Your refusal to take a life weakens you."

"Not as much as being murdering scum would." The woman's voice didn't betray any strain, though her hands shook and sweat ran in rivers from her face.

The sorcerers growled and pushed more effort into their staves.

"Troll." One of the sword-swingers yelled and pointed at Baz. The sorcerers spun and aimed their staves at Baz. One of them spoke a syllable; the other's mouth had just opened when the tree Baz still carried struck them and sent the pair soaring into the trees. One swordsman rode at Baz screaming, blue flames licking the edge of his weapon. Baz hammered him into the ground; the flames vanished. The other turned his steed and vanished into the forest.

Silence fell. Baz dropped the tree. Whatever he wanted, he was still a troll, and every human knew that trolls killed without reason. The remains of the swordsman and beast accused him. The other beasts must have fled. Their masters' mangled bodies hung from branches high up in the trees.

"He said you don't kill." Baz turned to the woman, who gazed back at him out of eyes which might have been cut from sapphires. "I apologize for the shedding of blood." He lowered his head and turned to leave.

"Wait." The woman crouched beside her companion and checked him. "You took no oath, and there is no blame for aiding strangers. If Willard hadn't been injured, he would have championed me."

"Your champion, Willard. He is badly injured?"

"I'm afraid so." The woman sighed and wiped at her eyes. "Beyond my ability to heal at any rate. I must go for help."

Baz looked around at the wilderness.

"I have ways of traveling swiftly, though the price is high." She adjusted the man's cloak minutely. "I'm loathe to leave him alone, but traveling the ways would kill him."

"I will stay with him." Baz stomped over to where he could get a look at the man's pale face. His cheek twitched as if pain were torturing him even in unconsciousness.

"The Council is *not* going to believe this." The woman spun in place and vanished. Baz caught a glimpse of a tunnel formed of light, then he stood alone in the forest.

He didn't like the corpses lying around, proof of his murderous ways. Baz dug a hole in the soft soil of the forest floor. His hand tingled oddly when it got too close to the sword, so he used the tree to push sword, swordsman, and beast into the hole. Since the bodies of the sorcerers repulsed him even in death, he left them in their trees and filled the grave, tamping the soil down.

"My lady Qwyneth?" The man's voice rasped. Baz stomped over to look at him. Brown eyes pleaded with him.

"She has traveled the ways to bring you help."

"It is just like her." The man let his head fall back. "Wins an impossible battle, then kills herself to rescue me."

"The lady said you were injured beyond her ability to heal."

218

"Did she now?" The man's eyes closed. "I suppose even she has limits. The Rahadlian death curse is incurable. I am glad not to die alone."

"I promised to wait with you until her return."

"You are a most unusual troll." Willard's voice weakened.

"You've met others?" Baz couldn't stop the question. Quar was the only troll outside the village he'd ever met.

"A few." Willard winced and gasped. Baz guessed he would die soon.

The troll looked at his hand. Though his litany of questions made him an outcast, he wondered: what was it that kept him alive? He could almost perceive energy running through the black rock forming him. Death was so easy. Why did life have to be hard? Baz put his hand over the man's chest, now barely moving.

The light flashing through his hand wasn't much different than the light fading from Willard. Baz experimentally tried to push light from his hand into the human and suddenly lightning flashed from one to the other. The man arched his back and screamed, black fog lifting from his skin and vanishing in the lightning.

Then the light vanished with a snap.

Baz's hand crumbled into gravel. The disintegration traveled up his arm. Willard sat up and reached toward Baz, his pitch-black eyes open wide in shock and grief.

It was the last thing Baz saw before the rest of him fell into a heap of rock.

***

Qwyneth jumped from the roc then helped the Healer down. The great bird walked to the edge of the clearing and sat. Qwyneth ran to where she'd left Willard and the troll then stopped in shock, the healer bumping into her. The Arch-mage had ranted at her for risking her life for a dead man, but curiosity made the Healer willing to fly on her roc to meet a troll who apologized for killing.

Qwyneth had prepared herself for anything but this.

Willard looked up from the rock in his hand.

"I see you made it through the ways." He dropped the rock on the pile and knelt at her feet. "I'm not deserving of that level of risk. I'd rather die than live knowing I'd caused your death."

Qwyneth pulled him to his feet.

"How many times must I tell –" Her words broke off in a gasp as Willard looked at her. His warm, brown eyes had become hard, black stones. Yet he clearly saw as well as he ever had.

The Healer stepped around Qwyneth and laid her hands on Willard's arm, then snatched them back like they'd been burnt.

"What happened?"

"Don't rightly know." Willard sighed and sat on a rock. "I woke enough to talk with Baz. I could feel the curse working its way toward my heart, and thanked the troll for being there with me at the end."

"But where did he go?" Qwyneth looked around as if he'd step out of the trees at any moment.

Willard pointed to the pile of black rubble.

"The darkness was coming for me when a bolt of light struck through me, blowing the curse into tatters. I sat up and watched as he fell apart in front of me." He put his head in his hands. "What do people see in me to be so willing to die for my sake?" Willard jumped up and stalked away into the trees.

"Willard isn't human anymore, at least not completely." The Healer slumped down on the rock Willard had vacated. "His heart is stone, yet the life energy in him is beyond anything I've experienced, and I've healed dragons."

"Artisan preserve us." Qwyneth picked up a piece of rock from the pile which was all that remained of the troll.

220

"I must ask you to release me from my oath." Willard stumbled into the clearing and threw himself at Qwyneth's feet. "I swore an oath on my life to serve you until my last breath, but Baz has been reborn missing most of what makes him Baz. I must make what is broken whole." His shoulders shook.

Qwyneth reached down and lifted Willard to his feet.

"You know I cannot release you from that oath." The buzz of energy in Willard's hand stung her, but she set her teeth and kept her grip. "So I will journey with you and give you what aid I can."

Willard opened his mouth to argue, but Qwyneth gave him what he called The Look. He sighed.

"Then let us set out."

The Healer mounted the roc and flew away as Willard led them vaguely north.

***

The troll crawled from the rock and roared at the heavens. He smashed stones with his fists then threw the pieces far out into the canyon. He knew he was a troll, but he had no name, only whispers of memories taunted him, just out of reach. A tug from far away pulled at the cavity in his chest, aching to be filled. The troll turned his head as if he sought a scent in the air. Crushing one last rock between his hands, he thudded away down the path, always aware of the distant need.

Baz. His name fit loosely, leaving unexplained gaps in his mind, not touching the emptiness inside him.

The path moved from bare rock to trees to open meadows. Valleys filled with green slowed him as he had to find a safe way down abrupt precipices. Massive trees grew on valley floors, big enough even a troll must go around. He walked when he had to, ran when he could. Always downhill, always toward the ever-stronger pull of what had been stolen from him.

Baz only paid enough attention to keep from running off a cliff. He didn't question his rage, or how a rock could burn with hate. The open spaces grew larger, the slopes more gentle. Baz increased his speed, leaving the ground shaking behind him.

Momentum carried him halfway through the army before he crashed to a halt. Men with uncertain eyes surrounded him, others on strange beasts gathered behind them. Confusion kept him in place. He'd seen these things before; the memory almost came to him.

"Surrender and serve me." A man carrying a tall staff and blue fire burning in his eyes strolled over to contemplate Baz. "You creatures are easy enough to kill, but how you live in the first place intrigues me. Imagine an army of stone warriors at my command. You could be my General."

The pull became painful. Baz shook his head. Then a memory struck him with the force of a boulder. A man like this stole his heart. He screamed his defiance. Rage and pain mixed. A man tried to stick him with a spear glowing with blue flames, and Baz spun and snatched him up. Completing the spin, he threw the spearman at the one with the staff. The sorcerer's bolt of red light was deflected enough to strike the troll's arm instead of where his heart should be.

The arm exploded sending red-hot rock toward the humans. Baz thumped the ground with his remaining fist, making everyone close to him stagger and fall to their knees, even the one with the staff. Baz threw a handful of dirt and rocks as another bolt shot from the staff. The blast left a wide circle of moaning humans.

The irresistible pull drew him into a run. The humans scrambled to get out of his way, and none followed him into the forest. He left a path of destruction through that day and the next. Pain ruled what mind he had.

In the night, he didn't see the cliff of black rock towering over him. Baz ran into it at full speed, splashing into the basalt cliff as easy as water.

It enfolded him, eased his pain, comforted the distress in his mind. When Baz moved to claw his way out of the rock, a voice whispered, *Wait.* So Baz let the rock cradle him, the first troll in the millennia since the gods had made them to return to the rock.

***

Willard opened his eyes to Qwyneth leaning over him, tears dropping on his face.

"It wasn't your fault."

"I swear you're a mind-reader." Qwyneth sat back and rubbed her face.

"The only time I've seen you cry is when you're blaming yourself for my fate. I made my choice; I'd make the same one again."

"If I'd just…"

"Just what? Been faster, stronger, able to see the future? Don't blame yourself for being human."

"But being human is such a nuisance at times." Qwyneth stood up as Willard laughed.

"It has its good points too, my Lady." He rubbed his arm, surprised to find it still attached.

"What happened?"

"Pain, like my arm had been torn off, a spear stuck in my back. Anger, grief, fear–whatever happened to Baz hurt him badly. It's stopped now, but he's still out there."

"I can only think of one thing which could hurt a troll like that." Qwyneth stared north as if her vision could cut through forest and rock to show her the Rahadlians.

"I will take care not to walk into them." Willard stood, picked up his pack and let the way through the forest. He didn't dare ask how long he'd left Qwyneth vulnerable with his weakness. They didn't talk as they journeyed; Qwyneth was used to silence as a safety measure.

A deep valley beckoned, already in shade, an immense black cliff on the far side. Willard guided them on a roundabout route, avoiding open spaces. They arrived at the cliff without incident.

"Something about this…" Willard stretched his hand out to touch the smooth black rock.

"No!" Qwyneth reached toward him, but too late; his hand vanished into the stone, pulling the rest of him inexorably. Willard snatched at his sword to cut himself free and twisted to see Qwyneth's horrified face.

"Sorry, my Lady." The last thing he felt was her fingers sliding off his.

***

Memories floated in the rock. He couldn't tell if he was Baz or Willard. He wasn't sure there was any difference anymore. The panic of climbing from the rock with only half a soul washed through him. The guilt at standing between an arrogant young girl and those who would harm her, blood dripping from his dagger. He wanted to know. He needed to atone. *Why?*

Amusement touched him gently.

He lived the memories of Baz refining his curious nature, desperate to find a purpose beyond existing. The worry as the trolls grew apart, uncaring even for each other. Then a memory of training floated to the surface.

"Dying is easy." The instructor had paced in front of him. "Life is hard. I'm training you to live. *They* told you to be prepared to give your life for your mage. I'm telling you that if you die, you've failed."

The knowledge that he could always be reborn – he saw how it weakened him, made him careless of his life. What had he done in the thousands of years as living rock? Only died and been made new. How had the world been changed?

His first meeting with Qwyneth as a mage. Against all advice, she'd bonded him as her companion.

224

"Guilt is not a good reason to do things." The Arch-mage had looked into her eyes. She stared back, unafraid.

"It isn't guilt. It's the desire to make the world a better place."

"You almost believe that." The Arch-mage had dropped his head, then took her hand and Willard and incanted the words linking their fate. He would not survive her death. She could not kill even to protect herself; he was her shield against danger.

"I must find her."

***

His heart raced, his hands shook, and he gasped for air. Willard fought to ease his fear then opened his eyes.

Baz stood and put his hand on his chest, then turned his gaze to Willard.

"This is what it is to be human?" He tapped his finger against the rock. "So frail, but so determined."

Willard stood and swayed on his feet. "Trolls do not lack courage."

"What is courage?"

"The choice to live a hard life instead of taking an easy death." Willard pointed to the ground. "There was a squad of warriors riding fell-beasts. They've taken Qwyneth."

"How do you know she lives?"

"If she were dead, you'd be standing alone here." Willard looked around, but they must have taken his pack along with Qwyneth. "We follow this trail." Baz thumped along behind as Willard loped toward his Lady.

***

Mic looked at the village; discontent filling him. The trolls could be so much more if they would just listen to him. A scant hundred out of the Thousand lived in the village, most of them going through their life as if they were alone. Baz's words before he left irritated him. The only thing needed was a little discipline.

Gran and Slate loomed behind him. They'd followed him for millennia. Mic didn't know what they found by serving him, unless the occasional chance to toss someone from the cliff was motivation enough.

Mic didn't really want to be a human, but he wanted what human leaders had: respect, obedience.

"Mic." Felds thumped up behind him. "A human army has been spotted at the bottom of the pass."

"Gather everyone you can find and bring them to the canyon. We'll discourage them." Felds departed, bellowing to the others in the village. Trolls left the village looking for others who lived close by. "This is Baz's fault. I warned him."

"Should've pitched him," Gran rumbled behind Mic.

"He was right about one thing." Mic clenched his fist, sending flakes of mica falling to the ground. "He'd have just come back. We need a better way of dealing with him."

"Deep hole," Slate said.

Mic turned around and stared up at Slate for a moment. The troll hadn't spoken in a hundred years. Then he shrugged. "We'll deal with that when we've sent the humans running." He headed off toward the canyon.

The edges of the canyon on both sides were lined with loose rocks of all sizes. Trolls on the other side waved. There had to be almost a hundred there, watching the pass intently. Almost as many stood on Mic's side. If he'd known an invasion would bring them out, Mic would have sent Baz out himself. He rubbed his hands together in anticipation. This would alleviate his boredom, at least for today.

The sun dropped below the horizon, but the trolls didn't move. What did rock need with rest? It rose again, showing a small group of humans riding beasts up the path to the canyon.

Mic held his hand up, waiting until the invaders were too close to escape. The humans didn't look to be in any rush. None of them looked up. They wouldn't live to regret their foolishness.

The sun had risen halfway to noon before Mic dropped his hand. A hail of boulders plunged toward the interlopers. Trolls threw one, then picked up another to throw before the first one hit. They went through half of the boulders placed for this purpose before Mic saw that not one rock had hit its target.

They slid to the side or off to the rear of the group. The humans were pointing up and laughing. One stopped and made a face up at them. The human in front, carrying a staff, turned and made a cutting motion with his hand. The impudent human returned to following, but as the train reached the end of the canyon, he turned and made a gesture at the trolls.

A boulder lifted from the edge and plunged down in a blur wiping the warrior from the trail. The leader didn't even look around.

"Wait here." Mic told the trolls. "I'll go find out what the humans want." He eagerly walked back toward the village. Gran and Slate followed, in step as always.

The humans waited in the village. The one with the staff stood a little in front of the others.

"I suppose I should apologize for the manner of our entry." The human nodded to Mic. "I didn't want damage any of your people, but did need to demonstrate my power to do so. The fact you are here shows you received my message."

"What do you want?" Mic glared at the man. He could squash the human with one fist. But a glint of challenge showed in the man's eyes.

"To the point." The man planted his staff on the stone. "I am the High Sorcerer of Rahadlia. If I am going to rule the world as I should, I need an army unstoppable by any normal means." Blue flame danced in the sorcerer's eyes. "That army would need a general."

Mic smiled. His face wasn't used to the expression, but it felt good. "Let's talk about what the trolls would gain from being your army."

***

Baz and Willard slipped through the forest. Baz watched Willard move and emulated him. The longer they went the more separate the two became. Baz knew without a doubt he was Baz, the troll, and Willard, the man. Willard glanced back and nodded in approval.

Baz watched for the human to stop and rest, but he moved as relentlessly as any troll. Maybe there was stone in him now. Was there flesh in Baz? He nudged at the memories trying to find something to show how he'd changed, but they were as confused as he was. Something tightened in his gut. Baz stopped to put his hand on his torso.

"It's fear." Willard didn't turn around. "While we are our own selves, it seems we still share some things."

"Fear?" Baz explored the sensation. It made him think of landing in the water, unsure if he'd survive in one piece.

"I think you trolls have as many emotions as any other race, but how long have you told yourselves stone can't feel?"

"Forever." Baz put his hand on his head. "Yet we live, and rock should not live either."

Baz explored his memories with his new insight. How could he have missed it? But looking back his life, it took on shades of emotion, many he couldn't name. Was this true for the others too?

Willard held up his fist and Baz froze in place.

"Let me go forward alone. Your skills are amazing for someone of our size–your size–but this is beyond you."

"I will think on what I've learned."

He stood still and sifted through his memories, comparing them to what he'd gained from Willard.

***

Willard ghosted through the forest, avoiding sentries. They were good, he'd give them that, but none had the training of a companion. Close to the clearing, Willard climbed a tree high enough to get a view of the camp. Warriors bustled setting up tents and corrals for their beasts.

In the center of the camp, a wagon sat surrounded by two layers of guards holding swords or spears, some burning with blue flame. On the wagon, Qwyneth had been chained in a kneeling position, arms bent awkwardly. Willard's shoulder twinged in sympathy.

Qwyneth's head lifted, and the guards in the circle rustled. She knew he was watching. He had no idea how she did it, but she always knew he was watching. Her head dropped again and the warriors relaxed.

Her hand stretched as if she were trying to relieve pressure on her shoulders.

Danger, trolls, sorcerer. At least Willard expected she meant "troll" when she signed "golem."

He wasn't sure if she meant danger to the trolls or from them. Maybe both. He couldn't see the High Sorcerer anywhere in the camp. The man had made Willard's skin crawl when he'd visited the Council to leave his ultimatum. Willard had thought he was used to magic, but the sorcerer felt like a viper among rat snakes. The man intended to rule the world, no matter the cost to the people who lived in it.

A fragment of memory drifted into his mind–Baz confronting the Sorcerer; the High Sorcerer inviting Baz to join him and lead the trolls. Willard's stomach sank as he imagined even a few trolls marching against the Council forces. Only magic could stop them, and the Mages were forbidden to kill.

Willard slipped down the tree and crawled his way out of the forest to meet Baz.

"The sorcerer wants the trolls to fight for him," Willard said without preamble.

Baz nodded. "Mic would like that. Not the fighting, but the importance of leading."

"Mic?"

"A troll who wants to organize us into–something. I'm not sure even he knows. A chance to be a General would be irresistible."

"How would the sorcerer know about Mic?"

"He wouldn't need to. He would just have to keep asking until someone says yes." Baz clenched his fist. "I need to go talk to Mic."

"The High Sorcerer may be there."

"It won't be the first time we've met."

"I remember. Go safely." Willard turned away as Baz vanished into the trees. Willard sighed, then turned to sneak back to the camp. This time he needed to infiltrate the Rahadlian army. It would be easier with the High Sorcerer missing, but there were others he'd need to watch for: he wouldn't have Baz to heal him of any death curse this time.

Getting to the camp was child's play compared to taking a sentry silently. They were warriors, strong and alert. He'd only have a short time before the gap in the line was discovered. Then he spotted a warrior headed to the woods, unlacing his trousers. In any army Willard had seen, he'd be disciplined for his actions, but his laziness served Willard well.

The man leaned against a tree making noises of relief. Willard waited until both hands were occupied with putting his clothes together. The warrior never knew he died. Willard hauled him farther from the camp, but not far enough for the first ring of sentries to trip over him. He changed clothes as quickly as he could, hiding his own knives out of sight.

A man in a brass helmet stormed over as Willard entered the camp. It wouldn't be good if he ended up in the stockade.

"What the blazes do you think you were doing?" Brass Helmet didn't give Willard time to respond. Just as well, since his Rahadlian was rusty. "March double time! You can stand in the inner circle for a day. Maybe the witch will strike you first. The sorcerers say she's bound not to kill, but that still leaves a lot of nasty." He pushed Willard, who marched over to the circle. The men thumped him as he pushed through to the inner circle. He'd chosen his entry point to end up in front of Qwyneth. The others held weapons at the ready and stared steadily at the wagon. Willard drew his sword and waited.

Qwyneth's hand moved in the circle she used to tell him he was being especially crazy.

You're one to talk.

***

Baz climbed up the back ways to get to the village. The first thing he noticed was the number of trolls present. They'd at least doubled in number since his last visit. Mic must be happy – and there he was, with Gran and Slate behind him, talking with the man who'd used magic to take off Baz's arm.

The sorcerer stiffened and pointed to Baz. He looked ready to fire a bolt, but Mic stopped him. They argued briefly before the sorcerer waved in disgust and stomped off.

"I told you the next time I saw you, you'd go over the cliff." Mic looked to be holding himself straighter, more confident.

"Need to talk to you." Baz ignored Gran and Slate, who'd taken his arms. "Maybe you can walk with me, and make sure they do it right."

Gran growled, but Mic shook his head. "You've always been a strange one, Baz, but I should thank you for sending the High Sorcerer to me."

"I'm guessing he's told you he's out to conquer the world. Wants you as his General commanding the troll army."

"That's right. The others are bored, and a little destruction will provide some new and interesting memories."

"I can see that. Any troll would love to be torn to pieces by magic–then the dragons. They'd be a lot of fun."

"The humans won't expect us, Baz. They won't have time to respond."

"They have short lives, but their race has a long memory. They adapt fast."

"You would know." Mic sneered. He looked to be about to turn away.

"If you're their leader, you need to have a plan for every possibility," Baz told him. "Including a plan for what to do if that sorcerer decides that conquering the world includes ruling the trolls."

Mic fell back into step. "He's just one more human."

"He fired a bolt of magic that blew my arm off. His men have swords and spears that will cut rock."

"It will only take one blow to kill him."

"Then plan that blow well, Mic, because you won't get a second one."

They arrived at the cliff. It wasn't the first time Baz had seen this view. Through the ages, he and Mic had never seen quite eye to eye.

"You're their leader, Mic. It's your job to have plans. He won't expect trolls to think ahead."

Gran and Slate picked Baz up and threw him over the cliff as easily as he'd toss a pebble. They'd given him more distance than last time.

Curl into a ball. Willard's memory prompted him.

Baz obeyed the thought. As high as the cliff stood, it didn't take more than handful of seconds to hit bottom. He crashed in the pile of shattered trolls sending shards in all directions. Baz rolled to a stop almost buried by rock. He stood up and inspected himself. He'd taken a few chips here and there, but that was all. Mic would not be pleased.

Let's not do that again soon.

Baz laughed, stunning his memories. They could not recall any troll laughing before. The day was filled with new things. Baz pushed his way out of the rock pile and headed down the valley. He'd be able to cross over the ridge and get back to Willard.

***

Willard stopped himself from falling by sheer willpower. Something had happened to Baz, and it had sent echoes through him. Not as bad as the first time, but he'd come close to fainting and giving himself away. Now all he got from Baz was a vague feeling of happiness.

Qwyneth looked at him, her eyes concerned. Willard lowered his brows briefly. Not much could be communicated with such miniscule expressions, but Qwyneth relaxed slightly.

Time for patience and endurance; even with his training, Willard couldn't imagine being forced into such a position for hours – never mind days. Qwyneth once commented that mage training made companion's schooling seem mild in comparison.

Willard knew two things for sure. First, that Qwyneth had a plan, and probably several plans; second, that he wouldn't like any of them. The High Sorcerer had grossly underestimated the Lady, and Willard didn't intend to let the man learn from his mistake.

Later in the day, the High Sorcerer returned, followed by a collection of trolls. More than a hundred of them accompanied the Rahadlian, if Willard's count out of the corner of his eye was accurate.

The Sorcerer strolled over to the wagon and waved the guards away. A single troll followed him. Where Baz had been formed of chunks and columns of black rock, this one was made of sheets which reflected glints of light from the sun. He picked at the stone of his arm. That must be Mic, the leader Baz had mentioned. If the troll had been human, Willard would have guessed he had a case of the nerves.

"For now, you are a useful hostage against the Council." The High Sorcerer's voice carried to Willard's ears. He held a cup of water and made a point of ignoring the soldiers. It didn't matter, as most of the guards broke into groups to sit or lie on the ground and rest. Willard sat and put his head on his knees. He missed Qwyneth's reply, but he could imagine her response to being thought of as a hostage.

"The Council *will* surrender, or my trolls will tear down their city around the Council's ears."

A grunt came, sounding like rocks grinding together, and Willard forced himself to stay still. Was Mic having second thoughts? Did he know how dangerous that was?

As the sorcerer left, the Rahadlian warriors reformed the circle around Qwyneth. This time Willard had a place off to the side, without any view other than the wagon, the camp, and the forest.

The sun dropped toward the horizon, and even Willard grew tired. He was seriously considering stealing a break when shouting at the other end of the camp roused him. Qwyneth's fingers twitched.

Golem, trouble, treason.

Willard forced his breathing to stay even as the younger warriors around him peered toward the source of the noise. More senior men thumped them and yelled for everyone to keep their eyes on the witch.

Be ready.

The chains holding Qwyneth's arms flared white and vanished in a shower of sparks that burned wherever they landed.

Willard jumped up on the cart and put his sword to Qwyneth's neck.

"Look scared," he whispered. Qwyneth snorted and began trembling realistically.

Willard looked around the camp to take in the chaos. The trolls were huge and fearsome, but no match for the trained warriors. He saw a huge troll shatter, and Baz racing toward an even bigger troll.

"Put a shield on me." Willard prayed his crazy idea would work.

***

Baz threaded his way through the forest toward the huge meadow where the army camped. Willard already had joined the army. He'd be near his lady. Baz put her out of his mind.

He bumped into a sentry and took advantage of the warrior's shock to hammer him into the ground. The blood on his fist accused him, but there would be worse to come if Willard's memories were anything to go by.

Baz watched for the second sentry and sent him after the first. A few more steps and he stood in the shadow of the trees with the sun behind him.

Mic stood in front of the High Sorcerer, looking in Baz's direction.

"We are not *your* trolls. We are not your beasts of burden."

"You are my General, and Generals obey their leaders." The High Sorcerer's voice made that uncomfortable twist in Baz's stomach worsen. Fear, Willard had called it. He'd also said trolls have courage. Baz readied himself to intervene.

"We obey your orders to fight, not to be servants!" Mic pointed at the High Sorcerer, who simply touched his staff to Mic's torso. As it reddened, Mic looked toward Baz and nodded, and then suddenly exploded. None of the shards hit the sorcerer.

Baz waited for the rest of Mic's trolls either to attack the High Sorcerer or to run from the field. They did neither. A troll bellowed *rockslide,* and they split up to move in all directions. Most ran into the camp smashing wagons and tents, swiping warriors out of the way with their fists.

The High Sorcerer raised his staff and sent up a bolt of light which boomed like thunder. In response, the warriors in the camp formed up out of the way of the rampaging trolls, some carrying spears and swords glinting with blue flame. Their beasts roared and growled, asking to join the fight.

That signal almost cost the Sorcerer his life. Slate leaped forward, both fists lifted to crush him. Baz ran across the field at top speed as the sorcerer swung his staff, red light flaring as Slate was cut in half. His legs fell into rubble, but his arms and head held their form.

The human turned toward Gran just as the giant brought his fists down on the ground. The ground shook, and the Rahadlian stumbled and almost fell into Slate's grip. He managed to twist out of the way, dodging both Slate and Gran. Rolling to his feet, he pointed the staff at Gran, and a bolt struck the huge troll and tore through to hit Baz dead on.

I tried.

To Baz's shock, however, the bolt splashed against him, causing no pain or damage. He didn't slow to wonder about it. Astonishingly, Gran took another swing at the Sorcerer, whose hair moved in the breeze of Gran's fist passing. This time, the blast took Gran's head off and sent it flying toward Baz.

Gran's head had a broad grin plastered across it. Baz laughed as he caught all that remained of Mic's bodyguard.

236

He hefted the stone before sending the head screaming back at the sorcerer. The human blew it to pieces with a jerk of his staff. His grin was identical to Gran's as he put both hands on his staff and aimed it at Baz.

Then Slate's hand swept the High Sorcerer's feet from beneath him. The bolt shot up into the sky as Slate's other hand crashed down on the human, driving him into the ground. The troll fell to pieces, and Baz slowed to see what remained of the sorcerer.

The human shot out of the ground with a shriek of fury. As he swung his staff in an arc, Baz rolled forward out of the way, coming to his feet with a chunk of stone in each hand. He fired them at the sorcerer's head. The man dropped as he cut the rocks from the air, but for an instant his staff was pointed up. Baz leapt forward and wrapped his hands around the High Sorcerer's waist, trapping the staff against his body.

A shield pushed against Baz's hands, stopping him from crushing the Rahadlian. Bolts of magic flew harmlessly away into the sky. The human fought, throwing every bit of his power against the troll.

"You may be a sorcerer," Baz ground out. "You may be the strongest man in the world. But I am made of the stuff of mountains."

The chaos in the camp stopped, and the warriors and trolls backed away from each other. Willard escorted Qwyneth through the center until she stood only a little distance from the raging sorcerer.

"You are going to burn out, the way you're behaving. Didn't they teach you any discipline?" Qwyneth spoke casually, almost in a friendly tone. "It doesn't have to be this way. Vow peace to the Council and you can go home."

"And be the weakling puppet of the Council?" The High Sorcerer put his head back and screamed.

Baz clenched his fists and the sound cut off. He dropped the crumpled remains of the human on the ground.

"I had a shield around him," Qwyneth said, "but that works too." She held her hand out over the remains of the sorcerer, and they sank into the ground. "Give me a minute, Baz." Qwyneth sauntered over to the stunned Rahadlians. "Go home. The Council has no interest in ruling you. They are lazy, and governing is a lot of work. Any who are sorcerers are welcome to visit, but only if you swear peace. Otherwise stay away."

"Tell your generals, your kings or sorcerers or whatever," Baz stepped up beside Qwyneth. "If they want to invade, they will face the trolls." He turned to look at Qwyneth. "That goes for your Council if they get too energetic. We trolls have been looking for something to do, and I think keeping the peace will work well enough."

Qwyneth grinned at Baz. "I will pass on your message. They may want to visit to discuss details. The Council is big on details."

"They can wait at the foot of the pass and fly a flag. We'll come and guide them to the village."

Willard's lips twitched, and his amusement tickled at the back of Baz's head. The rest of the trolls gathered around Baz.

"I've been thinking about you and Willard," Qwyneth said. "I had a little peace and quiet to do so." Willard rolled his eyes. "If you put the palms of your hands on the palms of another troll, you may be able to share your memories. Not as completely as with Willard, but enough maybe to give you a common ground."

Felds stepped forward and raised his hands. Baz put his over top. His hands tingled and memories buzzed in his head. When he dropped his hand, memories from Felds were being welcomed and given a place.

"Thank you, Lady Qwyneth." Baz bowed to her. The other trolls copied him. "Let's go home." Baz turned and walked away, the others following in his footsteps.

***

Baz looked up from where he talked in a circle of trolls. Mic was walking into the village, flanked by Gran and Slate.

"You were right." Mic said.

"But you had a plan." Baz held out his hands palm up. "Put your palms on mine."

Mic reached out slowly and connected with Baz. The other troll's memories flooded in, his centuries of frustration trying to do something—he didn't know what—with the trolls.

Mic dropped his hands and stood still. Baz waited.

"What do you want me to do?" Mic looked at the circle of trolls behind Baz.

"We've been waiting for you. We want you to lead." Baz put his hand on Mic's shoulder. "It is, after all your gift." He led Mic to the circle; they shifted to make space for him.

"Let them tell you what we've been doing, then you can give us your ideas from there."

Baz backed out of the circle and headed out of the village. He'd be able to make the pass by sunset. Maybe he'd find a campfire and hear some stories.

THE MOOK

I had to rob the bank at exactly 3:35 pm on the Friday afternoon. I knew that because that was when I was sitting at the ballpark with my face plastered on the Jumbotron. A guy couldn't be at two places at the same time, right? So, it had to be some other mook. Someone who looked like me.

I even have the tickets from the game. The Yanks lost, but what do I care?

Marvin came up with the caper. He had this thing where he could send somebody back a day. Only a day, but that was enough to make both of us rich. He had his lab in an abandoned subway tunnel in Brooklyn. It was creepy, but he stole juice from the transit people without them even knowing.

So, Saturday at 3:00 pm he put me in his chair and turns on the juice. It looked a little too much like an electric chair, but he let me watch him send himself back. So, no sweat, right?

The chair goes buzz and I'm sitting in an empty station shaking like I'd gone cold turkey. I have thirty minutes to get to the bank where we happen to know there is an unusually large amount of cash being moved. It helps being from the future and all.

Twenty minute's walk to the bank, a few minutes waiting for the right time and then I get to rock it old school. I look at the bank and shake my head. They just don't know how to build a bank anymore. The old days they had pillars and white marble. There was class to robbing a bank in them days. Now, you might as well be knocking off a gas station, only the gas station don't have security cameras and armed guards.

A gas station also don't have three million in bills from a charity drive.

The watch on my wrist beeps slightly. It's time. I pull my piece and run into the bank. Marvin has told me where the guards are and what they are doing. I knock the first one flying with my shoulder and shoot the other in the leg before he can think of getting his gun out.

"Everyone just stay put," I yelled and put a couple of round in the ceiling. Not even plaster, geesh.

The bags are just sitting there. I'm supposed to grab them and run out of the bank.

Only they have the game on TV and it's almost my big moment. There's a long foul ball and the kid next to me catches it and gives me a high five. How many times am I going to get to see myself on TV?

That's when the guard goes all hero and tries to shoot me. Only he misses on account of he's shaking from the bullet in his leg. Instead, he hits the TV and I see the kid miss the catch and that ball smack into my head. All of a sudden, I don't feel so good, like my head is going to burst, so I grab the money and run out of the bank. I don't make it very far before the world turns black.

* * *

I'm sitting in an empty station shaking like I'd gone cold turkey. I'm supposed to be back with Marvin, but he isn't here. It's just me and the shakes. I decide to take a walk and maybe clear this headache I still got.

I just get out of the station when I see this mook walking along the sidewalk. He's about my height and build, but he couldn't be more obvious if you gave him a dancing monkey. He already had his hand in his pocket where his piece bulged just he was happy to see someone.

Come to think of it, I should move mine, the back under the jacket is less obvious if you don't have a job. The mook stands in front of the bank watching traffic. It's still an ugly bank. Now he's running across the road and kicking the door of the bank open. He shoots the guard and shoots the ceiling.

What a mess, who stops a bank robbery to watch TV?

I do. My headache gets worse as he grabs the money and runs down the road toward me. A guard pops out of the bank with a gun, so I draw mine and shoot him first. I can't let him shoot me in the back, even if that me is a mook who deserves to get shot in the back.

" Get away from me," I say as I approach. I'm not thinking that I still have a gun in my hand and next thing he drops the bags and pops between the eyes.

I'm sitting in an empty station shaking like I'd gone cold turkey. Shaking that that mook got the drop on me. He might be me, but I wasn't going to let that stop me from finishing him off the next time I saw him. I headed out the door and saw I wasn't the only one following the guy. The guy in front of me discretely moved his piece to the back of his pants and I knew. He was the other me. I mean the other me that got shot by the first other me.

"Hey," I yell to the first other me, "watch the guard, he's a hero type."

You'd figure that I'd be thankful for a little advice, but this other me must be nervous or something, cause he turns and starts shooting at me, so of course I shoot back. Both of us, at ourselves. There's screaming, and a guard comes out and plugs me.

I'm sitting in an empty station shaking like I'd gone cold turkey, but I'm up and out of that chair hopping mad. What kind of mook shoots himself when he's just giving good info? Me, that's who, but I got it figured now. I shoot the me and the other me and that first other me and run into the bank. Only now with all the shooting the element of surprise is kind of blown. I'm in a full-blown shoot out with the guards when I see that kid miss the catch and the ball hit my head.

Then the guard's bullet finishes the job.

I'm sitting in an empty station shaking like I'd gone cold turkey. I swear and shoot the walls and kick the chair. What a ugly mugged up farce of a job this is! I'm still

242

smashing things when a mook me shows up in the chair. I slug him good, but he's still loaded and all my bullets are in the wall.

I'm sitting in an empty station shaking like I'd gone cold turkey and watch while two of me are fighting over in one corner of the station. The only thing I can do is shoot them both and get out on the road. I figure I'll run the other way, but there's a gun battle on the street and I don't want to take any bullets to the back.

I'm sitting in an empty station shaking like I'd gone cold turkey while dozens of me are fighting and shooting it out. I hear more gunfire on the street, so I head down the tunnel. Maybe none of me have thought of the tunnel yet.

One, but a bullet takes care of me. I figure I need to get to the ball game and catch that ball. I hear gunfire behind me and run faster, but I can't out run a bullet.

I'm sitting in an empty station shaking like I'd gone cold turkey.

I'm sitting in an empty station shaking like I'd gone cold turkey.

I'm sitting in an empty station shaking like I'd gone cold turkey.

GRANDFATHER'S PEN

Alister counted six ceiling tiles one way, eight the other. That was the extent of his known world after the crash. Straps, blocks, tubes and for all he knew, fuzzy handcuffs held him frozen on his bed. At irregular intervals a face loomed over him; a professionally cheerful nurse, or his perpetually morose fiancée.

Bekami had defied her family six months ago to get engaged to a poor, white author. They apparently were split on whether the poverty or his whiteness was worse. She'd given up her position as a literal princess to be at his side. Now he was reduced to a twitch of his right hand or blinking, and she had nowhere to go.

If he could have talked, he would have told her to go back to her mother in their home country and beg for forgiveness. The only communication possible was answers to yes/no questions, and Bekami never asked if she should stay.

Tears dripped on his face as Bekami ran her fingers across his cheek. They'd established he could feel her touch in that one location. "Alister, I've finished packing up the apartment." "Your mother has helped me move into the room over the garage. Everything is safely stored in the garage. Your father said he could park the car outside until winter." More tears and she leaned closer to brush his cheek with her lips. "I'll come back soon."

Uneven footsteps carried her out of the room.

I don't need anything from that apartment. It isn't like there is anything I can use now that I'm the next best thing to brain in a jar.

The view of the ceiling blurred until he blinked away the tears gathered in his eyes.

***

Bekami slipped something cool and heavy into his right hand.

244

"Your grandfather's pen."

He ran his fingers along it, awkwardly, barely able to grip the bronze cylinder. He'd always been fascinated by the carvings, sometimes he saw them as writing, other times as the outline of a dragon. At one time it must have been a fountain pen, but now it looked more like a roller ball. He'd never figured out how to open it to replace the cartridge, so it sat as a talisman while he struggled with deadlines and writer's block.

That wouldn't be an issue now.

"Never give up."

For a moment Bekami sounded like his grandfather. She leaned over him, brown eyes glistening. He wished she'd smile again. Since the break with her family, her beautiful dark skin had stilled. After a kiss on the cheek, she left.

A nurse came to do things which Alister was sure would have humiliated him if he could feel them. As a final action, he slid a pad of paper beneath Alister's right hand.

"See if you can write something with that pen. Wouldn't it be nice to be able to communicate with your girl?"

Alister couldn't tell him the pen didn't work, had never worked as long as he'd owned it.

***

Zcaxilq crouched on the mountain top peering down at the clouds covering the world as far as he could see. The dragons had legends about the Roof of the World. Air so thin even dragon wings couldn't grip it. Air cold enough to douse the fire in his heart.

The full moon mocked him with its silver light, showing a world in black and white, but not one he could trust. It had no dimension, no scale.

If no one had ever returned from the Roof of the World, there would be no legends. Zcaxilq crept forward to peer over the drop. Was the ground at the bottom of this mountain covered with dragon bones? There was only one way to find out.

He scuttled back from the edge and sighed. His body betrayed his heart. Maybe when the sun came up.

***

The rustle of paper woke him, and he forced his eyes open. He'd never imagined the weight of eyelids would tire him.

"You wrote this?" Bekami held a paper where he could see it, covered in barely legible scratches. Paralysis had done nothing to improve his handwriting.

One blink for 'yes', two for 'no'. What did he do for 'I don't know'?

"I know a legend about the Roof of the World." Bekami caressed the paper. "It is supposed to be a place of testing."

Alister blinked once, hoping she'd say more. Instead she repositioned the paper beneath his hand, then kissed him on the way out of the room.

His hand ached, but he didn't dare relax it for fear of dropping the pen. Could he continue the story? He'd once joked he'd die with a pen in his hand.

The pen lay heavy in his hand, the paper's slight roughness lay beneath, but he couldn't bring them together.

Don't worry about the mechanics, think about the story.

***

Zcaxilq stared into the fog. If he turned his head, he couldn't see the end of his tail. Day teased at him. He couldn't remember the shape of the drop. His heart pounded in him and his flame quailed. No echo returned from his bellow of frustration.

Even a dragon's limbs grew stiff from inaction. Zcaxilq paced the tiny area at the peak of the mountain.

246

Six paces one way, eight the other. No matter how he strained his eyes he couldn't make out the slightest shadow of anything below the peak.

Though he spread his wings and flapped, they gave no lift. His legs refused to carry him over the edge. Who knew what lay below? He might die, or worse, he might not. Could he face the prospect of lying broken and crippled at the bottom of the mountain?

***

A new face loomed over him.

"I'm Dr. Jeding. I was asked to consult on your case. You have paralysis caused by a compression of the spinal cord." A clipboard of writing worse than his fluttered briefly within his line of sight. She flipped a page and tried to draw something, but her pen didn't work.

"You mind if I borrow yours?" The pen slipped out from between his fingers. The doctor raised an eyebrow when no ink came from his pen, but she carefully put back in his hand. "I thought they said you were writing messages. I'll come back when I find a pen that works."

Bekami came as Dr. Jeding left. She lifted the paper from beneath Alister's hand, took the top sheet of the pad, then replaced it.

"You've written more." She read it, her mouth moving as she worked through the scratches. "I want to know the end of the story."

So do I.

"Your mother and father say hello, but…" Bekami's tears dripped on him. "They are so scared. I am too." Bekami closed her eyes and shuddered. "But I can't leave you alone to face this."

She leaned down to kiss him, her lips drifting down over his like silk over sandpaper. The taste of spices tickled his tongue. Hissing from his oxygen was the loudest sound in the room.

After she'd fled the room, Alister tried moving his lips, but he couldn't tell if he was successful.

The doctor returned to sketch a picture of a hose pinched by rocks, at least that's what it looked like to Alister.

"It may be possible to relieve the pressure on your spinal cord surgically." Dr. Jeding moved the drawing away. "You could recover some, or even all of your control over your body." Her blue eyes held his, unwavering. "Or you could die. Or nothing might change."

She rubbed her eyes. "I wish I could tell you the odds were in your favour, but to be perfectly honest, you get dealt a completely random card. I will explain the procedure to your girlfriend. You can talk it over with her. Don't take too long. The longer we wait, the less likely improvement becomes. Do you understand?"

Alister blinked once. She nodded and left.

***

A tiny red bird landed on Zcaxilq's claw.

"You been here long?" Its voice was musical.

"I'm not sure." Zcaxilq lifted his foot to bring the bird up closer to his eye.

"Don't stay too long, it only gets harder."

"Why am I here?"

"Why isn't important here." The bird preened its feathers. "Only what you choose." It flitted away, gone in an instant into the fog.

As the moon rose, the fog lowered into the clouds below him. Stars winked at him as they wheeled overhead. If they were any closer, he might be able to hear them singing.

***

"The doctor talked to me." Bekami looked carved from obsidian; liable to shatter if bumped. "What do you want?" She shook her head and wiped tears from her eyes. "Sorry. Do you want the surgery?"

248

Alister blinked once.

"You sure?"

He blinked again. He was lying to himself. If he'd been hooked up to the machines the movies show, the beep of his heart would have been a vibrato tone.

"I will be here for you." Bekami leaned to kiss him. He tried to move his lips, but she straightened with no sign she'd noticed. After taking the top sheet of paper from the pad, she left.

***

"You're a brave man." The nurse prepped him for surgery. When he tried to grip the pen, she laughed. "They're saying it's your magic pen. It doesn't work for anyone else." A bit of tape wrapped his hand holding the pen in place. "You need all the magic you can get."

As they wheeled him out of the room, he winced at the lights, but refused to close his eyes before he needed to.

The operating theatre buzzed with activity, people talked to each other in what might have been esoteric code. Firm hands moved him to a board and flipped him onto his front. Now his view was limited to two tiles each way.

"We're going to put you to sleep now." A new voice spoke to him and friendly darkness absorbed him before the end of the sentence.

***

Zcaxilq roared up at the moon, breathing in the thin air and using it to stoke the fire in his chest until he thought he might burst into flame. Before he could think, Zcaxilq ran to the edge and threw himself from the top of the mountain.

The air rushed past him, too thin to hold him up, then he reached the clouds and the world shrank to a space smaller than his body. Wide spread wings trembled as the air grew thicker, but at his speed he couldn't do much more than catch the barest edge of the wind.

He sent a burst of flame out ahead of him as he broke through the cloud into deep blackness. Live or die, whoever was below would know he'd crossed the sky.

***

The lights of the room were dim, but Alister could count six tiles one way, eight the other. He didn't try to move, being awake was enough for the moment. The back of his neck ached with cold, his cheek warmed beneath a soft hand.

"You're awake." Bekami's voice caressed him. "They've strapped your head and shoulders in place, you won't be able to move. Dr. Jeding said you needed to heal a bit first." Her fingers brushed over his lips. "I'm holding your left hand."

Bekami giggled. "Your grandfather's pen is still taped to the other one. It's too dark to see if you wrote anything."

A sensation came to him from far away, he couldn't even be sure if it was his own body. Pressure, warmth. Alister sorted through what he was feeling, then tried sending something back. Impossible to know if he'd achieved anything.

Until Bekami gasped. Her face appeared over him; he couldn't see anything in the gloom except the light of her smile.

"You moved!" The squeeze on his hand came through clearer and it was easier to squeeze back. Tears dripped onto his face.

***

Zcaxilq laughed as he glided through the night air then did a roll out of sheer joy. He sent out a blast of fire and streaked across the sky like a comet.

WHERE OR WHEN

First published online by Havok 2021

Dion and the Belmonts, #3 on the charts, January 26th, 1960

Hank wandered about the empty house, bored out of his mind, from the kitchen with a fridge full of meals, to the tv showing only reruns, to the shelf of books he'd read a dozen times, then all over again. He'd expected having his parents away for five weeks would give him a sense of ecstatic freedom. He'd been wrong.

Freedom was dull.

A knock on the front door broke him out of his funk. He answered it. "Hello?"

A girl in cargo pants and a checked flannel shirt tied up showing her midriff beamed at him. "Hi. I'm Jenny. My last hitch dropped me in this neighborhood. Didn't tell me it was the back end of nowhere."

"Hank." He put out his hand. Her grip sent warmth up his arm into his brain. "Yeah, life can be deadly boring here in the sticks. Like, it takes half a day to get to a cinema, then it's playing some John Wayne flick."

"He isn't much to look at." The girl tilted her head. "Though the horse he rides is nice."

"There you go. I'd never have known about the horse." Hank's heart beat frantically. His brain threw random things toward his mouth. "Hitching rides can be dangerous. I hope you know how to defend yourself." *What am I saying?*

"Yeah, there are a few creeps, but I know how to deal with them."

"A little kung fu?"

Jenny's laugh echoed musically, sending heat through his face.

"I grab, squeeze, and twist." She rolled her eyes. "Not the safest when he's driving." Then she smiled in a way that made Hank want to melt. "Can I have my hand back?"

"Oh, right." Hank let go. *Now what? I don't want her to leave yet.* "There's a bug on your shoulder. Hold still." He leaned forward and flicked the insect away. Close enough to smell the apple scent of her hair, he moved his face a fraction of an inch and let his lips brush across hers. She tasted of apples and honey. *What?* He braced himself for the slap he deserved.

As he pulled back, it struck him. *I've tasted her lips before.*

"What's wrong?" Jenny looked more concerned than upset.

"Déjà vu." Hank rubbed his head. "Like I've done this before."

"I know." Jenny's eyes lit up. "But I can't remember where or when…"

***

Hank wandered about the empty house, listlessly waiting for an idea of what to do. He'd expected having his parents away for five weeks would give him a sense of ecstatic freedom. He'd been wrong.

Freedom was dull.

His feet carried him to the door, and he opened it to discover a girl on the step her hand raised to knock. Her eyes widened, then she smiled.

"Hello." Hank smiled back. *Say something, keep her here.* "You like the movies?"

"Yeah, sure. The last one I watched had a nice horse in it. I'm Jenny." She put out her hand. Hank took it, and its warmth traveled up his arm to blow a few breakers in his brain.

"There's a bug on your shoulder. Hold still." He leaned forward to flick the insect away then—as if he'd done such things all his life—moved closer and kissed her, his hand holding the back of her neck. She tasted of apples and honey.

252

As he pulled back, it struck him. *I've tasted her lips before.*

"What's wrong?" Jenny looked more concerned than upset.

"It's like we've done this before." Hank rubbed his head.

"I know." Jenny smiled at him. "But I can't remember where or when..."

***

Hank wandered about the empty house, the hairs on the back of his neck on end. He'd expected having his parents away for five weeks would give him a sense of ecstatic freedom. He'd been wrong.

It actually felt a little creepy.

Something was going to happen. *How do I know that? A* knock on the door interrupted his thoughts. He strode to the door and threw it open. A girl stood on the step, smiling at him. Hank pulled her to him and kissed her. She tasted of apples and honey.

He pulled back and frowned.

"This has happened before."

"I know..."

His heart raced, something felt wrong. *Who is she? What does she want?*

***

Hank paced the empty house, his heart pounding. He'd expected having his parents away for five weeks would give him a sense of ecstatic freedom. He'd been wrong.

It was terrifying. He ran to the kitchen to find a knife, then waited heart pounding for the dreaded knock on the door.

***

"Jenny, you can't keep doing this." Paula tried to pull her back from the time machine. "You're changing the timeline. Each time, your knowledge of his death the next day taints his memory further."

"Nonsense." Jenny yanked her arm away. "There is no theory to support that." She looked at Paula's worried expression and sighed. "Last time."

"You have to let him go. It's been twenty years."

"I've never made another connection like that. I don't know where or when I ever could."

The settings were already in the computer. Jenny sat down and put the helmet on, then pushed the button to send her mind back to ride her body from twenty years back.

***

Jenny gave the driver the finger. How was she going to get a ride from here? Odd, the street looked familiar. She shivered. *Just déjà vu. Knock on a door and ask for a ride.* Hitching her pack into place, Jenny walked along the road to the first house. Her hand brushed across her lips, and she smiled. *What am I doing? I should get out of here.* The déjà vu struck harder, and Jenny tried to leave.

Her legs refused to obey. They carried her to the door.

"Oh, well. Now that I'm here…" Jenny raised her hand to knock.

THE DEVIL'S IN THE DETAILS

Meelchubak hated breathing. The way air moved through the human's body, marking its foolish emotions. It anchored it to the flesh of this world, forcing it to suffer until the humans were in greater pain than it.

His human, who called himself 'Steve' walked at a not-quite-brisk pace, matching his speed to the crowd around him, just as his grey suit and slightly askew tie fit in with the rest of the business crowd. Stopping at a large window, Steve checked his tie then straightened it and tugged at his jacket in a vain attempt to make the cheap cloth hang like it was a thousand-dollar suit.

Head up, shoulders back, you've got this. Steve sauntered into his office full of confidence in total control, only to bump into a woman carrying hot coffee, soaking both them in scalding liquid, his attempt to help her earned a slap and "I'm going to file—."

Steve sweated through the armpits of his shirt and buttoned the jacket with shaking hands. It wouldn't happen. It wouldn't. After a heavy sigh, he covered the last half-block to his job with the doleful gait of a man going to his execution. At the door into the room full of cubicles, he stopped and checked for people.

"Don't stop in the doorway." A woman spoke sharply from behind him. He muttered an apology and kept his head down as he walked to his desk.

"Jansen." The almost shout made Steve hunch over, his gut churning. "Get in here." Mr. Beldy, Hell take anyone who called him baldy by mistake, glossy pate or not, stepped back into his office.

By the time Steve slouched his way over to the supervisor's door, Mr. Beldy had seated himself behind the desk where he could glower out the door.

"Don't just stand there." Mr. Beldy deepened his frown. "Time's wasting away." He waved a stack of papers in his hand. "You call this a report? The numbers are all wrong." They made a rustle as he tossed them in Steve's direction. "I sent you an email with the correct figures since clearly you are incapable of basic accounting. The revised report will be on my desk before you go home." His beady eyes fixed on Steve's breaking down the human's will.

"Yes, sir." Steve's breath came painfully ragged, his heart banging erratically. Having him die in Mr. Beldy's office would be too much to ask for.

You can't breathe, your heart is stopping. He fell to the floor in agony. The manager yelled for someone to drag the corpse away.

The human turned and lurched out of the office to his cubicle, placed where Mr. Beldy could keep an eye on him. Not a keystroke or phone call happened without his knowledge.

The supervisor waited until Steve was almost sitting before yelling at him again.

"Get in here and clean up your mess."

Steve dragged himself back to the office to pick up the scattered pages then drop them into the shredder. The short walk back to his desk made him pant like he'd been running for the bus.

Everyone knows he's using you to rob the company blind. Meelchubak hissed, *when someone catches the mistake, you're the one they'll blame.*

Steve picked up the letter opener, the one he used in his daydreams to stab Mr. Beldy in the throat. His hands trembled as he gripped it tightly enough to pop his joints painfully.

Do it, go in to ask a question, then slash his throat.

Steve stood and hid the knife by his leg.

He walked into the office, not giving the bald man a chance to move. The knife slid through the man's double chin, red blood poured out.

256

His thumb ran along the dull edge of the blade. It wouldn't cut butter, never mind a throat. Steve went to the washroom and splashed cold water on his face, then returned to his desk.

The email waited for him, so he copied the numbers to a spreadsheet before the email disappeared. He painstakingly recreated the report with the new numbers. Each time Beldy fixed the numbers, he grew more brazen. What started as a tenth of a percent on the exchange rate of a million dollars for pounds became a half point. 'The devil's in the details,' his father-in-law always said. This detail could send Steve to prison. The pain in Steve's stomach grew to the point where Meelchubak became curious. He'd never had someone die of a busted gut before.

You're going to die, and they'll blame you, your family won't get the pension. A policeman knocked on the door to tell Heidi he'd died. Then the letter arrived saying he'd embezzled money and she had to pay it back, hundreds of thousands—"

He moaned and saved the new numbers, sending them to Mr. Beldy's printer.

***

At home, Steve put on his fake face and smiled as he walked through the door.

"Daddy, look at this." A young boy waved a math test in the air.

"John, give your dad a chance to sit down." Heidi laughed and tousled her son's hair.

Steve collapsed in his chair in the living room and helped John climb up in his lap. He would have a nauseating warm glow in him the whole time the human spawn spent explaining each question on the test and asking for help with the ones he'd missed.

Push him down, snap his neck. It would be so easy. They are fragile these young ones. Images of death and horror bounced away from Steve. Nothing Meelchubak did ever got through to Steve as long as the child was with him. It loathed the spawn as much for that as for the warmth easing the agony in the human's gut.

Meelchubak's agony grew worse, so desperately he whispered suggestions, each more horrendous than the last, at the human's unhearing soul. With every word Steve ignored, Meelchubak squirmed. Misery was his job, and failure meant pain. His boss wasn't nearly as understanding as Mr. Beldy.

He's going to miss you when you're in jail.

Steve stiffened in his chair, then hugged his son tighter.

The children mocked John. "Your Dad's a crook. Loser." He became hard and bitter silencing his tormenters with his—"

The human spawn twisted out of the embrace and dashed away.

He doesn't love you, love is a lie. You'd be better off without them. He drove along a curving coastal road in a luxurious car.

"Supper's ready." The woman poked her head into the living room.

Meelchubak dutifully tried to make it taste of ashes, but Steve ate, as he always did, savoring the first bite, then cleaning his plate mechanically. Fortunately, the spawn had to go to bed soon after.

The TV show Steve watched after supper while the spawn was washed, then bribed into sleeping, featured an accountant slowly being cornered after embezzling from his company. The grinding in Steve's gut returned as the man in the show became ever more desperate. It ended with a satisfying violent clash which left most of the people dead or dying.

That's going to be you. Go buy a gun, get lots of ammunition. Don't wait for them to catch you. Steve

258

marched into the office to shoot Baldy, then his uncaring fellow slaves. Blood spattered the industrial gray room. Taste of iron on his lip—".

Steve jumped up and ran to the bathroom, barely making it before vomiting up his dinner into the toilet. Even more deliciously he spent the time wishing he was dead.

That's right, no one cares. He swerved into a tanker truck on the highway creating an explosion which killed dozens of people. He bought a gun and loaded it. The barrel tasted of steel and oil.

"Dear, are you all right?" Heidi knocked on the door, concern oozing out of her voice and banishing the thoughts of self-destruction.

"I must have caught a bug." Steve wiped his mouth, then rinsed it out before flushing the toilet. His clothes were covered with puke, so he stripped them off, vaguely embarrassed at wearing only his underwear on the ground floor of his home.

When he opened the door, the woman took the reeking bundle.

"You go upstairs and take a shower. I'll bring up some ginger ale for you."

The icky warm glow burned away his embarrassment.

How many times are you going to make her clean up after you?

Meelchubak tried to break through the man's mewling gratitude, but if it had eyes, they'd be rolling.

The shower did far too much to settle Steve's nerves. He went from thinking how to kill himself to other ways of extricating himself from the mess. Quitting his job was high on the list. Meelchubak gleefully took the reins.

Steve explained to the boy they had to move away because the bank was taking it back. Heidi took her son and moved home. Steve sat in tent under the bridge holding a shard of glass. The life insurance would keep

them comfortable. Quick is better than slow. It replayed
the truck, the explosion, the outpouring of grief, but then
the woman marrying someone else, the spawn forgetting.
Interspersed were scenes of the police knocking the door to
drag him away in handcuffs. The family in court, visiting in
prison, the divorce papers.

The wheels spun in the human's mind. Meelchubak's
manifestation in hell - the endlessly spinning cycle of
despair, anger, guilt then despair again was so satisfying,
and once started became impossible to stop. This wheel
carried no joy, no hope. The demon laughed in glee.

Steve lay on the bed with the towel still wrapped about
his waist holding his head as Meelchubak made the
thoughts spin ever faster and more out of control. Tears
leaked out of the man's eyes and his breath caught as he
tried to silence his sobs.

Failure, weak, coward, fool. You can't even die to
save them. Steve mouthed the words as Meelchubak put
them in his mind.

"What's wrong?" The wife put a glass on the bedside
table and sat beside him, stroking his hair.

Don't say anything, she'll hate you. She threw the
glass at him then stormed out passing the door with a
screaming boy under her arm.

"I'm in so much trouble." Steve choked on the words.
Meelchubak threw shame, guilt, humiliation to silence
them, but to no avail. All its work had pushed the human to
the point he had nothing to lose. The whole sordid story
tumbled out. The wife never stopped stroking his hair as
Meelchubak shrieked.

Kill her, then kill the boy, keep them from suffering
because of you. Steve reached up and wrapped his hands
around her neck. Why hadn't he done this earlier? So
easy—.

Steve lifted his hand as Meelchubak panted with
desire, but his fingers caressed her cheek.

260

"I love you." Steve smiled as Meelchubak cringed. "I should have told you earlier."

Steve couldn't be hurt, couldn't be pushed. The sickening warmth slowed the whirling thoughts. The human shoved everything away and clung to his wife.

"Daddy, did you have a nightmare?" The spawn tottered in, dragging a ragged teddy bear. He climbed on the bed and hugged Steve before putting the toy in his hands. "You hold Albert. He keeps the monsters away."

Reject it, throw it away, punch the kid, what does he know?

Meelchubak's words burned away in the glow coming from the bear. Steve hugged the bear and his son.

"Thank you," he whispered into the spawn's hair. "It's working." Steve carried his son back to his bed and tucked the already sleeping boy in, with the teddy bear wrapped in his arm. "That's right, you charge him up again for me."

"Why don't you call my dad? He works in a different division, get his advice." Heidi spoke from the hallway.

Disaster, the old man hates you, this will make it worse. Be strong, deal with it yourself. Be a man. The stern father ordered Steve out of the house, never to return.

Steve's heart skipped a beat, and Meelchubak tried to make it a full-blown heart attack.

Then he brushed the spawn's hair, and his heart slowed. Last time they visited his father-in-law they'd watched a movie. 'Courage is being afraid, and still doing what is right.' That was the moral.

Meelchubak wanted to gag but had no throat.

"Can you call him, ask him to come over?" Steve took his wife's hand, interlocking his fingers with hers. "I'll get dressed and come downstairs."

Meelchubak cursed, shouting that his father-in-law would be disgusted and have him fired, but it couldn't break through the human's determination.

The demon gave up as the doorbell rang. Disaster, punishment, pain. The world was supposed to be a dark and ugly place, as close to hell as demons like Meelchubak could make it. Failure was not tolerated, nothing was tolerated, the only goal was for others to suffer more. Meelchubak kicked itself from the wheel. It couldn't afford fail. Exquisite suffering threatened his being.

Steve stood straight and strong, accusing the evil, giving evidence... There would be a long investigation, plenty of opportunity to create anxiety.

Meelchubak wasn't defeated yet. It told itself that over and over, whimpering as Steve took a long deep breath then started down the stairs.

Damn, but Meelchubak hated breathing.

Tim Cratchit's Christmas Carol

Tim sat in the pew next to his father on Christmas day and listened to the familiar story and joined in with the Christmas Carols. He knew all the words to all the verses without needing a book. That was one of the things he liked about himself. His memory was better than anyone he knew. Not that he knew very many people.

As usual people stared at him as he stood on the pew and sang out the hymns with his raspy voice, stopping once in a while to cough. The other worshipers continued to watch him after the service was complete and he walked out with his father, using his crutch.

"I'm sorry so many people stare at you." His father put a warm hand on Tim's shoulder.

"Perhaps they would see me and like to think of who made blind men see and lame beggars walk." *Except for me.* Tim put on his best smile. It wasn't his father's fault Tim was weak and lame, though Tim didn't feel broken. He had always been this way as long as he could remember. It was just a part of him, even if it was the part everybody saw first.

His father lifted him to his shoulder, and they walked home from the church singing silly songs. This was one of the very few times in the year Tim had his father to himself and he wished it lasted longer. For this time Tim was just his father's son, not Tiny Tim the cripple who caused so much worry by his weakness.

They reached their home a tenement in a long line of tenements. A small space which was kitchen, dining room and living room and two even smaller rooms where his parents and he, Peter, and Martha slept, along with a bathroom, though the water was most often cold.

They sat together and shared in the Christmas goose, and even more importantly the Christmas pudding. The pudding was his mother's greatest worry and proudest achievement. As every year his father sampled the pudding with a face which told them he was savouring the quality of this year's offering.

"Oh, a wonderful pudding. It is the best one yet." His father said and his mother sighed in relief.

They ate the grand pudding in a very short time. Then it was time to clear up and gathered around the fire. His father poured the steaming liquid from the pitcher into the few cups that could hold it.

"A Merry Christmas to us all, God Bless us."

The family echoed the sentiment, but the breath caught in Tim's throat, and he spoke after rest.

"God bless us everyone." His family looked at him, his parents' eyes shining with almost shed tears.

His father cleared his throat. "Mr. Scrooge! I give you Mr. Scrooge, the founder of the feast!"

"The founder of the feast indeed," Tim's mother cried. "I wish I had him here. I'd give him a piece of my mind."

Tim shrank into his chair by the fire beside his father. Christmas was the one magical day when a rare joy suffused his family. The one day they ate all together and could eat their fill. But this day always held this same argument which cut through the joy like a cold knife and stole the warmth from Tim's heart.

Tim drank the toast, but didn't care about it. Scrooge was the ogre of the family, simultaneously the reason they had anything at all to eat and the cause of their poverty. Yet the icy thought of Scrooge couldn't hold back the joy of Christmas for long.

His father mentioned that there was a perhaps a position for Peter, which would pay a small portion of the measly salary Scrooge gave Tim's father for his work on every day but his one. They laughed and joked. Martha talked about her apprenticeship at the milliners, and how she had seen a countess and a lord just a few days before.

264

The thought of Mr. Scrooge fled from Tim's mind as he laughed and teased with the others.

He looked forward to next year's Christmas, but the thought of another year before the day made Tim weary. No one would talk about it to him, but he'd heard whispered conversation about whether Tim would survive to see another Christmas.

The idea of dying didn't bother Tim. His family would be less poor with him gone. He suspected they might cry a little, but children died and life moved on.

These glum thoughts accompanied him to his bed and tried to keep him awake, but his weariness dragged him into sleep.

***

The next morning Tim lay in bed. He had little to get up for. It would be only himself and his mother to drink weak tea and nibbled on the remnants of their Christmas feast.

The noise from the kitchen finally made him crawl from beneath his blankets and hop with his crutch to find out what was going on.

"Hey, sleepy head." His father ruffled Tim's hair. You're getting up awfully late on Christmas Day.

Tim stared at his father while he took his seat by the fire. Had he slept a whole year through for it to be Christmas again?

"You don't look quite awake yet," his mother handed him a cup with tea it had the slightest hint of sweetness which he only tasted on Christmas Day.

Surely his family would tell him if he'd slept a year away. Not that he cared much for the rest of the year. He would cease his questioning and enjoy this second Christmas.

The morning went as Christmas morning always did with them peeling potatoes to boil for their feast. They chattered about the feast and the pudding to come.

There came a banging on their door and a man stood with the largest bird Tim had ever seen.

"Turkey for you." The man looked as puzzled as the Cratchits. He handed them a note which simple wished the Cratchits a Merry Christmas.

Tim's mother shook herself and started giving orders. "We'll have to work hard to have this ready to go to the baker, to be cooked in time for supper. Won't Martha be surprised."

The flurry of activity filled the tiny home with joy and Tim soaked it all in. Such was the feast this day that his mother didn't baulk at a toast to Mr. Scrooge and there was no argument to suspend the celebration.

Tim's father carried him to bed as he'd all but fallen asleep in his chair. Tim wondered what he would think if he woke to Christmas yet again in the morning.

He didn't, the day was as dull and dreary as any he'd lived through, until his father arrived home with the oddest look on his face, like he'd woken to find the sun rising in the west.

"You will never believe this." His father fell into a seat. "But Mr. Scrooge has raised my salary this day and offered other things I can scarce bring myself to relate they are so strange."

The family buzzed with excitement and wonder. This was better than a second Christmas. Tim sat in his chair and soaked it all in. The year stretched ahead of him like a shining road. Perhaps he would live to see another Christmas after all.

GANYMEDE FARMS

Jack came in from burying the last cow and saw the flyer on the kitchen table. At first, he thought it was for a vacation and almost threw it in the recycler. He noticed the back just before he let it go and took it over to the table and sat down. He was still sitting there when his wife and partner in the farm returned from town.

"I couldn't get the quota for the chickens," she said, "There's a new beef plant going up behind the Mart and they are going to grow chicken as well. I would never have thought that farming would be replaced by test tubes and factories."

"They can manufacture the meat cheaper than we could grow it, and they don't have to worry about disease killing off the herd."

"I suppose it's good for the environment, what's left of it." She sat down across from him. "We all have to make sacrifices."

It'd be nice if it weren't always the poor farmers making all the sacrifices."

"Isn't that the truth." She took the flyer out of his hand, "What's this?"

"It was just sitting here. It must have come with this morning's mail."

Jack stood and walked around the worn kitchen. It wasn't likely to be his much longer. His herd was gone, and without the permit to grow other livestock he wouldn't be doing much bill paying. The bank would have a 'bot here within the week.

"I don't know that we can afford to uproot ourselves and go into space," Marta said, "Even if we could sell this place, we'd have nothing left."

"They aren't asking for investors, Marta," Jack punched the button on the pseudo-caff machine and made a couple of cups. He put his on the table; then added a drop of milk to hers. "They want farmers who know animals. You know there aren't many of us left who work with real animals."

"But it's in space, we'd be living under a bubble."

"When was the last time we went further than town?"

"But the kids…"

"The kids have their own lives. They haven't done more that vid us for years."

"I don't know, Jack, my knees are what they used to be."

"The news lines say that the low gravity is easier on the old folks."

"But this is our home!"

Jack put his hand over hers.

"You know it won't be for much longer. Without the cattle or even the chickens the collection 'bots will be here in a week."

Marta put her head on the table and started crying. Jack put his hand on here shoulder. Even after forty years of partnership, he still didn't know what to do with her tears.

They showed up at the spaceport with their bags packed to the last gram. Jack had spent hours walking through the house vidding everything before putting his print to the paper that turned it all over to the bank. All they owned was what was in the tiny bags they were allotted.

They had two days to check in before the flight. They had to be frozen and stacked in the hold. Where they would stay until they arrived at Ganymede Station.

"Look," the young woman in white explained to Jack, "If you sign this rider on your ticket, it will allow us to cyber-copy you in the case of a malfunction. You'll be loaded into a 'bot. Some people just choose to go as cybers."

Jack looked at his hands and imagined them as metal tools. He shook his head.

"I don't know," he said, "I have a hard time imagining being a 'bot."

"I know," the young woman sighed, "people do, but the numbers are cruel. We'll load a couple of hundred people into the hold, and I'll tell you right now that at least five of them won't wake up. If they haven't cybered, then they're just gone. We promise that we won't bootleg your cyber. If you wake up, we'll wipe the backup, and you go on in the flesh."

"OK," Jack said, "I suppose it doesn't hurt."

"No, Sir," she said, "We'll take the cyber copy just as we freeze you. You won't feel a thing.

***

It was a strange thing indeed, Jack thought, to watch the cow bound across the pasture in low gravity. It didn't seem to bother Bessie any and she still gave top quality milk. Of course, the cow had never known anything but the light gravity so she had an advantage over Jack.

Jack was still getting used to everything about Ganymede Farms. The gravity was the least of it. Watching Jupiter hang over the horizon still filled him with awe. There were other adjustments he was making as well.

That reminded him. It was lunch; he'd better go see how Marta was doing with her chickens. He turned and spun his wheels a bit in the soft earth before he shot across the pasture.

Maybe if Marta was in the mood, they could do some polishing tonight.

MOASH THE WARRIOR

First published in 'Words on the Rocks' The Flin Flon Writers Guild 2015

Moash MacThane came to the tiny river that was the southern boundary of his holding. He tied the lead rope to a handy tree and began stripping off the battered armour that had served him so well in the months he had been gone. As each piece was removed, he turned it over in his hands, then placed it into a rough sack.

When he was standing as naked as the day he was born, the tall muscular man walked out into the river and lay down in the icy water. The water flowed past him and gradually cleansed him, body and soul. Lying on the smooth rocks he remembered the face of each person he had killed in the struggle to put the rightful King on the throne. When the last face had faded from the inside of his eyelids, Moash sat up and gasped in a huge breath of night air. He splashed to the shore and put some homespun clothes that had travelled in the bottom of his pack all this time. He tied the sack of armour and his claymore to the saddle of his horse, then picked up the lead rope of the cow that munched mindlessly on the grass by the tree. The returning hero led the beast across the river and up the hill.

It was a matter of minutes before he reached his home, and only a few more to settle the animals in the barn. He put the clanking sack in an empty stall, then walked to the door of his home. He stood at the door and took three deep breaths. Only then did he open the door and walk in.

"Well, it's about time you got home," Mae looked up from her spinning. "Did you remember the milk?"

"The new King gave me a cow," Moash said, "We'll have our own milk now."

"And who do you think is going to milk this cow?" Mae set the wool she was spinning down.

"The Princess showed me how to milk a cow."

"Did she now? And what does a Princess know of cattle?"

"She was living as a dairy maid while she was in hiding."

"So, what was the Prince being, a swineherd?"

"No, he was being schooled in some foreign land."

"Ah well, at least one of them will have some sense." She went over to the fire and stirred it up. "I kept your dinner warm. I was about to give it to the dogs, but you might as well have it." Moash sat in his chair. His son had built it to fit him perfectly. The heat from the fire warmed him to his bones. His wife plunked a bowl and a spoon in front of him, and he began to eat the savoury stew. A chunk of bread appeared at his elbow, and he used it to wipe clean the bowl. A tankard banged down at his other elbow and he took a long draw on the dark ale. The bowl had been refilled and more bread beside it when he put the empty tankard down with a sigh. He tucked into the stew and once again cleaned the bowl with the end of the bread.

"I've missed your cooking," he said.

"So that Prince has been skimping on feeding you?"

"No," Moash said, "but no palace cook can compare to you."

"Now you're just trying to get on my good side 'cause you forgot the milk."

"But..." Moash sighed, "Sorry, I should have stopped at Thomas' holding and picked up some milk."

"And a good thing you didn't or you would still be there telling tales while the dogs ate your supper."

She poured more ale into the tankard.

"Faugh, you smell like an ironmonger." She pushed a large iron kettle over the fire and put some more coal in. "Go draw some water for a bath."

"I bathed in the river," he said.

"Likely you did, and you may catch your death of the cold too, but if you want to sleep in my bed tonight, you'll bathe in warm water with soap." Moash got up and fetched the buckets from the corner and went out the door. When he returned, Mae had the wooden tub pulled out. By the time he had filled the tub, the kettle had boiled, and she poured the hot water in until the tub steamed. He stripped his clothes once more and stepped into the tub. He folded himself into the hot water and sighed as aches he hadn't known he had melted away.

"Couldn't anyone cut your hair in that army of yours?" Mae kneaded soap into his greying hair.

"Didn't have much time for that," Moash blinked as she poured water over his head to rinse his hair. She started scrubbing his back, tracing each new scar as she did.

"So many scars," she said quietly, "I swear you'll fall to pieces someday."

"It is what I do," Moash said just as quietly.

"Aye, but I don't need to like it." She slapped his back, then started scrubbing his arms and chest. He lay back in the tub and looked up at her. Her hair was all grey now, but her blue eyes could still see through a stone if they took a mind to.

"So," she said, "Is this one going to do any good?"

"He's better than most I guess." Moash stood up and used his hands to strip the water from his skin. Mae wrapped him in a thick wool blanket.

"Leave the water, Mae," he said, "You know what I need now."

"And what would that be?" she said smiling impishly.

"Tell me," he said, "Tell me everything that happened since I left."

"Well, Thomas's wife caught him spending her egg money..."

"No!"

"Yes, and she won't let him inside until he's paid every penny back..."

Moash sighed and let the stories of the people he loved flow into him and make him whole.

OUT OF DARKNESS

My children were running wild with anticipation. It seemed like there were hordes of them. I had stopped trying to count them. The desire to go on this outing would be enough to get even the most obstreperous on the bus. Whoever said that children were angels hadn't met my brood.

I laid the last layer of necessities in my bag and closed it up. I am old fashioned. No wheeled luggage for me. I liked to feel the weight at the end of my arm. I didn't need it, but it set me apart from the others. I climbed the steps of the yellow bus and sat behind the driver. He was sweating in the heat, or perhaps it was nerves. He was rolling his eyes like a steer being led to slaughter.

Whichever it was, he honked the horn quick enough when I tapped his shoulder.

The children screamed with excitement and ran toward the bus. They pushed and fought to get on, then continued their battle for the best seats. I saw a grossly fat boy deliberately sit on a waif thin girl. His smug grin turned to a pained grimace, then panic. I allowed myself a smile. She must have found some tender part. The boy lumbered away, and I saw her sit up and wipe her mouth. She saw me watching and gave me a cheeky grin. Clever girl; I would have to watch her.

An especially brave imp chose to claim the seat beside me. There was one on every trip who foolishly thought they could claim a part of my space. The others watched to see what I would do. I smiled and patted him on the head. He made the mistake of looking at me. They all do. His grin faded, then the rest of him until I was alone on my seat again.

The level of chaos on the bus dropped far enough that I tapped the driver on the shoulder again. He closed the door and shifted the bus into gear. I could hear the wailing

274

of those left behind. The children always wanted to know how far it was, though they would never dare ask. The truth was that I couldn't answer. Far didn't have any meaning where we were; neither did long. The ride felt like an eternity because it was a piece of eternity.

Yet it wasn't quite eternal. I felt the sudden heady pull of time and knew we had arrived. The driver lasted long enough to put the bus into park before entropy took over and he fell to pieces. The children poured off the bus into the light of the created world. Some of them couldn't hold themselves together in the time stream and vanished. Most managed to adapt and spread out into the world to explore and play.

The mortals that surrounded us were unaware of our arrival. A couple of the most sensitive wrinkled their nose at what might have been a smell of death. Even if they could see us, they wouldn't believe. We have been relegated to the status of fairy tales appearing in a certain class of fiction. I watched some fights break out between mortal children who had been playing peacefully. My children were quick learners.

I looked around the park and spotted the person I was looking for. They were always there; torturing themselves with their temptations. His desire oozed from his pores. I sat beside him and soaked it all in. The furtive looks, the aborted searches on the web, the fear that someone like him would find his own children, the envy of the ones who dared to act on their desires. I left him staring avidly at a little blonde child who played in the sand while two bigger children threw sand and punches at each other.

While the man clenched and unclenched his fists fighting either his desire or his fear, I sauntered over to a woman eating an ice cream while she watched the children play. I stood beside her and watched too. My children had thinned out. Causing strife was easy, but once it was done, it was done. There was no real sustenance to it. A punch, some tears and then it faded away. The ones who didn't learn that quickly faded away and learned that the trip back was much shorter than the journey here.

The real food was in the struggle to choose between desire and restraint. The woman beside me frowned as she saw one child, larger than the others, struggle to keep up. I glimpsed her view of herself in the mirror. Buried deep was the loathing for all the perceived imperfections; a wrinkle here, a bulge there. Even the ice cream she was eating tasted of both guilt and vanilla. The woman wanted to throw the cone away, but she was even more fearful of wasting food than eating it. The turmoil was delicious.

There was a disturbance on the other side of the playground. A tall thin woman was berating the man who had been watching the little girl. I could feel the waves of self-righteousness from where I stood. The ice cream woman gathered her children and took them protesting away. Her internal struggle over the sweet forgotten in fear for her children.

The waif like imp from the bus was standing to the side of the arguing pair. She saw me watching and shrugged then went back to her feast. She was more subtle than the others, but still had a lot to learn. The shouting match drew in others, and I heard the sound of sirens approaching. There would be plenty of drama, but it would vanish as quickly as it built.

I walked away from the park. The tiny blonde girl followed me.

"Why do you do it?"

"You know why," I said. I wanted to be anywhere but here, talking about this. She was new, probably on her first trip.

"I know what they tell us."

"It sustains us," I said.

"You don't need it," she said, "The light would sustain you."

276

"The light!" I said and choked on the word. For a brief moment I felt the cloying light that permeated everything. I felt the pull to let it in, and the fear of what it would reveal.

She shook her head sadly.

"It would set you free," she said. She reached out a hand as if she were going to actually touch me but stopped. The last thing I saw were the tears running down her face.

The familiar darkness and fire surrounded me. Others surrounded me sensing weakness. I growled and disemboweled one while I tore out the throat of another. The rest backed away, this time.

The girl was right, the light would set me free, after it opened all the shadowed depths of my being and cleansed it of the envy and pride. The mortals think hell is fire and brimstone, but it is worse than that. Hell is knowing what I could be, and what I have chosen to become.

AGGIE'S SWORD

First Published in 'Mythical Girls'

The chill of Dozmary Pool had penetrated far enough for Aggie to decide to get out. The unusual warmth of the English sun had sent Aggie paddling in the nearby pond. Her father was napping, the first rest he'd had in the months since the babies had come home. This picnic, away from squalling twin baby brothers and the constant urge to help, was to celebrate her move to Year 7 and a new school.

She splashed back to where she'd climbed into the pond, a microscopic bit of beach. Something stung her foot, and the surprise made her fall face first into the water. It tasted mossy, and not at all nice.

Sitting up, Aggie looked at her soaked shirt, now marked by blotches of green algae. She twisted her leg to inspect the bottom of her foot. A scratch more than a cut—not enough to wake her dad.

Aggie crawled back, feeling with her hands for whatever had toppled her. A long, narrow thing took shape beneath her fingers, with enough of an edge to make her wary. Another piece crossed the first, then the thing became cylindrical. She couldn't budge it from her kneeling position, so she stood one foot on either side of the round bit, got both hands around and heaved.

It wouldn't move, so she tried again, and it wiggled just a little. Once more then. The thing came up out of the water making a squelching noise. Her arms wouldn't stop lifting it until she held it high over her head, where it dripped stinking mud on her face and hair.

The sword—Aggie had watched enough movies to recognize it immediately—blocked the sun, and for the briefest second it looked as though it had flashed with brilliant light. Then the weight of the mucky sword made her arms tremble and she fell to her knees.

278

A croaking voice startled her. "Well it ain't a rock, but it'll do. Awfully foolish way to choose a leader if you ask me."

Aggie let the tip of the sword drop back into the water and looked around for the source of the voice. The only living thing besides her and her dad was a rather large toad, which jumped off into the grass as soon as she'd met its eyes. She shrugged and stood, wiping mud from her face, then limped toward the sand, holding her find with both hands, sticking it into the muck, stepping, moving the sword. Her foot hurt worse now.

At the shore, Aggie rinsed the mud from the sword and herself as best she could. Then she tossed the sword onto the grass and sat on the bank to push herself out of the water with her uninjured foot.

With most of the muck sloughed off the sword, Aggie could see it was plain, with no gems or anything else to relieve its utilitarian lines. She stood up and hopped toward her dad, using the sword to keep her balance. She puffed for breath, vowing again to exercise more and lose weight—or at least turn it into muscle.

"It's a sword, for Pete's sake, not a crutch." The same cranky voice came from the grass. The toad glared up at her.

"You going to carry me up the hill?" Aggie pointed at the toad with her free hand. *A talking toad? Maybe I've had too much sun.*

"That wouldn't be wise." The toad bobbed its head. "My apologies." It jumped along beside Aggie until she reached her still slumbering father. She dropped to the ground beside him and used a napkin from the basket to clean the cut, then wrapped another one around it, tying it on top of her foot.

"Am I really talking to a toad?" Aggie looked around for the toad but couldn't find it.

"If that's the strangest thing to happen, you'll be lucky." The voice came from further away this time.

"Who are you talking to?" Her dad woke up and stretched. He saw the sword in Aggie's hand and stared. "What on earth is that?"

"A sword. I stepped on it wading in the pond." She waved her hand at her bandaged foot.

"What do you plan on doing with it?"

"Well, I'm not throwing it back." Aggie ran her fingers along the flat of the blade. "Maybe someone at the museum will know more about it."

They packed up the remains of the picnic, with Aggie eating some of the food left over from earlier then tossing the rest into the tall grass.

"We'd just have to throw it out anyway," she said when her dad raised his eyebrow. He nodded, then picked up the basket with one hand and offered the other to Aggie. She lifted the sword in her left hand, then limped to the car with her dad's arm around her waist. He made her put the blade in the boot.

***

Their first stop was at a chemist's, to buy proper gauze and tape for her foot. With her shoes on, the cut hurt less, so she made her dad drive to the museum in Bodmin, where she carried the sword in to lay it on the desk where a woman stood arranging brochures.

"I'd like to talk to someone who can tell me more about this." Aggie tried not to giggle at the woman's wide eyes. Her name tag read Karina.

"May I?" At Aggie's nod, Karina picked up the sword and held it carefully while peering at the blade and hilt. "Doesn't look very old," she muttered. "Machined, not forged. The wrap on the hilt's too even."

In the woman's hands, under her inspection, the sword didn't look as real as it had dripping mud into the pond.

"I found it in Dozmary Pool."

"If this was Excalibur, you'd be the Queen of England." Karina grinned at Aggie. "I expect it's a movie prop. We've had our share of King Arthur movies here because of the legend." She put the sword down on the counter and handed Aggie a booklet. "You can keep it if you like, or leave it here."

"I'll keep it, thank you." Aggie put her hand on the sword.

"Careful," Karina said, pulling out a tag and writing on it. "Get too deep into the Legend of King Arthur and it will consume you. I've got three different history degrees, and I still want to learn more."

"Wow." Aggie picked the sword up, trying to emulate the way Karina had handled it. It felt right in her hand. "If I have questions later, can I call you?"

Karina wrote something on the back of the tag. "There's my email. Ask away. Maybe send me a picture of it when you've cleaned it up; I can hang that in the museum here. Keep the tag, it certifies I've looked at it and said it isn't something the Antiquities people need worry about." Karina walked with them back to the car. Aggie put the tag in her pocket and the sword in the boot.

"Thanks for your help." Aggie waved as she climbed into the car. As her dad put the car in gear, Aggie looked over at him. "Now we need to convince Mum to let me keep a four-foot sword in my room."

"Don't look at me. It's your sword." But from the look on her dad's face, he was already planning what to build to display the find.

***

Aggie had misjudged her dad. He'd bought her a book on King Arthur. A thick one with footnotes. The sword leaned against the corner of her room as she slogged through the book. Keeping her find entirely depended on reading through the tome. That was what Jenny had called it. Aggie looked at the book through the afternoon light with much more interest than the sword itself.

Jenny sat in the corner, her feet tucked up into what had to be the most uncomfortable position, reading her own book on Arthur. She flew where Aggie plodded. They were the perfect opposites, Jenny with her black belt in Taekwondo, Aggie with a belt that no longer made it around her waist. She could have gone on to compare hair, skin and everything else, but what was the point?

Jenny had welcomed Aggie the first day in Year 1 with a brilliant smile, as she had every year since. Six years later they were inseparable. Aggie only wished this extended to the others in the class. After Jenny's board-breaking demonstration no one bullied Aggie, but neither did they go out of their way to be friends.

"Aggie Farrier, you're moping again." Jenny's eraser bounced off Aggie's book. "The book isn't that hard. It isn't like you have to write a report."

"My dad keeps asking me what I've learned." Aggie stretched, holding the book tightly in her pudgy hands. Her toes had already been bruised when it slipped from her grip.

"Well, what have you learned?"

"Arthur was this kid who pulled a sword from a stone and became King, only no one can agree on what sword or what stone. The movies show him in armour, but the book says he lived way before armour like the knights wore was invented. He had a bunch of knights who went on quests and did all kinds of weird things."

"That's a start." Jenny grinned at her. "Think your mum would let us try cutting some water bottles out back?

"She's out cold with the twins, but Mrs. Hathway will throw a fit." The old woman was their neighbour on the council estate, who had no hesitation expressing her opinions on proper behaviour.

"It's Friday, she'll be at the pub a while yet."

"How do you know these things?" Aggie stood and put a bookmark in the book. It wasn't even close to the quarter mark. *Oh well, swinging the sword has to be more fun than reading.*

***

They filled bottles from the recycling bin with water and balanced them on a stump behind the house, the final remnant of what had been the last growing thing in the tiny backyard.

Jenny went first, as it was her idea. She swung the sword like a bat and launched the bottle into the gate to the alley.

"Oops. It looks easier on YouTube."

Aggie took the sword and tried to hold it like one of the diagrams in her book. Her fingers tightened and she stepped forward to slash at the bottle.

"You missed." Jenny giggled, then gasped as the top of the bottle slid away to land with a splash on the dirt. "I didn't think it was that sharp."

Aggie tested the edge with her thumb; still the not-quite-sharp it had been when she found it.

**

They spent the rest of the afternoon cutting bottles. Jenny got to the point of cutting them in two as they launched, but Aggie's strikes always looked razor-edged. She could slice a bottle into rings before it fell.

The slam of a door warned them Mrs. Hathway was home, so they cleaned up and returned to Aggie's room to study the sword more.

"You think it might actually be Excalibur?" Jenny ran her fingers along the blade.

"Right." Aggie snorted and stood it in the corner. "The museum lady said it was all the wrong shape and stuff."

"If it had looked real, what would have happened?"

"She would have kept it; there's some law or other. Dad looked it up."

"Agatha." The shout came from downstairs. "Can you help with the boys?"

"Sure, Mum." Aggie shrugged at Jenny. "I'll see you tomorrow."

"I have a tournament." Jenny packed away her books. "It's at the Rec, so you can come and watch if you want."

"I'll ask Mum."

**

After watching the twins all next morning, Aggie was allowed to head down to the Rec to cheer Jenny on.

People of all ages and shapes in white uniforms crowded the place. A couple of moms were talking about a rumour that the council housing had been sold. Aggie was tempted to stay and listen in, but she didn't want to miss Jenny's match. She found Jenny covered with red foam armour beside a mat. A girl on the far side wore blue. A wide smile lit up her ebony face as she trotted out onto the mat.

"Wish me luck," Jenny said. "She's *good*."

"You can take her." Aggie slapped the red armour.

Jenny flashed her a grin and went to meet her opponent.

They bowed to each other, then the round started. Aggie couldn't follow the flurry of kicks, but once in a while a scorer would hold up a red or blue card.

By the third round, they were tied and the crowd was cheering wildly. At the end of the round, the other girl landed a solid kick which sent Jenny staggering back onto her butt. The bell rang for the match. The other girl went over and helped Jenny up. Aggie ran out from her side.

"*C'est domage*, you fought well."

"I've never lost before." Jenny took a deep breath. "That was brilliant." She went into a discussion of the match, which lost Aggie within the first few words.

"I must go. My coach will wish to speak to me before my next match. My name is Lamkay."

"Jenny."

"Aggie."

The girls turned to look at her and she reddened.

"Lamkay, Aggie is my best friend." Jenny put a hand on Aggie's shoulder.

"I'm sorry you came out to see your friend lose."

"If Jenny isn't worried about it, I'm not going to. We'll look up your match and cheer you on." Aggie grinned at Lamkay.

"Right, you have to win now. I want to have been defeated by the champion." Jenny slapped Lamkay's back.

"I will do my best."

Aggie lost her voice before the end of the day. Lamkay won the championship and Jenny the B side tournament.

"Come back to my house for ice cream," Aggie begged them.

"Sure thing."

"Where do you live?" Lamkay's coach asked.

***

The four of them ended up in the coach's car to drive up to Aggie's house. She worried suddenly about her mum's reaction, but the twins were playing quietly and her mum was in a good mood. They took the ice cream out back.

"You're very good," Lamkay's coach said. "As I'd expect of someone from your school. Sensei Joe is a terrific instructor. I've been trying to convince Lamkay to join your school. She needs a different instructor to round her out, and since she moved here, it's much closer."

"So, should I join yours?" Jenny asked.

"You can, but better yet, just drop in to visit once in a while. Keep us on our toes."

"I will do as you ask, Sensei." Lamkay jumped up and nodded. "Now that I've seen how good Jenny is."

"Could I join too?" Aggie put a hand over her mouth, but glared at Jenny and Lamkay's giggles.

"Black belts should have more respect for learning." Sensei Mack's voice didn't get louder, but the giggling cut off and the girls blushed deep red.

"Taekwondo is expensive." Aggie's mum collected the dishes.

"She can come out for a few lessons before she has to pay," Jenny said. "I'll talk to Sensei Joe."

"We have some spare doboks; Lamkay will bring one by for her."

Next thing Aggie knew, they were teaching her the basic stance. It made her legs tremble, but Aggie bit her

286

cheek and endured. The praise of her friends, old and new, was better than ice cream. She had to wonder why she hadn't asked before.

***

The end of the summer vacation arrived, and Aggie walked to school. A block from her school, she saw a crowd of boys around someone on the ground. She jogged over, marvelling that she could move faster than a walk after just a couple of months. When she recognized Lamkay, her fists clenched.

"Back off, Ben—and your cronies too," Aggie yelled. The biggest boy turned and laughed.

"If it isn't everyone's favourite tub of lard." He looked around for Jenny, then grinned.

"Really, Ben. That's the best you can do? Sad, sad, sad." Aggie had no idea where the words were coming from, but she wasn't about to stop them. "After all this time, you can't come up with something original?"

He stomped over to her, fists clenched. "I don't have to listen to your tripe."

Aggie put her hands on her hips. "Go ahead and hit me." She stuck her chin out, heart pounding as he towered over her. These words, she wasn't so happy about.

"Do not touch her." Lamkay walked around to stand beside Aggie.

"And what are you going to do abo—"

"She beat Jenny for the Championship at the Rec." Aggie grinned at him as he stepped back. His buddies snickered and Ben frowned.

"Why didn't she beat me up then?" He cracked his knuckles. "Maybe this Taekwoncrap isn't—"

While he was nattering, Lamkay jumped and kicked out, flipping the cap off his head. He paled and stumbled away, his gang following him.

"Thanks."

"*Merci*."

They spoke at the same time, then laughed and sauntered after the boys.

Jenny met them at the school outside the gates.

"I saw Ben and his boys practically run into the school."

"Aggie took him down a notch." Lamkay opened and closed her hand, like it was talking.

Soon after they settled into class, the headmaster called Lamkay to the office. When she didn't immediately reappear, Aggie stood up.

"I should go to the headmaster; I'm a witness. It will save time." The teacher waved her on and returned to history.

***

Ben scowled as the secretary ushered Aggie through the door. Lamkay stood head down and hands clenched behind her back.

"—using martial arts is very serious." The headmaster frowned at Lamkay.

"Sir," Aggie winced ready for a rebuke for interrupting, but the words poured out of her. "I expect Ben didn't tell you how he was pushing her around before I got there and she didn't hit back, nor that he was thinking of hitting me when she stepped up to my defence. Probably not that he was ready to start a fight, when she kicked his hat, not his head."

With each word Ben turned redder. "Of course, the girls are going to stick together."

"You didn't mention Aggie's presence." The headmaster frowned and Ben's red face became white. "We spoke about this. You can't be bullying students. I'll let the coach know."

"Please don't kick me off the rugby team." Ben all but fell to his knees. His eyes actually glistened.

"Kicking him off the team won't help." Aggie said. "His problem is that he has too much time. Make him

288

coach the juniors or something." She laughed at his gobsmacked expression. "He can eat lunch with me and learn how to make conversation."

This new mouth is going to get me killed.

"Very well." The headmaster pointed at Ben. "This is your last chance."

***

At lunch, Ben came over to their table. Jenny and Lamkay frowned at him, but Aggie slid over and patted the seat.

"Ben is turning over a new leaf." Aggie giggled at the dumbfounded looks from her friends.

"I thought you were joking." Lamkay shook her head. "So, what are we talking about?"

Ben had to be reminded more than once that insults didn't count as conversation, but when the subject turned to rugby, he brightened and became part of the dialogue, not just a sullen observer.

***

Over the next month Aggie spent lunches learning about rugby, Taekwondo, and Lamkay's home country of Cameroon. Ben's friends came by to tease but ended up joining them, though Aggie had to pull him back into his seat a few times. Life was as good as Aggie thought it could get.

Then the paper came out with the headline.

Local council housing to be demolished.

"Where are we going to live?" Aggie demanded at the dinner table, her stomach in a knot.

"We're looking for a place." Her dad sighed. "We might have to sell your sword to help get the deposit. We have three months."

Aggie went upstairs and fetched the sword. She put it on the table, anger and fear pulling the knot tighter.

"Here it is, if you need it."

"Thank you, dear, but it doesn't belong on the table." Her mum smiled and dabbed her eyes. "Put it back in your room for now."

Aggie stuck the sword back into its corner, somehow disgruntled that it hadn't immediately solved the problem.

"Don't be thinking you can give Excalibur away that easy." The voice from the pond came from under the bed. "That's what they want. Take Excalibur and take your power."

"Power?" Aggie flopped in her chair. "I haven't got any power." *I forgot about that talking toad. What's going on?*

"All those new friends... You don't think you did that on your own?" The voice's compassion took the sting out of the words. "Of course, you aren't used to such things in this day."

"I'm supposed to believe that chunk of steel is magic..." Aggie trailed off as the sword glowed briefly then changed shape. Now it was shorter but deadlier looking, more like what the illustrations in the book showed. Then blinked back to the familiar blade and she rubbed her eyes.

"There are more things than you can imagine with power to change the world."

"What am I supposed to do with it? I'm not killing anyone."

Laughter came from beneath her bed. "You won't be killing; far from it."

Whatever was under the bed left. Aggie could feel its absence, but it would be back. Maybe it was Merlin. Merlin always knew what King Arthur needed to do.

***

Aggie wasn't very good at Taekwondo—the warm-up was torture, she could hardly kick above her knees, and sparring was terrifying. Her reward came at the end of the class, when they broke boards. She loved smashing the wood into pieces. Her hands stung briefly, but it never stayed; and when she stomped on the boards, the shock of the break never made it past the heel of her foot.

She wanted to try the bricks, but the often-bloodied hands of the black belts held her back.

"You are improving rapidly." Lamkay rolled up her belt and put it in her bag, then folded the dobok before putting it in too. She never wore it outside the dojang. Jenny and Aggie walked to and from the dojang in their doboks.

"Why don't you wear the dobok home? You wouldn't sweat as much without the extra layers."

"I was born in Cameroon. Sweating is a reality of life." Lamkay laughed. "In Douala, there were boys who would challenge anyone they saw wearing a dobok. It is hard to avoid fights, so I never wore it outside. *C'est la vie.*"

"What was it like moving from there to here?" Aggie blushed; maybe she shouldn't be asking.

"Douala is a big city, so a lot of things were the same. But a lot of things were different too. There, I was the normal looking one, and some days I wished to look different. Here, I stand out…"

"But you're beautiful," Aggie said.

"So my father tells me." Lamkay grinned. "It is not so hard now I have good friends." She hugged Aggie and kissed her on the cheek.

***

They walked home, talking about the class. Aggie could follow the conversation now, but she mostly listened. A notice in a shop window caught her eye.

"Look, a Mr. Mori from the company who's redeveloping the council homes is coming for a public meeting."

"That's going to be trouble." Jenny frowned, clenching and unclenching her hands. "A lot of people are angry."

"Mum and Dad aren't; they're looking for a new place. I told them they could sell my sword for the deposit. We may even get a bigger place."

"Sell your sword?" Jenny's frown deepened. "I guess, if that's what you want."

"What I want is to help my family." Aggie's stomach boiled. "It's not like it does anything but collect dust in my room."

"Helping your family would be stopping the redevelopment." Jenny rounded on Aggie. "My mother has a petition she's taking to Council."

"Good luck with that," Aggie rolled her eyes. "It had to be their idea in the first place."

"What do you know?" Jenny shouted at Aggie and ran off.

Aggie moved to follow, but Lamkay put a hand on her shoulder.

"Friends fight; I argued with my friends when we were moving to England. I wish we had made up before I left."

"It's my fault." Aggie's eyes leaked hot tears. "I should have known Jenny and her mum would fight it; they can't afford to move."

"Perhaps we need to aid their fight." Lamkay took Aggie's hand. "Come, we'll talk to my father." She dragged Aggie away from the window. Lamkay's hand was hot in Aggie's, and Aggie reddened as she saw people from her school. *No, I've already hurt one friend today.* Aggie relaxed her shoulders and walked with Lamkay. Once she stopped worrying about it, holding hands was pleasant—not like she imagined it would be with a boy, but easy, a connection between them.

***

292

Lamkay stopped in front of a law firm and Aggie's eyes widened.

"It's okay, my father doesn't mind visitors." They found out from a woman at the counter that he had a couple of minutes between clients, if they didn't mind waiting.

"Please do not speak of anyone you see in the office." Lamkay put a finger on her lips. "Confidentiality is important."

"I won't." Aggie peered around the waiting area, too open to be called a room. Expensive-looking paintings hung on the wall, and the chairs were leather and steel. The men and women wore clothes Aggie thought her parents might wear out on a special night.

"Did you and your friends hold hands in Douala?"

Lamkay dropped her hands and looked down.

"*Je suis desolé*, I forgot it is different here."

"I'm not upset, once I stopped worrying about it, it was… nice." Aggie lifted her chin. "And if it reminds you of your home and your friends, I don't mind."

"Mr. Batoum will see you." A woman came out from behind the counter to speak to them.

They walked into his office—not as plush as the waiting room, but Aggie liked it. Vivid paintings hung on the wall, along with sculptures she was sure he'd brought from Africa.

"Hello, you must be Aggie." He smiled, brilliant and warm like Lamkay.

"That's right." Aggie grinned back. "We wanted to ask you about the development."

Mr. Batoum's smile faded.

"I'm sorry, but I can't talk about it."

Aggie opened her mouth to ask why, but Lamkay put her hand on Aggie's knee.

"We understand, Pappa." Lamkay stood. "I am glad you got to meet Aggie."

"So am I."

They left; this time Lamkay didn't hold Aggie's hand as they walked down toward Aggie's home. Lamkay's shoulders shook, then she sniffled.

"What's wrong?" Aggie stopped and took Lamkay's hand.

"The only reason Pappa wouldn't talk about something is if they were a client of the firm." She threw her arms around Aggie and sobbed. "*Mon père est un ennemi.*"

"Listen, you can't help who your dad works for. We can still help Jenny."

Lamkay shook her head. "It would embarrass Pappa."

"He should be embarrassed." Jenny stood red-faced across from them where they'd turn toward Aggie's home. "He's helping them." She threw a ball of paper at Lamkay. "And you," she poked Aggie in the chest with a hard finger. "Traipsing about holding hands like a daft kid. I don't want to talk to either of you again."

She stomped off, curses floating back to turn Aggie's ears pink.

Aggie picked up the paper then stood, trapped between the fire in her veins and the ache in her heart.

"It is hard, *mon amie*." Lamkay's voice broke. "It was so, when I moved. The rage, it burned in my friends. They felt I'd abandoned them."

Aggie smoothed the paper. It was a petition with no signatures on it. "I'm not leaving it this way," Aggie vowed, her heart burning. "We've been friends since forever. I'm not letting something as foolish as this be the end."

"You are brave, Aggie." Lamkay hugged her, then walked away.

***

Aggie went home, filled up all the plastic bottles, then fetched her sword.

294

Slicing the bottles into thin rings wasn't as satisfying as when she'd done it with Jenny. *Why did we only do this once?* When she ran out of bottles, she started attacking the stump, slicing it down until a tiny green leaf standing out from the stump made her pull her cut.

Just like the fight between her and Jenny. A little bit of carelessness and look what happened. She threw the sword into the corner of the yard with a clatter.

"It isn't the sword's fault." Mrs. Hathway's voice made Aggie's blood chill. She turned to her neighbour. *I'm in for it now.*

"Please don't tell my mum."

"What, that you are slicing bottles and stumps into slivers, or that you tossed the blade away like trash?"

"You're right, it isn't the sword's fault." Aggie went to pick up the sword and examine it for damage.

"It would take more than that to dent old Excalibur," the toad voice said.

Aggie spun, almost dropping the sword. An immense toad sat on Mrs. Hathaway's shoulder. "It was you under my bed?" It puffed up and looked ready to explode.

"Relax, Albertus, she didn't mean to insult you."

"No, no." Aggie tucked the sword under her arm and came over to the fence. "You are a fine figure of a toad. I've just never had the privilege of conversing with one such as you, at least not knowingly."

"Well, ye got the gift of the gab alright." The toad deflated.

"Come have tea. Bring the sword." Mrs. Hathaway opened the gate.

Since when was there a gate there?

Her neighbour's lips twitched.

"Let me clean up my mess." Aggie put the plastic in the bin and tossed the sliced-up bits of wood into the corner of the yard with the weeds. "There, that's better."

"Indeed, it is."

Mrs. Hathway's home shouldn't have been much different than Aggie's, being the other half of the semi. But it felt larger and cozier. A small fire burned in the grate. Mrs. Hathaway used a cloth to lift a kettle from the fire and pour water into a teapot.

"You've been doing marvellously so far, dear, but the hard bit is about to start. Don't turn back."

"What am I supposed to do?"

"I can't tell you that." Mrs. Hathway poured tea and handed a cup to Aggie.

"Use what you've learned," Albertus grumped from the cushion he sat on as though it were a throne.

"Now, would you like milk or sugar?" Mrs. Hathway asked in a tone which made it clear the subject was closed.

"Neither, thanks." Aggie picked up the cup and inhaled the perfume of the tea. She sipped at it.

"How do ye know it ain't poison?" Albertus asked.

Aggie deliberately took another sip while she considered her answer.

"I don't, I guess, but what would be the point?" She shrugged.

"To take Excalibur from ye, dimwit."

Aggie picked up the blade and offered the hilt to Albertus. "Do you want it? All you need to do is ask."

Mrs. Hathway laughed as the toad scrambled back.

"I keep telling you it isn't about the sword, but the person."

"What kind of queen offers to give away 'er sword."

"Aggie's kind."

"Wait, queen?" Aggie put her cup down. "Queen of what? We already have a queen."

"Of course, dear—you did draw the sword after all."

"From mud, not stone, and the lady at the museum…" She picked up her cup and took a long sip. Her heart slowed and she could think more clearly.

"It is the drawing. You will learn in time of the rest."

"Right." Aggie examined the sword closely. "In my room, when Albertus was talking to me, it looked different for a moment."

"It takes what appearance it needs to."

"What would happen if I did give it away?"

"It depends on why." Mrs. Hathway stared into her cup thoughtfully. "If it thought you were dishonouring it, it would vanish, and you'd have a much harder time being queen. If the reason were honourable, it would find a way to come back to you."

"Okay, that makes sense."

Aggie finished her tea, lost in thought.

***

She didn't see either of her friends at school the next day or the next. The first lunch alone with Ben felt awkward, but he didn't treat her any differently.

On the third day, he asked why Jenny and Lamkay weren't around.

"It's complicated," Aggie said. "We had a fight, and I don't think any of us know how to start to make up, so we just kind of keep drifting further apart."

"You can't let an argument break up the team." Ben looked at her seriously. "Everyone gets angry or stupid at times, just look at me."

"I don't think you're stupid, Ben. You just needed a nudge to see things a new..." Aggie trailed off. "You're brilliant." She jumped up and kissed him on the cheek before dashing away, then saw a poster on the bulletin board telling the community that Mr. Mori would be talking to the people from the council housing at seven o'clock that night.

Aggie drifted through the afternoon alternating between chills of excitement and a hollow dread. By the time they were dismissed, she felt sick.

"You don't look so good." Ben came up. "Maybe I should walk you home."

"But you'll miss practice."

"I'll explain to Coach. You wait here." Five minutes later, he was back, and they started down toward her home. Their fingers brushed together, and Aggie took hold of his hand. His strength settled her, so by the time she got home, she could smile at her mum's shocked face.

"Thanks, Ben." She gave him another kiss on the cheek. "It means more than you know." Ben walked off—was he *skipping?*

"I'm going to the meeting tonight," Aggie said. "Can we have supper early?"

"Sure, I think." Her mum shook herself. "We'll have a talk when you get home, right?"

"Of course." Aggie headed up to her room, where she picked up Excalibur. "Could you try to look like something which won't get me arrested?" Excalibur shifted into a butter knife. "Great!"

***

There was a large crowd in front of the council building. Aggie went around to the back. A single light illuminated the door and the path to the parking lot.

"What are you doing here?" Jenny stepped out of the shadows to hiss at Aggie.

"I figured you'd be here." Aggie took the butter knife out of her pocket. "I came to help."

"What?"

"You're here to confront Mr. Mori, maybe bruise him a bit if he won't listen."

"What of it?" Jenny's chin lifted.

"So, I'm going to help." The butter knife became the sword. "This will do the job properly."

"Are you crazy?" Jenny tried to push the sword out of sight. "You'll get arrested."

298

"And you wouldn't?" Aggie gave a twisted grin. "You know what I can do with this thing."

"But you're all right. You don't have to worry about losing your home. I have no choice. We can't find a new place; we can barely afford the dump we have."

"My sword is at your command." Aggie held it up. "Tell me what you want."

"I want you to go away," Jenny said. "You can't do this."

"You're my friend. If we go to jail, we go together."

Jenny stared at Aggie, then fell to her knees. "I'm so scared, Aggie. I don't want to be homeless."

"What is going on?" A tenor voice spoke from behind Aggie.

"Friend stuff." Aggie held the sword out. "Can you hold this for a moment?"

"Uh, sure." A tall man in a suit looked at her uncertainly before taking the sword and peering at it.

Aggie knelt beside Jenny and wrapped her arms around her friend.

"I know it's scary. For years, you stood between me and what I was afraid of. Now it's my turn. You won't be homeless; you can have my room wherever we go."

"I'm an idiot."

"Everyone is sometimes."

"Very true." The tenor voice said. "Did you know this is the sword from the 1998 *Arthur and the Vampires* movie?"

"It is?" Aggie looked up. "That's nice. You can have it if you promise me something. Whatever happens, my friend and her mum have a place to live."

"I see. Perhaps for your friend's sake, I should rethink the way we are planning the development." The man was still examining the sword. "Mr. Batoum did suggest we could stagger the work so there is less hardship on the people. We do plan to build some units for the Council's use. It won't add much to the cost, but it is priceless in P.R just as being seen to make families homeless would be a disaster. I will have a word with him before we start. Maybe we can fast track tome "

"Mr. Mori," came another voice from the shadows, a deep bass matching the huge man who sauntered up to them. "You are running late already."

"Right. Halad, could you put this in the trunk for me?"

The big man took the sword, making it look hardly bigger than the butter knife Aggie had been carrying.

Mr. Mori knocked, and the door opened to let him in.

"You know I wouldn't have let you harm Mr. Mori," Halad rumbled at Aggie.

"I sort of expected you'd be here, or someone like you." Aggie stood and helped Jenny up. "But she's my friend, you know?"

"You have quite a friend there," Halad said to Jenny. He looked at Aggie. "I'm going to put this in the trunk. When I get back, you won't be here, right?"

"No, sir." Aggie took Jenny's hand and dragged her away to the front. Lamkay stood forlornly outside the door. She brightened as Jenny and Aggie ran up.

"I was worried I'd missed you."

"Your dad is amazing." Jenny flung her arms around Lamkay and spun her in a circle.

"He is?"

"He suggested a way for Mr. Mori to change things so we won't have to live in the car."

"We had a little chat with the man," Aggie said.

"A chat—you offered to chop him into pieces!"

"He didn't seem worried," Aggie said. "He was more interested in the sword than anything else."

"And Aggie gave him the sword in exchange for him making sure we aren't ever homeless. I was an idiot. Do you forgive me?"

"But of course." Lamkay grinned broadly. "Without you and Aggie, I wouldn't have had the courage to call my friends in Douala and talk to them."

***

Ben grinned as he sat down.

"Good to have you back, ladies." He gave Aggie a quick hug before digging into his lunch. Her friends stared at her open-mouthed. Aggie winked at them.

"Oh, I saw this in a shop, and for some reason I had to buy it for you." Jenny held out a tiny, bejewelled sword brooch. Aggie pinned it inside her jacket.

She reached across the table to her friends.

"I have something to show you at home."

After watching Ben practice, the four of them walked to Aggie's home, where she led them past her mum to the yard.

"Look." She pointed at the stump. "I diced up all the bottles, then I sort of got mad and chopped up the stump, but now…"

The remnant of the dead stump was covered in green shoots.

WHITE WINE IS FOR BUZZARDS

Clotheslines hummed in the wind as tempers flared in the Gravestone saloon.

"Everybody knows that the '89 Cabernet is the best vintage this side of California!"

"Only if you're drinking it with roasted buzzard."

"You darned fool, you know buzzard calls for a white wine! Like that horse pee you're drinking now."

"I'll have you know that this," the huge man waved his glass at his opponent, "is a Reisling from Germany." He took a large sip. "A very nice '95, or at least it was before all the hot air you're spouting warmed it up." He finished the glass and refilled it from the dark glass bottle on the table.

Okay, so it's fancy horse pee." The equally rotund man sitting across from him shook his glass sending red liquid splashing across the table. "A real man drinks red, and there's none better than this '89." He gave a last shake before he went to refill his glass from the clear glass bottle.

"You got red wine in my Riesling!" The first man looked close to tears as he peered at the drop of red rapidly spreading through his wine.

"I'm, I'm..."

A flood of tainted white wine that poured down his throat drowned his next words. He swallowed, then licked his lips.

"There is only one way to solve this," the white wine drinker roared. "Where are my guns?"

"You hocked them to pay for the wine," the red wine drinker said.

"Bartender! I require my guns!" The two men pushed and shoved their way to the bar. The saloon owner sighed deeply and pushed the guns across the counter.

"I'll tell Johnny to clear the horses out of the corral," the man said. "Mabel will meet you there with the bullets and the doctor." He pointed toward the door. "You'd better get started."

The wine drinkers snatched up their guns, then realized they made a mistake and spent a brief moment wrestling to regain their own weapons. The finally made the exchange and thundered toward the door. Guns in one hand and bottles in the other.

The entire town assembled at the corral to watch the duel. Some looked at their watches and tapped their toes with impatience, but finally a young boy spotted the duelists staggering toward the corral and leaning on each other for support.

Once they arrived several people helped them buckle on their gun belts.

"Now, gentlemen," the doctor said to them, "is there no way to resolve this peacefully?"

Both the duelists gave a firm shake of the head, each taking a swig from the bottles they still held.

"Then stand back-to-back and take ten steps. On the tenth step, turn and fire. He carefully loaded their guns, then hightailed out of the corral.

The duelists began counting their steps, on ten, they spun and snatched their guns out of their holsters. At least they tried to pull their guns. Such was their girth that it was all but impossible for them to reach the loaded guns at their side.

Finally, the red wine drinker freed his weapon from the holster and emptied it at his enemy. Sending dust clouds spinning and shattering the bottle of white wine.

The white wine drink stared at the broken glass and burst into tears. The other man, smitten by remorse, ran over to him and embraced him.

"Don't worry," he said, "we'll hock our guns and buy you another bottle."

AMANDA

Accepted in a Summer Anthology by the Authors of Manitoba 2016, but never printed.

I am the kingpin of the neighbourhood lemonade stands. After two brief seasons every kid selling lemonade within bicycle riding distance was using my recipe and paying me ten percent of their profits. I had a franchise that teenagers would envy, but it was as dust in my mouth; lemonade was last year's fancy. This year's goal is...

"Look, Dimitri." My friend, Amhil peered over my shoulder. "that's why no one gets you. You go from lemonade to dust in your mouth. Yuck! Who eats dust?"

"It's a metaphor, Amhil." I put my pen down. "I am not talking about really eating dust. That would be extremely unhygienic. Though," I spun in my seat to look at my best friend. "the Victorians insisted that a child should eat a tablespoon of dirt in a day."

"That's gross." He stuck out his tongue to fake gag.

"Again," I said, "I believe they were speaking metaphorically. They meant being too fastidiously clean was as unhealthy as being too dirty."

"I don't know," Amhil said, "all the Victorians are dead. They probably died from dirt overdose."

"The Victorians are dead because they all lived in the time of Queen Victoria who reigned between 1837 and 1901. They died of old age."

"Oh, I thought they were a tribe, like the Mohawks."

I shook my head and went back to my journal. Amhil was my best friend by the simple expedient of being my only friend. I wasn't sure why he stayed around. Not that he was slow, but I was cursed with exceptional intelligence, and unexceptional social skills.

This year's goal is to befriend Amanda Plumbston.

"Like that will ever happen," Amhil said, "You have as much chance being asked to pitch for the Mudville Slingers."

"Hmmmph."

"Well, she was third runner up at the Mudville Mall's Got Talent contest. Though there were only five contestants, and two of them involved hamsters."

"She was the youngest, at least if you don't count the hamsters." I looked up toward the ceiling of my room. "She has the voice of an angel."

"The one judge said she was flat." Amhil shrugged. "I thought it was mean since she's only ten."

"I think he was referring to her intonation," I said, "not her physique."

"Oh," Amhil said, "I wondered, since the others were definitely not flat."

"As I said." I rolled my eyes." She was the youngest."

"If you are off mooning after Amanda, who's going to run the lemonade stand business?"

"You are. Remember we are an honest franchise opportunity. If other kids want to open their own stands, they are quite welcome to do so as long as they don't use any of our materials."

"It would be pretty hard to make lemonade without lemons," Amhil said. I spun around and looked at him. He put his hands up. "Joking, joking, I know you mean the advertising."

I nodded at him and forced a smile. I have to admit that I don't completely understand what passes as humour, but I was willing to learn.

"Do you have any suggestions on how I should befriend Amanda Plumbston?"

"Divine intervention would be helpful," Amhil said, "I will light some incense to Parvati."

"Thank you," I said, "any *other* suggestions?"

"Not really, though you can usually see her at the baseball games. I think she's a fan."

"Very good." I typed in a quick inquiry on Google. "I will read up on the game."

"One thing," Amhil said, "You might not want to tell her that she's your project for the summer. Maybe something more along the lines of you always dreamed of getting to know her. Anyway, I will leave you to your research and go contact last years customers and see if they want to buy into the franchise again."

I didn't reply. I was already deep into my research. Amhil was used to it and made sure to close the door on the way out.

***

The air was surprisingly chilly in the stands. The Mudville Slingers were up by two runs in the fifth. From my location in the bleachers, I had an excellent view of Amanda sitting behind the bench. Occasionally one of the players would turn and chat with her while they waited their time at bat. This was the Bantam League, and the players were all leggy almost-teens. I sighed and pulled my coat tighter, beginning to think Amhil was right. She was out of my reach.

I shivered through the next few innings. At least I had a rudimentary understanding of the game. When it was over, a Mudville victory, I watched Amanda stand and stretch then walk away from me. She wore a satin Mudville Slingers jacket a little too large for her. She held her arms crossed in front of her like she was cold, or as if she had heard the judges' comments the same way Amhil had. The blonde hair that she had worn in fancy braids for the talent show hung in a simple ponytail falling almost to where her slim legs appeared from under that jacket. In spite of the cold, she wore sandals, and I caught a quick glimpse of red toenails.

306

To be honest, I was smitten, and I didn't have the least idea what to do about it. Until I heard her sing at the Mall, my plan for the summer had been to expand my business. Now I had just handed over the business to Amhil. I had said my fantasy was to be friends with Amanda, but what I really wanted, was for her to be as smitten with me as I was with her.

I gave myself a smack on the head. All those romances I had read in research were rotting my brain. I went home to hot chocolate and plans.

That was how my life progressed through May and into June. The only difference was I went from shivering to sweating. Amanda's outfit never changed -always that satiny jacket and slim jeans. Occasionally she wore a ball cap.

Amhil in the meantime made good progress with the lemonade franchise. He had signed up all last year's customers and one or two new kids. Everything was good. Well it would have been good if I could figure out what I should say to Amanda. Clearly, she was friends with the ball players. I couldn't imagine anything I could say she might want to hear. So I sat and watched her and the Mudville Slingers. At least the games began to take on some interest as I grasped some of the strategy. The Mudville players weren't a lot better than the visitors, but they made the little differences count and they racked up the wins.

I don't know if it would have been easier or harder for me if she went to the same school as I did. I went to East Creek where I was relegated to the 'gifted' program. Competition for the position of class brain was fierce. Maia led going into the home stretch. Normally I would have been jostling her for the title, but my heart just wasn't in it.

"What's the problem, Dimitri?" Maia plunked herself down beside me at lunch. We have been companions and competitors since kindergarten. I couldn't say that she was a friend, but she wasn't a stranger either. At least she understood all the words I use, but today I just shrugged and opened my lunch bag.

"Come on," she said, "either you're sick or you're in love." I must have paused briefly in laying out my lunch because she started chortling. "Oh boy," She bumped against me, "tell me all about it."

"Even if you were correct and I was in love." I laid out my lunch on the table. "Why would I tell you about it?"

"You know I will figure it out anyway," she said, "Would you prefer to spill the beans now, or have me poking around in your love life?"

"I don't have a love life." Suddenly the healthy hunger pangs rumbling in my stomach curdled. I looked at my carefully nutritious lunch and couldn't imagine eating it.

"Ah, but you want to." Maia bumped me again. "I know the feeling." I looked at her and raised my brow. "I'm a girl, we're not only smarter than boys, we grow up faster."

"What did you do?"

"Nothing," Maia took a huge bite of her sandwich, then washed it down with her milk. "but I wish I had at least talked to her."

"Her?" I looked at Maia.

"Don't even go there." Tears hung in her eyes.

"I'm cool." I bumped her gently.

"No, Dimitri." Maia gave me her more usual vicious grin. "You aren't cool, and you probably never will be." She bumped me back.

"Just like you?"

"Just like me," she said. "We are the brilliantly uncool kids. Talk to her, Dimitri and at least you will know what would really have happened."

"Talk to her, huh?"

"Yep."

308

"OK, I will." I picked up my sandwich and took a bite. This would take all the strength I could get.

There was a game that night. I went early and sat on the seats behind the Slingers' bench. For the next fifteen minutes as the crowd shuffled in I tried to think of what I would say. My lemonade empire was built on my ability to talk my way around any objection. The teacher in my classes could always count on me for a reasoned and detailed argument of my position. Customarily, the opposite of Maia's.

Amanda wandered in and didn't look at me. We all stood while they played the national anthem over the loudspeakers.

"Um, hi," I said when the music had scratched and hissed its way to the finish.

"Hi," she said and sat down.

"I saw you sing at the Mall," I said. Amanda shrugged and turned a little away from me. "I thought you sang beautifully."

"The judges said I was flat."

"You'll grow out of that," I said.

That's when she turned and slugged me. I fell backwards and got tangled up in the legs of the person behind me. They dropped their drink on my head.

"Hey, Mandy!" one of the Slingers said, "is that creep bothering you?"

"He's just leaving," she said.

The tears on her face glistened like diamonds in the harsh lights of the ball diamond. That hurt worse than my eye. So I dragged myself to my feet and tripped and staggered my way out of the ballpark, sticky, humiliated and heart-broken.

"I see you talked to her," Maia said the next day.

"How is it possible for someone as intelligent as I am to be such an idiot?"

"I'm not sure. I'm not aware of any scientific studies on the phenomenon."

I went back to sitting up in the gallery where I could see Amanda, but she couldn't see me. Every night I dreamed about her. I would say terribly clever things to her and she would punch me in the eye, every time, without fail. Most definitely I was in love. Who knew that love would be so uncomfortable?

The Mudville Slingers were doing so well that people talked about playoffs. Someone decided it would be brilliant to have a live singer for the playoffs. A few people each sang a song during the seventh inning stretch. The crowd would vote for their favourite. The night's winner would go to a semi-finals, then finals. I wished that Amanda would sing, but I was afraid to talk to her, not wanting another black eye.

Amhil came to me with a problem that for a moment put Amanda out of my mind.

"I'm having some trouble with the lemonade business," he said.

"Someone not paying the franchise fee?" I asked.

"Unfortunately," he said, "it isn't that. Someone who isn't one of ours has copied our sign and is using it to sell their own product."

"How close is the copy?"

"Pretty close," Amhil said, "but they said that since they are selling limeade instead of lemonade that it is OK."

"I guess I'll have to go and talk to them. We'll go tomorrow."

Amhil and I peddled out to the extreme edge of my lemonade domain. Sure enough, there was the sign that said 'Sweet Refreshment' but the lemons were green and it said limeade. The kid who sat behind the stand glared at Amhil.

"I'm not giving you no money," he said.

310

"Allow me to purchase a glass of your product." I pulled fifty cents from my pocket and dropped it into his jar. The boy stuck his tongue out at Amhil and poured me a glass. I took a sip. It was at least as good as my lemonade.

"What would you say to a different kind of deal?" I said. "I'll let you use my signs, and you give me the recipe for the limeade."

"It's my gran's recipe and you can't have it."

"I see." I put another fifty cents into his jar and he handed me another glass of his limeade. I closed my eyes to savour the taste of summer ambrosia.

"Why are you bugging my brother?"

I opened my eyes and choked on the last bit of the drink. Amhil thumped me on the back while I turned red from coughing and embarrassment.

"You're the creep from the ballpark," Amanda said.

"Sorry," I said. "I came here to try to make a business deal with your brother."

"You don't own this sign," she said.

"Actually, I do. It's trademarked," I said, "but I will make you a deal. You sing at the ballpark, and I'll let your brother sell his limeade under my sign. I'll even buy whatever extra he can make."

Amanda's mouth opened and closed several times. I wondered if she was deciding whether to hit me or not.

"OK," she said, "but only if you sing too."

"Deal," I held out my hand.

"Deal." Her hand was strong and warm in mine.

"There is one minor problem," I said. Amanda glared at me. Prudently stepping out of her reach I lifted my arms up in surrender. "I don't know how to sing."

"Everyone knows how to sing." Amanda put her hands on her hips; her eyes smoldered. "We had a deal. You shook on it."

311

"I have no intention of reneging on our deal." My hands stayed up, but my shoulders were getting tired. "It is just that I hoped to get a few tips on singing so as not to embarrass you at the stadium."

"Does he always talk like this?" She looked at Amhil.

"Always," Amhil grinned widely. "You'll get used to it. I learn much from Dimitri."

"Right," Amanda looked at me. "And the smartest thing you could think to say to me was 'um, hi?'"

"There are some things that even my intelligence can't deal with." I put my arms down, but watched in case another punch was coming.

"Right," Amanda said again but somehow it became a completely different word. "Stand up straight and take a deep breath." She demonstrated, an angel in shorts and a T-shirt. Her eyes started to burn again, so I gasped in air and tried to push my shoulders back.

"Hold your stomach like I'm going to punch it," she said, then punched my stomach, My air went out with a whoof. Her brother giggled. Amhil bought a limeade, then leaned his bike against a tree and sat on the ground to watch.

"Again." Amanda demonstrated. I decided not to punch her in the stomach. She breathed out a single note that hung in the air like a bubble of purest sound.

Once again, I breathed in air and tightened my stomach before she slapped it lightly. She nodded and strange warmth climbed from the place she touched me to my heart and up my neck. I opened my mouth and sang. It sounded like a cat strangling. The brother laughed and fell off his chair. Amhil hid his grin behind the empty glass of limeade. Amanda looked pained.

"Relax. Don't force the note out. Let it free."

I tried again. A kid on a bike stopped to snicker at me and buy a drink from the brother. And again. A girl walking a dog stopped to watch with her hands over her ears while her dog howled. By the time Amanda gave up, most of the kids in the neighbourhood gathered around making what they considered witty comments. Unfortunately, I had to agree with their assessment. I sang as well as a brick floated.

"You don't have to..." Amanda said.

"A deal is a deal," I said, in a voice that was more croak than speech. "We shook on it."

"Keep trying," Amanda said. "Relax, find a video on Youtube and sing along. I'll see you at the game."

"Deal," I held out my hand.

"Deal." Amanda's hand squeezed mine all too briefly, but she smiled at me before Amhil and I collected our bikes for the long ride home.

Once at home I locked myself in my room with a large glass of water and looked for the perfect song. I had three days before the game. My parents begged me to stop. Amhil told me he was too busy with the lemonade business. I practiced and drank water until the day before the game.

That's how I ended up standing on the pitcher's mound with a microphone in one hand while Amanda gave my other hand a squeeze. She didn't let go. Heat traveled up my arm to envelope me. I squeezed her hand back and grinned what I absolutely knew was the most mindless grin on the planet.

"Break a leg, creep." She winked at me.

I took a deep breath and sang in the dulcet tone of crows at dawn.

THE BOTTLE

First Published online by 'Cocktails' 2024

Erik juggled the phone and glanced at his notes.

"Yes. This family is on social assistance, but they have an excellent—" The person on the other end hung up.

"Erik?" Andrea stood in the door. "Someone to see you at the front desk."

"Fine." He pushed himself to his feet.

He walked through the door into the lobby and stopped short. A young man in a suit which had to have cost more than a month of Erick's salary stood waiting.

"Saladar Mossetti retained us as executors of his estate. He gave unusually explicit instructions."

"Really?" Erik glanced around at the many eyes gazing at them. "Maybe we should go to my office."

"Very well." The lawyer followed Erik through the halls with boxes of files piled in corners and up against the walls.

"Mr. Jorund. You will receive a package this evening. In thirty days, you are asked to report what you have done with the item to the firm." He laid a card on the desk with a snap.

"What do you mean report what I've done? Is this a game?"

"I am only required to deliver the terms of the will, not explain it." He stood up. "I'll see myself out."

***

Erik devoured a peanut butter sandwich, still irked by the lawyer's visit.

"Typical, Great-uncle has to cause trouble even after he's dead."

His wife, Helen held up a hand. "Calm down. They'll deliver some package, then you do whatever you want, and you're done. It's no big thing."

314

"Why does Great-uncle want me to report anything to the law firm?" He pointed his sandwich at her. "He's still meddling, playing with me."

"Why would you think that?" Helen took his empty hand. "Lots of people were closer to him."

"The old coot had it in for me. Every time I visited; he'd find another way to insult me. I think he never forgave my father for marrying his daughter." He threw the last of the sandwich at the wall; the peanut butter left a brown spatter on the beige paint.

Helen let go and went to the kitchen coming back with a washcloth to clean up the mess. "There's no more bread, but we have a few crackers—"

"No, it's my fault. I'll deal with being hungry." He tried to get a grip on the flood of anger, humiliation, and love flooding through him.

The knock on the door, interrupted his struggle to find words to explain.

"Mr. Jorund?" A women stood outside holding a wood crate little larger than a wine bottle.

"That would be me." Erik tried to paste a smile on his face.

"Great, sign here." She winced slightly and Erik's gut tightened. He signed and took the package.

"What is it?" Helen came to the door behind him.

"The package from Great-uncle." Erik pointed at the crate. "A little underwhelming."

"What's going on?" Helen wrapped her arms around him. "Talk to me."

"Last birthday, Great-uncle Sal asked, as he always did, what we were doing with our lives. He would then delight in dismantling our aspirations. When it was my turn, I told him as always did that I worked to provide housing for marginalized people. 'That's why you're poor, you can't feed people on good feelings.'"

"Good grief what did you do?"

"I yelled at him I'd rather be poor and caring than a cantankerous, manipulating excuse for a human being, no matter how much money he had. He laughed at me and went on with dinner as if nothing had happened. I left right after supper."

"Then he died a month later. Maybe he'd heard from the doctor and didn't have any other way of dealing with it." Helen rested her head on his chest.

"I know you're trying to make me feel better, but he was always like that." Erik pulled away. "Let's go to bed, I don't think I can talk any more about this." He immediately missed the warmth of her arms, but something in him was dangerously close to breaking.

If only he knew what it was.

***

The crate sat on the table as they ate the instant mac and cheese someone had left on his desk at work. Erik hated taking these occasional gifts, but he hated letting Helen and Meredith going hungry more.

Was he being fair to his family? With his Bachelor's in Social Work, he could get a better paying job. Child and Family Services were always hiring.

"Penny for your thoughts?" Helen peered at him; her head tilted.

"Should I get a job which would pay more?

"Why?" Helen furrowed her brows slightly. "Don't you like what you do?"

"I do, frustrating as it is. But is it fair to you and Meredith?"

"It's tough, but we're getting by, she's a happy little girl. When she starts school, I'll get a job and will be able to help with finances."

"That's another two years, how can you take this that long?"

"It's the commitment we made to each other."

316

Erik looked up at the bottle and sighed. "It's my fault for running through our savings buying all that expensive scotch trying to be Great-uncle's equal."

"It's done." Helen frowned at him. "We're all right. You kept your word and became a husband and father I am proud of."

He put his head on his arms and fought back tears. What had he ever done to deserve her?

"Let's open this thing and at least figure out what we're going to do next."

Erik straightened up, then fetched a screwdriver from the junk drawer.

"I'll try opening the top." The screwdriver made quick work of the staples holding the wood pieces together. In a few seconds he lifted out a velvet bag with a bottle in it.

"What is it?" Helen leaned forward to get a better look. Pushing the mess to one side of the table, Erik avoided looking at the bottle in its bag. Great-uncle was reaching out from the grave to make one last jab at Erik.

"Only one way to find out." His voice shook as he untied the string holding the bag closed. A paper was wrapped around the bottle. Picking it loose gave Erik time to try to compose himself. The handwriting on the inside of the paper was his Great-uncle's.

"Great-nephew, some time back you refused a drink because you said you'd made an agreement with that wife of yours. No more scotch, or she'd leave. Foolish to let a woman steal your one enjoyment in life. Do what you will with this bottle. It is, as far as I know, the longest aged scotch ever bottled. Figure out what you are going to do with it.

"P.S. I know you all hated me, maybe I should have cared, but I didn't."

Helen stared at him wide-eyed.

Erik picked up the bottle of deep amber liquid. Before his mother had been born, someone had filled a barrel with scotch to age it. A simple handwritten label identified the now defunct company, the date on the barrel and the date of bottling. At the bottom it read, 'One of One'. Erik put it down carefully before he dropped it.

"He loved scotch and was tickled that I of all his descendants shared his love. When I refused to drink after I chose you, he never offered me another drink."

"You stood up for your convictions." Helen put her hand on his arm. "I'm proud of you."

"He was wrong. Scotch wasn't my only enjoyment in life, that's you and Meredith."

***

"I looked up on the internet," Helen greeted Erik at the door. "A bottle of 50-year-old Macallan sold for fifty-thousand dollars." She grinned at him.

"You're thinking we should sell the bottle."

"Of course, don't you?" Helen crossed her arms. "We could invest it and not have to eat leftovers and cheap food."

"Are you angry that we have to eat leftovers and cheap food all the time?"

"No of course not, but if we don't have to?"

"I don't know." Erik tried to find words to express his misgivings.

Helen turned and walked to the kitchen. "I picked up some celery on the past-its-date sale, so we can eat our peanut butter on something other than cheap, white bread."

Erik forced himself to eat and smile. Meredith played with her dinner until she was covered in a sticky mess.

"I'll clean her up and put her to bed." Erik said. "I haven't had a chance for a while."

"Okay." Helen looked down. "I'm sorry, I'm not being fair to you. It's just…"

"I understand." Erik picked up Meredith. "I'll investigate how to sell the bottle tomorrow."

***

318

After consulting with a few auction houses and experts in scotch, Erik wasn't any further ahead. All of them talked about provenance and authenticity. A few offered to give him a few thousand for it. He turned them down.

A couple of days after that a man called him at work.

"I got your work number from your lovely wife." The man's voice was everything Erik's wasn't. "I hear you have a rather unusual bottle of scotch. I'd be happy to pay you ten thousand dollars for it, today."

"We have no proof it is what it claims to be on the label."

"Are you saying Sal Mossetti is lying about that bottle?"

"Thanks for the offer, but—"

"Twenty thousand."

Erik hung up the phone and went back to work.

At home, he walked in to find Helen sitting at the table with notes all over it. Meredith watched TV.

"Daddy!" His daughter screamed and ran to him. He picked her up and swung her around. "How's my girl?"

Meredith pouted. "No park."

"I'm sorry, honey." Helen came over and gave her a kiss on the cheek. "We'll go tomorrow."

"Ice-kweam."

"Sorry, we can't afford ice-cream." Helen spoke sharply and Meredith hid her face in Erik's shoulder.

"You go and watch your show while mom and dad talk." The little girl walked over and plumped herself down in the living room. "What happened?" Erik went to look at the table.

"People have been calling all day." Helen pointed to different piles of notes. "These people aren't serious. This pile is people who didn't sound like they had the kind of money to pay our price, and—"

"For this you didn't go to the park with Meredith." Erik's chest felt hollow.

"All the calls, I didn't want to miss anyone."

"We have an answering machine. Meredith is more important than selling the bottle. In a week we've gone from a family to a business."

"But Erik, if we want to sell the thing, we need to work at it."

"Not if it means becoming less of a family." He flipped one of the piles with his finger. "I hung on someone today who offered twenty thousand for the thing."

"You hung up on Mr. Brasdin?" Helen searched through the piles. "He's famous for paying extravagant prices for what he wants."

"If he wants, he can call back." Erik sighed. "Don't give out my work number anymore. I don't want to be interrupted by nonsense."

"Nonsense? This is our daughter's future."

"Are we trading in her present? What do you think she's going to care more about when she's older?" He walked over and sat beside Meredith, effectively ending the conversation.

A few days later a man showed up at Erik's work, even more out of place than the young lawyer.

"I'll only take a few minutes of your time, son." The man pulled a check from his breast pocket. "Fifty thousand for your bottle."

"Sorry, I have work to do." Erik turned away.

"You'll regret not taking my offer."

"I will regret taking time from my work finding people places to live."

"You could find a lot of homes for seventy thousand."

Erik stopped in the door. "I suggest you give the check to the board."

"They have nothing I want."

"No, of course not." Erik went back to his cramped little office and tried to imagine doing his work in a spacious office. It felt like a betrayal.

Mr. Brasdin called back and offered a hundred thousand. When Erik got home, Helen informed him a man had called from Japan and offered a hundred and fifty. Meredith sat in front of the TV, not turning around to greet him.

Erik opened the cupboard to take out the bottle. He put it on the table. Then he lifted down the Glen Farcas.

"Three years ago, you put this bottle on the table," he tapped it with a finger, "and gave me a choice. I could stay with you, or I could keep collecting scotch. You were right, I was being a fool." He put his hand on the ancient bottle of scotch. "Now, I'm giving you a choice. You can have this bottle, or you can have your family. Let me know what you decide." He left her staring at the bottle and went to Meredith.

"How about we go to the park?" She jumped up and ran for her shoes. Erik let Meredith play until she crawled into his lap and fell asleep. He carried her home and put her to bed.

In the kitchen, Helen sat with her head on the table weeping over piles of shredded slips. Erik sat down and wrapped his arms around her. She clung to him, sobbing even harder.

"I –I'm sorry." Erik tightened his grip. "Great-uncle always got under our skin to show us the worst of who we were."

"I won't take any more calls." She hiccupped and lifted a tear-stained face.

"I'd like you to make four calls for me. Invite Brasdin and the other top offers here in a week. Then call this law firm and ask this fellow to come. He'll be interested in what happens." Erik sorted out the three slips from the rest, then crumpled the remainder to put them in the trash. "Tomorrow, take Meredith out for ice cream."

Helen nodded her head. "Thank you."

***

Four men in expensive suits sat around the kitchen table their eyes fixed on the bottle in front of Erik.

"I'll give you two hundred," Mr. Brasdin said.

"Two-fifty," Mr. Sakamoto frowned at the other men.

"Three hundred." The third man, Mr. Hacken snapped. He glared at Erik. "You're getting greedy. I am a very bad person to have as an enemy."

Mr. Sakamoto opened his mouth, but Erik held up his hand and the men fell silent.

Erik put his hand on the bottle. "I used to drink scotch with my great-uncle Sal. When I made a promise to buy no more, I wouldn't even accept a drink. I regret taking away the one thing we enjoyed."

The men stared at him like he'd grown a second head.

With a quick twist of his wrist Erik opened the bottle. The three collectors paled.

"Sit down." Erik went to his cupboard and picked out six glasses. He carried them to the table and poured scotch into each of them.

"Gentlemen." Erik lifted his glass. "I invited you here as people who love scotch as much as Sal Mossetti did. Drink to the memory of the nastiest man I've ever known, but he did enjoy a good scotch."

Hesitantly, reverently the three collectors lifted their glasses and breathed in the aroma, they sighed in unison, then smiled at each other.

"To Sal." They sipped at the amber liquid.

Erik didn't have the words to describe the flavour. It shifted and changed as it moved in his mouth. The next sip tasted different; it warmed him down to his toes. The men argued like old friends.

When the glasses were empty, they stood up.

322

"Even with all my money I wouldn't have considered opening the bottle and sharing it." Mr. Hacken shook Erik's hand. "Thank you." He nodded at the others and left.

Mr. Brasdin handed Erik a card. "If you're ever in New York, give me call and we'll share a drink."

Mr. Sakamoto bowed slightly. "I will cherish the memory." He left Erik alone with the lawyer.

"Does that count as a report?" Erik sat down and played with his empty glass.

"I'm not a scotch drinker, but that's beside the point." He pulled out a letter from his breast pocket and handed it to Erik.

Hey kid, if you're reading this, you've just had the most expensive drink in history. Good on you. I watched all my grandchildren and nieces and nephews shaping themselves into something to impress me. You were the only one to stand up to me and be what you wanted. I liked that. I could have tried to tell you, but I didn't think you'd listen. This was a way to see if you really were who you said you were. Only a caring fool would invite others to drink in the memory of a man you hated.

Great-uncle Sal.

Erik put the letter on the table beside the one full glass.

"So now what?"

"Mr. Mossetti put careful thought into his will. After the usual bequests, the residual of his estate will be given to *From Street to Home*. He trusted you would appreciate this as a belated commendation for the work you do." The lawyer smiled. "The firm will be in touch." He nodded and left.

The man had barely touched his scotch. Erik pulled the glass over and clinked it against the one he'd poured for his Great-uncle.

"I wish I hadn't refused that drink."

Erik put the empty bottle up beside the Glen Farcas.

"How did it go?" Helen came in with Meredith.

"We went park." Meredith ran over to the couch and fell asleep.

Helen carried the empty glasses over to the sink.

"What are you going to do with the last one?"

"Take Great-uncle Sal his drink."